I0681968

# Skin Overcoat

**Skee Morif**

Searchwell Books

*relevant ideas*

Published by Searchwell Books
PO Box 52175
London E8 9AX
editor@searchwell.co.uk

Dedicated to Ellen and Elvie

# 1

Gridlock. And a bleary overcast. Tall clouds mute a shape over London. Hard to make out what; it could be more than rain. Swallows veer past a dust-stained windscreen. And all the time, the motorway from here's getting later and later.

Jimmy kills the engine. Grabs the mobile. And dials Arleene. "Weird sky," he says. "Could almost be a woman up there. Looks like a woman in blue jeans. But that would be pure fairytale, right?"

She laughs. "You said it, not me!"

"Good thing about a fairytale woman is she wouldn't quote scriptures all day. She'd zap this gridlock."

"Stop daydreaming! Gets in the way of what you do."

"My sky woman would have a big laugh. I'd want a laughing lady, somebody like you, but high over cloud cover. Yeah. I'd play hide and seek with her."

"When will you stop that mystic stuff?" Arleene says.

"Well, I'll have a hundred miles in my strides when I get there. Long motorway miles. Should get there before dark. I don't have sat-nav, not easy to scheme from here. But I can see what swallows do with London in August."

In one car, a sax solo plays from the hi-fi. Charlie Parker playing a taut tenor. Louder now. A loner sax preaching in summer air, pouring out to scud at rain clouds. Some drivers haven't heard Charlie Parker. Not before today. Tempers fray. Somebody yells, 'Hey, Neanderthal! London Zoo's only a shout from here!' And straightaway, the gridlock gets a clue how fables come out of nowhere.

Scoffing at the kerb, Jimmy starts the engine. And shunts the steering. Then inch. Inch by inch, climbs the wheels over. Then a dizzy scoot. In other cars, they don't like this. But he shoots down a side road. The motorway will wait.

It would be different at the coast. A day like today the sea gets bigger and bigger. Yachts whiling or darting. And that blue water! Way too deep for even the lanky sky to wade. Masts taller than telegraph-poles, but not too tall to run the whole ocean down. Someone ashore would watch this; a loner gazing at spinnakers, seeing them puff salt breeze.

Jimmy lights a quiet smoke. Turns the music down. Understands. Parker solos say it all. From here, thinking of the ocean is remembering fairytales.

# 2

London Zoo is a place with windows open yet closed; a jailhouse edited by summer. And something else. Hard to pin it down. It could be flesh. Could be perfume. A woman-like smell here. Or just like pulling up in a country lane and getting fresh daisies on a verge.

After ten minutes in a zoo anybody sane would leave. But to Jimmy these cages are business. And the big thing, nobody else black. Not here, not right now. Not during the gridlock outside the gates.

Cheetahs don't pack well. Gazelles meant for these cats are out on the plains a hemisphere away. Cheetahs have their eye. A nod, a cheetah taps the motorway speed limit before any Aston Martin. From 0 to 60, it out-guns a Ferrari. But a grown cheetah wouldn't get out the blocks in a zoo.

Smiling, Jimmy gets a good picture here. A picture of plenty women. Woman after woman, moving round in this zoo. Some way too nice to let pass by. This place could be just right for a loner to while away. Score. And the sky pitched like asphalt. Mobile twitching, he chats away. Thirty seconds into the phone-call, lightning struts from cloud cover. Baby-blue, slashing, pale. Wronged light. Lethal. The mobile cracks.

"Minims in Britain is _ "

"*Minims*," Jimmy says, "it's called Minims now. Remember?"

"Sure. Sorry about that."

"C-sharp is the thing. It was B-flat, but I changed my mind."

"Oh, right."

"Hear me OK? I'm at London Zoo. Rain anytime now."

"Minims, well it's not what this is about."

"Sharp keys cut through any weather. C-sharp zaps the lot!"

"Your line's breaking up, so let's get to the point. Minims, we like it Jimmy. We all think it's on the ball. But it's jazz, mate."

"Yeah, I know."

"Then why get difficult?"

An elephant trumpets in the zoo. The mobile slams close. "What's difficult?" Jimmy yells.

"Jazz isn't folk."

"You don't like the theme?"

"*Theme*? Theme doesn't come into this. Jazz is not folk!"

"Got something against jazz?"

Quiet loads up. A sly hush streams the void. Silence swallowing the line like snake-skin.

"As it happens," the voice drifts back, casually, even obliging, "some of my favourite music is jazz."

"So what's the problem?" Jimmy says, knowing what's up, but feeling like playing along. "Think bebop will make a comeback?"

"It's never gone away, you know. This is 1999."

"Yeah, last year of the old."

"Tell me about it! By the way, how old are you?"

"Twenty-four."

"*How* old?"

"Twenty four."

"Wish I was that age again!"

"Age? Isn't that the tracks you play. I think bebop was it!"

"Bebop brings it home. Max Roach is still around, keeping it safe."

"Got those old tracks of Max?"

"Naturally. The ones with Charlie Parker. Classics!"

"Ever see him play?"

"Yeah, yeah. New York. London."

"London?"

"He did the Barbican. But we could talk about that all day, so let's cut to the chase."

"I know," Jimmy says. "Time to talk about the festival."

"The *folk* festival."

"Yes."

"The Millennium Folk Festival."

"Sure."

"It's about folk music, got that? There's obviously places for your sort of thing."

"Any ideas?"

"Loads of gigs out there, Jimmy."

"Like which ones?"

"Lots to choose from, pal."

"Name a few."

"Well, there's obviously places where _"

"Like where?" Jimmy says, vacant now.

"Look!" the voice spits. "I've had enough of this. Try Brixton!"

# 3

Today was to be a good August day. Not sunny, the weather looks like a flip-flop already. Just like a flaked-out somebody operating rented rooms. One year Jimmy rented from one but every day she flopped on the stairs, deep-dived the gardening magazines. It was a big eye-opener, getting past on the narrow stairs.

Today is storm-clouds. But only two days back, Heathrow was over 90 all day. Now rainstorms snatching at southern England. And anybody wanting to get wet will have this big sky to grab at. Even after a putdown phonecall, Jimmy can tell some things are still the same. Wild animals here colder than steel.

A group of women collect and chat. Not bothering with the animals. The zoo's only backdrop to them, like sunlight on a wet pane. Talking and talking, the unsmiling ones try to steady those with a damp question in their eye. One girl rubs and rubs her eyes, figuring why anyone would choose a zoo to complain in. She doesn't know it, but everybody's in a hold-zone here. Every visitor killing time, posing, sloping.

A squint of raindrops. Shadows as thin as sighs on the ground. Rain. Sky-water won't wait. Summer rain heading this way, feral, crazy. Scatting water will fall.

Bulked in the mid-ground, fresh hay gets piled high on a cart. But as it gets nearer, the keepers pushing it look lost. Voices lower than knees, two sad keepers pushing a failed foetus under lush hay.

Trying to switch off, Jimmy takes a long swig of air. But the air's too bare; more like stale fairgrounds than air. Two slow breaths confirm it, slower this time. It would be cage-doors all day to dwell on Brixton. Not here. Not today.

Arleene. Far up the motorway, the tamarind woman waits for Jimmy. Just thinking about her makes the motorway a dream, open miles to slice. That woman, sweet up the free motorway. One tamarind widow to reach by asphalt miles today, a boogie special, never talking talk. Cooing down the phone she set this evening aside. And all tonight.

In the sky, lightning divides like eels. Cold blue fire, lasers looking just like eels in a storm-filched sea.

Teeth clenched, Jimmy looks for the exit. A keeper comes up to him. Asks if things OK. His throat clears. But nothing to say. This keeper is a good-natured woman.

"Why the long face?" she wonders.

His head shakes. "A blues day."

"What?"

"Millennium blues."

Stock quiet, she looks around. Wondering. Her eyes are kind. Quiet eyes, calm. The zoo's her home from home. Her crinkled eyes turn from Jimmy and mock the clouds. Then she says, "Cheer up! What a nice day!"

"Yeah."

"Whatever it is, it makes you too sad. Don't take it personally."

"You wouldn't understand."

"Listen to me," she says, *"nothing* can be more desperate than people forming queues in August for the winter sales."

"What?"

"A winter sales-queue is on Oxford Street."

"Already?"

"Right this minute!"

"Clowns?"

She nods. "Outside one store there's six or seven clowns, morons, queuing up for the millennium sales."

Jimmy wants to laugh. The woman laughs. Her eyes check his. With a quiet smile she swaps a bunch of keys, hand to hand.

"Queuing for the winter sales," he says, "in *August*?"

"The store promises Pacific cruises. New Year's Eve, first ten punters get on board for a quid each."

"New Year, that's over four months away!"

"Woad," she sighs, "is so, *so* silly!"

Jimmy frowns. "What is woad?"

She turns to walk away, then, puzzled, turns back. "Woad is the start of every troubled thing in England. Bad things. Understand?"

"Not really."

"Millennium blues, eh? Well my dear, 2000 is only a number. Winter vigils on Oxford Street, so ridiculous in the heart of summer!"

# 4

Everybody wants the rhino to move: 'Do something, rhino. What part of *move* is your problem!'

This rhino could prove it's no sculpture. The tail will flick, a keeper says; a gaunt keeper, saying rhinos are a kind of pig but actually more kin to horses.

"Far away and tropical," Jimmy says, "a hummingbird gets tricked from thin air. In a bad fairytale, Stephen Hawking kicks hummingbirds from his wheelchair."

The keeper frowns. Turns away. Somebody tells him this rhino was made for politicians. Why? Because they're just as thick skinned, and would want to milk the crowd here, preach some blanks, get the rhino to move a rhino part. This is a lady rhino, the keeper says; he'd like to see a politician enter her enclosure to milk.

Outside the zoo, the gridlock's a knot of knots. Some people are only here to blank that chock outside. But pig or no pig, kin to horse or not, this rhino is no joke. This is a military pig. Flicking its tail now. This thing's so steroid-fixated, a muscle-clad lady with a slow tie; rain will wash her stray milk away.

Penguins are lithe as marble. They know they get laughed at. They know the zoo, own their slosh space. Some architect had a problem here, a chatty girl says; according to her, whoever designed the penguin space must have nursed mermaid heartbreak, codged this space to spite a wave, but the zoo put penguins round it because the architect didn't get the sea, was a dry-land swimmer, and penguins don't get that; they know about the visitors. Lighting a smoke, Jimmy laughs.

"Hey!" he yells.

Straightaway they turn. Look up. But not like to a ringmaster. He mimes what he's thinking: 'Quit splashing this fake place. Face down the crowd, front the shaming of your penguin race.' He knows they know. But they're only wet toys here, splashing. Sometimes their small black wings shrug like weary arms. But they never dance. Never face the crowd to snap their wings, move their feet. Never, ever want to tap dance: shuffle-shuffle, one, two, three.

He turns to them, again, says, "Hey!"

Then grabs the mobile. Dials Arleene. "I'll be later than I thought."

"Where are you?"

"London Zoo."

"You're supposed to get here before dark," she says.

"Animals could escape a zoo. But a rhino would have to polevault."

"*What?*"

"Even with a hundred tries a day, every day, rhinos would need a long time to learn. Trillion years. Then again, they aren't the only ones that can't vault. Too wet, penguins can't."

# 5

Over the zoo, clouds gaze like zebras' eyeballs. They stoop in a slow dream-state, a cage dizz. Animals beat the air.

And wide-eyed chats through roaring and growling, trumpeting, snarling. Birds singing high in a cage. Giraffes are the high chit in a zoo. But they don't sing. Leaves are their thing. Leaves sing out for them. Green, on the open plains. Those hot savannas humming with leaves. Long-necked is business here; without that neck giraffes wilt like the morning star, somebody says.

Jimmy checks the time. Motorway time. That sister tarmac waiting. And then. Arleene. Owner of tamarind. A day'n nighttime woman. He turns to go.

But bad ground. Worry. A bad feeling. Worry like a mange dog. A dog that talks, 'Hey you! Remember your tune? Yeah, that Minims. Well, it's not folk!' He kicks out. Minims is a jazz-opera, dog! But the dog won't reply. Dog-tongue in use, licking busted ribs where a boot cracked hard.

"Dogs hear higher notes than clouds," Jimmy tells a keeper. "Jazz is the biggest folk of all. Any place with TV, radio, nighttime, daytime, Shepherd's Bush, Mongolia, Chicago, Cape Town, straightaway folk know jazz."

Going past the rhino with a fresh cigarette in hand he's getting away from here, knowing nobody kicks rhinos to death but a clown steps into a pet shop to traipse round, buy a hamster.

Somebody complains. Says it's a chilly day; saying a jacket would do it here, even a scarecrow coat to button and pull together. A kid with loose laces steps shorter and shorter, saying summer or no summer this place is cold.

A furrowed woman comes up to Jimmy. Hurries with two little girls, freckled twins. A camera pouts in her hand; will he take some snaps, please? Already the camera's in his hand. Through the viewfinder her red hair looks easy, let go, lax, not trampling daylight; belle-red hair, changing light round it like a flush hello. Her eyes, deep-set but happy and soft as moss, yet laced by regret. A redhead woman clinging to something. Five paces back, and the viewfinder changes everything. That red hair looks like a haystack on fire. Squinting, she's confused about where; this zoo could be any place. Flecks of drizzle wrangle summer air.

# 6

Tigers are bigger than lions, the keeper says; they're more catlike, but nobody leaves a zoo before seeing the maned cats.

Jimmy turns back. Wanting to reach Arleene but must see the lions; they'll compete with her today. And compete with bad traffic outside. *Gridlock* is not the word; roads outside the zoo add up to disdain.

Rain stalls. One minute clouds shape up and look clean, then soon get stark. And that's painful. Especially for someone at odds, panning round, wondering, trying to figure how weather works, how clouds fling apart then close. Jimmy agrees. Today, clouds look like a woman. Not the wisp kind, the gaunt; they'd stacked that way a while, looking like haunted widows with elbows every place. But now they look like round women, lady after large lady; clouds looking like heavy women that sing trad songs or, if they croon, dream out jazz standards; one lady large enough that their dress stalls an albatross on her belly.

"Bernstein would have composed here," Jimmy tells a keeper. "Nobody's moved jazz-opera on since Lenny. He'd run the cheetahs, then splice a theme, a jazz theme, the road from West Side Story. You know that? Bernstein, he'd see deep at a zoo and call it *Cage Side Story*. Then there's Mingus. Know about him? Charles Mingus with thunder hands, he'd tear this place apart! Elephants chasing the shock wave. Hands big as industrial lifting gear, but Mingus is dead. Bernstein's the same, you know, polishing clay with his bones."

The keeper shrugs. "We get a few like you coming here!"

Thunder in the ground. The sky's holding on. A taste of tobacco in animal air. Bitter smoke cropping, gnashing. Smoking is not allowed here, the unsmiling keeper says.

Jimmy's weary. Teeth clenched, smoke billows from his lungs. He can see the reason why a zoo: 'Look at me, I can come and go!' The rapture. Steel. The putdown phonecall was a 'go, don't come.' Arleene. She'll understand. He phones her.

"What's the matter now?" she wonders.

"Today," he says, "these clouds over London couldn't be bigger. Rain. This water can't wait. It wants to play. Big in the sky. Biding time. Waiting to do it. And nothing can match that. Ever. Some days rain hangs round, killing time. Or it looks down, sees only targets. But mostly, rain's nice. New sky-water. Nice and cool."

"Cooling like suntan oil?"

# 7

Two lions. Straight ahead. One blink to move.

But a cage. For a blink it was only lions. Now it's clear: steel round them. Lions in a big steel room. Jimmy's whole life yanked to them, somehow. Every eye blinks. Every eye says, 'So, this is lions!'

The male gaze is a butcher's gaze. Visitors are only meat to that eye. And the mane. The lioness paces her space, left and right. Granite in that eye. Her eyes are like granite honey. But wasps don't make honey. Her gaze is more than her mate's; wasp's eyes mocking honey, whisper, saying 'Fear torture!' With no fooling she'd suck visitor-bones while they bawl the sky out. Talk is, some nights a live cow gets tossed to the lions here.

Nothing domestic in the cage. And nothing cross or like a ball of wool near old ladies getting greyer in a chair. A secret collects in the gaze of the lioness; all moves depend on that. The next move. Everybody's scared but glad; steel of the enclosure looks good. It reminds the lions: a different space for big cats here. But something like a message, a note at the cage. Hurt wells up. Blood at the back of their watchers' eyes. Everyday they hear zoo birds singing a high cage. Jimmy steps back.

Giraffes don't mope, a keeper says; but elephants do. The keeper laughs, saying elephants get maudlin. Straightaway somebody wonders how laughing in a zoo can throw a big question away.

Every now and then a loner visits the cage, dreaming of lions going home to the plains. Keepers always know the dreamer; man or woman, black, white or child, keepers watch as the dreamer sleepwalks from the cage. Lions don't refuse meat.

Water is no help here. Not for the thirstiest thirst. Penguins have it. They're so out of place, cozying up to anything, getting the sea in any old puddle, clean or dirty. But here they're a wet cabaret. And seals are so discarded; they should be conning predators in open seas instead of poolside party tricks. Their eyes dampen air like cold sea plums.

Going your business some place like Oxford Street, your face is on a thousand CCTV screens. But if a lion walked that same thoroughfare, tarmac would up and scoot. To Jimmy, the putdown phonecall was only the most recent thing.

A woman's hand. It moves closer to his. Hand, next to hand on cool steel. The woman's lion gazing. The hand is small, pale brown. He wants to ask. Anything. Even ask if rain might come this way, or ask the time, some stupid thing, anything so she'll turn round. And then. Just by thinking it he gets to see her face as she turns. Now the woman. Quiet, her eyes let go of lions. Before swinging full round, she gets his cut in one take. Her eyes fix his. Amber eyes.

Folk looking at this woman will see mixed-race. This bothers Jimmy, making him sorry she turned round. She looks gashed. What brings her to the lions? He thinks she's like two people, a two-ness all over. And something else: maybe she escaped a bad night, a night with no mercy; looks like she walked from a pitiless night where some guy tried too hard.

Her mouth smiles. "Wonderful, aren't they?" she says, nodding at the lions.

Jimmy can tell. Straightaway the looks they exchange tell him. She doesn't want him to speak. So he turns to the lion hunger and steel. Something to reach for in the enclosure, but he turns round. And looks the woman over, wondering. Maybe she's here to go after lions, going with all she's got. She stands so still, only the nano-circuits in her body move.

Some folk have lions in their heart. Jimmy didn't know. Not till now. Everybody gets the same TV, the same camera panning wide to pick these cats lying round or yawning in shade, or moving cubs place to place, or doing the lion groom. But hungry lions are a dread sight. And the greatest part is a big hungry pride, sly, tacking, sectioning, cutting down a savanna that's as heart-stopping and tawny as them.

A summer day, but Jimmy's kind of cold here. Suddenly feeling cut off. Especially from the woman. Her suit's a black shade of grey. This like-two woman in a near black suit set off by the bare arms of everybody else in the crowd. Now she's closer by half a step. Hoarseness in her eyes.

He turns to face her. "How d'you deal with a putdown?"

"What?"

"A racial putdown."

Her face pops. Face like she's been hit, like a rhino in the question. She doesn't turn round. Whatever she'd say, she makes herself hold back from. Her lips a cage. A woman with steel for mouth. Lips confining something wanting a chance to leap, to get away. Her lips full zipped. And, big surprise, she turns to face him. A blank. Her eyes pointblank. A knowing face, but still withholding. Jimmy shrugs.

"Don't forget where you are," she says, nodding at the lions. "You're in a zoo. Don't forget!"

He can't tell: did the woman answer him, or talk to lions? Her suit could mean a trip to Oxford Street; maybe she went past the beseeching eyes of mannequins.

A thick crowd at the lions' enclosure now. But nothing. No gladness. No nerves. No amazement. Nothing but blank stares for tawny life to paint on. Maybe this is love. Or fear. Jimmy's a loner wanting lions, to get their eye, watch their moves, gaze at their stillness. Their loom is the colour of just-washed hay. The same loom that gets blood red every time they eat; but that's the price to pay. The two lions brace. And in all this, only a sneeze ticks by.

A huff from the crowd. Raw, human, indigo. Somebody says you can't be jealous of things in a cage. The mane of the lion is work that never happens except by savanna thunderstorms. A flurry of raindrops nags, a wet swish taunting yawning air. Something will happen.

The lioness shifts. Her eyes move from the crowd. A honey gaze, cool, it dapples air then gets back to the crowd as a clumsy child moves. Straight-away she wants child meat. A spray of anger shrugs from her shoulder.

Nobody speaks. The business is lions, the mane mystic. The hushed crowd gets a heavy mane that turns away to leave them watching. This is reverence. Some folk are jealous. But quiet. The quiet a congregation makes before closing their eyes. Now, his heavy lion gait shovels him sideways. Then sideways some more, over to the lioness. Who pays her any mind? She's seen the whole thing a thousand times, watchers arriving in ones and twos. By now she knows. No, no chance to kill them. This lioness knows lion space.

At the back of the enclosure, something fluorescent and white; an old ribcage stripped bare. Nobody in the crowd knows what it was. And if a chair was near, nobody would sit.

Thunder! Rumbling that blunts gaping air. The two little twin girls get anxious with their mother, the woman with bright red hair and camera. It's going to rain, one twin says; and they don't want to look at lions anymore. The woman mentions ice cream.

One keeper steps up. Nobody asked, but he says when the weather's too hot lions get ice-lolls in the zoo. Vanilla or chocolate? Blood, the keeper drawls. *Blood?* Yes, blood. He explains: lions don't want to feed if the weather's too hot, don't want meat to eat in the heat, they want to drink. They like ice but there's got to be blood, so vanilla or chocolate wouldn't do, so the zoo makes shafts of ice; about the same size as this, the keeper says, extending his arm. Somebody sighs. The redhead woman steps back, miming 'lions licking blood-laced ice.' Another step back, then she looks at the cats, wonders about that ice-loll strangeness.

Lightning strafes the overcast. Lightning flickering in eyes. Laser to laser.

The like-two woman's afraid. Her hands smooth at her suit. "That light-ning," she pants, "it makes the zoo seem like it's up on a screen!"

Jimmy nods. "Yeah, like old silent films you can't turn from."

Her eyes don't follow his. His eyes long for clouds. Hers prefer the cage. His check the time.

"There's something childish about you," she says, eyes settling him.

The lightning could smile. On cue, the psycho light smiles; lightning smiling slick and high. The woman's hand is like a vice on Jimmy's arm; hand wanting muscle from his body. She's scared. Thunder. The sky explodes. Thunder mowing ground. Jimmy holds the woman. But the strangest part is he won't look at her face; what's she want?

And then. It's over. Three, four seconds. Lightning gone. Thunder gone. Nobody saying a word. Bleary eyes. The light fades to twilight. Now a strange scent in air. Strange, but really only the scent of scared air; air round two lions no longer wanting to kill anything that moves.

They turn from the crowd. At the back of the cage now, settled and quiet. Ignoring the crowd, the lioness squats the ground. But her eyes remember. And now the lion connects, gets the join, and humps. His teeth claim her neck. Somebody says his mane is like a bush umbrella. Nobody knows what to make of this. Part of it is the lions don't want to waste time, getting it on because of sudden twilight. But the keeper tells it: these cats mate forty, fifty times a day when the female's in season.

Jimmy checks the time. Arleene. She's so far up the motorway. Far and waiting. But this like-two woman is nice. He knows if they meet again there'll be talk of what happened today; chat the whole lion thing. And that's to be glad for.

Heart thumping, she asks, "Glad for what?"

"It's hard to explain," he says.

"Lions?"

"Them, and a day like this. Yeah."

"The way they did their thing was like any longtime couple in their living room."

Drizzle cuts through air. The big rain gets closer. He wants to ask the woman if they'll meet again. But lions in her heart. His shoulders roll because of her phone number he won't ask for.

# 8

Alone in the carpark, Jimmy's wondering. Weighing a weird day. The weather blinks. Arleene phones.

"How's the traffic?" she says.

"I think it's a bit better. I'll grab a few minutes sleep, then hit the road."

"What's that rattling noise?"

"Me, checking out what's in the glove-box. Music tapes. Pens. A chewed-up old map. But it's the shells. Seashells. I love them. Some in the glove-box. Old nacre, as tender to look at as a dove's eye."

"Get yourself here!"

"Can't wait. But there's that gridlock. It's still there."

"Then forget me, play with your stupid shells!"

"Seashells are strange. They look like they could explain. Getting left behind, tell why."

"You still feel stranded on a coast?"

"Yeah. These shells look like my feelings. One's like sheet-music, two like dice. Whatever lived in a shell listened to the ocean round it. Magic! I mean, shell-life compiling bearings from the sea."

"Get on the road, Jimmy. Ring me when you get near the motorway."

The engine starts. Clutch bites. Wheel turns. But quick! Another feeling. A bad feeling. From this carpark, suddenly all roads might go to Brixton. Nothing what it seems. Maybe not a carpark, not even London. Only one place: the North Pole and polar bears, 50 below. The engine stalls.

Arleene. For a while he let the road to that woman get fallow. Too long a while. So today it's broad daylight. No sneak moon, no nighttime boogie. Not tonight. She wants tonight to be homing night. She knows the score. He'll bring the motorway. Tonight she gets a motorway with voltage tensed by miles. She'll pull that, whisper low.

Rain! The water itch. Rain jumping the limber green as birds hurry past the lowest sky. Jimmy's jealous of bird life. That lightness. Not jealous of birds being light but jealous that birds know where to go. His eyes close. Arleene waiting. Blink open. Slow to close. But close. Sleep a nod away. A quiet nod. One quiet nod. Sleep. Rainwater falling grey and light. And seashells in a glove-box, far from the ocean.

Something. Not a dream. Somebody tapping. Tapping hard. Not exploring. This is no blind someone with a cane. Somebody at the driver's window. He's wide awake.

No more rain. Rays of a new sun tweak the carpark. Through globules of water on misty glass, the face of the woman who was beside him at the lions' cage. The like-two woman, watching.

Her lips part. "You OK?" she says, eyes worried. Her mouth softens. Quietly she repeats it. "You OK?"

"Yeah."

"Sure?"

"Must have dozed off," Jimmy says, eyes open wide. The window winds down. But only part way. "No sleep last night."

"Well, that's it then. Just a nap, top-up the daydreaming?"

"Didn't think I'd see you again."

"Me too."

"Want to go for a drink sometime?"

"Not really."

"Then have a seat. Chat a while."

"Back in the zoo it was like you wanted to yell."

The window winds down all the way. Jimmy blinks. "What?"

The woman shucks rainwater from her hands. Her gaze tells him. She understands. Women read Jimmy. And this one reads him in a wet carpark. He was asleep maybe twenty minutes and, all told, been away from the road two hours. The gridlock will be gone. He hates emotion, fussed emotions. Part of the survival game is emotions, but cut down, stuff that must never get loose. He holds back, watching her eyes. Her decision about him stills her mouth. She weighs the invitation one more time. Her eyes say 'Are you sure it's only to sit and talk?' Weighing him still, she smiles an easy smile. Then steps round the car.

"Lorna," she says, getting in the passenger seat. "Lorna Stanley."

"Jimmy-Lines."

"Jimmy *who?*"

"Jimmy-Lines Dell."

"Nickname, right?"

"No."

"What part of the world is it from?"

"My birth certificate."

"Jimmy," she says, like tasting the name, "and Lines. As in lines on a page? Lines in the sand?"

"Not really. It was travel. Dreams of travel."

"Travel lines?"

"Yeah, latitudes."

"North, south?"

"My old man had a thing for travel. Kind of a weird story."

Her lips press to a smile. "Crisp, meeting you."

"What's in a name? Hey, they might have called you Molly."

"*Molly?*"

His eyes meet hers. And normally this would be it. But the weird thing now is having nil to say. She gets this. It annoys him. But he knows: this is a lot more than babe in a suit. A woman. One that won't bring the day down with small talk.

She turns to him. "You looked desperate in the zoo. It was like you wanted to do an Androcles with those lions."

Jimmy should relax. But something dims the woman's eyes. Some self-denial thing. And the way her eyes just take the right amount of light, all she wants is talk.

His hands grab the wheel. "Desperate, like how?"

"Like you'd *die* if you couldn't get those lions out of there."

"And you wouldn't?"

"The poor things! Even those elephants. Did you see the elephants? Those unbelievable giraffes. The whole affair."

He knows where this chat could lead. Knows the best thing is to back off, better go easy. Pointless trying a chat up, everything about her tells him that. Things always going on in this mid-ground. Even face to face. Maybe it's the way she sits, looking ready for takeoff as robins on a twig. Only a fool would scare her away. "What's the big deal?"

"The deal," she sighs, "is freedom. Ring any bells?"

"Come on! Most people would set those animals free."

"And me and you, we have our hands tied, eh!"

"Yeah, even Mike Tyson's in a cage."

"I've probably got this all wrong, but you're too sure of yourself."

"Like how?"

"It's like you'd want those lions to thank you for it."

"For what?"

"Getting them away."

"What's *that* supposed to mean?"

Lorna's fingers duel the clasp of her shoulder bag. A fidget, wrestle. Finally, the clasp jumps. "You don't get it. Not a clue what's out there, have you!"

"You a teacher? Or is it animal rights?"

Her hand jumps to his arm. A light hand, from a kind heart. A simple hand. Not a prop. Not from a song. Not like a falling leaf. A soft touch moves to his hand. A clenched fist. He can tell; this woman's lived.

"Got a man in your life?"

The hand grabs away. Straightaway. Like from fire. Her body pulls side-ways.

"Woah!" she says. "Slow down! One step at a time. Relationships and things, anybody can do those, you know, have a great time. But it always happens. Breakup time and it's 'How did I *ever* get into that?' Makes me sick!"

Jimmy frowns. This woman confuses him. Her hand was like the touch

16

of a good aunt, a relative, someone close. But she's not auntie, not a relative. Who is she? She talks prophet talk about the zoo, how this place started; but she could be talking bible here.

"Only a Noah could get the animals out."

She sucks her teeth. "You're a pessimist!"

"Caged lions," Jimmy groans, "all they do is run their rails."

"What else can they do? They're in a zoo, true or false?"

Turning away, she eyes the carpark. He wonders about her age; thinking she's as much as thirty two, but maybe only twenty five. Her suit hints a toned feminine body. The body troubles him. And her face; even more to that far-away sideways than her full frontal face. But as she turns round, the body stuns him. Her skirt rounds over a mystic mound. The skirt's like from a hidden faith, like made by an alien seamstress, far from penance, spooking. The near-black cloth looks scarier than a soundless night. Her lips move. But only to mention lion cubs; the life they lead in a zoo. His hands clamp the steering wheel.

Parker's Mood plays. Quieter now. In the pokey car quiet, the tune makes space. Lorna wonders. Somebody gave her a John Coltrane CD and the liner notes talked of Charlie Parker.

"It's the improvising," Jimmy says. "Charlie P was it, way ahead!"

"Ahead of what?"

"Of anybody else. Solos you can see."

"See music?"

"Yeah. Charlie Parker plays blues from blues."

"What?"

"Blues brings jazz. Jazz always gets back."

"*What*?"

"Charlie Parker's solos always get back," he says, trying again.

With the woman in the seat beside him, haunting but not aware, something happens. He wants to find what. Not her body. Not anymore. But the story in her eye.

"What do you do?" she wonders.

"You mean work?"

"It's music, isn't it? You're a music man."

"*That* obvious?"

"A mile off!"

"Well, yeah. Music it is. Piano. Jazz, mostly."

"Jazz?"

"Yeah."

"Come to the zoo for inspiration?"

"Nah!"

"Then why?"

"Music it is."

"Is birdsong music. Birds in a cage?"

"Yes, and no."

"Not sure?"

"Look, sometimes I don't even know what it is."

"Music?"

"Yeah."

"Music is good sound."

"Not that simple. I mean, music is a cage sometimes. There's other stuff. Even music can't reach."

"Like what?"

"Stuff. You know, up to here!"

"Music man," she sighs, "what's wrong?"

He fumbles for a smoke. But none there. "Really want to know?"

"Talk to me!"

Jimmy can't confide. But something Lorna's eyes; he knows she understands. But. She can't know the half of it, can't know what starts in a man's head then trips him.

"It's all pent up," he says. "Bad genie, pissed off!"

Worry in her eye, she turns to him. "What's caused that?"

"There's always stuff to deal with. Weird, weird."

"You mean racism, don't you."

"Yeah."

"So, what's new?"

He turns away, gazing at the carpark. "What is woad?"

"Woad?"

"Yeah. What's it mean?"

"Some people I know never bother saying racism. They say woad."

"Where's it from?"

"It's a plant."

"*Plant?*"

"A long time ago woad made the bluest dye. Bluer than the sky. When Caesar's army came here, 2000 years back, they saw flint-eyed Brits, bodies painted blue with the stuff. Caesar laughed. Had to see for himself. And it rocked him. But the shock didn't last. He was, you know, a man of the world so woad made him laugh. Those bloke Brits smeared with it."

"What about women, the lady Brits?"

"Yeah, the same. Painted their bodies blue with it."

"Then checked their reflections in a stream, no doubt."

"No doubt. Anyway, with Caesar, his southern tan almost fell off, laughing. 2000 years down the road and that blue stuff, it's still here, blue as ever. That's woad."

"Blue die, angry with black skins!"

18

"Yes."

Jimmy sighs. "Ever seen a rhino polevault?"

"What?"

"Rhinoceros on a pole."

"Don't be daft!"

"Rhinos would polevault."

Hands wringing, Lorna's lips dither. "You mean polevaulting, as in *pole-vaulting*?"

"Yeah, run with a pole down the runway. Like a plane."

"That's terrible!"

"Yeah."

"*So* much pain!"

"Yes."

"Makes you want to laugh. But it's serious, isn't it?"

"Laugh if you want," Jimmy shrugs.

"Some guys can't cope," she says, eyes narrowed. "I've seen it before. Flake-highs."

"What?"

"Flake-highs."

"What's that?"

Pulling the skirt below her knees, she steadies herself. Wipes her forehead. "Guys get it," she explains. "British black guys are the worst."

"Giddyness?"

"You guys, it's what you get."

"What is it?"

"Some guys that are confident of the stairs, sorry at the top."

"Vertigo?"

"There's other words I could use."

"Posers?"

"Eunuchs!"

On the tape, Charlie Parker takes a solo. A solo like never heard before: far, desolating, reaching out, wailing through wet weather. A dab at the volume switch and it gets the level it wants.

As the track ends, Lorna and Jimmy sit back. Wordless, spent. Silent, numb, gazing past the windscreen.

His throat clears. "This carpark is only a frown wet weather wears."

"What?"

"I'm no talker. And as for being a listener, well, there's too many guys that don't compose well."

"What d'you mean?"

"Flake-highs sounds like a mind game, or a tower-block tumbling."

"But it rings a bell, true or false?"

Jimmy must find out who Lorna is, where her life. Simple things will do.

Like why she wears a winter suit in a summer zoo.

"Crafty stuff," he says.

"What?"

"It's a doddle, tucking into lengths of it."

"*What* are you talking about?"

"Some of them don't bother with colour."

"I haven't got a clue what you mean."

Weary, he grabs twists her torso to face him. "There's no winks, no nudges. None of that stuff. Some of them listen to jazz, know the snazziest bop."

"Who?"

"Hypocrites. They've got all the moves."

"What d'you mean?"

"Things can be going OK, even great, but when push turns to shove, they jaw."

"They *what*?"

"They jaw," Jimmy says, shrugging.

"What's that?"

"They expect you to be from Brixton."

"Brixton?"

"Some days it's like a hod of bricks. You never feel it?"

Suddenly her tongue is dry. It troubles her mouth. Staring down her hands, she turns them over and over, doing guess work with her palms. And then her eyes. Her brown eyes settle on green things past the windscreen. Still saying nothing, not with her mouth. A kleenex pops from her bag. It wipes the part of windscreen. Clearing the mist. Then she reaches over, wary, wiping misty glass in front of him. Her bag hugs her thighs. Now her hand reaches into it and brings out a postcard. Not saying a word, she writes on the back. Heedful writing. The card passes to him: a postcard of the Tyne Bridge in Newcastle.

Across the carpark, the woman with red hair waves. She's one of the last to leave the zoo; she and her twin girls waving goodbye. Jimmy waves back. The woman and her twins are going home to remember. So much to talk. Way into evening they'll talk what happened at the lions' cage.

Rain stipples the carpark space. Only three cars here now. Quiet sunlight wades through. Jimmy checks the postcard. A brand new card. Lorna maybe meant to post it, but he won't ask.

Then, without a word she steps from the car. Not even saying goodbye. She's crossing the carpark and never looking back.

"If you want to know," he yells, "those lions got me thinking. It should be me and them. Lions and me, leaving, going to Brixton!"

# 9

Instead of straight to the motorway, Jimmy laps Regent's Park. He answers the mobile.

"London Zoo is part of Regent's Park. I'm checking out the Outer Circle. Millionaire apartments going by. The folk here have a story, they live only right next to the zoo."

"You promised," Arleene says, "to get here before dark."

"These apartments must be a buzz," he says. "They probably have crazy parties, really late night stuff. Hear elephants trumpet, and lion danger so near."

"Jealous?"

"Not jealous. On my way to see you, right? Woman, you should see the way lions' eyes are. The gaze. Honestly, this lioness clocked me, sized me up for a feed, and it was like she smiled. I tried to look away, get her to check somebody else, but it was me she wanted to chew. Weird, but I stood there. In another world really. Felt like I was getting a message."

"Yeah. And getting sized up for dinner."

Jimmy's old car goes one more lap round the park. Things were clear in the zoo. Sharper focus. Steel cages clearer than a roadway. Finally the car turns into Albany Road. The motorway's only 5 miles away.

"What happened with your piece for the folk festival?"

"They won't let it in," he says. "The organizer, what a crafty guy! Talking folk, you know, but meaning something else. I'd have shrugged off the usual race words. But Brixton?"

Arleene laughs. "Sociology geeks swap notes over Brixton. White liberals check the nightlife there, sweat the sweat, some wouldn't live anywhere else."

"But nobody says 'Enough!' No geek. Nobody. No astronaut. It's the Brixton bile. Spewed like bad wine. It's like from a gut wanting a garment home."

"It's the skin overcoat!" Arleene says.

Jimmy's going to see a cool woman. Arleene, a clean woman bathed in tamarind. Nothing must spoil it. No skin coat. A hot shower first. Then two baths. Searing. Then dream of a swim in the ocean. He can see: the Brixton putdown was weasel in a steel yard. His fingers click. The ocean's somewhere. To float, or surf in a bay. Or meet a quiet woman opening a door tonight. Late. Arleene, far up the motorway.

# 10

Autumn. A little late this October. But getting set for bluster; arriving more in a leaf every day.

Two trains crashed at Paddington today. Eight dead. At least eight. Being on rails meant nothing to them. More than two hundred injured. More counting, more dead to log.

Jimmy's alone in the flat. At the $8^{th}$ floor window of a north London high rise. Flat broke. Wondering. Seagulls soar. Between the grey tenement blocks they soar today. Some days only a guitar could compete with that; blues guitar, getting down to indigo soul. Electric blues, soloing higher than gulls fly. Or crows.

Listening the blues and considering, testing autumn, he's sure. No more playing for money. Not the hustling. It's clear. Playing for money breaks some players. So no more session work, no more hustling stage. Money's the big smiling-the-smile. Even BB King. Even somebody like him mimics himself on stage. And all because the deal is habit money. BB borrows his own old clothes, Jimmy thinks.

He checks the coffers. Things starting to squeeze. Money down to one week's supplies. And a razor line. Wake up and take a shower, check the time, get to the station to get a train, something on rails all the way, a sure thing. Do that without a blink. Then Paddington happens.

Through the tenement windows, one bad thing is cement. Some days the sky's heavy as cement. Windows are shatterproof. Glass is more like bullet-casing than glass. Some tenement windows have the speckled look of salt. Seagulls go past them. The ocean's too far for salt spray, but breezes grab enough sea to dump on high-rise window panes. Concrete life. Seagull conceit.

Funny enough, it was only after the first news of Paddington that Jimmy weighed stuff. Weighed the tenement box, knowing only fatal livestock can be some place like this; cattle lowing, unknowing, waiting for the last shipment out. It could be Peckham, Hackney, any place. But this time it's in a Tottenham tenement.

Then the dogs. Tenement dogs. *Bad* dogs, psychos, deadeye. Barking louder than cement contains. Mean dogs. But other noises here. Starting with quarrels: shouting that flares any day or night. But the worst part is music. Some folk in the tenement only hear their music when too loud for anyone to listen. And that happens all the time. Bad noise in the block: war cries, human fire, heart flames, cauldrons blaring through concrete five levels away. And noise from drum machines that could be gunfire on a battlefield. Noise so loud that nobody hears what's said, not hear some faithful thing, exactly what must be said quietly to be true.

Jimmy's OK on the 8th, the one they call Neptune. It's always a joke. This tenement's like the solar system, somebody said. Mercury the first floor, Venus the second, then on up past more planets till the top floor. Folk on the 10th got left out; they deal with every kind of alien scare some nights. And somebody can get scared, wondering where gulls go when they swoop past. City gulls mistake the sight of windowpanes for open water; gulls soaring, getting fake ocean from vertical glass.

Drunk, Jimmy talks to a whisky bottle. The bottle-spirit talks back, says 'Them organizers at the festival, the folk festival. Who, them? Big mistake! Minims is crotchets out-paced. Britannia's lips would tell. But her mouth is stone. No black man her boyfriend. No black man her son. But one day she'll respire, in, out, in. Shed stone tears.'

He no longer believes. Not in religion. It bugs him that the whole millennium fuss goes back to a man with a cross to die on, a preacher that some folk refer to by the nickname of Faran.

# 11

Kew Gardens. Jimmy's at Kew, checking out what autumn can do to trees.

All morning, asphalt clouds over London. But getting here by river was a breeze. A riverboat from Westminster. The old Thames was grey and khaki. Longing for the sea, but clinging hard to England.

It was near the Pagoda Vista. That was where he saw her. A shy girl, bevel-eyed and calm; in a whole crowd of women, but still shy. Alone now, her bevel eyes enjoying palm trees of early autumn. She checks them again. Then clocks him. But turns away. Then changes her mind, turns back to him. Her eyes say 'Climb?' Jimmy could laugh. But only nods.

The girl's eyes are serious. He tries a smile. Knows she knows. Her bevel eyes know. Learning from the mirror in her face, he must say something. She bites into a toffee-apple. He fumbles for a smoke. Smoking not allowed here, but already sly tobacco stacks like black silk in a greedy mouth.

"You lost?" he says, closer to the girl now.

A slow smile. Then she squares to him. "No, I'm not lost. I come here often. My third time this year."

"Didn't believe these palms when I first saw them. They're for real."

"The main reason I come. Their sense of hope."

"We all call them palm trees. What's *your* name?"

"Mona."

"Like the Mona Lisa?" Jimmy laughs.

Her eyes roll. "Actually," she says, "I'm Eleanor Rigby."

"Lady, you're a gambler."

"What makes you say that?"

"In a card-pack you'd be in a red suit. Queen of Diamonds."

"I'll settle for the song."

"Then you're Mona Rigby, daughter of Eleanor."

She grins. An elliptic light in her eyes. "You're a smooth one!"

"Butterflies should be coming and going."

"Mmm. There *is* a southerly trace of breeze, isn't there? Nice."

"They call me Jimmy."

"Somewhere in Kew today a carnivore plant's getting fed red meat."

Stepping back, he thinks she can go any place. She's just right for jazz. But maybe not. Mona wraps the apple core in a tissue, puts it in her handbag. Some other loner would tap her shoulder, ask if she walked from a convent. But Jimmy's wondering if maybe she came to gaze at people going by. Lonely people. His throat clears.

"If all you're doing is being a watcher, counting lonely people, then these palm trees would wail."

Ignoring him, her eyes stream the plants. Her eyes gazing like a searchlight. She can't decide.

Closer now to Eleanor's pretend-daughter, he says, "The millennium could be ace. Like a woman. The festival on New Year's day could be like ace women."

She turns right. Then left. Right again. Eyes not easy to read. Not easy to read such eyes, not as before. Eyes, not searchlights. But eyes that could chase sparrowhawks through thickets. Realizing this is a chat-up, a searchlight smile on her face.

"You again?" she says, trying to read him.

"Yeah, me."

"Where's it come from?"

"What d'you mean?"

"Festivals. How can a festival be like a woman?"

Jimmy wants to answer. But talk lets him down. Mona's question is a surprise. Her lips get in the way. Her lips exclude what he could say. Her lips test him. They want something. 'Answer me!' her bevel eyes say.

He shrugs. "Everybody checks festivals."

"You a festival-head, carnivals and all that?"

"Festive stuff is OK," he says. "Fireworks do it for me. But the big one, they're saving that for New Year's day. It'll be huge. There'll be guys goggling gunpowder in the air. Makes me think of handrails, a woman. Something to haul with from the cold."

"What?"

"Handrails," he says, "or women."

"Look!" she snaps, angrily.

"You want me to look at you?" Jimmy laughs.

"It's the way you talk. I mean, *nobody* talks like you. Not even close. I've never come across anybody that talks like you. What's this about?"

His shoulders heave. Half-heave. Then take set. Mona's head levels with his shoulders. He wonders if she was a little taller or less plain if there'd be a plant that she was like. "From your face," he says, "you lag behind what you want."

"What I want?"

"Yeah."

"What's this about! You a fortuneteller?"

"I don't believe that stuff. You?"

"Then what *are* you saying?"

"It's your eyes. You're a serious woman. But you have a long way to go. There's things you don't know."

"Nobody knows everything. But I bet *you* do!"

"There's attendants," Jimmy shrugs, "and there's what gets kept."

"What?"

"The plants. Look around."

"These plants have a great time."

"So you say."

"They obviously get looked after. It's about conservation, isn't it? Kew keeps the rarer species going."

"Politicos talk that stuff."

"I never do politics. Ever!"

"Knee-deep bull to wade."

"Yes."

"These plants are a sideshow."

"I still don't get it," Mona says. "I mean, if not about the plants what were you thinking?"

"It was, well, you know what I'm saying."

"No!"

"Things, the way things pan out."

"Like *what*?"

"If it wasn't for water these plants wouldn't be here in the first place."

"Straight out of genius college!"

"Another millennium, another splash of bull."

"What's this *about*?"

"What more can I say?"

Near to Jimmy and Mona, somebody wonders out loud. Wonders if some plants can walk round or even run, saying elephants can't run but only walk, reaching the speed of a racehorse, but even then the elephant's only walking.

Mona's eyes flit from the palm trees. "Tell me about fireworks. You like fireworks."

"And I like women, right?"

Shy again, her lips relax. "Yeah, I can tell."

"Can you?"

"I bet you play the field. It's all over you, you wicked!"

"Wicked?"

"Oh, come on!"

"Where we off to?"

"Think you're amazing, don't you!"

"No complaints. Not too many."

"Know what? I half believe you. Yeah. So, tell me about women."

"Where shall I start?" Jimmy says, grinning.

"Tell me all you know."

"Well, there's cherry trees and me to pluck them."

Weary, she wilts. Suddenly miffed. Her eyes veer away. They check the cloud stack. "Can I ask a question? Why d'you always look up at the sky? Got your magic carpet on its way?"

"No. But I met a woman one day, a sky-diving woman."

"Well, I am *not* her."

"It's the rain," Jimmy blinks. "Rain makes me think of nakedness."

"What?"

"No magic carpets in your sky?"

"Look, I don't know what you want!"

"What's wrong with a few magic carpets, now and then?"

"Where did they get *you* from?"

"Here at Kew, they have pineapples ready to eat."

"Well," she sighs, "OK. So that's what this is, is it?"

"How d'you mean?"

"Who sent you to torment me?"

"Hey, everybody does magic carpets. Music rides on it."

"Then get on yours, and magic off!"

He turns to her. And starts to sing, *"When I get older, losing my hair, many years from now_"*

*"*You don't look like somebody who likes the Beatles.*"*

"Woe is me."

"Where's the magic carpet?"

"We can make it happen. I'll share yours, ride it with you."

Stifling a smile, she studies him. Steps back. Head shaking, again. Then shrugs. "OK. I give in! If it'll make you happy I could always do with a bit of magic."

"*Now* you're talking!"

"You're not from the sky, then?" she laughs.

"No sky, no stars."

"What about rain?"

"No rain. No birds."

"Not kites!" she says, suddenly chilled. "*Anything* but kites!"

"Race is only a kite."

"What?"

"Kites, stuff with strings attached."

She turns away. Looking at the palm trees as if for help. This is the weirdest day in her life. Looking round herself. Checking where. A journey starts in her eyes. She's far away. Thinking. Wondering. Squinting at the palm trees. Looking left. Looking. Then right. Then. She gets back from her voyage. Got the answer. Her lips lick. But before she talks, the look in her eyes makes Jimmy worry what she might tell.

"Kites scare me," she says.

"How'd kites get into this?"

"You and your magic carpets, weird skies!"

"Not as strange as millenniums."

"Hoo-hah about the millennium? *So* silly. Fireworks are so expensive.

And the fact that nothing will have changed will be a *horrible* let down. You'll see."

Jimmy knows Mona's disappointed. She expected more. But knows nothing about him.

"What's going on?" she wonders.

"How d'you mean?"

"If you want to ask me out, why not ask?"

"Well, yeah. You're it. Beautiful."

"*Not* beautiful."

"No, seriously. You are."

"Look, I'll have to go in a minute. You interested, or not?"

He won't ask why she's scared of kites; no time, not for the jolting answer she could give. He tries again, low this time. "With music," he says, "I get what I need. My life's from music. It's what I'm about. It's there all the time for me."

"And?"

"Music shakes the crap out of kite-flyers, chucks them like rubbish in a hurricane."

"*What?*"

"Elephants can't run, they only walk."

Hand to her mouth, she stops short of laughing out. But giggles. Giggling the kind of private space where a secret trips. This goes on a while. Sometimes her eyelids move as if dreaming. Jimmy likes her. She's a serious woman, a worrier, not the kind to carry cement from a shed.

"Where will you go after leaving here?"

"I don't know," he says. "People can come from only one place at a time."

"So, where do *you* come from?"

"Music land."

"Jazz?"

"Yeah."

"Then where does jazz come from?"

"A brothel. Flowers in brothels. Jasmine."

"*Jazz?*"

"Yeah. It started in a brothel. Jasmine were the flowers they used to cut the scent of flesh. But jazz, the music, that comes from any place. Anytime. You could be looking at trees, or notice somebody scared."

"I don't understand!"

"Rivers always have some place to go."

"Rivers?"

"Yeah."

"Why pick on them?"

"Ask your coach-driver."

"*What?*"

"A coach-driver brought you here today. Then must get you away."

"Look, I haven't got a clue what you're on about!"

"Try a man and woman," Jimmy grins.

"Why?"

"Man and a woman together, doing the business."

"This is madness. You're *mad*."

"So they say. So some say."

"I've never come across the likes of you before. Never!"

"A man and woman have one great place to be alone."

"And where's that?

"By the river, on the river. Any river."

"Because?"

"Rivers go down to the sea."

"You don't say!"

"They meander down. Got to get to the sea, the sea."

Resigned, her head shakes. "The banks of the old Thames."

"What?"

"The river Thames," she laughs, "it's the nearest river from here."

Listening to Mona laugh, Jimmy could close eyes here. Her laugh making him almost forget Arleene. Arleene's in London tomorrow. But today, well. This girl won't carry cement. Her eyes say 'Your move!'

"How did Brixton get like it's my home ground?"

She blinks. "*Where?*"

"Brixton."

"Be serious!"

"I'm joking?"

"A big fat chip on your shoulder!"

He grabs a smoke. Her lips itch. She's never smoked. Not once. But he can tell. Something about the mention of Brixton worries her. The cigarette's alight. A quick furtive drag.

"The Thames," she says, wanting to change tack, "it's so mythic. I hear somebody plans to swim the length of it."

"It flows past this place."

"Yes, but Brixton doesn't!"

"Dolphins swim in the Thames."

"Now and then. But dead bodies float on it. Gross!"

Somewhere in the British Museum is a manuscript in Nile papyrus. And one of the pyramids holds a mortgage on the solar system; that's the talk going between two people standing near the palm trees.

Mona says, "I work in PR."

"A glitzy job like that?"

"PR does lots."

"Like?"

"Toothpaste, trains. The rest of it."

Jimmy checks the time. "Long day."

"Say you mean it!"

"Mean what?"

"Chatting me up. That's what this is, isn't it?"

"Dolphins are great."

"Wall!"

"Dolphins, beautiful as you."

"If you don't stop it, I'm leaving!"

He checks the time. Again. Then checks the girl beside him. "Next time they talk about immigrants, you know, some moron going on about boat-loads coming to the country, tell them about the Thames after rain. Raw sewage floats on it after rain."

"Is that true?"

"Heavy rain, London's old drains overflow into the Thames."

"What's that got to do with immigrants?"

An attendant approaches the palms. The cigarette trips from Jimmy's fingers. Hits the ground. Resolute, his feet click. Not tap-dancing. But quickening feet. Chasing fire.

"Immigrants get treated like shit."

"They come by the planeload these days," Mona says. She laughs.

"My father's an immigrant."

Straightaway, a cough. It escapes the heart in her mouth. Her eyes are sorry. Bevel, a quiet hazel. Misty, older eyes. "Sorry," she whispers. Knowing eyes. Her voice lowers. "Honestly, I'm sorry. I know what you mean. That terrible Brixton thing."

Jimmy hates this. Hates to see this ace girl detached. Wants her back on track. Maybe even get her from here. To break the ice, he tells his full name. Then, to test her, admits it. Admits being a womanizer, got a woman or two, saying one woman's far up the motorway. She asks if the women are black or white. He says he could spend the whole day with a Mona Rigby. She turns away. Disappointed. But wondering. Thinking. Smiling a shy while away, a whole life in her quietness.

"And," she says, "after leaving here, we'd go back to your place?"

Any loner could listen to this voice. Mona's voice. She's so close. But more far than near, like at sea. Jimmy can tell. Fairytale or no, she wishes for the sea. She could sail solo or crew a yacht, go the whole ocean. But not today. He'd gallop her like a mare. He wants to get her away. But.

Her friends are back. Made their excursions, and want to sit on the coach and chat. Her friends are back. Closer and closer, gathering round. Tugging at Mona. Jimmy steps back as they tease her away. They know she's not ready to go. But eke her with them. Her eyes say she mustn't go, not yet.

Looking over her shoulder. Looking back.

He wonders if her friends thought of Brixton, seeing her in the frame with him. Her eyes say goodbye. One final time. Sad eyes. Torn.

"Sorry," she says, moving with the crowd. "Got to go. Hope you get there, you know, wherever. And good luck with it, whatever!"

Spit pits ground. Jaws clenched, Jimmy grabs a smoke. Watching the girl fade to her crowd. Her wordy crowd. Never see her again. Then he remembers: elephants can walk fast as a horse gallops. One last nod. He's alone in the footprint of palms. Checking the time.

# 12

One old song claims autumn is for weather playing. Autumn is about old songs. And new songs. Autumn sheds a leaf or garden shears.

Today the jobs' pages didn't work. Not for Jimmy. Money's tight. Some things must go. Great things. Ganja. None from now; for a while spliff-life is over. Even tobacco must cut back. He's taking stock. Wondering. And playing Drifting On A Reed. Learning from Bud Powell. Learning from JJ. But still can't believe Charlie Parker. JJ Johnson was the first guy to bebop trombone, and trombone was the first thing Jimmy played. Way before serious piano, it was trombone. But it was never the lung power, the monk-like to bulk, it was the clown side to playing it. He jotted a reason on a record sleeve: 'Playing trombone,' the note says, 'is not the kind of thing you do and keep a straight face, not while a room of nice looking women are looking at you. So play piano from now. Playing piano, you never look up halfway through a solo, catch folk reading your life.'

Last night Arleene didn't show. From the phonecall Jimmy could tell. She may never show again. Now he remembers how they met. Two years back she was going down the street one day, minding her business, looking like a tamarind tree. Drifting On A Reed plays like that first chat with Arleene.

'Woman!' he said, and it was one autumn day like today. 'Mmm, what's your name?' Arlene said zil. Holding her head high, moving along, fast and proud. That day was gold. Autumn leaves everywhere. So he tried a new tack, pointed at leaves. Arleene was moving faster but couldn't get away. So she swiveled round. Fire in her eyes. But then surprised herself. Because, well, her lips glowed. Heady lips. She said 'OK, you want to play? So play!' Jimmy smiled. And got to play that woman that same day. Arleene can play. Every now and then it's the way it should be, play-that-woman time. Note after note, note, note.

A music man, Jimmy knows things can never be bad like two trains colliding. Not at Paddington. Any place. Three days since lifesavers got there. Now some sly official logs the dead, talks weasel. Industrial cleaners are at the crash site still. And a big sponge wiping away that caked blood. 31 dead, 400 wounded. A solo train crash is bad. But not two trains. Not colliding on rails.

Arleene heard about the crash. It made her worry. She didn't get on the train to London. When she phoned it was about angels, saying angels could be for real, they carry condolence, or tug at weather like pulling a shawl. Then it was Parker time. Charlie P soloing a conduit.

# 13

Last week should have been a dry run for Minims. And a midnight gig. Would have been good money, but Jimmy didn't show. Alone, standing at the window. Broke.

One job advert puffs out: *£1000/week. No experience necessary.*

"You sound like a hurdler," he says.

The voice gulps. "What do you mean?"

"It's like you're reading post-it notes on a running track."

"What?"

"You could be a scene in Piccadilly, bouncing on a trampoline. It's like you have your mobile in one hand and knickers waving in the air."

"Mind how to talk to me!" she says. "Or I'll put the phone down!"

"What's the job about?"

"Nothing else like it. I mean, anywhere. Great money. A once in a life-time opportunity. Loadsamoney. *Gorgeous* benefits!"

"A grand a week?"

"Earn that here, yeah!"

"Doing what?"

"You're a fussy one! Nobody real sniffs at great money, meet some *unbelievable* go-getters."

Jimmy's not looking for careers. That's why the phone waffle. Mostly. But tomorrow's the interview, size the size of the money.

It was the voice. A voice that jumps like a water-hose in town squares. The girl's voice was like from Brazil, like a coast town where somebody sits a lifetime to watch weather walk. Maybe this explains Astrud Gilberto, Jimmy thinks. He was thinking Astrud black, singing the way she sings, like Vivo Sonhando or The Shadow of Your Smile. A big surprise, that CD picture of a white woman. Astrud, a white woman with old ocean voice.

The voice of the phone girl made Jimmy curious. New music waits for a voice like that. Maybe she's a singer already, a jazz-lone; maybe making ends meet by temping on the phone. From her voice she wants it to happen. He thinks behind that hurdling is good music, she wants to prove her worth. Maybe she sings in a nightclub, or singing some safe place. But her voice is a hill, a sunshine mound, fresh, ripe, a Margarita sunset. Maybe her roots in Jamaica. Maybe her parents come from that island place. Or she's white, English white.

# 14

Jimmy was born in '78. Same year of the disposable single-blade razor. And one blaring day the National Front marched in London, dead set against Britain joining Europe, waving banners, beating their drum, shaking fists, chanting 'Get the reds!'

Nathan was welding steel, working in Liverpool 6 days a week. And that's when the map got noticed; how Jimmy got named.

The map was in that dictionary they still have. It dropped to the ground a day after he was born. But it was only a sketch, line upon line connecting Jamaica to England. Straight-lines, sketched when Nathan was whiling Kingston away in the 60s, wondering what the next move was after Jamaica got independence from England.

Money. Or it was education. Moving to England was supposed to be a better life. Even now, Nathan says it was the money. But it was timing more than anything; time to quit the sun. Nathan made the trip in '65. Harold Wilson was prime minister a year already. Ten years later, he was doing a second stint at No 10 when Jimmy was born. His mother was 17, the adopted daughter of a black family in Liverpool. Nathan was 35. Straight from the hospital Jimmy grabbed out at music. And it was Charlie Parker music playing in the small house on the Wirral. Everybody milled round, looked the new arrival up and down, saying he'd never want to govern the Bank of England.

The big thing was a name. And that's when it started. Glad noise. One side of the family got a name, played with it a while. Same thing the other side. Everybody looking for the best name. And the first best name was Moses. That's a name with mission, somebody said. Moses from water, yes, the warrior part of the wise bible. But Nathan trumped that. He said a better name was Miles, a name out front. And that was that. Well, for the hour. Everybody knows Miles Davis but in England somebody called Miles would have to squeeze lemons to get sunshine. A black guy born here and then called Miles would get laughed at here, that's what they said; white folk would laugh at black Miles. Nathan built a spliff. He was going through a Dizzy Gillespie phase. Right alongside Art Tatum music. That's how Dizzy and Art got there as two names for Jimmy. Then it was Ellington, even Thelonious. Then they tried something else. Kingston Dell was it for a while. It had a shout. Loud or slow, it had a shout. But. They knew. It was just one step too far in England, getting called after some Jamaican place; too backward looking, they said. And then. The name got solved. The map.

It happened by pure chance. That map dropped out of the dictionary. Those straight lines, Jamaica to England. Everybody was stock quiet. Nice quiet. Bigger than luck, somebody said; just how it should be. And that was that. Because after all the shouting, coming and going, it was Jimmy-Lines Dell.

Later on, it was getting music education. Fugues and counterpoint, and some of the neatest notes anywhere. That music degree was higher than staves.

Hard to believe, knowing Jimmy, but it was theology that was the first academic thing. But after one year theology was only a jester to him, nothing to think. So it was straight off to music. 'Why music? Why now?' the dean asked. Jimmy said theology wasn't getting any place, marking time, but getting nowhere. The dean said machines mark time, even a budgie can mark time. Jimmy wrapped that music degree in two years. And now, if only one advice he'll give it's that serious music is Ellington as much as Bach. But only people way down the road from their own shadow should try composing.

The rest of the way's been up and down. Nothing to write home about; not far enough out front. Not yet. Stopgap job after job. Stirring water when money runs dry. But travel gets the full ten by ten. And woman, woman, woman. Just because of the wildness, that stuff never gets home.

The only down side is losing absolute pitch. Jimmy had great ears. Could tell any tone. But lost it early this year after a bad flu. Doctors can't explain why. But he gets by on relative pitch. More than gets by.

For now, it's life in a high-rise block. A loud place. Most days, checking out that book by the wheelchair man: A Brief History of Time.

# 15

Autumn could bring a bout of flu. A northerly wind gusts in the streets. They said the interview needs suits and ties. But Jimmy's going anyway. No suit. And no tie. For one whole hour there's only traffic to chide.

Taking a chance, he turns off the high road. Sudden quiet. A tree-lined avenue. Everything reserved. Nobody would connect this easy place to traffic. A straight roadway, the avenue whispers by in a blaze of trees.

The trees are different here. Some show by glistening. But something deeper than being a tree. The avenue loves them. These trees look like an invitation: 'Forget the interview. Stop. Grab some quiet. Look!'

Newton was on the radio earlier. Jimmy dropped the whole world just to listen, transfixed by the spat Newton had with Leibniz. Looks like the German was right, the radio said. But Isaac unpacked a prism one day. His head flashed. 'Good God!' he must have said, as the prism in his hand untwined light, carding it like wool. Light was only a weave, Isaac said; light was never white, it was a weave of coloured thread. Shy in front of the naked universe, lovelorn, Isaac looked bleary-eyed at the prism. Fondling it. And ambled to a window to scan, clear tears from his eyes. Nothing the same again. Not the sun. Even the sky was no more a virgin. A light-mystic now, Isaac starts a song to the sun, wanting to undress light one more time. Just by a prism in his sweating hand.

The car stops. Jimmy checks. His fingers tap the steering wheel, quietly click. Jealous of Newton. Jealous of Hawking's eyes. Jealous of how Isaac was first to see light beautiful and naked, his voice starts: 'Hey light, don't be shy. Take off the rest of it! Come on, I've seen it all before. What, you want me to turn the light off?'

The radio didn't put the story that way. It was Isaac under that apple tree one day. Then the prism.

Checking autumn in the avenue, Jimmy gets a feeling the story's been only half told. Newton could have done it with autumn. More leaves than apples fall. And smart women would want to talk autumn more than eat apples. Isaac could have reached gravity quicker; like maybe if he was out walking with a woman one autumn. A smart woman. A real headstrong woman. Jimmy makes notes:

The woman say, 'Something or other obviously accounts for leaves falling, but light is deeper.'

Sulking, Isaac ask, 'Why?'

She say, 'Dear Isaac, don't think I'm trying to be Eve. Don't think I want my private little Eden, but it's not normal to pull light down like apples in a garden.'

'I am Newton!'

'But of course!' she say.

Isaac growl, 'Here, take this prism. It'll remind you.'

'Remind me?' she say. 'Of what?'

'Because of this little prism the whole universe is a coach and horses to me, a mere machine. Here, take the reins!'

Jimmy grabs a smoke. Music in the avenue. Somebody could do an opera, call it Newton And The Woman. In one bay-window bronze leaves defy a glass vase. The cigarette lights. He should be hurrying for a job interview. But this place, this autumn mood's bigger than that.

After the avenue the rest is a blur. Somebody else would head to Newton's tomb, check what's said there. But Jimmy shoots the car to an air hole. The radio volume's too high. The road's clear, moving along to somebody scatting.

Suddenly, a weird sign. It cuts through roundabout haze. The logo does not boast. But it wants to star. Bolted over a dizzy stairway, the sign comes straight down from a dimwit door that somebody believes looks prophetic. Metallic-orange, it glints: Homes, Homes & Homes.

# 16

Only one empty seat in reception. She shrugs. She's the hurdler on the phone yesterday and guesses who he is, maybe because of not wearing a tie. Her eyes tease. She's not content here; nods when asked if she ever listens to Brazilian love songs.

Her voice doesn't matter to Jimmy. Not now. Too much in her eye. Learned the tease game here. She's maybe twenty six but should get told why teasing is a bad mistake. But he won't preach.

"I'm not a painter," he says

She frowns. "What's that to me?"

"There's ace painters out there."

"So what?"

"A painter would get the art in your face."

"Most people mind their own business!"

"You have a yearning. Get it tagged, or it'll bring you down."

Turning away, he shrugs. Looking round the squat reception, only odd-job faces gazing back. Empty face after face. Most of the chairs don't belong in reception. Jimmy takes the one empty seat. But not at ease, shuffling already. This is nerves. Wanting-to-leave time.

"Would you all like to come this way," a woman says, gliding past the reception desk. She wears it well, a spick beige suit wanting to smudge light. "Kept you all waiting. Been a terrible, terrible 2 o'clock. I'm so sorry. Not to worry. We'll just be a minute. We'll get acquainted in a minute. One little minute."

Everybody looks past the woman. Look up at the wall clock. Twenty past two. She's a big dresser. But doesn't connect. Some people here think she could be a chat-show host on TV. Everybody gets annoyed by the loud tinkling. Her earrings make a baubling noise; they're big as mini-coconuts, the biggest earrings any place in London. Earrings this big could be heartless.

Earrings clattering, she leads the way to an airy room. Most guys here already know; this woman likes it hot. Rhythm, hot and lots. A woman with those earrings could keep time with a rock-band, somebody says. But not past limits. That's because what a bebop drummer can do, or a bebop bass, well, just too much bop for this woman to ever keep time. Then again. Maybe she's not for razzle. Maybe she never got naked to real rhythm. Maybe she's eye-line, liking to look. And one thing's sure: she wants to get gazed at. Earrings, tinkling like ride-cymbals. Max Roach could set them, get a 5-4 over 3-4, get them ear things to ring! She looks the kind that goes to Land's End to watch birds migrate.

Strict at the head of the room, she says, "I'm Colette Core. I'm the sales manager at Homes, Homes & Homes. I started where you all are. And that's plain scared, apprehensive. I was a single mother, a single mum with a part-time partner. Bills everywhere. That was six years ago. So relax, I've been there. Please, relax. I'm also on the board here."

Close as looking allows, every male reflects on the woman. Her name should be Maybeline; somebody says it should be a country & western name. Something about the way she holds herself is cut to order. Huge danger. She's maybe thirty-eight. But could be more. Her body holds her clothes. A bozo model practicing years wouldn't manage it. But something else. Colette is tabloid, somebody says; her clothes are cut from good cloth, but a show-off. Maybe she gets hot sun for holidays. Florida.

"Nothing like gender matters here," she says, hips dipped to the table. "We don't care where you come from. You, your parents, anyone. We want good people. People who communicate. The first lesson is to know what our customers want. Are you with me? That's how we achieve our goals."

Everybody upright in a chair.

Colette sips water, wary. Her eyes get every face in the room. "When I started here," she says, "our turnover was under two million pounds. Way under. Last year we topped thirty million. This year we'll hit thirty five. Yes, five mill sunny side up! All the experts said you couldn't do it. So-called experts. They all said it can't be done. Know what? I can't stand clever. What do they know? *Anything* is possible! We're looking to share our success. Want to work hard? Yes? Then we want you! I mean, work hard *all day*! The rewards are here. Everyone of you can earn fifty grand, anything! Is there anyone here who can't work hard enough to enjoy a thousand pounds a week?"

"What do we do to earn it," says a woman's middle-class voice.

Everybody looks round, checking this out. Checking the completion in the voice. A class act. Her hair is close cropped. What's she doing here? She cropped that hair to get forgiven? What's she done? Jimmy knows if she ever listens to jazz then it's Brubeck or Stan Getz. Maybe she can play some instrument, even piano. Or she can play lute. Something solo about her. Something bitter. Maybe she makes instruments. Or the lute was what turned her to a cropped-hair, closing her eyes at home to listen Gregorian chants. But a class act, out on her own in a room where women outnumber men by more than two to one. Colette doesn't like her.

Cropped-hair tries again. "The person on the phone, quite a pleasant girl, but it was all very cloak-and-daggerish. Can't you tell us what the job entails? Could we start with how the earnings come about? I so need to know the facts."

"What's the problem?" Colette gags, eyes narrowed like blinds. "Aren't you all salespeople?"

Thick quiet in the room. And somebody getting queasy, remembering a boat trip one night. It was the English Channel. The way back was queasiness because of the water; looking at the wind on water was what caused the problem. The water was deep and black, deep, deep black, its own creature, able to ride its own back. And only water can ever do that. Seasickness was on the boat. And a drunk shouted, 'Don't look at the sea! Focus on the stars!' Somebody shouted straight back, 'Where the hell are the stars tonight!'

The forecast this morning was via satellite shots. London warmer than Athens, and Malaga hot all day. Then Sydney. In less than a year the Olympics in Sydney. And that means class. Getting to know. Sports genius. Great runners, greats. Michael Johnson, Haile Gebrselassie.

This group-interview's getting like a queasy boat ride. Looks like the way to the money is over water. Only a minute back, the room was all Colette. Now a dizz. Only one open-water swimmer here. And that's the old sales hand, a wary guy pushing sixty.

This man must have seen the likes of such spiel before. Turning round, his wry eyes wonder where the stars. "Looks like we're wasting our time," he says. "The job-advert said *No experience necessary*. The papers must have got it wrong."

Colette's hand shoots the air. "Hang on! Just a sec. There's got to be a mistake. I'm positive! If there *is* a mistake then we'll refund all your expenses. You'll get your traveling expenses. We'll have this sorted in a sec. One minute, no more."

As she quits the room the old sales-hand whistles. Low and slow. His whistle grabbing at the woman boss. Even her suit doesn't disguise the hips. But 22 suspicious folk, quiet now in a suspicious room. Nothing getting said.

Eventually, throats clear. Random chats start. But nobody walks. And nobody mentions how the doorway sliced Colette's symmetry as she went through it. She's made for pirates, somebody says; pirates making a good take would heave-ho, row dat boatload body bay.

Worry in the room. Nobody's waiting for transport fares. Money time. That grand a week, now. Folk in the room are a job-lot. Weird, hungry. Only halfhearted chats start. Guff. Student types squaring off with wary middle-aged. Everybody's going through hard times. One man looks like a big time bank manager visiting a country fair. Some here are too mishmash to describe. Jimmy accepts that maybe he's the weirdest of all. Some under twenty, nervy, joking. Three big on grey hair. Some don't talk. And maybe only the cropped-hair woman's worth talking to anyway. One girl trashes the whole room just to take her coat off. Somebody else looks for what to see through the window. But only cars out there, all from the up-side of the market, gleaming in a smudged afternoon. Jimmy's hand in his jacket pocket, encountering the postcard Lorna Stanley handed him at the zoo.

# 17

Colette moves one pace before the spent man. A grey, drinking man. His gait breaks down and jump-starts, short strides with no knee-lift, not the type that was ever fit. His aftershave chugs the room. Then the champagne grin. His gaze telling the women they're already in his eye.

Colette turns to the room. "This is Mr Core. Our MD. He'll say a few words."

"Afternoon!" the man grins, signing the room in a checking applause. "Good afternoon. Welcome, welcome. It's Clive Core. Clive. Apologies for the mix-up. All my fault."

Something wrong. Nice looking goods through the window; through glass a white Porsche and red Maserati dovetail a yellow Bentley in the car park. Then the easy tailoring on the woman, bespoke suit on the man. But the place itself. It looks clunked, not success. Nothing wise is here. Nothing reserved because of good taste. The big Bentley could be green, blue or black; anything but yellow. And the Porsche silver or grey, the Maserati blue. Everybody in the room sits back. A show is starting.

"Homes, Homes & Homes," Clive says, "is a byword for, yes, *homes*. Aha, ha, ha! Ladies and gentlemen, we're into homes here. We do home improvement on the outside, home improvement on the inside. Beautiful, or what? When I started this game, I was running errands in a little architect's office. That was what, 40 years ago? We do your conservatories, your extensions. All your double glazing. You want? We do!"

No ashtrays, but the old sales-hand asks if smoking is OK. Clive nods. Then steps back, rubbing his cufflinks. With enough rubs, those links will make a genie appear. The room expects a puff of smoke.

"To continue the good work," he says, "we're looking for excellent people. The best."

Cropped-hair says, "What's the job?"

"The job? Ah, yes."

"Is this about sales?" she says.

"Well, now. That's why you're all here. The job is our customers. Meeting them on their doorsteps. Tell them the *great* news at Homes. Ah, ha, ha! We want marketing executives. Only the best people, mind! The ones with the dog's bollocks in their eyes. They'll know who they are. Earn a lot of money, a *lot* of money!"

Wry, the old sales-hand smiles. "What's a lot of money?"

Clive steps to the man. "You tell me. Name me a figure."

"That grand a week in the advert would be handy."

"Want a grand a week?"

"That's why I'm here!"

"Well, you'll have to work for it. Ladies and gentlemen, only one trick. What you earn is down to you. Your bottom line is in your own hands."

"The more you graft," Jimmy says, "the more you make. Easy!"

Straightaway, Clive stops. Suspicion. Puzzle. Looking at Jimmy. Frowns. Hand to jaw. Weighing. "Now then, what have we here!"

Jimmy shrugs. "I believe in hard work."

Cold craters in his eyes, Clive grins. "This guy, this man without a collar and tie, he tells us he can work hard."

"It's how I've always made my way."

Clive points to his neck. "You must have the balls of Branson, coming here without a tie. Never seen anything like it. Never! Think you're Richard Branson, do you? That good? Sure of yourself, are you?"

"I never need ties," Jimmy says. "Hold my own without them."

Hand on chin, Clive steps back. But only to study the loner with no tie. Jimmy's in the circus-master's light. Getting rattled.

"*You,*" Clive says, halfway approving, "you'll do all right here. Yes. Believe it, my friend!"

Jimmy turns to the room. Turning round and round, checking. Cropped-hair winks. Clive ambles back to the room top, his circus eyes collecting the assembly. Colette lights a smoke.

"You all want money," she says, slapping her hands together. "You all have a need. So let's get there together. You all with me?"

With one voice, the room says it aloud, 'Yes!' And straightaway a money wad jumps from Clive's pocket. The wad flexes. Flexing and flexing. The room belongs to him. The room is numb, in a cage.

"Anybody not sure what this is doesn't need to be here," he says. "Come, here's fifty quid, call it traveling expenses. Fifty quid each for anyone who doesn't want to be here. Come, take your fifty quid. Please, leave now. No hard feelings. What, no takers?"

The old sales-hand smiles. "We're not going anywhere."

"Well, OK! Looks like we've got winners here today. My friends, let's get ready to rock and roll!"

"How long," Jimmy says, "before we start getting the money in the advert?"

Following Clive's gaze, the room gazes at the carpark through the window. Quiet gazing.

"See that Porsche?" he says. "Brand new. Cash! Young guy from sales. Been with the company, what, 18 months? Only just turned 23 and, know what? Earned 150 grand in 12 months! Kid that age pulling more wedge than the prime minister! Our marketing execs do very well here. Commitment. We call it success, the kind you hold with your own hands. Wouldn't trust any other kind!"

Colette's eyebrows raise. She lights a new smoke. The old sales-hand sizes her up. One more time.

Clive turns to the room. "My friends, that grand a week is down to you and you alone. Want those things you deserve? Really *want* them? Want to show you can get 'em? Get legal, mind! Your own property. Weekends in Moscow. Easter in New York. A lovely new car. Aaah!"

Cropped-hair puts her hand up. Wanting to be polite, but she needs the end-game. Her cropped hair looks neat and sandy in the blonde room light. A nervy cough, and she's ready. "What do marketing executives do? Not the same as canvassing, by any chance?"

Clive frowns. Wrangling his braces, eyes turned on the woman. "*Canvassing*? What's that?"

"Well," she says, "if it's houses, it's probably knocking on doors all day."

"Oh dear, oh dear! Must be something wrong with my dear old ears. Canvassing? My friends, that word sounds like, well, it sounds like one of those screens you used to get at a lido. No. No, we don't have those here, thank you very much! Would be, like what, twelve Ford Mondeos in the carpark at Saatchi."

"So what's the difference?"

"Between?"

"Canvassers and marketing execs."

Clive's chin struts, juts from a Mussolini to a bear-fist. Proud at the window, chin up notch by notch. His right hand jumps to his temple and salutes the carpark. "The difference, ladies and gentlemen, is thirty-five grand a year. Earn fifty grand here."

The old sales-hand shrugs. "Why only fifty. Why not sixty?"

"I know where this is going," Clive says, teeth clenched. "See any rubbish in that carpark? Look again, my friends. Any Mondeos, even one Escort? No, and no! *Canvassing*? Do me a favour! At Homes we're into the mind. My friends, a marketing executive is someone of the mind. Not academics. Our best sales guys, the best sales people, most of them don't have any paperwork to speak of. But tell you what, some go on to employ the best of them with degrees and what have you. And that's down to just one thing. Commitment. Sexy, or what!"

"But what do we exactly?" cropped-hair demands now, not asking. "What do we *do*?"

Clive's eyes project to the carpark. Everybody must love the hardware outside. He turns to the room. Hollywood sun in his eye. "Want some of that carpark?"

"Who," she groans, "would say no!"

"By the end of your second week, you will each do 300 quid a week. But I'll tell you now, only the totally committed will stay the course. Only the best gets that grand a week. Tough old world. If you've got any frailties this job finds you out. I must tell you, of the 20 of you here today only one will be here next year. Only one. That's the bottom line. Only *one* of you."

Cropped-hair's eyes narrow. "Which one is that going to be? The rest might as well not bother, go now."

"The fittest!" Clive yells, banging the window sill. "Fittest gets the money! Couldn't be simpler, could it? Man or woman, the fittest. All down to that Charles Darwin. *Where* would we be without him? Where, indeed. My friends, a quick hand for Charles Darwin!"

Everybody gets it. This is no longer about jobs. A great show here. World class. A place where rabbits will jump from a hat. But. Clive doesn't convince everyone. Face sweating, he's in reverie. A woman mumbles, saying he trips over his own capacity, a talent that could make it in burlesque; his name should be 'His Hollywood' she says.

Clive grins. "Never underestimate me. Never second guess me. We're a growing company, top dog in the M25. But watch this space! You will all work in London. Those lovely, millions of lovely homeowners. We're after them. Want them! Lovely people, *lovely* people!"

The old sales-hand frowns. "What's the plan?"

"Plan?" Clive says. "We've got a nice little motto. Simple. There's more readies out there than anyone can collect. We'll show you how to crack it."

Cropped-hair's pen shuffles to hand. "What's the motto?"

"Now, now!" Clive snorts. "No need for pens."

"There's nothing on these walls," she says. "No logos, no mission statements. Not a word."

"I'll tell you what the motto is. You all ready for this? Our motto is 'It won't matter what plans you make if you don't own your home!' Get it? Coined that one myself. And please, let's all be happy. Earn loads of money. Beautiful, or what?"

# 18

Clive slams the £1000 wad of brand new fifties on the desk. Money in a dream light, the wad lights a spooky bloom in the room. £1000 sitting high. Who's the one? Everybody looks at every face. Hunger in the room. But only the old sales-hand has ever sold a thing.

Moving like a swallow, Colette splits the room into groups. Guys here clock the swaying as she walks the space. Somebody asks if she's related to Clive. Yes, they're brother and sister; 18 years apart, she says.

3 o'clock. Coffee break. Clive packed every miracle into half an hour. This is maybe how Hollywood preachers pack it, hurrying a herd to get saved. Everybody here was hired on the spot; part of the show now, at Homes, Homes & Homes for wads of cash.

The woman next to Jimmy smiles politely. "Hi! I'm Geraldine. Looking forward to that lovely dosh? Spent it already?"

He takes the woman's outstretched hand. A handshake like a voice, like somebody with a stutter. He wants her to be tragic. To him the more stuff to a woman, the more tragedy must be. Geraldine's eyes are bird's-egg blue. But no tragedy. Nothing holding back. She gazes at the clasp of her hand in his. He won't ask, but thinks she likes clarinets at night. Her hand pulls away.

Some people walked to get here. Some have mortgages. Everybody bills to face. Two do cocaine. But a £1000 wad of virgin fifties is no joke. Top football players earn ten, fifteen the likes of that every day. Seven days a week. Some earn more. But this wad taunts people here. Everybody in the room grabbed by it. Wad, so bespoke, ready to tuck to a pocket. For Jimmy, nine or ten of those and it's run time! For a good year. One woman says people do sales because of revenge; somewhere along the line salespeople have messed up. Meeting people is not why they go into sales; that's the front, the excuse. Not even the money. The sales game is to blot pain. One woman says autumn makes her cry; she's better off at work than alone at home. A man says the sales game is basically for heartless people.

Through the window, Clive's Bentley looks glitzy now. Earlier the car was the kind that a pride of lions could gather round, nuzzling it in autumn light. The paint was the hue of autumn leaves. But out there in the cramped carpark now, the big Bentley looks like a plate stained by mustard swipes.

# 19

A flare-up at the tenement tonight. This time from Uranus. The police darted over the block.

Caribbean skies are too far away, too much ocean from a tenement. All islands have their sun. But nearly everybody's born in England these days. Easy, knowing the ones born somewhere from those born here. They get back from their home island and always have a tall sun to talk. The sun there, how high the sun, how blue the sky. Women mostly. They get to Jamaica, never quite believe the tall sky. Barbados, St Kitts, St. Lucia, some place. They get back to the England tenement and only talk of the tall island sky; the sky so blue, man, that thing so, *so* blue. But they never talk of the gap in a life, like how come all they have in the tenement is grey skies. Tenements collect clouds like duties.

Jimmy mulls the spiel at Homes. Tomorrow is grab-the-cash time. Wad after wad. The lights turn off. Then the hi-fi. He's alone. Settling back, but getting a rap blast from the flat below. His mother phones.

"Don't know how you stand that noise," she says. "*What* a racket!"

"They've got nothing else. No money, no brains. Got left behind."

"They should keep their noise private."

Jimmy laughs. "Private noise?"

"You know what I mean!"

"Anybody could get that way, greet rap."

"Greet?"

"Yeah. Home from home."

"Inside, we're all far from home."

"Rap's closer to bulletproof than pain. Had to happen. It's like a jack-hammer. Clears rubble away. Noise, yes. But not just noise, not always rant. Not all the time. Rap's a laughing-gas. Humphrey Davy, that laughing gas guy, he nailed it. After the high of his first trip he could hear every sound in the room, lost all connection with the world."

"What happens next?"

"Rap?"

"No, the Humphrey Davy bloke."

"Some clever chemist cracked it, got painkillers from laughing-gas. 200 years down the road, black guys have rap to zap pain."

"Rap is bling!"

"In a way," Jimmy says. "Yeah, in a way."

"It's too much. Too loud."

"That pain will go."

"You *must* get away!"

"Yeah, I was thinking the same."

"Where?"

"Brazil."

"Samba?"

"That's me!"

"Your generation, my God! You can burble Oxford or Cambridge, drive a new Merc round Marble Arch."

"The law was here this evening."

"Drugs, or violence?"

"Dunno. They crawled all over the tenement. One more set to pose. Wearing stab-proof gear. Cold eyed with every man but wanting tenement women to see them as regular guys."

"How can you live in a place like that?"

"This place, that place! One thing's always the same. When coppers turn up here, nobody doubts what could happen. Something serious enough every six, seven weeks for them to bother turning up."

"I'll give you ten grand. Pack your things. Go to Brazil. Ten grand!"

"That's probably all your savings. No way I'd do that."

"Listen, you can't look back. I saw somebody, you know, visiting after getting away from their community, but now realize it's time to move on, look back less and less."

"Get back to your community, but only to visit?"

"That's how it works. Shelter from the rain."

"What?"

"Here's the thing. Someone's out some rainy day, easy in their new car, tuned to Mozart or Ellington, going through a few old-time streets, then they glimpse somebody, a onetime friend running in the rain, some old pal chasing down a bus."

"And?"

"From inside the car, one somebody moves to a different speed now. Out in the rain, the old-time friend's hurrying on foot."

"Then stop the car!"

"Yes, yes! Then what?"

"Give them a lift. Whatever happens, happens."

"Tell you what, tell your neighbour to turn up that rap volume!"

Jimmy frowns. "I *will* leave. Give me three months."

"Time," she says, sighing, "you lived under taller skies."

# 20

All recruits show. Except one. Today, the new workplace. The new rock'n roll.

The reception girl grins. She wears a tight dress today, snatch-pink, looking to shed Marilyn Monroe blood as she jigs the reception space, shiftless smiles, slaps magazines on the coffee table. A crazy dancer. Not who she could be. She's a stick-tease, somebody says; she knows there's gaps between a dress and body-toy. Idly, somebody murmurs 'Wear it, witch. Wear it!'

Colette calls from the salesroom. Recruits have doors to knock, spiel to spin. And evident dogs in driveways. The £1000 wad's still waiting. Tidy and patient on the desk. With that thing somebody here will clear their arrears.

The cropped-hair woman arrived late. She's probably seen too much life already; maybe even as much as an astronaut or deep sea diver. She could take a lute to space and while. But today wants to be by herself, only half nodding when somebody says hello. The room can tell. She hates being here, hates being preached at by a Clive Core. And especially hated having to show hands.

All recruits had to choose one word. A word to describe themselves from now on. First word was predator. The second was striker. Everybody showed hands for striker. Clive's was the vote that counted. So the name is predator. Arriving at Homes on two legs, recruits must see themselves in the simplest survival game of all. They're all broke, all hungry. So eat!

Jimmy won't need a tie. Clive said it was OK. That was a surprise. No racials, nothing about Jimmy's locks. As he looks around him, his eyes impact the cropped-hair woman's. She's forty years old and just back from the Alps. But knows. She knows what he's thinking.

Stippled sunlight through the window. Chain-smoking, Colette talks of money dreams; but tells it like salt lemonade. She gets a tray with steaming cups of coffee brought to the room. And lights a smoke.

Geraldine taps Jimmy's shoulder. Says hello, again. His eyes stay fixed on the money wad.

"A thousand pounds a week is daft," she says, sighing.

"Daft?"

"It's not real. Not for knocking doors. And, you know, flounting it in that wad, that's vulgar!"

Straightaway, Jimmy can tell. This woman doesn't understand. Head shaking, he says, "I'm here *for* that money. That wad. Get a few like it."

"And then?"

"Disappear. Lie low for a year."

"Disappear?"

"I write music."

"Need to be alone?"

"Yeah. Get some quick readies so I can knuckle down."

"Don't you do gigs?"

"Sessions, now and then. But only if I respect the outfit. It's a hassle."

"Then why don't you go on the dole?"

"No way!"

"Free up time for your music."

"I don't wanna get called a scrounger."

"What," she smiles, "can that matter if we get a masterpiece?"

"Well, yeah. I believe in myself. But it's not up to me."

"No! Tell you what. I've changed my mind. A composer *should* do a job like this."

"This?"

"Absolutely! Talk to strangers. Do you good. That's why they're a stranger, eh?"

"What d'you mean?"

"People on their own doorsteps," she says, "they aren't the same as out and about. That's got to be good for a composer, hasn't it?"

"Philip Glass went through that stuff. Know about him?"

"Who?"

"He drove a New York taxi, didn't he?" cropped-hair says, butting in. "Did it for years. Year after year. Even a stint as a plumber. The people he must have met!"

"And the crap," Jimmy says.

"Then think of the end-game."

He frowns. "Well, yeah. Maybe."

"Only *maybe?*"

"Definitely. That science piece, it's good work."

"Yes, yes! That's it! Oh, what's it called?"

"Einstein On The Beach."

Her eyebrows raise. "Came out in '75, didn't it?"

"That's the same year I was born!" Geraldine says.

Jimmy steps back, says he was born the same year. Cropped-hair slips away. His eyes attach to the way Geraldine turns and turns the wedding band on her finger. That ring could melt down.

Clive is a plain man. To him the selling trick isn't what folk want. Not even need. The trick's what they can find money for. Never matters to him how they find it. Borrow it. Beg. This guy's a raider, cold-cut eye, quick to pick up on a wounded thing. And nothing in England's ever wounded as a Jones or Smith having a complex over their property. But something's changed. Already some faces in the room look like big cats on the open plains. Hunger. And the money wad lying still on the desk, that's the prey.

Jimmy turns to Geraldine. "TV's good at predators. I like lions, watching them on a hunt. Seeing predators in rain is the beautiful part. But just as they close the kill, a rainbow might appear out of nowhere."

# 21

"*Recession?*" Clive howls. "That sounds bad. It sounds like what you catch from a lavatory seat!"

Geraldine blinks. "That's what the newspapers call it. They all say home-improvement is in recession."

Clive tugs his braces. Tugging like at guy-ropes in a storm. "My friends," he says, "no negatives, please! No rubbish about recessions. That's so, what shall we call it? Sad. So very sad. It is loser-speak."

Cropped-hair says, "But recession is what the experts claim!"

"Look," he says, "let's be honest about it. Some of us wouldn't make a few bob if everybody was clued up, would we? If everybody was street-wise we wouldn't be here now. None of us. And I mean *none* of us! No banks, no TV, no motorways, nothing. Know why? We'd all be in animal skins, still living in caves, my friends. Now there's a prospect!"

"I don't see how that follows," Geraldine says.

Clive's arms fold. Lazing to the window, he strides along it. Then struts. Heavy skips. Then faces the room. His cufflinks flash like wolves' teeth. "Geraldine? That's your name, is it? Nice try, Geraldine. But no thanks!"

"What if they can't afford a conservatory? If they can't afford it there'd be no point trying to persuade them, surely."

"Look, it's never what the punter tells you. What you worry about is what they've got in their head. That's the bottom line. You with me? Not what he's got in the bank. You have your house, the biggest investment of your life. A lovely home. So, tell me how you protect the value of your property. Anybody? What, no takers? Well, what a surprise! You, the man without a tie?"

Cropped-hair coughs. "Could be a ten answers to that. Personally, I think it's maintenance."

"Own your own property?" Clive grins.

"I rent. A little flat."

"Well, now! How did I know that? Deary, deary, me! Some of us sit on the fence in this life. Me? Well, you all know the answer to that! My friends, let's get back to business. Homeowners will always want to protect their property, add value. That's where we come in. Because with a *lovely* Victorian conservatory, you've got tradition, a property to be proud of. Even your grandma's kippers could appreciate that!"

Cropped-hair doesn't laugh. Clive looks fed up with preaching. He rolls back his cuffs and elects Geraldine for the first role-play. Reluctant on her feet, she removes her scarf and prepares to be the homeowner. The willow green silk slips her fingers and hesitates, then swoops, drooping to the ground.

"We don't need a conservatory," she says. "No space. Too little room in the garden. And it's way beyond my means, honestly."

Turning to the room, Clive winks. A boozer's wink. Spins back to Geraldine, the homeowner. "Mrs Smith," he says, "times are difficult. Difficult for everyone. We understand that. We've done our homework, believe me. And what a charming home you have! Beautiful place! A tidy little conservatory is all you need. And what a *lovely* picture that will be. Now then! If we're talking value then the right conservatory puts 10, 15% on the value of this lovely property. For a beautiful home like this we'll definitely help with the finance. Tell you what, we'll spread it, arrange a comfortable package. That'll be a big help, won't it?"

"Well, I'm not so sure," Geraldine demurs, giving in as a homeowner. "You make it sound so easy. By the way, what's the interest rate? How long would I have to pay?"

"Just a sec!" Clive yells, standing back. He collects room daze like biscuits from a plate. "Pay attention to this! I want you all to get what happens next. I cue the bit about a finance package and the punter gives out a buying signal. Lovely! If that happens, *when* that happens, what you say is 'I'm not qualified on finance, Mrs Smith, but someone from our Customer Services Department will explain the details. What time are you at home tomorrow?' Everyone got that? You never ask the punter if they've got spare time, *never!* You ask 'What time are you at home tomorrow?' Better still, 'What time tomorrow will be convenient for you?' Everybody got that?"

Geraldine saunters to her seat. Gets the scarf from the ground. Then turns to Clive. "What happens after we arrange the appointment?"

"The kaycee turns up," he says, strutting a new Mussolini.

"The *what*?"

Quickly, Clive writes 'k-c' on the white-board. "In a word, a kaycee is the dog's bollocks."

"A salesman?"

"Well, now! Some words are never up to speed."

"What is it?"

"We could be here all day with that one."

"A k-c is a salesman," cropped-hair says.

"OK, OK," Clive grins. "Let's get on with it. Salesman, yes. But not a blagger."

"But a salesman!"

"A breed apart. Peak predator. Part wolverine. One whiff of the money, and he's in there! One whiff! Ladies and gentlemen, you make the appointment and your k-c is a friend. Gets you the *money*!"

"Yes, yes, but what does it mean? Is it Chinese?"

"A k-c is a killer-closer. Aha, ha!"

"Killer?"

Disappointed, Clive rolls his sleeves. "We don't kill anyone, OK?"

"Then why *killer*?" Geraldine moans.

"Because we kill their money, that's what! We slaughter the stuff! Kill 'em without bloodshed. Aha, ha!"

Marketing execs get the k-c a foot in the punter's door. Smiling, but efficient, k-cs call themselves customer services managers. Nothing ever gets been them and the money. Nothing. A top k-c is the type that gets into the punter's house and straightaway strides to their TV and turns it off. Then invites the punter to sit. Inviting punters to sit down in their own house.

Not every punter is a warmed-up mug. But enough out there as dead meat. To Clive, punters have no sense of self, even in their home. Neat profits stem from that. The biggest profits come from people who get upset if their chat with a power-salesman is only talk; they're the punters looking for a star to quicken their humdrum with sizzle. They don't know it, but are exactly looking for a k-c to call.

Now and then Clive hankers after the old days. Hankers after the time he was a k-c. Sometimes, His Hollywood does the rounds to reacquaint the kill.

One somebody with eyes shut here. Not squeamish. What's happening in the role-play room reminds Jimmy of a dream. It's always a bleak space, a frontier, stark, with slow-motion borders and wounded angels hurrying on the whisper-thin shoulders of others. The outlines of their faces just visible, but their eyes impossible to see.

His eyes should open now, but Jimmy tells himself this is a survival deal. Something is here. Bloodless. This is no scam. Real glass to sell. But k-cs lay into punters, take them down. His eyes open. Something heathen here. But welcoming. A cold but beautiful doom saying 'This way, you're invited!'

He turns to Clive. "Are homeowners like angels?"

"What did you say?"

"Angels, wisp-like things."

Clive's brow furrows. "What?"

"Angels."

"What the 42$^{nd}$ Royal Fusilliers is an angel?"

The room laughs. In the role-play room everybody laughs out. Falling apart with laughing. The next move could be rolling in the aisles. But not Clive. Something holds him from the fun. He's afraid, wants to brush the question aside. Like on a tightrope between bad heights, a fly could kick him off.

Hand blunt to jaw, he says, "What a funny question!"

"*Why*?" Cropped-hair asks.

"Tricky question," he says. "Nothing daft about it. Not at all. You don't get a question like that everyday."

"They say," Jimmy cuts in, "it's the chance of seeing angels that makes religions work."

Clive shrugs. "I wouldn't know a thing about that. And come to think of it, let's not get soppy."

The chase is on. Clive talks of the bull's-eye on every middle class home in England. Bull's-eyes to get aimed at everywhere. Up and down. Doors are doors. Doorbells all the same. Even in London, the know-all city. Homes, Homes & Homes is out and about. Taking aim.

# 22

The money hour. Recruits gulp coffee and head out. Going by van to get dropped on suburban street corners. This is where it starts. This where prospecting starts. The gold trail.

As the afternoon rustles by, light and shade intertwine. Daylight and quietness. And remnants of conscience in autumn leaves. Quiet in the van. Slow-motion in the street. And, after forty minutes, gold-brown leaves on silent lawns. Random, beautiful. The van slows to another drop-off point.

Jimmy starts to worry. Hard to think. His turn to go. But no homing signs. Not here. This place, not the kind where somebody black owns any of the houses. Only middle class white folk live this quiet place. Only seasons change. Time to go, but he's too visible; that's how it feels. Having to walk quiet driveways, getting nervy. This is no game. The folk living here probably never had anybody black knock their door. Jimmy's nervy. Not stage-fright nerves, but like-a-child-again nerves, not-wanting-to-go nerves. How come he's here? The job advert said *No experience necessary!* But this is where experience would do it. How to judge the blink when that first door opens? Best remember the role-play, get polite, show the Homes, Homes & Homes ID card and say 'Good afternoon!' No ad lib. Just the script. Get set in eye, ask if this is the homeowner. That's the easy part. But what if they see him through their curtain, or CCTV, will they still open the door? Black, dreadlocks and no tie.

Geraldine can tell. Others in the van don't know. Or care. But somehow she understands. Volunteering, she gets out the van. Happy to work alongside Jimmy. He wonders why.

"Simple," she says.

"How come?"

"Because you're *so* going to be lucky."

"Think so?"

"I do! I do! You *will* get that grand a week. Remember it?"

Jimmy knows she knows. The white woman knows. She sees panic over him.

"Grand a week?" he says.

"Absolutely!"

"Well, that's the plan. I admit it. But you, what's the real reason you pair off with me?"

"I hate hypocrites," she says, eyes narrowed. A wistful but clear pair of eyes. "Frankly, there were little nudges about not wanting to pair off with you. I'm not into anything like that."

Nervy, he says, "Thanks. Again, thanks."

"Well," she says, "it would be nice if we could just get on with it. Not become little diplomats with one another."

"Never!" Jimmy says, tall again. "Best tell it like it is."

"Agreed!" she says, as they step towards the first house.

# 23

Doorstep canvassing isn't for everyone. Not the knocking, ringing, not dogs rushing past the owner wanting blood. Not postman miles.

By the evening of the first day, four recruits walked. Cropped-hair was first. Lasted one hour. From gossip back at base, she was halfway through a pitch then looked the punter in the eye and said 'Forgive me!' Then hurried down that driveway. Maybe she went for a gin. Or shot straight home to look herself in the mirror, watch sin bloom in her eye. Except for Jimmy, everybody agrees: cropped-hair was weird, never the kind to settle for Clive's spiel or that the canvassing game is a show, that folk want to get their doorstep feted, liking frolic there. But she didn't want to feed herself and killer-closers this way.

A walk contagion. By the end of the second week, only 9 of the 22 starters still out and about for Homes. The others could be anywhere. Or checking the jobs pages. One or two maybe grappling with that Hawking book. Cropped-hair definitely cracked it. Instead of getting conned by the title 'A Brief History Of Time' she grabbed her pen, changed it to 'Synoptic Time, By Time Changing In Respect Of Time.'

Jimmy and Geraldine are top. The ace canvassing duo at Homes. Taking glass spiel to suburbia. The weather's getting colder. Trees bare. Six weeks at Homes already.

Race is never far. Not only where polished pewter gleams. Mostly these folk have the likes of Led Zeppelin playing on the hi-fi, think Jimmy's the central-heating man come to check the boiler. Or a woman grins, talks domestic, mentioning this and that, baking soda because of the bubbling when water hits the powder, or asks if he can get stain from her carpet. Maybe because they've never had a black man on their doorstep before, but race flusters them. Now and then a woman wants to flirt-talk, but knows the line, calls it quits. Then again. From the longing in some eyes, even the bluest blue, a herd of suburban white women wanting to spread it for a black guy. Furtive, hard. That's one thing. But three or four times every day Jimmy gets other race attitudes. The political kind.

Geraldine is troubled by the predator game. For a woman who often cries when Joni Mitchell sings, the folksy Debussy-like tunes, this kind of work is unclean. Jimmy agrees with one thing. Joni is clean to listen to. But to him, the job is a way to get even.

One evening after work as they walk along he asks how she can stomach being a predator.

The lady spreads her arms. "I hate that word. *So* melodramatic."

"You're in denial."

"This job *is* an out-of-body experience, isn't it! "

"It's all legal."

"Well, yes."

"So there's got to be morals to it."

"Where?"

"In the contracts, stuff the punters sign."

"Oh, we can all do morals. All it takes is a bucket."

"Your spit?" Jimmy laughs. "Or theirs?"

"Moralizing is for coffee tables. Tell you a little secret. My energies go into Brian, getting my head round the idea he might have gone for good."

"This job takes your mind off that?"

"Yeah."

"Loads of other things you could do."

"Like what?"

"Anything!"

"Like?"

"Why not give teaching a go?"

"Yuck!"

"Language grad like you, they'd beg you to teach."

"I'd *never* teach," she says, foot slammed into the cold pavement.

"You miss translating farm brochures."

"Wasn't *that* bad."

"Can't see you sucking up to dirty great German tractors!"

"Not as bad as it sounds. High pressure language skills. Machinery can be so life & death. Operating instructions. Critical. Got to get it right. Snotty kids in classrooms? No thanks!"

"I was thinking older kids, A levels."

"Tractors, any day!"

"Why not turn up for work in a tractor?"

"This job," she laughs, "is about quick dosh. Full stop."

"What's the other reason?"

"Other?"

"There's *always* some other reason."

"Let's not play morality merry-go-rounds. No high horses, OK? Oh, look, I didn't mean that the way it came out. I mean, can't we find something better to talk about?"

"Better than morals?"

"It's so, you know, subjective."

"Lines in the sand."

"I draw the line with this job, believe me! Anything lower than this I couldn't do."

"This is only a step from the gutter."

"One giant leap for mankind!"

Jimmy shrugs. Not mean enough to deny the Neil Armstrong line, he scans to the skies. "What's the German for gutter?"

"What?"

"The German for *gutter*."

"Where the hell is the gutter, anyway?" she says, brows packed. Her eyes turn to the cool street lights. "I've heard of that place somewhere."

Somebody, maybe it was Nathan, told Jimmy the gutter's the one place to hint at to feel better. He remembers lions at the zoo, wondering how they keep warm in winter.

"What's wrong? You look so sad."

"Sometimes," he says, "I feel like shouting Brixton out loud."

"You'd get arrested!"

"Yeah, me and my shadow."

Geraldine laughs. "Two sets of handcuffs?"

"No, they'd cuff my shadow. I stay free."

"That bad, eh?"

"Some days."

"While we're at it," she sighs, "I've always meant to ask something. Why do so many black people bother staying here. The older ones. I'd take the sun. Believe me, any day."

"There's a fairytale about a giant bouncing the sun."

"What're you getting at?"

"Oceans cut folk in two."

"When I was little we borrowed a boat, sailed it to Malta."

"Look at the moon."

"Mmm, half-moon this evening."

"Stints and hemispheres."

"*What*?"

"Everybody started in Africa."

"Who's everybody?"

"All the races. So says DNA research."

"You sure?"

"Yeah."

"So what?"

"Millions of white folk have gone back to Africa."

"What?"

"White folk in South Africa," Jimmy smiles, "gone back to roots."

"Are you trying to tell me something?"

"Me? When did I get a say in what's what?"

"What d'you mean?"

"Black folk, staying here."

"I don't understand what you mean."

"This is your society."

60

"What *are* you getting at?"

"How would the likes of me know where's where?"

"I don't know what you mean."

"Black people, we do *not* miss a bit of sunshine somewhere."

"What's brought this on?"

"Your society."

Weary, Geraldine turns to the houses. Glazed, regards them. Scans them up and down. Like maybe they'd know.

"This is your society," Jimmy says, again.

"You," she groans, "were born here. Same as me."

He grabs a smoke. Time for a sear. Time to burn some bridges down. As the match flames up, he remembers Lorna Stanley. Dizzy for a chat last week, made a quiet call to Lorna. A weird call. Bad suffering down the line. The only reason she was at the zoo that day was to see what a cage is. He remembers how she looked like the lions' cage was only there by mistake.

Geraldine eyes the fire. Her gaze follows fire searing in tobacco. She must find out. "Can I ask a question, a personal one?"

"Anything you want."

"Why," she wonders, "don't you try a little more to belong?"

Wondering where to start, his teeth clench. Example after another, he talks it, saying Brixton is a fault-line, black folk have places they never go. Not if too far from the likes of Brixton. And the likes of Stephen Hawking, a man in a wheelchair but can steer round the universe while Jimmy, six feet tall, able bodied and quick of mind, gets Brixton as a hold zone.

She doesn't understand. She knows town and countryside, villages, hamlets, places where only a thousand people live, or few as a hundred. Her relatives and friends are in parts of England where no black person ever goes, let alone lives. This never occurred to her. Till now. He thinks when she talks of rural England, she could as well be talking the sleep-like distances to stars. She doesn't know the hurt. Doesn't know the pain of folk not getting close, only seeing countryside on TV, or watching it from a motorway, or wanting to walk a country lane, maybe even chase butterflies, but not get gaped at because of being black.

Jimmy explains. "Black people only happen in London. Or spots like Liverpool, Birmingham, the rest."

"I know what you mean," she says, wiping her nose.

"The black thing is simple. Simpler than people think. Black folk shuttle from one hot-spot to another, use that other map of England."

"*Other* map?"

"The good old Ordinance Survey, that's not the only map. The other one is the black archipelago map."

"The what?"

"Inner-city ghost lines. Ghosting, not living it."

"That's *terrible*."

"Yeah."

"Why do we never see this discussed?"

"Because it *is* so terrible. Too many snakes in broadcasting."

"Yikes!"

"Nobody talks it. Not out loud. Quarantine round it."

"And you, you've got this all pent up."

"Yeah."

"Same for all black people?"

"Even simple things never happen."

"Like what?"

"Well," he sighs, "simplest things hurt the most."

"Yes, but what?"

"Like not having a cottage."

"What the bloody hell are cottages to do with anything?"

"I'd live in a cottage tucked in the New Forest, the calm that's there."

"You mean," she says, "you just want a quiet life, really."

"Plain, ordinary."

"What can we do?"

"We?"

"We can change that."

"All *I* can do is take the money. That's why this job's great for me. Love it! This predator game was made for me."

Geraldine's lips bale, a wide O-gape. "I don't know what to say."

"The folk in those houses! They make a fuss, polite, best manners, but don't really want me knocking their door. Except if I was the electrician. That's why I turn k-cs loose on them. Payback time!"

Frowning, she fakes applause. "Some enchanted evening!"

"I don't want to get preachy about it."

"Then don't! A dog-collar would *so* not be you!"

"This winter light," he says, "it's like blue zinc this evening. And somewhere, zest in hard bluish-white petals. Far away, or near as Kew Gardens, palm trees spread in a message: 'Blue seasons, intermittent.' And in a marketplace, imported things bring fire to wear a gentleness."

"So," Geraldine blinks, "now I know! Mysticism aside, I know now."

"Yes. You see it from the other side now, but know it."

"That chap," she says, "the little creep organizing the folk festival, at least he didn't tell you to go back."

"Go back?"

"You know, to wherever."

"Where I come from?"

"You know what I mean!"

"To some folk, Brixton *is* go-back land!"

"Oh, not necessarily," she pouts, eyes gazing her feet. Her hands are restless, shuffling her coat. Turning to Jimmy, her eyes are pained. "The poor guy, he gagged didn't he? Ran out of ideas. It happens."

"He was talking woad!"

"What?"

"Little England," he says.

"Woad?"

"The silent majority at home."

"Brixton is *part* of England!"

"Yeah, the spice part. Tropical condiments."

"It's as much a part as any."

"Oh, yeah!"

"Occasionally things are, well, in the margins a little bit. But it's still on the page. These things take time. Take it on the chin. Why ruin your whole life?"

Watching Geraldine meet herself in a cold evening, Jimmy chucks the smoke. "Nazis made the Jews sew the Star of David on their garments. But a skin overcoat is different."

# 24

Jimmy's mother started in a Liverpool orphanage. Eventually a black Scouse family came along. Adopted her. But even now they don't know where her birth parents were from. At 41, she's young enough to have more. But will not; says she was born to have children with one man only.

"What's Nathan up to?" she says.

Jimmy yawns, cradles the phone. "Dominoes all day."

"He's your father!"

"Dominoes, that's all he does. Can't get him to talk, discuss. So we play dominoes. I don't mention the canvassing job. He'd be too upset. Feel a failure."

"Then it's up to you. You do the talking."

"He'd guess, know I was patronizing him."

"How's that girl, the one from South Africa?"

"OK. More or less."

"Trouble?"

"No."

"What's happening with Arleene? I liked her. Good for you."

"Women can wait. Other stuff to deal with. I mean, it's bad seeing your old man fumble, look for words. He wants to be ace, but scared of not being the big father, not wise. Every time I visit it's dominoes, ritual playing, have a drink, listen to the greats. Ellington, Ornette Coleman."

"Art Tatum?"

"Yeah, his jaw still drops."

"My thing is Willow Weep For Me, what Tatum does with it."

"You shouldn't have stopped playing. Could have been good."

"Come and visit. Teach me some chords."

"Yeah. I was on your knee when I played my first tune, Jingle Bells."

"Does Nathan still listen to Japanese music?"

"More than ever. Even got one of their flutes, a bamboo thing called the shakuhachi. Nice! Hard to explain it. It's so *scant.* Like a Samurai sword. When you listen to it, it's like going about your business in the old days, moving past rice fields, and a bozo wants what you have, so you call that blade and, zap! Your dreams get delivered."

"Stop it! You sound like a little killer!"

"What were you doing, I mean 17 years old with a man 35?"

"Made *you* happen, didn't we!"

# 25

As the dominoes collect, one man hears orphans in a bamboo flute. The other man wails inside because of sounds he can no longer get from a trumpet. Nathan tries hard. Doesn't want to think the music he would have played; even now, wonders what could have happened, what if it had been America instead of England. Some nifty Jamaican musos went to America. Ernest Ranglin, Monty Alexander got it right. They upped to the States, got a good reception. But not Harold McNair. He skipped to England from Jamaica in '60. And that was the clincher for Nathan. Harold was another muso from Kingston, came to England and got a residency at Ronnie Scott's. A serious flute man; not primal, but he bossed that thing. Nathan plays Harold tracks, likes Flute And Nut. Listening to it with Jimmy, all he'll say is 'Man!'

If Nathan's in a bad mood the dominoes get black, black. Dominoes talk instead of talk.

Nathan's sorry about the hands. Arthritis in his hands more and more. Too hard to take. Pain on two levels. Still at the welding job but some days the pain's so bad he can't work. Welding was supposed to be the back-up. If music was just smiling the smile, shuffling on stage, or mickey-mouse in a studio, then welding in England was always there. That was the deal. That's how it was when this proud man first arrived. With music, it was to take six months. Welding was to be five years of graft. Either way, the mission was to get back to Jamaica and run clear. That was the plan. But way beyond money, Nathan was into vision. Clifford Brown was dead. America was still coming to terms with that. Clifford was dead 10 years before Nathan arrived in England. And Miles Davis was the big man, edging Dizzy because of cool. This made Nathan think England was the place. On a good day he could take trumpet to where maybe only Clifford used to take it; the speed, tone. The plan was to show it. But just in case, welding was on every building site in England.

To Jimmy, hearing Nathan talk is it. the broad Jamaican accent. Talking in near-standard English or gritty down-home patois, either way a true Jamaican always in the talk. Nathan only talks this and that, stuff going on, ducking, diving the street. But that slow Jamaican accent, that's what's really what, who's really who.

And then locks. What to do with locks. Locks in England. Nathan got rid of his dread one day; the first time Jimmy ever saw the shape of his head.

He laughs. "Only genuine Rasta should manifest locks. Rasta start in Jamaica. Cover your locks, man. Any Jamaican that show locks in England is a smalltime poppy show."

Jimmy blinks. "A what?"

Nathan slaps a domino. "Poppy-show is Jamaica talk for a fool, a mascot. Any Jamaican away from the island can have locks. But use a hat in public, get me? Show respect. Cover your locks, man. That means your bag packed, ready to go. Same for the son of a Jamaican, yeah, abroad any place."

"Locks got anything to do with lions?"

"Domestic cats every place, Jimmy. And panther, tiger. Only lion have a mane."

"Still going back next year?"

"Yes. Back to Jamaica. Man, we made a big mistake! Yeah, the music was OK at the start."

"Jamaica borrowed stuff from Americans."

"Rhythm, rhythm."

"Dance shuffles?"

"Louis Jordan. Those guys handed that stuff down. Rhythm that will always set a dance-hall alight."

"Did you know a guy called King Jammys?"

"King Jammys used to build shortwave, tune to rhythm & blues from the States. That stuff got to Jamaica and, man! Guys tried it on guitar. It was the *ska, ska*, that guitar chip. It turned into ska music. Next step, melody, you know, blue-beat, rock-steady, reggae. But the guys on the island should have learned Ellington."

"The boss!"

"Learn from to the Duke," Nathan says. "Good tunes stack easy on jazz chords. If more musicians do that, even now, especially now, then more respect to go round."

Jimmy's eyes narrow. "In England, showing locks is a mistake?"

"A true Rasta is a humble human. But a hypocrite can mimic that."

"I'd love to see hypocrites mimic a nuclear warhead."

"Dreadlocks inflation! Guys walking round with empty suitcase. The bigger dreadlocks, the bigger the empty suitcase. Suitcase-head. Nobody laugh like suitcase-head. Dem no understan' wha' go'an."

"Locks was never religion. Not for me."

"Tell me something. What is music?"

"What d'you mean?"

"What is in-tune music?"

"Don't know how to answer. Not *answer*."

"Dub is to blame. Right now dub is the problem. Dub know the score, but don't talk it. Bad business in de basement. A million cockroach, but dub-man slam de door, run upstairs, check folly."

"Scary!"

"If mimic get hit by a racial, that mimic talk shit. Man! Dem claim England is Babylon. But dat? Jive! Mimic man talk empty suitcase talk."

"Some dub guys are educated, got good degrees."

"Dem man deh! Dem seh locks 'ave nutt'n to do wid Babylon, not even religion, not now, not de modern world. But suitcase-head? Dem move round wid dem empty suitcase. Understan'?"

Jimmy nods. "Got it. Loud and clear."

"Mimic shout 'Birmingham!' or 'Bristol!'"

"Inner-city places."

"Yes. But if the question come from the eye, a suitcase-head can not reply."

Nathan's eyes mist. Remembering. Eyes this side of life. But he should know. He was one of the first to have locks in England. Before dreading-up was fashion, before any suitcase-head twisted a knot of hair to tag along for the high ride, Nathan was a locksman. And those days a locksman always had a travel-bag ready, always packed.

Everybody could tell. It was plain. A locksman did not arrive to grin sunshine in England. Never wanted a house and car here to fake forty years before age and a pension. New false teeth in a coat pocket.

"Dem run for cover!" Nathan says.

Jimmy jumps to his feet. "*What!*"

"Dreadlocks in England was a big divide in the 60s. Hard to believe now, but most black folk run for cover. Somebody like me, man, I was too black. Then Bob was on the scene. Bob Marley. White folk loved that guy. Talent, yes, but skin tone was the deal. White folk accepting Bob locks, that was how black folk accept."

"That was then," Jimmy says. "A *long* time ago. Not seeing locks now is plain impossible."

"Rasta content in a tent. But a suitcase-head is Mr Bling the Ritz."

"That's why there's no room for jazz at the folk festival."

"Which festival?"

"Some bash they plan, calling it the Millennium Folk Festival."

"They who?"

"Whoever they are, jazz is a bad-mouth prophet to them. *They* call the shots. So that makes it jazz, not folk. They listen to Radio 4, go to the Tate, expect tradition, saying the past is key to the future."

Nathan laughs. "Next time you open your front door, check the key!"

# 26

New scissors in hand, Jimmy squints in the mirror. Scissors that will never get used again.

For five minutes it was only gazing, blank, checking, gazing, admiring the resemblance to Nathan. The scissors will do it. Lethal, cold, but a friend, not hari-kari blades.

The first lock lops off. No going back. Not now. Nowhere to back to. So, one lock at a time. Cut. Cut that empty suitcase away.

Now something ebbs in mirror mist. The mirror misty like open sea. In two minutes a stranger on a misty shore. And one empty suitcase gets set aside. Suitcase no more.

Maybe it started at the zoo. Or maybe it was on a doorstep. Hungry women on a doorstep. Two plum-talking women at their door one day, but not wanting glass talk; not with Jimmy. They just wanted to be nice, but inside. Right on the doorstep one woman couldn't wait. She wanted to feel dreadlocks, fondle dread. The sly one. Blood-red nails. The other woman just talked her mind. A threesome, she said; fancy ten minutes upstairs with Genesis playing? Maybe Jimmy would've gone with that. Thinking that wildness was wild on a doorstep. He was just about to step inside when Geraldine arrived through the gate. Just finished her pitch next door, she was coming to correct folk she supposed must be giving him a hard time. Then it was four on a doorstep, with different ways to go.

Fronting the mirror for a full hour after shearing, a stranger stands watching. Checking. A different man. More serious, wary. Worried, confident.

Eventually, a relieved somebody looks back from the mirror. Disappointed, but relieved. The face is different. The bearing different. At exactly six feet tall, this guy's nearly 2 inches shorter. But no mascot, not now. Poppy-show is a scared show; Jimmy talks it a while to the mirror. Now he can see. Having locks was like someone else was always there.

Deep into night, a shorn man gazing from the window. He lights a smoke. The night's so near it could ring. Streetlights beam like tapered wings. A long exhale. Then the woad song: *Hey, woad-man! Yeah, you! You flick a switch and icebergs thaw. You look at waterfalls, even rain, but all you see is floods. That's all you see, all you want me to see, want me to see, to see. But more colours to jazz than blue, woad-man. Yeah, more colours than a rainbow could weep at.*

# 27

Agnes. A business-like woman from Cape Town. Jimmy's number one lady. She gave him a copy of A Brief History of Time. And that was the clincher.

Arleene is number two. She knows that. Knows about Agnes. Knows the whole thing. But only sucked her teeth, said, 'So what!'

In her last letter Agnes swims every morning. Jogs three miles most evenings. Four miles. Jogging because of something to do, wanting to get too tired to think London and Jimmy's flat on the eighth; or so she says. Before she left they talked about making it last. Make what's going on between them go a long while. She's having a neat time. This time of year Cape Town's like a crystal lozenge, the letter says. She's cozy in the new South Africa, loving being back and black. And loves the opportunity they give her in the bank. More and more, Jimmy thinks Agnes could be the one. But if she ever hears about Arleene, how he plays Arleene, she'd never write again.

Jimmy's got the blues. Agnes left being faithful up to him. And living up to that is too hard.

Locks or no locks, he can't figure why she left her slippers behind. Two crimson things, tucked under the bed like a joke. But that's Agnes. She used to step from her shoes at the door. Then go straight to the shower. Quick shower, then braid that hair. That was always the same. Hair's a big thing to that woman. One minute hair was wild. Then she gets the jar of fourteen oils. Next thing, the neatest corn-rows outside Africa. And only lightning's ever quicker than that.

But she's a hemisphere away. She loves whispering. And dance. Even break-dance. Jazz is beautiful but unpredictable, that's what she whispered one day.

Being alone helps Jimmy. But he sent a note. It said 'Agnes! you should be here!' Missing the way she moves. That woman doesn't walk. She rolls, just like mangoes in a breeze. He remembers. Wishing it was home. But Agnes in far South Africa. Too far. The day she left was hard to take. At the quayside the mist was like old curtains on the ship. She'll be true, she said by mobile as the ship slipped from sight. Might take as long as a year but she will get back to England; that's what she said. And Jimmy said 'Hurry back, woman!' And now her memory on the sheets.

# 28

Geraldine talks of a neat way to spite tenement dogs. Then mentioned another way, the moat way: get to the estate of the nearest Lord Bloggs, then throw the dogs into his moat.

The better way for Jimmy was cans of beans. Feeding baked beans to tenement dogs. That will quieten down, she says; bad dogs shut their noise, depending on the amount of beans you feed them.

The dogs on Pluto are the worst. Attack hounds. Lethal by inclination. Most days they try waiting. Can't wait for their master to get back, the quiet guy that never talks, the one with the baseball cap low over his forehead, not wanting to get recognized. Somebody says he was a rich man, one upon a time.

Jimmy tried Geraldine's trick. Loaded the tenement dogs with beans. Seven huge cans, jumbo-cans of baked beans got shoved down a tube through their letter-box.

The trick didn't work. After just one hour those hounds got angry. More than ever. They howled through the whole concrete block, howling on their master to get back. Dust termites gnawed their eyes.

Jimmy didn't figure it. Tonight the dogs get diarrhea. Hounds letting fly, nine feet up above a new unlocked head.

# 29

Christmas next week. From the road, every house looks beautiful. Lights glowing. One garden's got winter-flowering shrubs, Chinese witch hazels.

"These shed their leaves in autumn," Geraldine says, "but look so good now. *Love* those petals. Pale yellow. As you get close to them, a delicate perfume's in the air."

Jimmy turns away.

She adjusts her coat, tucks the scarf. And shrugs. Wondering, gazing at the ribbon-like petals. "Getting rid of your locks was one thing, but that's not the only thing you've lost."

"Still the same me."

"No! Now you're like, I dunno, a cynic with not much to say."

"Want me to be a wordsmith?"

"Say you'd like to live like this. In a house like one of these."

"Me?"

"These houses are up for grabs," she says. "Ones like them."

Jimmy looks again. Scans houses. House after house. The evening is not too cold. He agrees. Living some place like this would be it. He'd go for open-plan, wide, with a workout room and rowing machine. But the Steinway; that would top the list. A concert Steinway, Ferrari red, hot. Something even Oscar Peterson would smile at. Or Joanna MacGregor; she could drop by any old time, play Bach. Living somewhere like this means being next to top surgeons. Deep thinking theatre directors would be neighbours. His throat clears. "What would they think?"

"Who?"

"This lot, having somebody black next door."

"Never mind what *they* think!"

"Where did my tenement go?"

"That's just for now," she says. "Think yourself in a half million house. Or a million. Any problems with that?"

Jimmy watches Geraldine, coolly now. Not sure. In the cold evening light, her blond hair tucked into the coat collar, he believes she means it. That day three weeks ago she saw him with no locks, said he was like a young Denzel Washington. A true quiet was in her eyes.

But the thing he likes best of all is the laughs. Geraldine can be belly laughs. This evening, fed up with how canvassing was starting to wear her down, she tried a prank. The sucker was a pomp and circumstance gent. A real sucker opened his door. To crank the prank she got the look right, set the scarf to cover her hair, narrowed her eyes, and got high seriousness in a high-pitched voice. Then looked the man in the eye. But instead of spiel from Homes, she told him she's a grateful Eskimo. Who? An Eskimo.

What? An Inuit. Well, now! Then she said she got a great education in England, thanking the man for his taxes that made it possible but now she's doing research, so would he help? Well, she said, it's a little survey, just a quick questionnaire. Let's have the first question, the man said. Voice upped an octave, and still doing the unblinking, she said her tribe was wondering if they could try a few igloos here. Where? In London. Where? Yes, in this street. *Where?* Well, as close to your house as possible.

Geraldine played and played that gent. Worked and worked him. Moved him round like a leaf. At one point he was looking to tie his tie even when there was no tie to tie. And when it was over, he was back by his fireside, she was in the street the other side of privet. Laughing and laughing.

# 30

Effectively, night. Somebody in a front garden is winter pruning. And because this is surgery, the wounds on the tree need special care to heal. Trees standing still, wounded.

The pickup van's late today. Canvassers getting cold at junctions. This evening is like no sugar in cold tea. The van was never this late before. Geraldine is anxious.

Shivering, she returns to a longtime bug. "I've never heard anyone link jazz to folk. Why do you?"

Jimmy shrugs. Wonders if this is worth bothering. But knows. This woman is somebody to make room for. "Hard to explain."

"Try me," she says. "Start with jazz."

"People going by quicker and quicker. Going home to get warm. And somewhere in an airless observatory, bat frequencies milling on some nerd's oscilloscope."

"I can do without the mystic stuff. Answer my question!"

"You mean," he says, laughing, "I must say what jazz is?"

"Yes. What is it?"

"Jazz is based on the blues. Ever listen to blues? Blues is folk."

"*One* type of folk."

"Good! So jazz, well, this is the part where it's hard to explain."

"I'm not a dribbling idiot."

"Real jazz is never more than half a step from blues."

"I, er, don't get that. Run it past me again."

"With jazz, you live moment to moment. Imagine the next moment and it happens. You get past repetition. Way past."

"I don't understand. Sorry."

"There's always somebody imitating, living the past. That's not what I call living."

"What?"

"Look at my hands. What d'you see?"

"Hands."

"Yeah, two. But there's things between left and right. Subdivide and subdivide."

"*What?*"

"Some folk-music can get tedious, racial," Jimmy says, fingers clicking. Feet quickening, shuffling side to side. Then a scat. He scats a track Clifford Brown called Joyspring.

Geraldine's head shakes. "You're something else!" she says.

"Look, jazz is backwards compatible with blues."

"So, what is blues?"

"That's the part that's irreducible. The start. Africa in America."

"Is this going to get black conscious?"

"People indoors, they're looking forward to dinner. Checking the wine. Cozy, sipping coffee. Ogling the TV schedule. But me? I'm just displaced. Between wanting a smoke and a thought of lions."

Brows puckered, Geraldine scans the road. Jimmy tries to light a smoke. But cold weather blows over the junction. Both hands go deep in his overcoat. Her eyes say she understands.

He kicks the kerb. "Tell me why you do this bullshit job."

"Don't start *that* again."

"Why?"

"Because, because!"

"You get satisfaction?"

"Satisfaction?"

"Preaching at people. Preaching of glass."

"Well, you know, there's something I should tell you. And what a story *that* would be on a cold evening! Would have to be by a fire somewhere, with a glass of something. It's a long, long story."

"You can't tell me the end part?"

"Feel like a bit of agony columns?"

"That bad?"

"Pretty much. It's, well, I must sort out something."

"Is it what's going on with Brian?"

"Yeah."

"Like you must make up, or walk away?"

"Well, it's not clear at the moment."

"Why not?"

"How should I know? Everything's so cut and dried with you."

"You been married three years."

"Three and a half! Straight out of university."

"You want to *feel* married?"

"Well," she sighs, "of course."

"Why don't you visit him? I don't think the guy's hiding from you."

"Hiding, that's an unfortunate word."

"The stars over England repeat themselves. Repetition, stacked and stacked, measured by light years."

Geraldine bites her lip. "I think it was pretty much a lost cause. After the flop, Brian and me, we just lost it. We *so* wanted to keep our little agency afloat. But the tide came in and we went belly up."

"Must have been sickening."

"It was," she says, voice lowered, "like losing a child."

"Go and check him. He'd like that."

"He's all books at the moment. Resurrected his PhD."

"Bright guy."

"IQ, 160. Dropped his thesis so we'd set the agency up."

"What's he working on?"

"Information theory. Could take another year."

"That's why, then. It's the other woman in his life."

"But *I* wear the ring."

"You and me," Jimmy laughs, "we're the same age but you're ten years up the road from me."

"Oh, at least ten!"

"Yeah. So I don't know how you can do a childish job like this."

"This stint at Homes? Well, it's me on the rebound."

"A fine romance!"

"My adventure."

"*This* is an adventure?"

"What else? I mean, morality doesn't come into it."

"Sales morality."

"Well," she says, "at least *I* tell punters the facts. I say a salesman will call, not rubbish about customer services managers. Never!"

"You realize, in some of these houses there's probably the complete works of Beethoven. Might even be something on Hendrix."

"You're jealous!"

Jimmy shrugs. "Nothing wrong with jealousy. Now and then."

"I've got to think, do something."

"Why not give VSO a try?"

"Live abroad?"

"For a year, yeah."

"A whole year?"

"What's one year?"

"Can't wait to get rid of me?"

"Well, it might help you think. Somewhere far."

"Hmmm."

"Not a bad idea, is it?"

"I suppose."

"Afghanistan?"

"Don't know a thing about it, about what's happening there."

"Africa?"

# 31

Cars going turtle on tarmac. Want to turtle the evening. So move in cold turtle steps. Some switch headlights to beam. Cars going turtle, getting a closer look at the man and woman. Black man, white woman talking at the junction. Slow turtle eyes. And after every turtle gaze the same thing happens: turtles turn to cars again, speed off to turtle hiss.

Geraldine never mentions this. Pretends not to notice. Hard for Jimmy. He knows she understands. Wonders how a middle-class white woman can know. She knows how he keeps the hurt. But they don't mention it, gazing at Christmas lights in the houses.

"Every house here glows," he says. "And obviously they inherit every street. Those tarmac miles, connecting every house in England. Any old Smith can jump in a car and get to any place."

"Is that you being jealous again?" she says.

Jimmy mumbles a lyric: *Black tarmac, come with me. Yes, you. You know me by now, the cold archipelago.*

Geraldine yawns. "What's it mean?"

"I saw a right-wing pamphlet, it wants ethnic spots named the same."

"You're joking!"

"No. The name they site is Brixton."

"Don't be daft. I mean, they're obviously idiots!"

"Those guys are serious. I can see it now: Brixton-1 wouldn't be too desres; only down-home blacks and white liberals there. Brixton-2 would have the best jazz club. Anything beyond Brixton-9 would be still looking over its shoulder."

"Don't play their daft game!"

"No? But all the time in the lily white countryside, mint sauce and hot dumplings pile onto lashings of beef. Genesis plays, or Elgar."

"You're scaring me!"

Scanning the road for the pickup, Jimmy gets a brand new glimpse of Geraldine. Her face looks etched by arctic light.

"I think Hitchcock would've looked for you," he says. "Your specific English would've been great for his films."

Scanning for the pick-up van in the cold evening, Geraldine's face wracks with tension. "Go to Africa?" she says.

"Yeah. That VSO thing we talked about, does Africa count?"

"Of course!"

"Where would you go? I'm curious."

"Ethiopia, perhaps."

"South Africa?"

"Why not! I'd give it a go once things get more settled."

Stepping back, he wonders. Gets the play of light in the air round her. But quietly, counts to ten. Kicks the pavement. Then counts from ten to one. Tries to light a smoke. But gives up, again.

She frowns. "What's wrong?"

"You want a suntan on some South African beach?"

"Is this going to get nasty?"

"What d'you mean?"

"It was *you* who invited me to Africa. South Africa."

"I was curious. Wanted to see what you said."

"No, no suntans in South Africa. I'd just do the basics."

"If it's about you helping black people, I'd dissolve!"

"No," she laughs. "It's bigger than that."

"Bigger, in their own country?"

"Since I met you, yikes! Are all black men so suspicious?"

"What a big word!"

"Suspect, suspect! Me, everyone. Always on guard. Cynical. You never stop!"

"Where I go, I go in this skin."

"Where's the pickup van? I'm getting frostbite around here!"

"What's going to be so great in South Africa?"

"Guess what?" she says, trying her best sarcastic. "I didn't bring my crystal ball today. So careless of me!"

"Then just go for it, ad lib. I won't know the difference!"

"Look, can we stop now? Why're you being so hateful? You want the high ground. But that leaves me with, what? Bursting into tears?"

"There was a row at the party where I met Agnes. She was avoiding everybody wearing gold, and was just about to leave as I arrived. Wear gold, and you leave town. She'd put every ounce back in the ground."

"Good for her!"

"I'll be honest, when I think of South Africa it's still white privilege. The old apartheid. I hear it's still in the grass, the sea. I'd feel weird going there. My girlfriend's from Cape Town. Sometimes it's the same old. And now they have former freedom-fighters, black guys, forgetting the struggle and becoming billionaires."

"She's from South Africa?"

"Yeah."

"Black, isn't she?"

"Yes."

"Where did you meet?"

"Did her degree in London. King's."

"Did she like it here? Oh shit! You know what I mean."

"She thought it was fantastic. London, the big city of lights. No racial insults, nothing."

"She gelled here, then. Brilliant!"

"She got by."

"No, she didn't *get by*. She gelled. She obviously gelled with you."

"And I'm so hard to get on with, right?"

"If she can get on with you," Geraldine laughs, "she'd get on with *any* Brit."

"Brit?"

"What's wrong now?"

"*Brit?*"

"What's the problem? I mean, a woman from South Africa should know. She must have told you."

"Told me what?"

"Didn't she say anything?"

"Like what? That there's black Britons?"

"Naturally!"

"Like who?"

"People born here. You're a black Briton."

"So you say, lady," Jimmy says, yawning cold air. "So you say."

"Not what *I* say. It's a fact!"

"Hey, mentioning Agnes was a mistake. She never said anything about black Britons. Even on the phone. She talks of Brits, meeting them, their highs, lows, visiting their monuments, but she's talking white people. When blacks talk of Brits, they mean the white man."

"Shut yourself out, then wonder why the door's closed!"

"How many white people talk that talk?"

"What?"

"You didn't hear?"

"Then what are you, if not a Brit?"

His hands rub together. Rough rubs. Trying to warm them. "How many white people see somebody like me and say *black Briton*. Not black British, I mean black Briton."

"Then," Geraldine frowns, "who *are* you?"

"Neil Armstrong stepped on the moon and was soon clearing stardust from his visor. But back at NASA, at base, on the earth, somebody was thinking 'Hey, Neil! Who are you, now?' Buzz Aldrin was skipping near the Stars & Stripes, waving back at home."

"You *are* a dreamer!"

"Yeah, a dreamer."

"And when you're awake, who are you?"

"I dunno!" Jimmy blinks.

"Who d'you think the world thinks you are?"

"Black. Born in Liverpool. British."

"British!"

"Yeah."

"So, you are a Brit. QED."

"Look, if I was born in China that wouldn't make me Chinese. If you were born in Delhi it wouldn't make you Indian."

Geraldine turns away. Eyes hesitate. What she wants to say hesitates. She can't say it. Her hand reaches at her face. The hand knows the face, steps of whey. The evening hesitates. Turtles could hitch a ride from the cold hesitating evening. The stars hesitate. And headlights hesitate from traffic hesitating. In the end, nothing left that can hesitate. It could snow tonight. But chances are snow will hesitate one more week.

Her eyebrows raise. "Briton is the noun," she says, "and British is the adjective. If you accept the adjective, you already have the noun."

"Cozy!"

"What's the problem now?"

"All that grammar. I could wrap it round me and still freeze to death!"

"I was only joking!"

"*British* is what the BNP use when they mean white. Down the road from my flat, I heard this BNP guy doing a sermon. It was 'Britain is for the indigenous people of these islands, the English, Welsh, Irish and Scots.' A bright guy, serious preacher."

"Come on, I said I was *joking*!"

"To me, a Brit is like a soldier in Boadicea's army."

"What?"

"Brit is heavy-duty English. Bald-head Tory, like Margaret Thatcher."

A fluorescent light stutters in the front room across the road; the only house with no Christmas lights. A tall woman walks to the computer and sits down. She doesn't draw the curtains. Wanting it that way. She wants to be seen from the street. Standing again, she removes her jacket. Folds it on the chair. And wipes the computer screen with her palms. Then takes a sheaf of papers, puts them in a drawer. Bending, she gets something from the floor. Jimmy won't upset Geraldine; she's too good to him. And mostly it's not her fault.

Hands deep in coat pockets, her mouth in a wry smile, her eyes turn to his. "Thinking in the past again?" she says.

"Yesterday I got dealt a hand of the woad-game."

"What happened?"

Remembering, he turns away. "A bloke said I can't be English. A big red-faced guy. I asked him why not. He said because my ancestors don't come from, I can't remember the name of the place, it was somewhere in Germany."

Geraldine gazes her feet. "Angleheim," she says, hoarsely.

"Home of the Angles, right?"

"What did you tell him?"

"What could I say?"

"Didn't you say anything?"

"He was all facts and figures."

"That's so shocking. Shocking. Didn't think there was that much rubbish. That's interesting."

"As in *jolly* interesting?"

"What d'you want me to do?"

"I don't know."

"Have I got a halo?"

"Your country, not mine!"

"I should shampoo my halo, head-butt a few diehards? Come on, let's hear it!"

"That's not what I mean."

"These things take time. Why can't you be patient? Be *patient*!"

"Wait a hundred years, right?"

"It'll happen. You must believe that."

"So I take a seat for now, make a nice cup of tea. And wait."

"Sooner we get started the better."

"Then one day me and my neighbour go off into the sunset together?"

"You sound like some horrid little drama you want to act in!"

"My life isn't a drama already, a tragedy?"

Arms in the air, Geraldine groans. "What can I do?"

"I need a smoke."

Slowly, she steps closer. And cups hands with his. Making a windbreak for the match. The cigarette lights in the cold evening air as she looks him in the eye. "You're too cynical!"

"Why'd you stop smoking?"

"Not me. Let's get back to *your* tragedy."

"Ever do marijuana?"

Angry, she turns away. Scans again for the pickup. Jimmy takes a long drag. Then laughs.

Geraldine frowns. "Your girlfriend, you said she hates gold."

"Not the mineral. Hates what they do with it."

"Here's a little puzzle for you," she says, eyes scheming. "Try getting from 'gold' to 'dust' by changing only one letter at a time."

"Fort Knox!"

"Scared of a bit of brain work?"

In the cold evening, Jimmy opts for nicotine. Lungs getting older and could die, but only exhale. "Somewhere," he says, "some nerd like Stephen Hawking wonders why nobody from the future ever comes back, you know, to prove time travel. They've got Ron Mallett in America, trying for a time machine. Could be a while to get it right. Then I could go back a few centuries, pretend being a slave."

"What's your answer?"

"To what?"

"The puzzle!" she says, exasperated.

Across the road, the woman in the window turns from the computer. Hurries from the chair. Now coyly at the door, she switches off the light. But forgets something. Back in the room, she's at the desk again.

After loud grumbling, reaching through tobacco hoops, embarrassed, scribbling on the cigarette packet, swearing, Jimmy says, "The puzzle is to get from gold to dust, right?"

"Yes!"

"I've got: gold, told, toll, doll, dolt, bolt, boot, loot, lost, lust, dust."

Hard, seeing the half-hidden sky over London this evening. But talking with Geraldine makes Jimmy feel less cut off. He reads her eyes. Likes watching the way she looks at trees. Mostly her eyes are kind,  seeing the big picture, understanding. And she knows names of trees he'd never know: oleander, hawthorn, hollyhocks.

"By the way," she says, "what's an uncle tom?"

Big surprise for Jimmy! Dragging smoke, inhaling hard, dragging with no mercy, tobacco more than lungs will bear, watching the ember sear to him, trying to think. This the end point. The terminus. The cigarette's a cypher. No lungs left. "Uncle tom?" he says, billowing smoke. "Where'd you come across that?"

"Who, or what is an uncle tom?"

Trying for the best way to answer, watching night play her eyes, he drags more smoke. One more drag. Then nods. "Toms are hypocrites. Stooges. Grinning black hypocrite-stooges."

"Yikes!"

"They're every place."

"Not an old tomcat, then?"

"Nah!"

"Where's it from?"

"Jeez!"

"A long story?"

"Yeah. It started ages ago. Toms were slaves grinning from the master's house, doing the master's chores, cooking his food."

"Wiping his arse?"

"*That* is an uncle tom."

"Yikes!"

"The other slaves were outdoors. All day. Fourteen hours every day, busting their guts in the fields."

Geraldine's eyes are busy with Jimmy's face, studying his face like never seen him before. Her eyes want something. But the more she stares the more he could laugh. Headlights flicker. Headlights on his face. Turtle lights. And a puzzled woman getting evening from a face. He won't laugh. Her face is innocent. A clean face.

Backing away, he wonders if he should doubt her. He must try, must find out. "Why not say blacks should go back where they came from, the ones that feel so hard done by here? Bet you think that sometimes."

"*What*?"

"You heard!"

"I have *never* thought in such terms!"

"Want me to jump for joy?"

"Let's get this straight, is that what you think?"

"Me, know to think?"

"If you think that, then don't talk to me. Is that what you think?"

Across the street the woman's front room is back in darkness. And the rest of the house. Suddenly, a little Christmas tree flickers. Now she's at the front door; a tall woman, coming down the driveway, heading for the street.

Geraldine doesn't know the whole story. But Jimmy thinks her eyes are true. He wonders about her. Wondering if what she thinks comes from her mouth. But no need to inspect this mouth; no gobbets of raw meat cling to that mouth. He trusts her.

"In a fairytale, half the Arctic on fire is still the Arctic on fire."

She tugs his coat sleeve. "Answer my question!"

"No," he says, "you don't bullshit me."

"Then what was the fuss about?"

"I never know. No idea where that stuff comes from."

"Why say it?"

"It just comes out. Hard to know who's who, what's what."

"Know who your friends are."

As the van arrives, the evening sky is cold metal night. And mutely, a few stars reach out for who looks. Two people get picked up from a cold pavement, cold and quiet. Christmas, less than a week away.

Geraldine doesn't play the predator game. For everybody else in the van work days are measure days, weighing lightning to pounce. Where weeks before was talk of tree-lined roads, neat houses to prospect for double-glazing, now talk is of predator tracks. Tracks through docile herds. Houses are not houses now. But slow-moving prey. And punters warm and dumb, munching merry muffins, content cattle chewing cud.

# 32

On TV, the MC grins, 'Ten, nine, eight..' Pausing, tipping champagne. Ogling fireworks. Then gets on with it. 'Four, three, two, one. Happy New Year!'

"This it?" Jimmy says. "This is 2000? What, *this*?"

Lorna sighs. Presses the handset to her lips. "What did you expect?"

"Hugeness was supposed to happen, off the scale!"

"Dream on!"

"Then why the big fireworks? I mean, serious fireworks on TV. You watching? Nice as a tropic night. Multi-coloured, alive. Higher and higher. Beauty fire!"

"Not gentle as stars."

"Well, no. Not as far."

"And not so kind."

"The river through Embankment, what a cool scene! Stars getting drowned by water going to sea. And that same old Faran! That guy still gets a piece of it."

"Faran?" Lorna says. "Who's that?"

"Religion. Or card games. Yeah, sermons, the lottery. But, hey! Priests are the problem. They're all at sea. Everybody respects the ocean, so bishops drop anchor in baptismal water, talk crap, saying, 'The Lord walked on this.'"

"It's politicians. Psychopaths. Not axe-wielders, but congenital liars."

"Politicians? They're the ones! The shrillest preachers of all. One turned up on TV earlier, said this millennium is a fresh start. Talking crap like that! Those bastards, they go for beer. Hops, hops, hops. They shake your hand, grab a glass, 'Cheers!' But know what? As soon as you raise *your* glass, they're looking for your suicide in that beer."

"You're drunk!" Lorna says.

"Me? The TV's drunk! Brixton's drunk. Ding, bling, bling! Faran can skip, I mean sing. Yeah. Ever see Brixton on TV? They go for drool, you know, panting for that ethnic thing. Makes me sick! Media walking round, never chewing gum, but mouths like fish wanting wet. *That's* the Brixton the festival guy talked. But guess what? That guy knows jazz. Heard him snazzing it on the phone, snapping his desk with a 6-8 beat. But the *way* his voice got rid of Brixton, Jeez! No way talking culture. Not the highs, lows. Not advice. It was like phlegm in a plastic mouth. Woad talk."

# 33

1st January, 2000.

"I forgot to say it," Lorna says. "Jimmy, a Happy New Year."

"At your parents' place?"

"No. By myself."

"You OK?"

"Yes, fine. But you, you don't need any more to drink."

"Then what's bottles for? What's calendars for?"

"Look, I won't keep you. Go get some sleep."

"Could be better calendars," Jimmy slurs. "Other spots the big count could start from. Could start with Jesse."

"Who?"

"Jesse Owens."

"The athlete?"

"Yeah. He trumped Hitler's skull. That punk Adolf, he stormed away from the Olympics. Same year Edward quit the English throne, wed a yankee dandee doo."

"What *are* you talking about?"

"Instead of 2000, calendars could show 'Year 64, Owens Era.' Get it? Bet you know the score anyway. Folk wanting to keep it sky up. Then again, the count could start from when Neil stepped on the moon."

Lorna laughs. "Funny, what a few drinks can do!"

"Folk weary with Faran. He was a bit of a musician, cosmic player, said he could play anything, anytime. You believe that stuff?"

"I believe in goodness. God is good."

"Good is good! Faran, I mean, promising to play stars, galaxies to sing out. Folk still turning their ear to the sky. Who hears a star? You ever hear them? Even one star? Bet you hear noise from a bell tower. Faran tolling, saying, 'Turn the other cheek.'"

"If you're going to insult my beliefs, then goodbye!"

"Goodbye? God is good, goodbye?"

"If you're going to blaspheme, I'll hang up!"

"Hey, hang on a minute. Want to know the weird part? Weirder than Faran. His mother. She was the weird one. Pregnant with him, but no man. No man! Bet you know that stuff by heart. Then after Faran was born she got a common man's brood, you know, testing her nipples, unload that woman milk to wailing mouths, human this time. Now we have a donkey going down the road. Jackass blues! That donkey, I mean, it's still traveling. Next move, a blood-red Ferrari overtakes, shows a carrot on millennium highway. You still there?"

"Still here," Lorna whispers.

"Year 2000, but nothing different. Idiots on TV shouting 'Hooray!' Not me! The folk festival started an hour ago."

"You feel left out? Betrayed?"

"Nah! Doesn't matter now. Bigger music to say."

"Ring me when you sober up. Got something I want to tell you."

Three days with no sleep. Alcohol jugged down. And that call from Agnes. She talked a whole hour; a nervy woman phoning from the southern hemisphere, saying she got asked again but turned the offer down. Jimmy said, 'Agnes, if you want to boogie, do it right this time.'

Instead of sheep he'll count lions. The last bottle of malt totes. His eyes close. Slowly, one by one, lion cubs file by. Day-old cubs, going by, nuzzling by instead of sheep. In twenty minutes, one lion cub for every year of the past 2000. Honey-eyed cubs.

Still wide awake, wary, grabbing at black coffee, sardines on stale toast. Then phones Lorna.

"You're still drunk!" she says.

"Aren't you watching the concert?"

"*What* concert?"

"New Year's Day, the thing from Vienna. Magic music, magic!"

"Classical stuff?"

"Strauss. Danube. Mystic water. Turn your telly on!"

"I'll give it a miss."

"Great to look at, high art."

"New Year's day on a Saturday seems wrong."

"Watch the concert!"

"No. I'm going round to my parents, get something to eat."

"Ricardo Muti this year. Bet the audience are whispering how it's Maazel they like."

"Who?"

"Conductors. They're a big deal in classical. Like a ship's captain. The focus. Muti's doing great. Got to be a billion people tuned in. I mean, from everywhere. Europe, Japan. Africa. America. Every place. Music it is. And the discipline! Discipline could *not* be neater. High art. *High* art. That sense of order. Ace, ace. The technique of white folk."

# 34

4 o'clock. Donna phones Jimmy.

Through bloodshot eyes he remembers. It comes flooding back, exactly how vicious he was that evening last year. For the first time he can see the whole thing. And if just one word can do it, that lone word is desolation. That Donna, that large lady got laid waste. Genghis Khan would not lay more waste than how Jimmy was vicious to Donna last year. And seeing that, only now, after more than a whole year to think it, that's bad, bad. Maybe it wasn't Donna. Through her body he maybe was laying waste to something. Like a squandered life: this spite and that, this setback, that insult, door closed, or opened by a hypocrite. And the church. Every false thing doled by the church, like the part in the bible where slaves must obey masters in all things. And a preacher who was god, but played mortal blood on a wood cross; or wasn't god, but got his blood shed so his god would be content. And nobody today ever goes to church to ask why anyone should ever have a master in the first place. Or how a priest lives in a mansion called Lambeth Palace. Maybe that's what that weird evening with Donna was. But to have a kind-hearted woman on the end of that, a singing black woman from the church, that's bad.

Donna, the lady with her body as a house. She got the Christmas card. And, well, she can't stop thinking the good part. Even after what happened.

What?

It happened last year. Donna was in the church choir. She got stoned by Jimmy. To him, she always had too much to say. Every day, every time, more gab. But the great thing was her singing. Singing pure, singing full notes. Something was always kind about that singing woman; maybe her eyes, something deep in that woman singing in the church choir. So that evening last year Jimmy said it, asked if she'd check him at the flat. She was looking for something. Must have been affection, looking for tender things. But that evening last year only stone. Wicked wildness, a force-9 hurricane grabbed her down.

Donna is large, a heavy lady. Hard saying how big. 16 stone maybe. They call her Queen Donna because of size. Big as any lake. But not like a wet pullover. Jimmy knew she sung from the heart, eternally from the soul, every note full, even, her voice like a euphonium, singing to sing. But she never got the piece he composed for the church choir; every time she said 'The rhythm, the rhythm!' Fussing that the rhythm's always on the move. Look, she said one day, this thing is jazz, understand? This rhythm skips all the time. And Jimmy said 'The rhythm, on the move? Where else would rhythm be?' She wasn't sure. And that was hard to take. Because she's a music teacher. So no excuse. So that evening he showed where rhythm;

that church woman got all the rhythm she could handle. The personal kind. That evening was mist last year. Weird. Rhythm was key. In one hour she got stormed, wicked, rough, a tempest, slaying, a hurricane, lion killing in the dark. He owned all she had. Even stuff she never believed. In the bible David was a great king and as a boy dropped Goliath, then later had 18 wives and a son named Solomon. Solomon topped that. 300 wives and 900 concubines. But one evening last year Jimmy got from Donna all the moves Solomon never got. And when it was over, it was over. But not quite: he expected to get called *Maniac!* or get called *Animal!* Even evil. But all she said was 'You're confused.' You're a wounded man, you're alone, so alone, she said. Blankness was in the room. He had zil to say. And when she got back from the bathroom, it was in a low church humming. By now the spliff was burning just right. And he was leaning back, smoking that high-rise herb, watching yards of cloth fix to her body.

Now more than a year later. New Year's day. She calls him on the phone. Voice on edge, she says 'Happy New Year!' She's at her sister's place and a serious turkey on the dinner table. Jimmy, sprawled on a tenement floor, grunts 'Hello'.

Donna's going to Jamaica. Go in two weeks. She could go for good. Mumbling, he says she should drop by; yeah, before flying out, drop by for a shot of malt. But. This is bad. Cold quiet. Something on her mind. She wants to hang up. Something else there. And not even she knows what. Then the strangest thing. And that's Jimmy with a sudden feeling; a quiet, warm feeling for this woman. Drop by later, he says again.

Donna's breathing is low. She wants something. But scared. Jimmy won't speak. The next move must be hers. Her lips damp the mouthpiece. A blindfold on her heart. Eyes closed, but seeing a basin for sweat. Somehow. But, yes, she'll pass by tomorrow. But only to say goodbye. That bad evening last year floods back. The ache, loss, the worry because of how she got mistreated.

# 35

Getting left out the folk festival isn't too bad for Jimmy. Not now. Not after the Donna call. Outdoors, trees forlorn and a promise of snow.

He phones his mother. "Happy New Year."

"I hoped you'd be here. Half hoped."

"Next year, yeah. No matter where in the world, I'll get there."

"No need to promise. You're my son."

"I'm going through a bad time."

"Like what? What's wrong?"

"This and that. Stuff going way back. Bad vibes."

"Girlfriend trouble?"

"Well, not sure."

"Who is it this time?"

"Somebody I messed up."

"She trusted you?"

"Yeah."

"Tell her you're sorry. Mean it. Ask her what she wants you to do."

"She's special. I didn't realize."

"A musician?"

"Sort of. A music teacher."

"Then, she could be the one."

"Yeah. You might be right."

"Don't be a typical black man, whatever you do!"

"I'm not a typical *anything*."

"No. That's true. You could have done anything in this life."

"Don't start! Don't go on about how I should've been a doctor."

"You were good at school. Ace."

"Remember how I used to come home and bawl?"

"You were very sensitive, couldn't cope with racism."

"That golliwog."

"Yes, I remember. It was painted on the playground wall."

"The blood mouth on that black face. Part cartoon, part vampire. That still hurts. A cartoon was inside the vampire, for why the big grin? And a vampire inside the cartoon, that golli mouth so big with blood."

"Then the name-calling," she says, sighing.

"Yeah. Learning to ignore that stuff. Or pretend to ignore. Teen years were the bad part. Those wisecracks! Somebody should definitely have got their eye poked out for that stuff."

"Then where would you be today?"

"I know. I think about that. Then again. Later on, it was cold spite from the guy at the factory, that first part-time job I did. The boss was a bozo, totally dripped school because of being thick, but owned a factory and wanted to settle scores by dealing spite to the low-paid. That, and other stopgap jobs. Even a place where race stuff was scant, you know, the animal belching to show exactly what they mean when somebody black walks past a group of them."

"I'll *never* forget one thing. It happened to me. I was working at this place, a shipping office, and anytime I went into the pool room, a really well-lit room, some redneck always turned round and gazed at the light bulb, saying out loud that the room's gone dark. In broad daylight! Even with sunlight screaming through every window and door."

"And the police. Nathan told me how they used to be."

"Used to be? Listen, that uniform is a joke! Twisted white guys using their uniform to hide behind, winding down their police window to make monkey-zoot, or stopping you, saying you can't be coming from where you say, even when you show something that identifies you, even then, even when it's obvious you *are* who you say, even then, those psychos say you're lying."

"Never heard you so steamed up!"

"The worst part comes next. The mask you wear to pretend. You pretend not to see the mask devious folk wear when looking for something safe to chat with you. But when you slip your own mask, thinking it's safe to be yourself because you're sure who's real and who's lying, you can't hide the hurt. You've been fooled again. That's bitter. *So* bitter! All that and a mile more. Some half-forgotten, but still there, never going away."

"Nathan's got 50 racials for every two bits of kindness."

"It's still tough out there. The thing that hacks me off is if you tell somebody what's happening, make a stand, try saying you've had enough, then pow! You get told to piss off. If they want to be polite, they say you've got a chip on your shoulder."

"Or they parade some uncle-tom on TV, a sports idiot, you know, it's 'Look at that chap who's black but always smiling, never complaining, just getting on with it and, anyway, you're welcome to go back where you came from.' *That* gets up my nose!"

"They do it all the time. So matter-of-fact, end of story."

# 36

Nathan calls from New York. "Jimmy, what's your Minims lyrics? I get the music, just played Bobby the whole thing on trumpet but, man! I can *not* remember the words."

"The bandleader? Bobby Delaney?"

"Yeah."

Bobby grabs the phone. "Hey, Jimmy! I want those lyrics! I could be interested. Might cover your Minims."

Jimmy grins. "I'm still shifting stuff round, still going for the best simple. But the theme's the same. The same folk-opera."

"What's the theme?"

"Minims, it's is about black people born in England."

Bobby laughs "What? Man, that's too big! Just one little size too big. One theme can never fit *all* black folk. Not in England. Not no place."

"Not now, maybe. But one day."

"Never happen! Black folk in the States, we learned that the hard way. Understand? Black people never see eye to eye on what's gotta get going."

"The old black, brown and beige thing?" Jimmy wonders.

"You bet! That stuff, it'll happen to England too. Once you get more browns and beige, some days they step from black."

"I don't believe that!"

"Hey, let's talk music. Music must move free, Jimmy. No politics, man! Duke Ellington tried that reconciliation stuff. Mingus tried. But who thanks them?"

"Then forget colour!"

"What? Where?"

"Think of people with nowhere to call home."

"Who?"

"Folk that've never seen the ocean, let alone belong to some place across it!"

"That what happening in England?"

"Yes."

"Yeah?"

"Broken people. They need a fireworks day, their own song."

"What, in England?"

"Yes."

"Jimmy, Jimmy! That is kid talk!"

"The Minims theme explains," Jimmy says, getting urgent. "The theme is the blind lady and child."

"Blind? She young?"

"This is no joke. Look at longitude! It was the big joke at sea. Wrecks all over the ocean. No sure way to know if a ship was going some place or heading away. Latitude was the easy part, a bunch of lines from the sun. But longitude, ghost lines on the map. Then a guy called Harrison happened. That was the 1700s. He made make a clock to sync with the whole ocean. That's how it started. Britannia grabbed the waves. How you, Bobby, got a back-story in America, blacks picking cotton till it came out their ears."

"OK, kid. OK. I won't mess with your head. Not any more. This theme you have, it better be good. Let's have it."

Jimmy flits to the keyboard. Hitches the phone. Hits a C-sharp chord. C-sharp minor. Smiles. His throat clears.

*The child winks at the sky, saying fireworks are at home, at home. Sweet and low, the blind lady says Child, you describe it so well, so well! Yes, fireworks at home in the sky, carrying the timing of minims so high, so high. Tapping the cane, she sings it. Yes, she'd like colours of things, oh yes, things nobody can hear, not now, not how things rank by colour, by colour. Blue things, purple, green, yellow, and oh, there's puzzles in huddles. The child wonders, Which puzzles. Oh, lots, lots. Like which ones? The lady sings, Minims, minims, minims! Singing of people who huddle, gaze at fireworks, starry-eyed, up, starry-eyed, starry. Weary now, sitting a while, she sings the puzzle: Folk huddle, but not by the magic of seeing, no, no. See like a Cyclops, one-eye, one-eye. Run from two eyes, run, whimper, eyes shut tight, oh Lord, scared of two eyes, afraid, afraid! The lady seeks the child's face with her hands, two hands. Yes, my dear, two eyes can be hard sometimes, but always get there in the end, somewhere safe, safe for light, sunlight. Cane waving the sky, the lady cranks, singing of folk expecting others to work for them, for them, even work things out for them. The start of every problem, problem. Listen to this, she sings, tapping the cane with both hands. Tapping the cane, the cane. A white cane's so folk can tell, tell their story, tell. Cane-rhythm is everything, the minims' rhythm, minims' rhythm, rhythm! The lady sings it, saying the rhythm of minims is a beat to fit most things, even fits Parliament Square in the middle of what was nowhere, nowhere.*

Bobby smiles. Down the phone line, and way across the sea, the bandleader smiles at the theme. "Hey, that's not bad!"

Jimmy hears him turn to Nathan. Nathan laughs, proud laughing. And more laughs. Then talk, but too hard to hear. The phone hangs up. Jimmy taps the keyboard, thinking Marconi should get music for what happened; somebody should craft phone-crackle to song. The phone rings.

"Hey, kid!" Bobby hollers. "Minims is neat. No wonder they don't understand that over there. Handle it right, it goes places."

"You'd maybe give it a try, record it?"

"Why not! But look, me and Nathan go back a long way, so don't mess up! Don't dream your thing away over there."

"I'm no dreamer."

"Me and the band, we toured Europe last year and, brother! The black people you have on TV in England? Some of the ugliest mothers I *ever* seen! Nothing happens there. Not any time soon. Get the hell out!"

A good sign. Bobby Delaney rating Minims is the best thing on New Year's day for Jimmy. Far from a fake folk festival.

Bobby's voice lowers. "Look, the one thing you gotta watch is don't mess with the bible."

"The bible?"

"Yeah, your Minims theme. It's like from the bible. Like from inside the Good Book."

"It's only the theme," Jimmy laughs. "I'll kick some street into it!"

# 37

11 o'clock. Tuesday morning. 4th January. Donna's voice sings through the entry-phone. In three minutes she'll be at Jimmy's door. He looks around. The flat's in great shape. But the kitchen. It's a bomb. He gets back to A Brief History Of Time, marks a paragraph.

*Who* is this?" he says

Donna smiles. Wearing perfume before midday. She's different. Not the huge in this same flat that evening a year ago. She's maybe only ten stone now, like a poinsettia bloom. She says nothing.

Not really smiling, her eyes check. Alert, checking details of the head, the eyes. From her own eyes she understands, steps past, pretends not to see dishwater splashed on his shirt. This the first time any woman's ever seen Jimmy this domestic way.

"Happy New Year, stranger."

"I got rid of the locks. Been this way a while."

"Then happy new millennium," she says, eyes touring the room.

"What, the whole thousand years?"

"Loosen up!"

"Well, yeah."

"That's all you've got to say?"

'You look great."

"Thanks."

"*Amazing.*"

"And?"

"Never thought I'd see you again."

"That's why you sent the Christmas card?"

"Kind of."

"You sent the card to say sorry?"

"Well," he mumbles, "I didn't know any other way."

"What happens now?"

Jimmy's nervous, can't hide from Donna's eyes. "I was reading this, A Brief History Of Time. The idea of galaxies going down a tunnel. Funny thing, stars. They're luminous factories of the universe."

"The flat looks nice," she says, ignoring the book. "A lot tidier than how I remembered it. It's more, you know, sort of homey."

"I try basic tidying up. Most days."

"You've changed!"

"Getting older," Jimmy grunts. "Twenty-five this year."

"Ready for your pension?"

"Feels that way sometimes."

"Your eyes are nice and clear."

"My eyes?"

"You walk alone now, I can tell from your eyes."

"Yeah, on a mission."

"No detours?"

"No more locks."

"Come, let's have a feel of you hair."

"Fancy a drink?" he laughs, stepping away.

"No thanks! Whisky is still you, isn't it?"

"Malt. Got to be malt whisky."

"I've brought some sorrel. And turkey, some New-Year cake."

"You look *great*."

She turns to the hi-fi. "Mmm. what's playing."

"It's Ellington," he says, adjusting the volume.

"What's the track?"

"Sonnet In Search Of A Moor."

Biting her lip, Donna turns away. Moves to the window. And stands stock still. Wondering. She nods. Then turns back to the room. And grabs the carrier bag. Heads for the kitchen.

Jimmy's gaze settles on the settee. Hands quaking, nervy, a spliff starts. Things to remember. Big quota. Ganja lies on a tobacco trail as Donna comes back to the room. And a glass that she fills with sorrel.

"Your kitchen is a *mess*," she says, scanning the sitting room.

The window next to the settee has never had curtains. Except maybe from the other tenement blocks, nothing to see; only a high-rise watcher could perv. But the settee! That's where it happened. Donna got roughed there last year. The little settee making Jimmy nervy. Standing again, he remembers. The spliff lights.

Hard, figuring why it happened. It was not to crop, not Donna. But it happened out of nowhere. That evening last year happened by itself. She was at the flat after rehearsals and, to start, it was to watch him at the key-board. She loved the settee, curling on it while he played, playing this and that, wanting the right feel, lazing, gospel riffs, Ray Charles riffs, music from the solar plexus of a community. She didn't want any ganja. Sitting, not saying a word, she listened to the playing; dreamy playing, she said. So Jimmy played it. And smoked, serious and quiet. And played it true. 16-bar music, blues, unguent notes only for Donna, the woman, not the complainer, playing for the quiet in her heart. And when the music was over, when there was nothing to play anymore, the player said nothing. Then he realized. And said it was OK she didn't want to smoke, mentioning that some people can't handle weed and, anyway, look, it was rhythm time. Yeah, rhythm time. The hour of rhythm, Jimmy said, saying it was time for person time. Her eyes narrowed, shuttered by shock. She jumped from the settee to leave. But then. Everything changed. She bit on her lip, looked at him and wasn't shocked any more. I agree, her eyes said. His hands were faint, touching, holding, finding it difficult to believe; so much to hold. Then reaching for what was what. Even the room was holding, the whole room. And all the time Donna was humming a gospel tune. And when the humming stopped, she looked him in the eye. Then took a step back, checking, finding out. Then said it. The music was great, she said, yes, she'd come for as much as could get played. But she'd guessed all along. Yes, knew his mind. And, no, a woman her size won't break. Then. The gap closed. She said it one more time, saying again a woman her size won't break. Then it happened. Something snapped. He was like somebody waiting a whole life for that, to cut loose, no obligation. Affection was in her eyes. But what happened next was nothing to do with that. That whole thing's too hard to talk. Only a tenement can hold enough emotion to tell it, but that evening a good woman was just too plain, too day-to-day. Her clothes dropped to the ground. She was on the settee. What a night. Jimmy rid what had been angry all the time. She whispered like from the soul. Donna's body was her house. And somebody got to ring a bell in that secret dream. Then she said it again, saying his playing was dreamy. But that was playing the keyboard, playing blues, dicing gospel, reaching out. That was far as far can not go. Not far as a stone trombone. And that was bad. That evening was a stone trombone, and only because of one thing: bad regard. Bad! Everything was down to disregard. With one whisper she complained. But not about stone. It was the window; no curtains on the window, she said. He turned to the window. Then looked at how that body-house got worked. Lazing, he wondered who could ever see them all the way up on the 8<sup>th</sup> floor.

That late evening last year was one thing. Till now, too much fog. He doesn't know why it happened. Even now. Stone was in his soul that evening over a year ago. Something wicked; something wanting to play a heavy woman. Donna was the field of dreams.

Now she's here. Looking great. Only a song could say it. Music to say how she's so changed. She's a lapsed Christian. Sings gospel in a choir, but no religion to cross her life. Jimmy likes that. He remembers seeing her the first time. It was one morning at Sunday school. He'd just moved to London with Nathan, and Donna was sixteen, about five years older than him, and he liked her straightaway because of the gap between her two front teeth.

Now she's here. Again. And dividing the room with her woman eyes. He's ashamed. She sips from the glass of sorrel. But her eyes want him to say it. Narrowed eyes. Her hands approach his face, fingers touch his mouth.

"Say it!" she says.

This 4th day of January, Jimmy's scared. Wondering what to say. But Donna must hear it.

"Somewhere," he says, "a flower's in a vase by itself. And on a stem outdoors, that flower could be glowing in a garden."

"That's all well and good. Very pleasant. But."

His throat clears. "Donna, sorry about what happened."

Her eyes say there's more. Jimmy lifts her from the ground and her hat falls. But then. A new mood. Bad news. She wants to talk. Slipping to the ground and stepping away, she spells the whole thing out. Her life's been helter skelter. Since that freak evening, up and down. Sick for a long time because of it. She was even sorry for him. Then hate. Hate! Some days she could die. But then, wanting him to die. Her eyes moisten.

"When I got your Christmas card, it came right back. I hated you all over again."

"Somebody can go to a garden and cut flowers down. But nobody leaves them cut there, on the grass, not put in a vase."

"What?"

"Even saying sorry is small-time. This is shame. Maybe *shame* is not the word. Guilt is a better word. The rest of it too severe."

"At least you're big enough to admit it!"

Something else. Jimmy knows there's more. Donna wanted some of what happened. She was looking for affection, but all she got was stone. He knows she knows; she wanted affection *and* stone. She wanted one wicked thing to quake her body, her house, her church; wanted a quake through it. And he stoned that body-church. Bulldozed it because it was a church. Her body was her church then. Now, more than words can hold, a scent of evening primrose in the air.

"Why'd you come here today?" he wonders.

"Could be ten reasons."

"What's the main reason?"

"Doesn't matter now. Not today. Got so much to think."

"Jamaica?"

"Yes. My mother and father are from Portland. A green, green place. It's in the north-east of the island. They'll probably die in England. Know anything about Portland? It's a lot like Wales. The same feeling of mountains and waterfalls. Obviously, it's warm there."

"Take a tape recorder with you."

"Naturally! I want to talk to old folk, old-time songs they remember, get African words disappearing from Jamaica talk. I used to go to Wales to get at Portland. And I like Great Yarmouth. It's nice there. But nothing in Portland like great-crested grebes. And absolutely *nothing* in Great Yarmouth like a Jamaican hummingbird. I took a DNA test. Get the results in a month. Find out where my roots are. It's obvious, all my roots are in Africa."

"But the slaves got so diced," Jimmy says. "Probably different bits of Africa in your mix."

"That's me!"

"Tribe, rent asunder from tribe."

"The slaves lost their own languages."

"Ever wonder what language your ancestors spoke?"

"After just two generations in Jamaica, African languages got lost."

"Woman," he says, "you're the colour of summer. Beautiful as black olives."

Jimmy's never gone back to any woman. Nathan's advice was clear: a man dat go back to a flame is a man dat 'ave no fire. But something about this one. Maybe that's why he sent the Christmas card; a blank card, no emotion, not even his name. Yet she knew. Straightaway she guessed it was him. Something's going on. Spliff ready to light. The matches irate.

"No," Donna says. "No ganja!"

"It's herbs of the fields."

"A spliff is headlights in daylight!"

"Better than bishops lighting candles."

"This rubbish," she says, grabbing the spliff, "it's total rot. What you guys smoke in England is *not* ganja. Chemical crap. Coops up inside, turns you loose. No, no ganja. Not today."

Jimmy could get angry. But then. Donna's coat slips. She folds it across the old settee. A soft Jamaican sunset in a new red dress.

# 38

The ocean was angry. As he got out the car in Great Yarmouth yesterday the sea heaved and bucked. Folk in thick overcoats. And gulls perched on the sea-front, feathers puffed.

Getting there was touch and go. The gearbox scrunched the whole North Circular. But just the sight of the sign saying 'M11' and it was a goer. Yesterday was a good day for Jimmy. A road journey. 130 miles each way, thinking, flowing, watching motorway signs loom and disappear.

Donna's friend is from Great Yarmouth. Invited her to a fireworks display near the sea-front. But yesterday it was Jimmy on the motorway and Donna on a plane to Jamaica. Maybe she gazed down at the ocean, maybe thinking of rain. Jamaican sunshine spreads on her today. She prayed as soon as the plane touched down. Being away from faith was only pride; it was pride all along, she says.

Jimmy was cold in Great Yarmouth. Edgy, about time and longing. But walked the beach a while.

Donna was right; they have a big statue of Nelson in Great Yarmouth. Horatio had a thing for the place; sailed from the naval base to test ocean salt. Funny, but that statue was up a full 30 years before the one in Trafalgar Square.

The fireworks got canceled. They'd planned a sea-front bash. But it was too cold. So he toured the coast road, going from Hopton to Winterton, gazing at winter beach. The solitude. Fifteen miles of solo sand taking a winter break.

Somebody said hello. It was a lifeguard, part young, so ocean. He waved. Then she said he'd chosen a bad day, but windmills are only a mile inland. Traditional windmills, only a mile or two inland and still working away; take a look, the lifeguard said.

Before heading back he grabbed some quality time at a restaurant. A warm, tidy place. A hot plate of scallops, artichokes, herb risotto. Next, a steak & kidney pie; a whole acre of it with fresh peas and tomato through red wine sauce. Somebody said 'Try cheese with apricot compote and walnut bread.' So he gave it a try. And all the time the sea was breaking on the beach. Sediment was in the glass of wine. Then two lazy, lazy cups of coffee. Then a cigarette. And a giddy sight of gulls dicing the wing. Then back on the road, in a half-light turning quickly to evening.

# 39

Another week off. To start the new year, Clive wants punters' heads free of booze. No booze or mince pies to get in the way of business. Geraldine phones Jimmy. She's at her cousins' Hampshire cottage. Even helped them repair thatching on the roof, and learned strange things.

"Strange?"

"Like liggers," she says. "Oh, and spars and tarred cord. I've never worked so hard. What a buzz, getting the reeds to gel! I could start again as a thatcher."

"A bit of a Maggie?" he laughs.

"Thatching, it's pretty serious stuff. Highly skilled. But so much other work these days, most people don't bother with the old crafts."

"There's something about reeds," he says. "Water is the obvious part."

"What do you mean?"

"Papyrus comes to mind."

"Oh, stop being so deep! Guess what? I went to a fete, won two old fishing books. Wood-block books, really old. Then fell off a cooper's barrel. Bruises everywhere. But that's OK."

"Glad with life again?"

"Well, you know, it's so relaxing here. I mean, we sit in front of open fires, up till late, watching firelight play on the parquet flooring. It's *so* beautiful outdoors."

"Cold?

"Nice cold. Icicles, twigs underfoot."

"Glad for winter?"

"*This* winter! Yeah. We had a lovesick barn owl swooping around. And the garden gate's as old as the ark and, you know, the stillness of new snow."

"That's half a world from me."

"Oh, no! Are we going to get all soppy tenements again?"

"Nah! Christmas was fine."

"Anything special. Someone?"

He laughs. He'd tell it all to Geraldine. But only tells what happened on Christmas Eve. Nathan's in New York, still laughing about the fight Christmas Eve.

The run up to Christmas was lazy. Jimmy and Nathan in a pub crawl, talking Jamaica, mulling jazz. Nathan said 'Send a tape to the Marsalis brothers, Wynton the man.' According to Nathan, Wynton would have done more with sax than trumpet. And that's how it started. Three guys from America. Drinking together at the next table. One was ace, crown of a thousand scores, jazz scores, quote anything, scat or tap it, said to Nathan he'll buy the next round. Because it's Christmas, buddy. Ace parlay. And a whole oil-tanker getting sloshed down. Rhythms tapped out at the table that maybe were never heard before. Then more booze. And scat, scat, scatting. Then one more round. Nothing was getting said. And that's when it turned. Maybe it was the liquor. The American genius started it, saying no American would piss on jazz out of Britain. They can't play jazz here, he said, so how can they compose it, and, sure, some of the musicians in England are good, but only as imitators, but give these younger guys a solo and, oh boy, they can not *play*. Nathan turned to the genius. Being a genius must be great, he said, but being drunk and a genius won't cut it. Not here. That cued it. That's how the physicals started. Heavy-duty. Quick, the genius leaned over, head-butted Nathan. Jimmy aimed two kicks, evil mule. But then got dropped by a trained elbow. And a beer glass in Nathan's arm, two ribs zapped. But even with arthritis in his hands, Nathan handed down a bad penalty. The law arrived.

Jimmy laughs, remembering Nathan shifting down the road like a cheetah on fire. Even with two cracked ribs Nathan was moving. Then he shouted 'Send a demo to Wynton Marsalis' as they split up just before White Hart Lane. Two days later he was in New York, laying low.

# 40

When Agnes phoned last night, it was talk, talk, talk. Late. Then Jimmy said it. Admitted playing around. But not naming who she was.

Donna was at the flat every day. Right up to the morning before she got on the plane, that woman was living ten years her life in seven days. But she knows the score. And if things work out in Jamaica she'll stay. Donna and Agnes, the last two women in Jimmy's flat. Two serious women. Far across the sea.

"What's the problem now!" his mother says.

"I didn't phone you to get angry at me."

"Be quick. I've just come in from work."

"Today I've got a talky melody. Hurtful tune. A nagging samba."

"From that Brazil trip?"

"Maybe. From the north, maybe. Belem or Natal. I was in Recife. Salvador was a surprise, a mini Africa."

"Brazilians are all black in Salvador, aren't they?"

"Yeah. More or less. But they claim something big. Musos there say every modern rhythm comes from Salvador. Even jazz. Yes, friend, even jazz. And reggae. And funk, friend."

"You agreed?"

"Hard to disagree. There was one old rhythm-king, really scat and play. I looked at him and thought they'd smile in New Orleans. Jamaica would grin."

"Ten million Africans got shipped to Brazil."

"Yeah."

"Africans took that samba there, the basics of it."

"Somebody explained it to me. Samba was the dance slaves danced to fool the slave masters. White man thinking samba was stupid African, but samba was only dance up front. It was secret Africa talking."

"Is Brazil where your tall sky is?"

"I dunno. Two years back, I played jazz there. Remember? And I learned samba. Nighttime in Belem was the great place. Sunset. Listening to weather, that sea breeze running palm trees up to a hillside."

"And you toured the south, didn't you?"

"Yeah. Good gigs down south. Porto Alegre, the best place. One night at a cafe they played The Third Man. Played it all night. The jukebox playing it over and over. Somebody said a TV star was there and wanted only that one tune played."

"Only one tune? Strange!"

"Worth it, though. It's being watched it every night. The Third Man. Folk watching the movie just to hear that zither play. Heartbreak time. The plot's lame to the zither. I mean, no border scam, no alleyways, no watered-down penicillin, bootleg, treason. Only that zither. Old heartache. Folk getting Vienna in black & white, but it could be any place."

The tune nagging Jimmy doesn't render. Not like that zither. And a girl. A special beleza in Porto Alegre. A bad girl. Way off the scale. Her eyes hinted at almond trees, beleza body rolling like guavas in a tray. She wanted to be with the touring jazzman, the one looking out to sea all day. It was easy for Jimmy.

One morning she wanted to surf. Far from the city. Not on a surfboard, but on the inner-tube of a truck tyre. The water was turquoise and a mile deep. The girl the colour of roast almonds. She laughed on the ocean. On the black inner-tube, laughed. And the Porto Alegre sun gleamed on that body, magenta, sometimes she was ebony; whatever colour the sun. She loved the water. But was soon wanting the shore, get back to the small hotel up the coast, the watermelon waiting. Jimmy tried to tell her, said the water was like the sea off Ocho Rios in Jamaica. That sea. The almond girl talking only Portuguese could say four words of English but cried 'shark!' Far from the beach, way out on the ocean, the brown-black girl cried *shark!*

When they got back, she toweled her body down. And couldn't stop laughing. It was only a joke, her eyes said. Jimmy tried a laugh, knowing how hard the water would get from then. Then she explained.

'The shark, it's no problem, you can't daydream the sea.' That's what the translator said as the girl explained, laughing in the sun. The melody bugging Jimmy is that girl's voice. A voice like homing water. Samba was in her limbs, in her laugh, her eyes. That samba feeling was even in her hands as she toweled him. Small hands. Quick fingers. Then it was time to leave the beach. And somehow, her eyes suggested sharks are beautiful.

Back at the hotel, her watermelon was on the table. Smooth and cool, but just too quiet when she upped from the bed. When the knife prized it, opening a slice, a slim slice, something flashed. But instead of only melon, something to do with the sea flashed. Not like a melon slice; it was more the vermilion razor of a coast-shark.

# 41

Geraldine's head shakes. "Harold Shipman got it in the knees today."

"Should have been the neck!" Jimmy says. "Or his balls."

"Steady!"

"Murdering fifteen old people? They should take his limbs off."

"And use the dullest knife!"

"That life sentence is a mistake."

"They've got a penalty manual, do what the manual says."

"Shipman jumped out the bushes with a syringe."

"Last thing on earth!"

"Scary world."

"He's got to be mad!"

"Who else kills fifteen people! Innocent people."

"They think it's more like two hundred. Not sure."

"This millennium's a big let down," he says. "Stuff going wrong."

"Yeah."

"Instead of only Shipman, a Shuttleman could happen."

"Yeah, even a Rocketman."

# 42

One morning as Donna rolled over, her sleeping face was too much. She was like Agnes. Jimmy was worried. Wondering if it was time for South Africa. A trip to Cape Town could happen.

Agnes plays Ellington most days; so she says. On Jimmy's hi-fi now, Ella Fitzgerald sings the Duke: Don't Get Around Much Anymore.

Donna was born in London. But wants her kids to be Jamaican born; that's what she says. This visit she'll spend time with Maroons, spiritual vibes from them. She owns land not too far from one Maroon area, a place where runaway slaves defeated slave masters a long time ago. She's twenty-nine. But in Jamaica that's no age at all. Time with Donna pounced on Jimmy. Everyday that first millennium week was hour after hour. It was plain: things would be easier having a woman like that. Music, for one thing. Donna's way inside music. Not jazz, but music from inside all the same. And that, Nathan says, saves time. And the way she talks. Flipping from straight English to Jamaican patois. And then the cooking. Seven millennium days, she cooked the whole island away. Then it got serious. No condoms one day. But all she said was 'Let's go with the flow.' Her eyes said she got the score but wanted to go with the flow anyway. Then her lips said it, saying it was more sincere with no condom in the way. That's when the best part got going. Four days to go: four days of Jamaican cooking, four nights the acest bareback riding a man could have. Donna knows about Agnes.

Jimmy should tell Agnes about her. Not the whole story, but enough. She'll never find out Donna was like the sole woman in the world to him, how she was at the flat singing old-time Jamaican songs.

Far in Cape Town, Agnes is back to roots. And maybe she could settle for some quiet England. But the reason would have to be huge; that's what her letter says. Agnes got a first in civil engineering. And somebody like that here earns five times more than in South Africa. But she lets that ride, doing merchant banking in Cape Town. With five brothers and sisters, along with their mother and father, what she earns is at the centre of all things. In one letter she sent a hundred pictures of Karoo, a mystic South African place; the letter called it the surest place on earth. Visions take place there, she said. A place big enough for towns and villages, wider than wide, mystic quiet, where troubles get clarified. Looking at the pictures, Jimmy's never seen anything this beautiful, this pure. In a song the full moon was the first circle; the next verse claims it was the pupil in a woman's eye. Goals can get set in Karoo. And if a solo tree stands in the landscape it's a where a leopard can shelter from the sun. Rednecks used to believe they owned the place, claimed they owned that mystic.

Jimmy phoned. Praised the pictures. And promised to visit Karoo. Photographs are only paper, Agnes said.

# 43

"D'you realize," Geraldine frowns, "we're the only ones. Nobody else from the October crew still here."

Jimmy nods. After the newest intake Colette turned a crew over to him. A supervisor now. This hikes the money. If recruits drop out, their leads go to the supervisor; if they stay, supervisor gets a piece of their commission. In three months this could mean goodbye to work. Get away to score music.

Geraldine is bored. From the first day back after Christmas she said door canvassing's no longer the adventure it was. Wanting to work from base, she can go for it because Clive's growing the telesales team. Now she'll sell furniture by phone. But the main thing is Brian; missing him, moping day by day. She'd go to Ireland and settle in County Clare. Beautiful place. Funny, she runs it past Jimmy.

"Only ever seen Ireland on TV," he says.

Geraldine's head shakes. "Too confused here. Countryside is raped, getting too slick."

"Because of roving conmen?"

"Not funny! There's more than 30,000 listed farm buildings."

"So what?"

"Already more than half have been converted to residential for city types. Just too hotch-potch, so often out of place."

"City folk arriving in their Range Rover?"

"Urban morons, swooping in but never seeing the wood for trees."

"Rural spots."

"What?"

"I could get music done in a rural spot."

"Or disappear for six months in a space-station, eh?"

"Yeah!"

"I know," she says. "I've picked up on that, how you hate the urban thing."

"The human toll," Jimmy says. "Can't stand it!"

"Door-canvassing is the worse thing ever."

"If you're black, this is just another hoop you jump through."

"Like how?"

"Some days your guard drops. Things can be going great, the sun shining the same on everyone, stars the same nice at evening. Then whack! Some word, chucked like a brick. Whack! Word pain."

Geraldine turns to him. Her hand on his shoulder. Then half-sings a sad song: "*Starry, starry night, paint your palette blue and grey, this world was never meant for one as beautiful as you.*"

He won't embarrass her. Not by talking more about it. And mostly she knows the score by now. Sometimes she looks in his eyes, knows what's wrong. But says nothing.

Jimmy's the top predator now. The do-it man. All the k-cs want his leads. A big puzzle. But not to Geraldine. She says this is down to the way he smiles; *exotic*, she says.

But wrong. Jimmy's not smiling. He's smiling the smile. The doorstep is only a show. This man that was all locks until recently is smiling the smile now, weighing folk on their doorstep. For every two like Geraldine, more than twenty resent him; up front or behind the line of sight.

"In England," he says, "granite burns."

Geraldine frowns. "What?"

"Seashells are amazing, collectable."

"Oh, no! I can feel a sermon coming."

"The English countryside paces up and down the motorways, never gets short of breath"

"How long's this going to take?" she says, eyes rolled to the sky.

"Patrick Moore talks astronomy on TV. Radio 3 plays classical and jazz."

"Tell you what, let's go get a coffee."

"The smug English are easy. Always to the point. Sometimes they even know you know. There's a kind of ceasefire, even a handshake. But the hypocrite, *what* a different game! They use the best dentist, smiling their smile, saying 'Welcome!' But lying through their teeth."

"Here we go again!"

"The doorstep thing. Easy for me to talk spiel. Easy to smile the smile then send a k-c to take them down. Any crap, and I smile the smile. They never know it but I'm taking aim with that smile. You know, the k-c comes along with a coffin disguised as a briefcase, collects all their money. Every penny they can find. Then my commission, those readies, the golden wedge."

"Then who's the hypocrite!"

"What choices do I have?"

"Stop hiding behind phoney smiles!"

"Smiling-the-smile," Jimmy says, "is hard to explain."

"But easy to?"

"If it was music, it'd be E-flat."

"What?"

"Can't explain it any other way. And I can't smile one for you."

"Why E-flat?"

"That key is home to some of the biggest hypocrite music."

"*What*?"

"Smiling-the-smile is 'Hey, arsehole, think I belong in Brixton? Well go shit yourself!' That's the best I can explain it."

Geraldine scowls. "Anyone for potty training?"

"They've got Wagner playing in a house sometimes, wondering about the black chap on their doorstep. Or they're playing Elgar, Pink Floyd. Barbra Streisand's the one they like in a hypocrite house, wanting to believe I'm simple, you know, he's black so can't wait to whoop music in a loud high-rise. Want me to stumble, not speak. And they never, ever, remotely think maybe I could out-music any modern composer in their heart. They want the black chappie to talk dub. I know what they're up to. So it's smile-the-smile time. Hard."

"But some of those people probably like you. I mean, *genuinely*."

"I know," Jimmy says, voice lowered. "Yeah, I think about that."

"Then go from there. Not much, but it's something. A start."

"Yeah. And, you know, some days I get the feeling somebody's seen that smile before. Like on their travels. Maybe on a Caribbean beach they saw that smile-the-smile. But a hypocrite homeowner never gets it, me smiling the smile on their lily white."

"Well," Geraldine says, "I'd better take up shoe-shining!"

# 44

Smiling-the-smile tops up Jimmy's pocket. Spiel, doling out money to the smile-the-smile man. And another thing. Every k-c is white, every one in suit and tie, so nobody yells 'Black mugger!'

Geraldine invited him to her mother's house. A quiet place with a big garden in Hertfordshire, detached, part-rural and coppiced, with a proud little lake. Fox hunting round the nearby woods and fields. Mulling, he flips off the music. Closes the book. Builds a new spliff. And phones her.

"Even when I worked the doors with you, the same streets together, I always pulled more money than you. Must be a good reason for that."

"Simple!" she says.

"What's the answer?"

"Middle class English people. The world expert at pretence! They never let on about a problem, except to one another. And only now and then."

"*That* is the answer?"

"What else could it be?"

"I don't know!"

"It isn't always about stiff upper lips."

"No. Because sometimes I get somebody having a hard time. A door opens and there's no attitude. Only pain. But then, they always blink. Because there's a black man on their doorstep, right?"

"No. Not about black or white."

"What else?"

"Middle class people are *so* wary of strangers."

"Even a white stranger?"

"Yes, even someone white."

"How's that?"

"Well, it's the stranger they react against."

Jimmy wants to believe this. But disbelieving is easier, and a lot safer. "The stranger is the problem?"

Geraldine tries again. "Yes", she says, "it can be anything. Someone with a funny accent, or something simple as personal space."

"Like standing too close when you talk, too far?"

"Yes, that's it. Of course, being black gives the stranger quicker. Quite a bit quicker, really. But that's only because the black stranger sticks out more. Like a sore thumb, I suppose."

# 45

A rainy day. All canvassers collect in the sales room. And listen. Learning from telesales pros, watching how punters get reeled in down the phone line. Every door canvasser gets a turn on the phone; dud punters on the line, but on the call-list for a rainy day. Glass and smoking mirrors.

Then. A new sky. This never clicked before. Maybe because being on the phone is kind of out-of-body. Nobody knows who's on the line; talking glass but getting to *be* glass, invisible on the phone, so nobody knows Jimmy is black.

Later at the flat he thought about that. And lazed at the keyboard, doodling. Then checked A Brief History Of Time. Then finally, untangles the puzzle. And phones Geraldine.

"What's the answer?" she says.

"State it again. I want to be sure."

"What links an athlete to a physics man to a Nazi?"

"It's primes, primes, primes. Jesse Owens, Heisenberg and Hitler."

"Prove it!"

"At only 31, Werner Heisenberg got the Nobel physics prize. That was 1932, right? Same year Jesse Owens was 19, Hitler 43. That gives their ages as three ordered primes: 19, 31, 43."

"Knew you'd get it. It was Brian, he said it would stretch you."

"It nearly beat me. Then I surfed the net. The best thing was particles. Tiny stuff, way too small to get seen. So down where the universe cranks to basic bytes, there's no black and no white."

"No," she sighs, "not one Aryan. Only a Hitler gets Jews."

"You think Hawking's playing air-guitar with that wheelchair?"

"Don't be nasty!"

"Timbuktu was a book-place. Way before Oxford."

"So what?"

"Right now there's somebody working moonbeams like a tanner with cowhide."

"*What?*"

"A seeing man listening to a radio never sees more than a blind lady. If there's some tune like Fantasia On Greensleeves playing, coming nicely down the airwaves, then sighted folk never wonder, you know, who's playing that sweet music. They *never* think a person of colour. They say Vaughan Williams and, abracadabra! Only white."

# 46

Today, the workday at Homes changed. To catch more homeowners, canvassing is from 2 till 8 o'clock now. The first hour at base is still the same, still role-play.

Geraldine yapped it. Because of the tape she plays at work, they know there's a music man. And somebody in telesales is big on jazz, knows swing through to post-bop.

Jimmy eyes a new recruit; a timid woman. Their eyes meet. Her eyes look from some far place. Agnes is a hemisphere from here but this woman makes him remember; somebody in Cape Town is looking over Agnes; somebody there wants to marry her. But this little woman's here now. He'll make a play. She looks frail, wears her neck low because of nerves. Maybe a single mother. She's tired, weary. She could do with some help. But somebody should tell the score, tell the game at Homes; she'll make no money here. The canvasser game's too swervy for someone afraid. Somebody should tell her go now, get a fixed deal. Nathan would do that. Nathan would never let a woman suffer. Not for money. Years before, even after a stay-away court order, he delivered maintenance money to Jimmy's mother. Never missed it.

Colette's in a new mood today. She hands a peach each to everyone in the role-play room. As usual she takes charge. No drama society, but everybody's glad to clown before going to front doorstep miles.

Coffee in hand, she checks the room. Checks it again. Sees everything. She chats of Lancashire, that it was in those parts the spinning machine was invented, but now empty mills everywhere. She was there last weekend, checking out foothills of the Pennines, took the train from Preston to Accrington. Beech was too thick to reckon; oak was sturdy like anchors, holding onto England. Her parents are from Lancashire. She could talk about it all day. Now, she's round to Jimmy.

"Salty stuff!" she says.

"Sorry?"

"Your music. Geraldine lent me your tape. Hope you don't mind."

"Mind? Course not!"

"Oh, good."

"How'd you get on with it?"

"Might make a name one day, my man. *Some* talent. Shall we get your autograph now?"

"Well," Jimmy grins, "I can't find my pen."

"You're very talkative today!"

"Nothing personal."

"What's wrong?"

"Long day ahead. Things bugging me. Hard to explain."

"Give it a whirl."

Jimmy pans the room, taking in every new recruit. One by one. The look in each face is the same look on his own face October when he first got here. Innocence in every face. He wants to turn them away.

"Well?" Colette says, reminding him.

"Sorry?"

"Your music. Tell me about it."

"Like how?"

"Where you want to go with it."

"It's hard to explain."

"Doubt you'll get there?"

Stepping back, he gazes at Colette. Watching her eyes, her red mouth. The earrings. A lazy peach in her hand. Her eyebrows raise.

"When you compose," he says, "it's a burden. Huge weight. You hit on something. Bit by bit, it sort of fits."

"The magic happens?"

"I wish!"

"Don't be so coy."

"Well, some ideas work. But that's when the worry starts."

"Why?"

"Because the piece wants to bite you. You're thinking this is it, this new piece is the business."

"And you're hoping nobody's done it before."

"Yeah! How'd you know?"

"It's very jazz, your stuff."

He turns to face her. One minute back, he was wanting to get away, set a distance, supposing she wouldn't know how a clarinet is different from sax. But dead wrong. Peach in one hand and sipping coffee with no sugar, she smiles.

"Know any musicians?"

"Since you ask," she says, shuffling the peach to him, "I happen to know quite a few, yes."

"Really?"

"Don't look surprised! I know some first-rate ones."

"Rock?"

"Popular, jazz, classical."

"Jazz, *and* classical?"

"You look devastated!"

"Surprised."

"What did you think? Think I'm just some greedy bitch, is that it? Is that what they say about me?"

"I didn't figure you for classical."

"I was there myself, once."

"Singing?"

"Violin."

"*Violin?*"

"Yes. And my onetime partner is a composer."

Jimmy gives back the peach. "So, you know the graft. You know the heartbreak."

He scans the room. The timid woman half smiles. But something else there; hurt in her eyes. The expectation in every recruit is like fog in the room. How to tell them? They all saw the same serial advert in the jobs page*s: £1000/week. No experience necessary*. But no more than two will make half that money here. And even if seven or eight are still here after two weeks, three leave by the third week; that's when Colette takes the basic pay away. After two weeks everybody's on commission only. The timid woman will disappear. And Colette, Jimmy's surprised she's so into music. Her earrings seem dumb as a horseshoe.

"How's the job?" she wonders. "Making lots of money?"

"The job?" he says. "Yeah, something to do. Money in my pocket. What can I say? You pay me, so you know."

"You *might* try being a little more up for it, say it's going great."

Jimmy blinks. "It's going great."

"Let me tell you a little something," Colette puffs. "Think where your bread and butter comes from. Remember that. Never knock money. Ever!"

She turns away. Checks the room. Checking. Measuring every face. And measures again. Checking space. Her eyes dart this way and that. Colette runs a drama group on the side. Fringe. If it wasn't for this thing at Homes, she'd be a theatre producer full time. Her new Maserati bleeds in the afternoon. Red as blood. The sky was overcast all morning but through the wide window of the role-play room the weather's getting set. The sun shines for the first time this afternoon. Talk is, one day Colette upped from the office and went straight to the bank then walked into a Maserati showroom with a bag of cash. Jimmy shapes his hands, shifting long fingers this way and that, shifting till they exactly fit round the image of a low crouching thing in the parking lot, hands cupping a red gleam through the window; Colette's Maserati is like a scarlet rose in his hands.

Her eyes smile. "Like it?"

Jimmy frowns. "Sorry?"

"The car," she says.

"It's like a song. Sad song."

"What's wrong?"

"Nothing."

"Look, if it's money that's bothering you, then stick around. You'll make what you want. Late spring, early summer. Good dosh, promise. Then you can go off and do your composing. Zings in spring here!"

# 47

Role-play time. Colette clips to mid-room, dragging Jimmy by the hand. She shrugs her jacket. Straightaway taking the part of somebody ragged by the ringing of their doorbell. The room gathers round.

"I'm busy!" Colette, the-woman-at-her-door, pouts. "I'm washing my hair, or can't you see!"

"Sorry to disturb you, but I knew you were in. I didn't want to face my boss and say I'd left before giving you the good news."

"The good news? Ooh, you're from Littlewoods Pools?"

"I've brought something really exciting! Homes, Homes & Homes are sponsoring home improvement in this area. We're looking for the right sort of homes."

"You're not from the pools company? What a blow! By the way, what's the right kind of homes?"

"The right homes? That's so easy. Homes with the proudest owners. Homeowners in your area will put a smile on the face of their property. Some will use a coat of paint."

"Well now, what colour would you suggest?"

"Any colour you like," Jimmy grins. "Some homeowners go a step further. "

"Further than what?"

"Something to be proud of, more than a coat of paint."

"Come off it! What're you trying to sell me?"

"Because your home is one of the loveliest in this area, this sponsorship allows you to select a glass product. Anything you like!"

"Like what?"

"Double glazing, arctic-proof glass. A beautiful conservatory. We'll install you a conservatory for a full fifty percent below list-price!"

Hands on hips, she throws her head and laughs. Laughing the laugh of a fishwife. "Well, handsome," she says, "I think there's something you should know. I, er, don't own the property. I'm staying with family for the week!"

The role-play room laughs. Group laughing. Raucous and loud. Jimmy did a mickey-mouse; a basic mistake. Yapped, but didn't check if the woman was the homeowner.

Quickly, Colette's back to being Colette; strict, but something like kindness settles her eyes. As she leaves the role-play room her jacket rides high.

# 48

Role-play today was a free laugh for new recruits. Loosening them from mind cramp. Laughing, everybody innocent with hope. But their face will wrack with despair in a week. The timid one gets close to Jimmy.

"That woman likes you," she says, shy, nervy.

"Which woman?"

"Colette."

"*Colette*?"

"She fancies you. That role-play, she was trying hard to tell you."

Jimmy blanks the idea. He knows this timid woman's going through hard times. That's why she's here. Her suit is neat, but should've been binned a long time. Her nails are manicured but not painted. Her accent is flat Manchester. "No work in Manchester?"

"Nothing to speak of down here, is there? I've done this commission lark before. They're all the same. You get a bit of a basic to start, but that's how they rope you in."

"Ever worked doorsteps before?"

"I'm not a canvasser. Tried it once. I was still at college."

"Degree in what?"

"No degree. Furniture repairs, nothing academic."

"How'd the door-knocking go?"

"Terrifying. You just want to turn and run."

"Why bother with this one?"

"I'm here to do telesales."

"Then why role-play the doorstep?"

"It's Colette. It's canvassing for me this week."

"Which crew?"

"Might be yours, you never know! Been working here long?"

"Three, four months. A job like this isn't for everyone."

"I'm Carmen, by the way."

"Nice name."

"Thank you."

"Hey, what's on your mind?"

"I don't think you like it here."

"Nah, it's not that. You lose track of time. But, yeah, telesales is where the serious money is. Don't know that much about it but some guy in there is a monster."

"Big-hitter?"

"Yeah, 150 grand a year."

"My God!"

"Yeah, that's a lot of wedge. Been in London long?"

"Colette wants you. She's offering it on a plate."

Jimmy tries again. "Been in London long, or is it a secret?"

"No secret," she smiles. "Been here a week. Thing is, I was born in London. We went to Manchester when my dad got a job up there. You're from Liverpool yourself, aren't you?"

10 to 2. Road time. Everybody's still clinging to coffee cups. Jimmy and Carmen continue to chat. They know.

"Nice weather," she says.

"Not bad."

"You married?"

He laughs. Fingers clicking. "Me?"

Fingers clicking, doing a Max Roach on fingers. Carmen can sense it. He knows she knows.

"Naughty!" she says. "I know what you're thinking."

"Yeah, you've got *that* right. Could do it on a boat!"

"Boats?"

"The sea's where you keep your feet on the ground."

"Think you're dead deep, don't you!"

Carmen's sudden laugh surprises the room. Now a hush. Cold gazing. Jimmy likes that. Spidery eyes watching him and Carmen, but only from the outside.

He turns face her. "If I didn't listen to Charlie Parker before coming work, I couldn't hack this job at all."

"You talk about him like he was Jesus."

"Well, some prophets pay heavy dues. He was in a madhouse once. A place called Camarillo. Thought they were rid of him. But then he cut some of the greatest tracks music's ever seen. You listen? Great, great!"

"Like which ones?"

"Anything, starting with Relaxing At Camarillo."

She turns her back on the room. Reaching over, touches his hair. "It's a nice head of hair," she says. "Makes a change, doesn't it? Everybody's got locks these days."

"Time for brains, more honesty."

"I'm not the brainy type."

"Wig."

"*Wig?*"

"Yeah. Wig is what bebop guys called brains."

"Camarillo," she says, serious again, "I don't know why, but it makes me think of chocolates. Not like a mental hospital at all."

"You don't get it!"

"You patronizing me?"

"It's obvious. You can't see where jazz fits."

"You *don't* know me well enough to talk to me like that!"

Wanting to relax her, he quietly says, "Why sales?"

"That was quick!"

"What?"

"You give up too easily."

"I hate conflict," Jimmy grunts.

"Then how're you going to survive?"

"I *always* get by."

"You sure?"

"Yeah. So, now you know."

"What you say is not what's in your eyes."

His head shakes. "Lady, why d'you want a job in telesales?"

"Well," Carmen blinks, "there's a little wind-chime. A must have. Saw it in a shop on Edgware Road. Got to have it."

"Happy wind-chimes!"

"So, this is you? The big patronizing man?"

"Sorry."

"For what?"

"Bugging you."

Carmen was on jury service last month. Somebody in Manchester shipped too many mobile phones, made just one trip too many. When the sentence came, it was hard seeing the way tears welled in the guy's eyes.

"You've been spoilt!" she says. "Too used to getting your own way."

"I don't believe in wind-chimes."

"Boy, you really *have* been spoilt!"

"What's the real reason?"

"It's a brilliant wind-chime. Gorgeous, old."

"So, you're not a hard-up single mother?"

"Me, with kids? You're joking! Kids are what my mother had. I'm sick of loudmouth black guys, boasting how many women have kids for them."

"Yeah, I know what you mean."

"Nine out of ten don't support their own child. Kids should ask to get born, right up in your head. They must *want* life. Understand? You can't just turn up in the sheets, you know, just adding to the list."

"The baby-line?"

"Exactly!"

"Lady, you're one *serious* woman!"

"Too many black kids have gaping mouths, like hatchlings begging worms from the sky."

Jimmy lights a smoke. "I think they call that the blues."

"*Blues?*"

"Paying for stuff you can't buy."

"Look, I'm here to earn money. I need a job!"

Somebody should tell Carmen, 'Get a job some place else.' Jimmy wants to say the right thing, say the business here is a mug's game. But this is where the daily bread comes from. And then, she might wonder how somebody can give advice but not take it.

In a set tone, he hints at this. But doing it in a way that's fair for all. "Why *this* place?"

"This place, that place! They always hustle you. In telesales they don't have to know you're black."

"Yeah, you with that northern accent!"

"You get to London, phone up about a job, then, you know."

"Yeah, when you get there it's a shock."

"Every time!"

"They can't connect the black face to the northern accent on the phone."

"It's a joke, honest."

"Noir cinema!"

"When's it going to stop?"

"When the cows come home."

Carmen can hide in telesales. She's done the hide game before. She pulls a photograph of her family. "This goes where I go. My little piece of the other Bayeux Tapestry."

"The *other* Bayeux?"

"Yes."

Jimmy winks. "You know what I think about you, don't you?"

"Careful!"

"You're kind of nice.

"Nice, or kind of nice?"

"Seriously nice."

"Thank you."

"Married?"

"No, but I'm thinking about it."

"My mother wants me to settle down. But it wouldn't be fair."

"Why?"

"I compose. Music is where I'm at."

"A composer?"

"Yeah."

"Selling double-glazing?"

"That sad. But that's the way it is, me and jazz."

Eyes narrowed, she weighs him. "I'm not into jazz."

"You don't have to be. There's always nonsense to listen to."

"Look, I'm only trying to help!"

"Then tell me why jazz isn't folk."

"Folk is like protest songs, isn't it?"

"That's because you don't *know* jazz."

"Folk music is like, everybody can sing along."

119

"Even if you wear a skin overcoat?"

Carmen laughs. "You sound like my brother."

"A serious guy?"

"Look, if they haven't got a name for what you do, then they don't have power over you."

"Wise lady!"

"Common sense."

"What would you suggest?"

"Do something they know."

"Something *they* know?"

"That's how it works."

"Do what?"

"Compromise. Smile and compromise."

"Like try to be St Paul's cathedral?"

"Be serious!"

"I'm dead serious!"

"Can't you compromise?"

"How? Do reggae in pubs, covers of the Stones?"

Carmen's eyes raise to the ceiling. Jimmy stands back, watching a wish die in her eyes. No longer hunched with nerves, she's taller than she looked before.

"Try to compromise," she says.

"I've done that all my life."

"Then go the extra mile!"

"Where's that lead?"

"Don't turn your nose up at it," she says. "It's a start. Play the game! Nobody lifts a finger to help if you can't give them something. If I was you, I'd send my tapes to America. Better still, just go!"

# 49

Knocking doors and smiling the smile, Jimmy wonders about the rap with Carmen. America could be the place. Big music there. Gigging with the best. Meet up with Bobby Delaney. Concerts.

Sending demo tapes to America would be one thing. It could also mean going to live there; a year, maybe more. But Agnes. She wouldn't want to know. Would never go to America. England as far as she'd go.

Donna being a music woman means she'd understand. But happy in Jamaica right now, planting her two acres of Portland that's only five minutes from the Rio Grande. That, and rearing chickens.

But America. Black and turning up with a big English accent, and having to explain. And the way blacks in the south are still mostly poor and might as well be in O-gape Africa. Then again.

Serious women in America. Ace black women. They have the opportunity, go to Ivy League or the Juilliard. He can't wait. And that's the rub. With or without Ages, he'd say hello to the American woman. He was thirteen years old when that got started. Some will cry, Nathan said, handing over that first packet of rubbers. Nearly twelve years later and that's been mostly true. So far.

Problem is, Jimmy. Jimmy attracts some of the awkwardest women in England, the race denial kind, the type never letting go of fairytales. Zeal in their face, they sing the loudest hymns in church; the secular ones memorize cute slogans, go on marches to hoist placards higher in the sky than the whitest liberals hoist. The weirdest woman of all was the social worker, the one that always liked to keep her bra on. She was licking ice cream from a blue saucer one day, then said he should write classical; compose proper music instead of jazz, she said.

But on the whole, he's been lucky. Great women have happened by. He knows there's something about him that brings worry, even pain, to a good woman. And something else.

One day Geraldine said it. She wondered how she'd never seen him eye up a white woman. Wanted to know why. So he told her. Told it the honest way. Apart from one afternoon with a Jamaican white girl, and that was way back when he was fourteen, there's never been a white girlfriend. Lots of times when it could have happened; times when it would've been the simple outcome. But never. Eyes blank, she asked why not. It's always been women of colour, he said; black lindas, from light tan to steep jet.

# 50

Colette said it. Money will zing from spring. The take at Homes is starting to cut it for top canvassers now. That grand a week is still a way off. It never happens. But some days it's a little closer, not too hard to believe.

Jimmy is no salesman. Now he knows. Knocking on stranger's doors is small time, cap-in-hand. But something else wrong. Twinges. More and more, pangs of doubt; something like conscience happens. The predator game is no fun now. Far from Brixton, meeting middle class folk on their doorstep is taking him to the soft England belly. This is a turning point. Some of these people live big lives. Some worried. The meaning of the job at Homes is starting to oppress Jimmy.

Two things. It's only with spiel instead of a condom, but on every doorstep it's like sticking it to middle England. Hard. But something else. He can sense canvassing is getting like saying goodbye. Every time a door opens, the idea seems better and better. It could be time to leave. Maybe for America. One evening the fateful door.

Before this evening it was only spiel, guff about glass. But now. Knocking doors and talking bull, he can see it's a kind of begging. Some punters know he's lying. Some connect lying and begging. But the hardest part is one or two glimpse something that might even get called good. But it flickers out exactly the moment of smiling the smile, the moment Jimmy opens his mouth to lie. They know. They'd spit in that lying mouth, say the sales spiel on their doorstep is only victim cringe.

Smiling-the-smile is victim cringe, somebody said. It was a wrestler, not the kind to argue with. He spelled it out, 'You're pretending to be what you're not, something far less than you are, a shallow lie, and that's plain silly.'

Now and then on some clued-up doorstep it's as clear as day. Now and then some white person roots for black folk. Their eyes say 'Chin up, you can make it!' And in bare branches, birds often twitter as evening falls.

Jimmy slows for a smoke. Must think. First thing is what happened on that weird doorstep earlier. A weird, weird. So weird, that maybe quitting the job must happen next. The answer comes straight out the blue. But it was the chat with Carmen. What she said. All she did not say.

# 51

The message on the answer-phone plays. One more time. The fifth time. The voice is clipped, part happy. Looks like good and bad news. Hand shaking, he dials the number.

"Lorna, it's me."

"Jimmy?"

"Yes."

"*Nice* to hear from you!"

Nervy, he braces himself. "Any news?"

"Guess what! Justin opened his eyes this morning. Smiled. We couldn't believe it!"

"*Great* news!"

"Well, sort of."

"What's wrong?"

"It was only a blip. He's still in the coma."

"But him opening him eyes, that's still a good sign!"

"Yeah. Opens his eyes, next thing he's like 'What, me?' Then his eyes close again. The doctors reckon he can make it. We went again this afternoon. Too early to tell, but it's looking good. I can't take it all in. Funny, eh? How are things with you?"

Happiness is in Lorna's voice. Jimmy loves this woman. Maybe not the woman. But her happiness. She's on a rush. Her brother's still on life-support, having to get by on one lung, but he might pull through. The best that surgery could do. Nobody knows for sure who did it.

"Me?" he says.

"Yeah. How's it going?"

"This and that."

"You sound so far off. Anything wrong? You OK?"

"Can't complain. Picked up the phone thinking it was bad news."

"Look, why don't you come over? Did I give you the address? I've got goodies going in the kitchen. Can do for two, honest. Great if you come. Come round!"

"Well, I was going to fiddle round at the keyboard."

"You don't like people, I can tell."

He gazes at the tenement wall, at the new damp patch. It's mildew that a spray could treat, but bigger today; the wall looks like mildew might eat through to get outside and mildew a sheer drop to the street. Mildew that could almost be wisteria on the tenement wall. Lorna has just invited somebody from high-rise mildew.

He grabs the mouthpiece near. "Seven o'clock too early, too late?"

"Make it eight," she says. "Be hungry when you get here. *Very*."

# 52

Jimmy couldn't be happier for Lorna. But not wanting to visit. Things still a daze. That weird doorstep yesterday, still spooky. He walked from Homes. Colette was livid. After the happening on the doorstep he headed away, leaving the canvasser crew behind. A doorstep encounter, a moment feeling some emotion like mercy. She would've given him a chance, but he walked. And that means only one thing: the quickest way to money from here is gigs. Do gigs again. Or maybe give music lessons. Either way, no music at all.

He's no teacher. Hates folk getting instruments they'll never play. Morons can't do jazz, can not get from bozo box to set light on fire. A full bottle of malt in the flat. But today's a different day. A day to be glad for Lorna.

On TV, a crashed plane. It fills the evening news screen. But then. Lush lips of the news-reader. A passenger plane is nose-down on the runway, and a hundred folk in danger, but she's telling it through wet lips, talking through a wet lever. Her lips spread like clams. And all the time the plane's got journalists nearby, tending the slew.

Upstairs on Pluto, barking dogs. They demand a minute. Downstairs, heavy carpentry; somebody hikes a dull saw through timber. Jimmy ups, quick to the keyboard. The sawing is painful, but a nagging beat. His left hand grabs at chords, getting the chords right, comping the rhythm of the saw. Right hand hovers, waiting for clues. But nothing. When the sawing is over, an electric drill chews into flustered timber. The music tapes Agnes sent can't get played while this noise cranks.

Agnes was never jealous. Not too much. But dreads VD. AIDS is big in South Africa. Too many guys there never use a condom. If Jimmy must go with some other woman while she's away, then it's condoms every time; that's what she said. Her only rule. He agreed. But then. There was that thing early new year between him and Donna. It can't go away. But maybe Agnes would understand, look at Donna and how she's clean. Donna's so clean, inside and out. Agnes would be jealous of Arleene. Women resent Arleene, know she's way ahead. No brains to speak of but way ahead as woman. Agnes could be like a sister with Donna. And in Africa some guys have more than one wife.

After the noise, South African music plays. Five-part harmonies in a language Jimmy's never heard of. Songs that click. This is spiritual. African songs quietly washing over a loner in a Tottenham tenement, washing like the ocean over gravel.

He wants Nathan to check this Africa. The singing on this tape is new, intense. Only Africa does this. He phones Nathan, says 'Yo!' and chocks the phone to the speaker. Agnes said her five aunts are singing these tracks. One is a lullaby, unguent, Africa aching, mother pain. All are Africa calling in song. All those years welding by day and playing jazz at night, Nathan is nowhere. Before the move to England he was in Kingston and getting rated. But jazz was never big in Jamaica. Nathan should have checked America.

Agnes said they have 50,000 tracks that apartheid used just for black people: Ndebele songs, and Sotho, Swazi, Tswana, Venda, Zulu. The white man applied apartheid even to music. But good news. It got taped. Somebody saved the tapes. And now they plan to bring it out on CD. A hundred good CDs could come from all those South African songs they have on tape.

After ten minutes he grabs the handset. Wanting to talk of the music. But Nathan's gone from the line.

Agnes is a hemisphere away. Suddenly, Jimmy's got woman fever. Thinking that Arleene should be near. She was never here. Donna's in Jamaica. Lorna's a drive away but her mind's on grim things. But shy Carmen! That face, rude walk. No point to Lorna. Tonight she's with too much world, will talk of flake-highs. And talk of her brother. But Carmen. The flat's clean and ready. He grabs the phone.

Carmen doesn't recognize him. Not at first. But then when she knows who, she's surprised. A distant woman. Glad for the call, yes, but she's surprised. Jimmy should have guessed. She lives with someone; a quiet reliable guy, she says.

# 53

Lorna is a white man's daughter. She talks a lot about her mother, a black woman born in England to parents from Barbados.

8 o'clock. Wary, Jimmy stands outside a peach door. A basement flat. There was no place to park. And it was a bleary mile from where the car slotted. But a woman's cooking here tonight. The bell doesn't sound from outside. And he stands back, weary and wary; woozy from topic more than booze.

Knotty lights play the door surface. One play of light gives shapes too intricate to name, just like jazz cutting loose under a fluid melody. A pale outside-lamp syncs to one aloof streetlight. Light playing a cold evening in late February. The door half opens.

An easy grin. But she's worried. Hand over her mouth, she's shocked. "*What* happened?" Lorna says.

Jimmy steps back. He tries squaring this casual girl at home with the edgy woman at the zoo six months before. Five or six phone calls have happened between them since, but today's only the second time of meeting. She's disappointed.

"What?"

"Your locks! What have you *done*?"

"Got rid of them," he says. "Me with locks was like being a mascot."

"How?"

"Like being a trophy."

"I don't understand."

"Locks wasn't me. It was a cliche."

"You look so, so *different*!"

"Should have been like this all the time."

Lorna can't decide. Wondering who Jimmy. Her head turns this way and that, mouth wants to smile, eyes don't connect with where he's going. So she stares. But not at the stars over his shoulder. Eventually, turns and twirls. Slowly at first. Indecisive, wondering. Then nice and easy. "I made the dress myself."

"This wine is all I could think of."

"Come on, let's get you in out the cold. You look so different!"

"*You* look different!" he says, stepping inside. And always taking a closer look at the woman at home. She unnerves him. But it's warm here. And close. The hall-light fits like a hug.

"So, it's my kaftan that gets you?" she says. "That's what the gape is?"

"Me, gaping?"

"Okay, not a gape exactly."

"Hope it was civilized."

"It was. You looked like a little lost boy. Yes, outside a bread shop."

"Bread shop is *not* me. Too basic."

"A car showroom, then. Settle for that? Ooh, close the door!"

Four paces down the hall she dips to a room; her living room, but more office than chill zone. Things are small and tidy. And two steeply high-backed chairs look like bishops would want to sit. Jimmy sensing something wary about this space; this front room is the kind that would please a sharp old lady; an old bishop woman could remember from here, her bric-a-brac long gone. A tidy old bishop woman could prepare for death here.

But then. A parachute is on the wall. Looking more like a rucksack, but this thing's hard-packed for the sky. Photos of skydivers next to it. The one disorder in the room comes from two carrier-bags. They flop against the bookshelf, a jammed little library. A small flowerpot peeps between old maps on the top shelf. The flowerpot's empty. It's never been used, never alive. Lorna needs it this way, a handy symbolic, a prop; she wants to remember her feet on the ground. Jimmy closes to a mini hi-fi tucked on a shelf. She grins from the skydiving snaps. Even with goggles, her face lights up a mile.

Thud. A sudden thump between the shoulder blades. A hand slams him. More than a nudge, less than a shove, but it stumbles him. Lorna's hand. Waiting on his shoulder. He doesn't turn round, can't get what's going on. Standing right behind him is a playful woman. But something else. Her woman smell is near, nudging. His finger hits the hi-fi pause. And, as the sound kicks in, ice tinkles in a glass. He turns round. A slim glass in Lorna's hand.

"This is brandy," she says. "You like brandy? This is brandy mixed with cane-juice."

"Cane-juice chaser, or a brandy chaser?"

Bach's Goldberg plays on the little hi-fi. Music that covers the tidy room like sailcloth spread. Glenn Gould. A piano genie meting out, playing like the piano itself is in the room.

"Music like this is what ears are for," Jimmy says. "Glenn Gould. This guy plays like a monk-dervish."

"A what?"

"Black holes are poorly understood."

"What?"

"I read somewhere that light, well, it kind of sighs."

"*What* are you talking about?"

"Every sigh of light is info with codes of the whole world."

"Are you drunk?"

"Black holes gobble up star-clusters. Just like crows. But black holes croak in B-flat, fifty octaves below middle C."

"I haven't got the *faintest* idea what you're on about!"

"Somebody said astronomy's the final turning, purest reaching out. In nursery rhymes the only thing stars do is twinkle. Or twitter like birds. But the only sound black holes make is a croak."

"Keep that up, and I'll dial 999!"

"How'd you get into parachuting?"

"Parachuting?" she shouts from the kitchen. "It's what we do. My family. My father was a paratrooper. We go most weekends."

Sitting in one of the bishop chairs, Jimmy could load up here. Liking the way music's doing it in this neat room. But the hi-fi. It's so skewed, Bach doesn't get enough through these speakers. Time for a spliff. But something else. Nothing senses can fix. Not the music. What's here is maybe not even here. Brandy tied to cane-juice, and Jimmy nagged by a scent. A faint scent in the room. He remembers a woman in Brazil; she was smooching one cool evening in a Belem cinema. Beautiful. The scent in Lorna's living room is like the Belem woman: avocado, ripe, fresh, just like that Belem woman one Brazil night.

Lorna is fussed with space. Only one random space in this room, and that's the laptop screensaver; random-moving, the word *ricochet* smirks the cold laptop face. And the hi-fi speakers, they shouldn't be on the bookshelf, not on the same shelf together; any place else, and they'd sound better. Wondering, he sits high in a chair bishops would design. Then stands. Checks books on the shelves. Checks what Lorna reads. Hoping some title will leap out, a topic with disorder built in. From the neat neatness of the shelves something should surprise. This is a skydiving woman but only a bible shouts back from the shelf. A bronze bible. On the top shelf a book on Monet looks different from the rest. Is this the surprise? Jimmy flicks through image after image of teal Argenteuil; blue-green, limber water every place. But no amber. Not like brandy in a bishop chair. Not like chasing cane-juice through a nighttime sluice. Tucked between two books, a snap of Lorna falling from the sky. That day at the zoo she was a clenched woman. Her hand was beside his on the damp steel buffering the lions' space.

"Nice room," he says, as she comes back to the room.

"So, you like the music."

"Great music."

"*What's this?*" she blares, lips ripped with rage. "You've moved the speakers!"

"How'd you get into Glenn Gould?" Jimmy says, trying to head the anger away.

Lorna flits to the speakers, jockeys them till back where she'd left them.

"What?"

"Where you place speakers, it's the way sound works."

"Who says?"

"The speakers must agree. With two speakers it's a bit like dowsing rods. A best spot."

"I don't care!"

"Speakers should work together. Like your arms and your feet, so you can swim."

"Work together?"

"Yeah."

"Like lions doing the biz?" she laughs, mischief playing her gaze. "Remember those lions at the zoo, mating?"

The quick mood change makes Jimmy realize. Lorna's at the edge. Wanting to wane from the pain she hides. In a stuttering motion, he steps closer to the parachute on the wall. Then checks the computer screen. Checks the ceiling. "How come you went for Gould playing Bach?"

"I don't know, do I! That bit of Bach's the only classical I've got."

"When the Golberg came out, I think it was '55, they say it was so amazing it knocked Louis Armstrong down the charts."

"Honestly?"

"Yeah."

"Because of Bach, or was it this guy?"

"Both. Glenn Gould was a great piano player. All time great."

"It's almost like jazz, this music."

"Yeah."

"Kind of spiritual, isn't it?"

"Yeah. But people say things about him."

"Who?"

"Glenn Gould. You don't know?"

"Not really."

"Then why bother listening to it?"

"OK, OK! What do they say?"

"Well," Jimmy shrugs, "they call him disrespectful."

"Why?"

"Idiots. They've got nothing to say about him, so it's 'disrespectful'."

"What do they mean?"

"They think he was some kind of music terrorist. Morons!"

Lorna lopes to the hi-fi, ejects the Bach CD. Thinned voiced, she says "Fancy some Beatles?"

"Not now. Got any Mary J?"

"Who?"

"Mary J. Blige."

"Never heard of her!"

"She sings tenements away."

"I've got Celine Dion. Falling Into You. Fancy it?"

"Nah!"

"Mariah Carey? Whitney Houston?"

"No, and no."

Lorna doesn't play a singer. But gets John Coltrane going. And straight-away something starts. It tiptoes the carpet. Music wanting a woman to dance it. A minute ago she was almost warlike, but this changes that. Coltrane. Even under a kaftan tent, her body can't hide. This is no longer a lady bishop's room. This is a woman with trouble in her meat. But wires connect tubes connecting her brother. And her mother, Jimmy wonders what she's like. Lorna's skin tone is up from ochre, and her nose straight. That's from her father. Waist up, only hair and eyes tell of her mother. And she totes a serious African woman's body.

On the computer screen the word *ricochet* floats on. Jimmy frowns. "Why of all words, why that one? This who you are?"

She shrugs. Not like somebody who'd go looking for lions in a zoo. She grabs a video. In one flick, Barbados is on screen. Lorna and her cousins on screen. Next to their midnight black she seems pale as white. Open blue water is only a minute from the house. And far at sea, way past transitions of yachts, blue and yellow fishing boats biding the tide. She does a voice-over to the video. Some spare days her cousins leave what they do just to check the beach. Jimmy wants it to play again.

"A fabulous holiday!" she says. "I brought back a bottle of seawater. It was for my mother."

"When did you go?"

"July. About a month before meeting you at the zoo."

"About the same time Justin got stabbed?"

"Christ! That was the day after I got back!"

Jimmy should say something. Anything. Any word to make the hurt less hard to bear. Or he could leave now. Lorna understands the quiet between her and him. Old wounds flustering in her eyes as his tobacco smoke ties emotions of the room. The cigarette stubs out. And all the time Coltrane's Giant Steps is playing.

She turns to him. "What's up?"

"How d'you mean?"

"You look lost."

"Not lost."

"Could have fooled me!"

"Your brother's in a coma. Blood through plastic tubes."

"We go everyday. Take the bible to read."

"What's the odds he'll make it?"

"Let's, er, not go there," she says, sighing. "You like the music?"

"How'd you get into Coltrane?"

"Oh, it was a present. Somebody gave me Giant Steps and," turning wistfully, she hoists another CD, "this other one. A Love Supreme."

"Coltrane was a mystic!"

"Yeah. Jazz, but not jazz."

"That's about the size of it."

"What key's it in?"

Jimmy's eyes dip to the floor. "I only have relative pitch."

"What?"

"Never sure about keys. Not from listening."

"But you're a *composer*!"

"Yeah."

"How can you compose if you can't tell keys?"

"McCartney can't read music. Gershwin used only one key."

"OK, OK!"

"I've met seriously talented folk who cant tell right hand from left."

"Let's listen to the music," Lorna says.

"Yeah. Listening to 'Trane makes me think."

"Shall I play something else?"

"No."

"Then what's wrong?"

"I hope your brother makes it."

Brow furrowed, she steps to the hi-fi. Turns the music down. "Let's get Justin back on his feet, eh."

"Sooner the better."

"In Jesus' name!"

"Well, yeah."

"Can we, er, change the subject?"

"Your brother's all that matters."

"Tell me about your music."

"That old headache?"

"How's it going?"

"I can't do stuff I want."

"Like how?"

"I get an idea. Rush to get it down. Can't do stuff away from the keyboard. Only relative pitch. The great thing is absolute pitch."

"What's brought this on?"

"What?"

"You, I think you doubt yourself."

"There's people out there, proper ear freaks. They could figure it."

"What the hell are we talking about now?"

"It's Bach and Coltrane. One guy kind of leads to the other."

"*What*?"

"Wayne Marshall, he could figure Bach and Coltrane."

"That's a bit anorak, isn't it? *So* over my head."

"Anorak, well, maybe."

"But not a Brixton overcoat?"

"Yeah," Jimmy laughs. "Don't know how, but you can read me."

Through the kaftan, Lorna's hands guide skinny nylon over boulder hips. "Look," she says, "this is what happened. After you phoned, I was like 'Hmmm, will he like the music here?' You always go on about Bach, so, guess what? I dashed out and got this CD. And it's playing when you get here. That's clever?"

"Bach is different."

"*Please* don't start!"

"With no Bach, maybe no lasting music."

"As in forever?"

"He was a music prophet."

"*Prophet*?"

"Safer than guys walking on water, raising the dead."

In a lazing butterfly, Lorna's hands roam in air. Dreamlike hands. They wander her body space. Looking for home. Hands that could be searching the dark, like for a lamp, or a dress of sequins. Jimmy lights a smoke.

"You never slow down," she says. "Can you relax for five minutes? It's always 'Watch me, I've got another river to cross.' Take it easy, OK?"

"Somebody walking in a winter field might almost step on a hare. But the hare bounds towards the sky."

"What?"

"Where hares celebrate, the sky steps across fields."

"*Where* did your poor mother get *you* from?"

"Bach," Jimmy says, "some of his pieces cut straight to Coltrane. But there's nobody out there for Coltrane. Prophets, the same message."

"Look, can you do me a little favour?"

"Name it."

"Anything?"

"Yeah, anything for a woman that skydives over England."

"Don't go on about prophets. I'm glad you came. I didn't ask you to prove God or anything."

He laughs. Head shakes. "Yeah, that's fine with me. Religion is out."

"Come, let's get to the kitchen. Good, yummy!"

"Bet you don't know who Wayne Marshall is."

"Yes I do! He's a classical organist, plays Gershwin. My mother listens to that. Her family and Wayne's father come from exactly the same part of Barbados."

Now a surprise. Heavy-duty, world class. Waiting in Lorna's hall, and totally bossing the space is Mike Tyson. A picture of Tyson on the wall. All head and neck. This is early Mike. Only 20 years old. Straightaway Jimmy's jealous. He steps back. Stock still. Wondering who could get started with a woman who's got a thing for Tyson. Tyson's eyes almost smile. But a lion's gaze. Unblinking. No emotion or store. Only one function: life or death. A gaze like dice.

Jimmy squares to the photo. He'd swap all he's got or could have. All hopes, dreams of getting near to Ellington in the hall of fame, the whole thing, just for one fight in a boxing ring. A single fight, then walk away or die. For ten fitful seconds he's shadow-boxing the picture on the wall. Tyson doesn't flinch. If anything, the gaze on the wall is even more focussed. In the gaze, no flicker of the fall waiting down the road.

A quiet calm in Lorna's eyes. Not laughing. This makes Jimmy feel alone. Isolated, he turns back to Tyson's picture. And notices some neat writing on the space below the neck. And another snap; next to Tyson's picture, Lorna's in a photograph with two women. Tyson's towers like a mountain over Lorna with her mother and sister in the next snap. To Jimmy, the mother's a nice looking woman. Her eyes and open face, a black woman with lips beautiful as sleep. Lorna can guess. Her eyes say 'I know you're wondering about the fact my father's white.'

The hall light isn't bright. But bright enough to make out the writing below Tyson's neck. A calm script: *Every ton can fly!*

"Tyson could have been great," Jimmy says. "Even an all time great."

"I know what you mean."

"It was downhill for him, from the Buster Douglas fight."

"Japan, wasn't it?"

"Yeah. If the bloodsuckers had respected him, you know, the man not the cash flow, then somebody would've said 'Mike, how can you beat Buster in Tokyo while you have a dose? You dragged yourself to a slut and now you've got gonorrhea. Buster is no great, but he's a man!' Yeah, something like that would've done the trick."

"Had a dose, and still got into the ring?"

"Yeah. Trouble is, from the start he never had the right gloves."

"The wrong size?"

"No. Gloves from the hide of the cow that jumped over the moon. That nursery rhyme. Hey diddle diddle, the cat and the fiddle."

Regret in her eyes, Lorna steps to the picture. Her brandy glass tips. "One day there'll be a proper write-up," she says. "When they get it, see what they've done to this man, it'll be 'Oh, wait a minute, sorry, we didn't understand!'"

"*Far* too late."

"Maybe," she says, tipping the glass to the pitiless picture on the wall. "But this one's for you Mr Tyson. Every ton can fly. Cheers, Michael!"

# 54

Fresh cloves of garlic ride in blaring olive oil. Fennel seeds sizzle as Lorna empties a bowl of prawns in the frying pan. This the place. The smell of the ocean here. The beads in her necklace annoy her. She flings it under the neckline.

"This is prawn cocktail," she says, ladling plates on the table.

Jimmy grabs a spoon. And a lemon slice. "I love the sea, sea-food."

"Eat as much as you like."

In the flat upstairs, somebody tries playing Freddie King's Hideaway. But only fumbles it, fluffs the attack. This bugs Jimmy. Fists clenched, he turns to Lorna. But she doesn't mind the noise.

"*Every* ton can fly!" she says.

"That thing you wrote on Tyson's neck?"

"Yes."

"It's kind of brutal. Same words on a jumbo jet, no big deal. But on Tyson's picture, toasting him, that's weird. You look at Mike Tyson like he's a load-bearing beam. Wishing words, a kind of epitaph."

"Every ton can fly!"

"The bible could've said it. It's like from a fading road sign. Or a book on alchemy. Not a heavyweight champ."

"Ex-champion."

"Walking in beech forests must be a thrill," Jimmy says.

"What?"

"We have this poster on the wall at work, a dim forest."

"Beech?"

"I think so. But any forest. You know, seeing wild things. With my job all I get is cars posing in driveways."

"Suburban driveways?"

"Not too many driveways in Brixton."

"Every ton can fly!" Lorna laughs. "Yes, even Brixton!"

Head spinning, he tries a smile. But something else nags. More than Lorna's caption for Tyson, something nags. Maybe now's a good time to talk what happened yesterday. That last doorstep. Now looks a good time to unload it. He shoves aside the plate.

"Somebody broke down in front of me. A white guy."

"In tears?" she says.

"Yeah. Huge eye-water."

"When?"

"Yesterday, about 4 o'clock."

"Why?"

"Things went wrong."

134

"What happened?"

Disappointing himself, he'll lie to Lorna. His eyes lower. "Not sure."

"You don't want to tell me?"

"Hard to put into words."

"We all get those. It's 'I know what I want to say but I can't say it.' Happens to me all the time."

"I was there to sell double-glazing to the guy."

"So?"

"Him and his wife, their house is probably gonna get repossessed but all I did was talk bull. Crap about cut-price glass."

"Try this," she says, totting neat brandy in a tumbler. "Take a sip."

"I can still hear myself rattling on, being bolshie on their doorstep."

"And now you feel bad about it?"

Didn't get what he was saying. Wouldn't listen. I could tell something was wrong. But he had to spell it out before I backed off."

"Look, you're upset. Is it one of those commission jobs?"

"Yeah. Punters don't spend, you don't get paid."

"I'd sweep the streets first!"

Jimmy's no predator. He knows that now. A natural predator goes for the kill. Always. The doorstep encounter yesterday was scare marks. He remembers doling out the cold-blood spiel. Doled it out till the man and wife stepped back in their own house. Clive would've been proud.

"Do I look like a predator?"

"As in 'There's some meat, so let's grab it!' kind of thing?"

"Yeah," Jimmy groans, "something like that."

"The seven sins start with greed."

"In my job the more morals you have, the less you're a hustler. You can't be a predator if you're not even a hustler."

"Bit of a softie, aren't you, music man? You're *so* sensitive!"

"Somebody crying, that never really gets to me. But I got affected by it yesterday. The tough part was the guy's wife. She was a step behind him in the hall."

"Pretty sad, really."

"Yeah. If I was there strutting away like a bailiff or somebody, it would be easy to take."

"As in 'Nothing personal, just doing my job' sort of thing?"

"Yeah."

"But?"

"I was just a black guy, talking bull on their doorstep. That bugs me."

"*Just* a black guy?" Lorna shrieks. Her body disbelieves. Hands raise in disbelief. "What're you saying? You're having me on! *Just* a black guy?"

"I know how weird it sounds."

She shoves the jug. Kicks the sink cupboard. Eyes smoldering, blaring at

Jimmy. Hands angry, tight, clenched. She'd knock him cold. "I don't believe this!"

"I know, I know! Don't believe what I just said."

"Tell me one thing."

"I know what you're going to say."

"Is you is, or is you ain't got uncle-tom sickness?"

Jimmy vaults from the kitchen stool. "Me?"

"You! You come here, eat my cooking, insult me. Yes, you!"

He's like a ton now. One that won't fly. His hands fall, want to reach the
brandy glass, but can't move. Eyeballs feeling like sandpaper. The light in
the kitchen flickers. His throat clears. Hoarse, wanting to explain himself,
his arms spread. Lorna's eyes narrow.

"No ma'am, ah is no uncle tom. Ah don't need no tom medication."

"That day at the zoo," she says, eyes iced, "you shouted after me. I mean,
you were so sure! It was 'Look at this crap in the zoo, it's not for me.' You
wanted to leave with the lions."

"Yes, yes. I wanted to get away. From the zoo, from every place. I didn't
know where to go. Captivity all round. Then you. I noticed you. But you
didn't give me a chance, a load of small talk. I wanted it to be me and the
lions. Wanted to leave, take them with me."

"But now you are *just* a black guy!"

On the kitchen table, two avocados and a pear. A ripe bunch of grapes
nudge an earth bowl. Lorna gets a lemon from the draw and, silent but still
angry, chops it four ways. Then a slow squeeze. Drop by drop, in a jug.
Then neat cane juice. Diluting but not diluting. Mixing but uniting. A deliberate woman. She puts a spoonful to her lips. Slowly, other things in the
mix. A whole grapefruit first. Then a mango. Before he can talk, a half-
tumbler of brandy pours. She gazes at the jug, like a jug is one type of thug.
Maybe that's what Tyson's doing in the hallway, he thinks; maybe she's
the kind of woman going to Tyson's picture to check she can walk tall.
Hand to jaw, Jimmy wonders who stays overnight here, who's lucky to get
sugarcane on this woman's breath. But one thing's clear. No tom was ever
here. No uncle tom would ever get the chance.

"It's tough out there," he says. "Knocking doors, talking spiel. Middle
class English folk. It was only like a game to me."

"Till yesterday."

"Yeah, that punter yesterday."

"Never happened before?"

"Not to me!"

"Know what? I think you're at the crossroads."

"Yeah."

"All dressed up and nowhere to go."

"Tucked up in my skin overcoat."

"Take it off!"

"So you say."

"Wear what you want!"

Numb, he remembers the look in the man's eyes. The pain, the worry. The woman's eyes welled. Lorna watches cigarette smoke drool to rings. She pours the jug.

"On the other hand," Jimmy says, exhaling, "I know what that bloke was thinking when he got his house."

"Him and the woman."

"They probably didn't want to live next to blacks."

"So, what's new?"

"It's a bitch."

"Took your time, finding that out!"

"Still trying to get it right. It was only him and his lady."

"And they were just kind of ordinary?"

"That's what bugs me. How *ordinary* they were."

"Not simple, is it?"

"Nah. Not black and white."

Leaving the punter's house yesterday, Jimmy walked with weirdness in his heart. The man's eyes were like in his pocket, like glass marbles where eyes should be. And the woman. When the tears wiped, her eyes asked Jimmy to leave behind the two smashed eyes of her man. This was not supposed to happen. The job was supposed to be money, playing the smile game. Then again. Before the man's eyes glazed, cold resentment in those eyes. And that was the spur; it was 'Get the money, hard!' From that minute, the punter was going to get it, get a dose of how folk pay everyday for what they can't afford. For two minutes it was great. Fireworks. But it changed. Everything changed. Yesterday things got haywire. With no warning the man's resentment changed. Puzzlement was in his eye. Then puzzlement changed to strangeness. All of a sudden, trust was in the punter's eyes. But the strangest part was what happened next. The man said Jimmy should be ashamed; he could tell from the calculation in his eyes. This is when everything changed. The man said that smiling the smile was being content to be a slave, yes, a small-time slave, hustling, not running free. He knew about that smile-the-smile. He's a teacher in a tough inner-city school and now and then that same smile's on the face of black pupils; talented ones do the best smile, the man said as his eyes welled.

Lorna sighs. "It's hard. People are only people."

"Yeah."

"Where will you get buried?"

"*What?*"

"What if you died here tonight," she laughs, "who would I contact?"

"Death's on the menu tonight?"

"Relax!"

"That's the idea. So, how about a little question?"

"What is it?"

"Tell you what," Jimmy shrugs, "it'll wait."

"Drink up, boy. It's not the end of the world, is it!"

"No, not with cane-juice and brandy in a fat glass!"

"I'll tell you a story."

"Fairytale?"

"No fairytales, promise."

"The truth, and nothing but?"

"The truth," she says, crossing her heart. "Where my mother works, she's the only black face there. Normally it's like 'Let's get on with it, do what we get paid for.' But some days it's 'Oh look, we have a cute little black lady!' But when they've got a headache, a bit of flu, anything wrong with them, toothache, anything, they go straight to mum, nobody else. They all go to her. Even the gents and ladies that wouldn't give her the time of day normally. Then when they're OK again, guess what!"

"Yeah, she goes back to being wallpaper."

"So, what's that tell you?"

Jimmy takes a slow sip, then says, "Not sure. This and that."

"Guess!"

His hands fumble the jacket collar from his neck. "They want a listener, a stooge?"

"They want nanny!" Lorna yells, eyes angry. She doesn't rate him.

"Why a nanny?"

"A black nanny," she says. "It's Oprah they want."

"Oprah Winfrey?"

"Who else?"

"I don't get it."

"Think!"

"Of what?"

"Pain, aspirins."

Jimmy's eyes narrow. "Shit!"

"When it's pain time, they want somebody to cozy-up to. So they wheel out Oprah, run onto TV and bleat. Then after the big emotion, it's 'Who do those blacks think they are?' Get it?"

"Yeah, they're OK again. Don't need your aspirin now."

"Jackpot!"

"But that Oprah," Jimmy shrugs, "I don't think she cares. A *seriously* rich lady. Worth billions."

"Richest nanny on the planet, big deal!"

"I'd settle for half a percent of that cool dosh. Any time!"

"She's got nowhere to go but her toys."

"Know what? She can adopt me, be my sugar-mama. I'd stop all that dangerous money going to waste."

"Get real!"

"Anything more spendable than money?"

"Thirty pieces of silver!"

"I'm going for *gold*," Jimmy laughs.

"Stand on your own feet! What's a billion dollars but no respect? Richest nanny in the world but her place is dirty nappies."

In the flat upstairs, somebody's been playing Stevie Ray Vaughan. Again and again. Lorna saunters to the pause switch on the hi-fi. Then turns to Jimmy. "A house in the suburbs is a casino."

"Hey?"

"Some bloke living in a big house, getting tearful on his doorstep, what's that make *you* when he locks his door?"

"Look, I could use a spliff."

"No problem. Try some more of this."

As she tops up his tumbler, her hand is like a torrent. Electric teem, angry blood flowing.

"You've got nice small hands."

"My mother taught me how to knit," she says. "Must knit something."

"Knit me a pullover. For next winter. Yeah, if we're still friends."

"You must have had some odd experiences, doing that canvassing."

"One afternoon a widow invited me into her house. A listed place. She'd just got back from her son in Manilla. But was never going back. Getting too old, she said. Her arms were pocked from insect bites. Her son married a local woman over there."

"Grandmother to little brown grandchildren?" Lorna laughs.

Bit by bit, Jimmy's gets it. He understands what secret thing is here. Some unsettled thing stems from the tidy sitting room. Somebody tidy as this is afraid of dying; die all of a sudden, not wanting just anybody picking through personal things. So she lives a tidy space. Fears death from skydiving. This tidy flat is foil to a hair-trigger temper that flips, then straightaway calms back down. The bible on her shelf is not a trad bible, not black. The cover of Lorna's bible is mid-bronze, a charred tropical.

Night simmers through the curtains. Folk passing by in the street. And a slant beam comes from the lamppost, drizzled on now. But something troubles this sitting room. Maybe it's the strange plant on the sill.

"You OK?" he says.

Nodding at the plant, she says, "You don't like it."

"Not what this is about. There's stuff bugging you, things you don't face up to."

"Like what?"

"Things!"

"Like strapping my life to parachutes?"

"Yeah."

"Anything else?"

"Not really."

"Then what's the problem?"

"Now you mention it, yeah, there is *one* question."

"Can I lend you a million?" she says, laughing. "Two million?"

"OK, I'll get to the point."

"I won't blink."

"There's stuff!"

"Talk to me!"

Jimmy remembers a tip from Nathan: 'A black woman with a white father can be a problem. Sometimes, she can borrow her mother's eye, look straight past a black man.'

# 55

"Does it ever bug you?"

"Does *what* bug me?" Lorna says.

Jimmy shrugs. "Easier with a white father?"

"Oh, that!"

"Yeah."

"Bug me, how?"

"The skin overcoat."

Something in the room. Suddenly. Something else. Sly, arching over Lorna. Settling over her. No flesh or name. And if she moves, even one tick, then her skeleton crumbles. If she so much as blinks then her bones turn to powder. The tidy flat's not the secret. Some cryptic thing here. Jimmy steps close. His finger dots Lorna's nose. Her eyes flicker, recognize him. Her mouth stutters, lips part. Her mouth dry. Whatever she could say, nobody would hear.

Something from her lips. Not a sentence. "Man Friday."

Jimmy frowns. "What?"

She turns away. "Robinson Crusoe copped it. It was in the sand."

"That's bullshit! Stuff they made up!"

"Sand said 'Look where he's going, let's go there with him.' Get it?"

"Fairytale!"

"The footsteps copped a minute of madness. Juices flowed."

"Fairytale, some dreamer wrote!"

"And, what, all we have now is a load of reality?"

"You tell me."

"I love my dad. But that's not what you want to hear, is it?"

"I don't know your family. I don't even know you."

"Skin, it's got *nothing* to do with anything. We don't wake up and think 'Oh, there's this stranger in the house, a white man, got to get away.' Never!"

Jimmy turns from Lorna's eyes. Light brown eyes, empty now. He must leave. In two strides, steps to the hall.

She grabs at air, says, "Don't go! Stay for ten minutes. You and me."

He's at the front door. But weird, stalling. Something connects him here. Maybe lions in a cage, lightning and thunder one summer day in a zoo. Turning back down the hall he sets the overcoat back on the hook.

At Tyson's photo on the wall, he says, "I don't understand this."

"Sir," she sighs, standing like a shopkeeper beside him, "can I help you? What don't you understand?"

"Tyson. So full of himself. Cocksure. This guy's going to jail one day but can't see that far in this photo."

"Glad you like it."

"Well, there's why you even have his picture at all."

Lorna isn't the first woman to see more to Tyson than war machine. This photo is proud Mike, top of the pile the instant of becoming the youngest ever heavyweight champ of the world. But nothing in the picture that one day would get called guilt; no tyro they claim grabbed by force stuff he could get ten times better for zil. Whatever happened in that hotel room, didn't have to be rape. But. Evander Holyfield should not beat Mike Tyson. But did. Evander went to the fight with a religious belief, saying 'No rapist will ever beat me.' And all the time his eye was dead sure. His eyes fixed Mike. And maybe that was it. Tyson getting spooked by the *holy* in Holyfield's name. And when they got to the ring the man to lose was the one with bigger burdens in his heart. Tyson got a beating. Fair and square. And in the rematch was starting to hit back with dynamite. But then his demons untied. Demons up from inner-city hell, freaked him. Tyson so scared of losing this time, nowhere to go if this fight should end the same as the first. Bad punches. Evil intent. Boxing, bossing Evander with speed and power. But demons talked. They talked of shortcuts. And straightaway. Tyson chewed down in Evander's ear, biting a piece clean off. From there, it was Tyson spitting demons and Evander's ear.

Jimmy turns to Lorna, the woman with a bronze bible. "Tyson did that rape?"

"*Rape*?"

"Yeah, that thing he went to jail for."

"How would I know?"

"Got his picture on your wall.

"What're you getting at?"

# 56

Lorna's neighbours at the front door. Want to know if she can baby-sit their cat this weekend. She tells them, straight: last time was a one and only one-off!

"You know," she says, closing the door, "you take somebody as they are. It's what's inside."

"Tyson?"

"Of course."

"Think he raped that girl?"

"It's not 'Oh, see how clean *my* cupboards are!' Who's to judge?"

"Do you think Mike Tyson raped that woman?"

"No, I don't."

"White folk have a big problem with him."

"People who've got a problem with him don't get it. They don't really have a problem with Tyson. The problem is closer to home. Grace is the key."

"*Grace?*" Jimmy laughs, turning to the tense portrait on the wall. "What's that?"

"The start of every good thing."

"Grace can make a ton fly?"

"Two hundred years ago a certain John Newton was a slave master. He murdered African people. Tons of them into bondage. But he changed. He changed, and penned Amazing Grace."

"That's the grace you mean?"

"Yes."

"Is grace like bricks turning to snow?"

"Don't be ridiculous!"

"But it makes a ton fly, right?"

"Yes."

"A jet plane?"

Lorna's teeth grit. Her palms glide the wall, like half expecting a Braille definition. "The best way I can describe it, grace is selflessness."

"I'm not religious."

"It's like 'The table's here but where's the supper? Get it?"

"Hey, let's skip religion. Not for me. Not anymore."

"Is that a smirk?"

"Religion doesn't work. Not for me."

"And that makes you, what?"

"Just a guy."

"No, you're *not* just a guy. Tyson didn't have too much grace, but he will."

Lorna's hands move like doves' wings in air. Jimmy mustn't quarrel with this woman. Lately, instead of just tucking up, he's into talk that ends in quarrels. One night way past midnight, nearer dawn, Arleene said 'Why don't you leave!' That was three weeks back. She was tired of talk, said getting between the sheets with him was a heartless romp. In the warm of Lorna's hall this talk should stop. But then. What should happen next won't happen tonight. His throat clears.

"I don't remember the name of the girl."

Lorna frowns. "Which girl?"

"The one claimed Tyson raped her."

"Oh, her! Desiree. Her name is Desiree. Some kind of beauty queen."

"You sound like a feminist."

"What's a feminist?"

"They couldn't believe their luck when Tyson messed up."

"Who?"

"The closet racists."

"Feminists are the same as them?"

"Knew they'd get him. Race mongers. They got those feminists all wound up, picketed outside the Tyson trial. Ninety-nine percent were white females."

"And you think *I* could be part of that?"

"Tyson had just one way to go. Desiree must be a retard, thinking white women cared shit about her. She was their pawn. Their creature. A bit of a feminist yourself, aren't you?"

"Bit of a feminist? And a bit white?"

"They got on their soapbox about Tyson."

"Well, sort of."

"Don't fudge me!"

"Calm down!"

"You know what I'm saying. That's why the guy's picture's on your wall. Stop playing games!"

"People have a problem, so they get up and preach."

"Who's preaching for Mike Tyson?"

"There's always Roman candles out there."

The doorbell rings. Lorna's eyes say she'll ignore the door. Even if who's out there can hear her talking in the hall.

Jimmy's eyebrows raise. "What's a Roman candle?"

"Fireworks. But I was talking about when your chute fails."

"Fails, in this day and age?"

"Anything can miss."

"No failsafe parachute?"

"Even that. But you know the risks."

"What's it like? That falling, falling, falling."

"I could live up there."

"Like in a dream?"

"*So* quiet. You remember all sorts. Like the Christmas presents you got, presents you gave. What you were doing. Then before you know it the ground's coming at you."

"Your chute can fail and that doesn't scare you?"

"Not if you don't think about it."

"Parachuting is not for me!"

Lorna frowns. "What's your thing?"

"Aquaplaning."

"*What*?"

"Motorway sailing."

"How?"

"Wet motorway, great place to sail. Wetter the better."

"Stop being silly."

"Silly? You don't mean that!"

"How can you sail on a road?"

"Graphite road, turning to washed lake. Nothing can ever match that. I mean, nothing's ever like water lashing ground, whipping it to fever like a wild horse. Rain, hard to believe. Like a herd of reindeer in summer. Ever seen that? A reindeer herd turning back from winter to sweat as one. Get it their way, and they stomp all over you."

"You could kill yourself, other people!"

"That black roadway? That's what it's there for! You're minding your business on a stretch, eye on gyre, catching green country, way above miles. Or humming a song. And the road, it's so silk. The wet road looking like your personal name's on it, pulling you closer all the time, sighing, shhh! Graphite. Like a jazz solo, or sweet like a woman ironing her clothes. Rainwater turning road to ace river. Then you check the rearview. This a must-do. The speedo clips 80. Next thing, 90. One blink, and you're the one! Grabbing bad river. Then. Suddenly. It lets go. The whole thing lets go. You float the old road, have four tics to live, five to die. No clock, no fuss. Only the rush. You clear this black water, or your bones sing out in your car-coffin. Yeah, tarmac-sailing."

"You know," Lorna says, grabbing Jimmy's arm, "we had this video at training camp. Somebody filming his own jump. But the chute didn't pop. So it was 'Watch me film my life story.' Sad."

"He was a moron, yeah, rhino polevaulting from the sky!"

"Skydiving is what it is. Some people get carried away, can't wait. It's 'Hey, look at me!' But you get used to them."

In the flat upstairs a blues guitar plays. Robert Cray taking a solo. And now, somebody else steps up the track, ripping the ceiling apart. And only Albert Collins plays it that way. Lorna doesn't care. Her right hand strokes the Tyson brow in the photo, tracing the glowering ton of neck.

"It's the neck you like?"

"It's that testo thing," she says, sadly. "Idiots, thinking all the world's testosterone is Tyson's neck!"

Jimmy steps to the photo. Gets a closer look at the fight mechanic. "Is this guy a Roman candle?"

"Not half as much as that guitar music upstairs!"

"Good playing. Pentatonic cliches. But good, good."

Lorna would dance. Moving shy moves, but she's scared of what she wants. Scared to get what she could. Time to stop talk. To Jimmy, the next move should happen now. A night like this is get-it-on time. And all the time guitar music playing through the ceiling.

"Lions don't rape."

Her eyes close. "What?"

"One boss lion to more loads of lionesses on the plains. Flesh, limb from limb. Then devour."

"What *are* you talking about?"

"Desiree. She's lucky. She sold her Tyson night, a pack of lies. And that never happens on the plains. The first ordainment is the rule of law. But where's the rule of justice?"

"Reverend Jimmy!"

"One rule makes Tyson a beast. Him, raging in a cage. The next rule is he can take all the meat, wild, fresh, any. But the rule-maker gets to watch. Rule-makers grab the best ringside seat."

"I didn't know you had all this anguish in you!"

"In boxing," he says, "the fight can go the distance. You see what you see. But sometimes what you see is not what judges see. So you ask 'Who's refereeing the judges?' But with a man and woman, well."

"I know," she whispers.

"Man and woman. A different game. Man and woman, alone one night, room high in the sky, alone together, late, like Tyson and Desiree in that midnight hotel. Well, you'll see what you want to see, you know, when you yourself weren't in that hotel room."

"Why d'you think the jury believed her?"

"She was a witch. Wicked witch."

"Wicked is a bit strong, isn't it? The bible uses that word."

"She castrated the guy, made white folk gloat. That's not wicked?"

"No comment," Lorna groans.

"Sellotape on your mouth?"

"What can I, little me say!"

"Tell the ones that want Tyson's balls."

"Think I know such people?"

"They want all guys castrated. *My* balls."

"Slow down, please! You're going too far. This isn't a game." Reaching for his coat, Jimmy's teeth clench. "Then what is it?"

# 57

Clive storms into Colette's office. Fist shaking at the wall-chart. "This is bollocks!"

Her eyebrows arch. "Can we do this later?"

"All it takes is a new bottom line! That, or new sales director!"

Jimmy leaves the room. Gets away from the fuss blowing. Clive does a war strut some days, kicks walls around. Colette always seems cool.

A week since visiting Lorna, Jimmy's back at Homes. This time to try telesales. No more doorsteps. No more smiling the smile all day, rain or shine. Colette gives him one last chance. Would've been the sack but all she said was 'Normal people don't walk from money.' Her soft spot for musos was his lifeline. Jimmy played on that. And she agreed to give him a go. But only after an interview.

The interview must happen today. And getting here was a big up and down, wondering, doubting. The keyboard bore the brunt. It talked through gospel riffs all morning. Then he tried Ellington's Solitude.

Traffic from the 8th floor window was spidery. And the worst thing was him missing trees that must have covered this part of England a long time past. Back at the keyboard, chords tumbled out of nowhere. But the tenement dogs barked. Round after round.

Money to be made in telesales. But right alongside that, Jimmy wants to get invisible. Nothing like a skin overcoat's ever visible down the phone; not with him wearing it.

That visit to Lorna was neat. And when she talked about her family, that was the best part; their trip every year to the Northumberland village where her father was born, always having a great time in that prime home, fun every summer; and almost invisible on the village green. That's down to Alan Stanley, a white man with skin magic round a black wife and kids. Everybody knows the Stanley family. Now they know Justin's on a life-support machine. Sheep outnumber folk by five to one in Northumberland. So maybe, just maybe, they don't bother with talking herd there.

No smiling-the-smile in telesales. Talk this, that and that, like wow the weather. But no doorstep agony. Jimmy's going for being invisibly black.

Outside Colette's office, the corridor is quiet now. Storm subsided. No more gale. He lights a smoke as Clive huffs by, scowling, heading for the Bentley.

# 58

Colette swivels side to side. The office is warm and smoky. But her chair's got a reputation for how the leather squeaks; the kind of place a cat would curl in, lazy with spite, nudging sleep.

Bleary eyed, she says, "Sit yourself down."

Gazing at the earrings, Jimmy thinks they look like plates. They'd be the biggest on a market stall, twenty steps oversize; a jealous octopus would hold them. Studying her face, he gets no trace of the insomnia she's supposed to suffer from.

"Play cards?"

"Now and then."

"What d'you play, Jimmy?"

"Three-card brag. A bit of poker."

"Ooh, three-card brag! Deuces wild?"

"Not for me."

"Why not?"

"Honestly, I don't see how card games relate to telesales."

"Ah, telesales!" she grins. Her neat hands collect a wad of business cards on the desk and, one by one, begin to toy them. "Gambling and sales are the same sort of thing, really. I'll tell you why. It's winning with the hand you've got."

"How's it work?"

"Eager, are we?"

"Can't wait."

"Oh good! What sort of money are you looking for?"

"I'd like to get, I mean, it should be serious."

"Don't be shy!"

"I heard a grand a week happens a lot. A definite grand."

"Only *one* thousand?" she says. "Well, that's only middle-lane here. We've got three guys, on the ball, make a grand each in a *bad* week. A lot, a lot of money. One guy's a gambler. Earns an absolute fortune, the size of your house!"

"I live in a tenement," Jimmy says, smiling wryly.

Colette checks the time. The paperweight on the desk is engraved with the Ferrari prancing horse. She'll trade up to Ferrari. Even though her Maserati is brand new. She scoops a trail of ash.

"I'd want to make as much as poss. A lot more than what I was doing on the canvasser gig."

"Well, you *can* do that here," she says. "No problem. Hope you realize you'll be self-employed in telesales. We'll stake you a basic, a little something while you find your way. A month, six weeks. Then you're on your own."

Geraldine warned Jimmy what questions impress Colette. He doesn't remember them. "How much is the basic?"

"Wrong question!"

"I'm trying to evaluate."

"You say you play cards, yes? You don't ask that kind of question. Not if you want to win!"

"Sorry. How much is the commission?"

A cigarette coolly alight in her mouth, Colette watches him. Hard. The business cards are tossed aside.

"I want to earn big money," he says.

"*That's* more like it! Let's talk reality, the commission you earn."

"As much commission as possible!"

"When you start selling, the first fifty grand gets you five percent. Ten percent from there. You could be looking at telephone numbers! Fancy it?"

This bugs Jimmy. To him it sounds too easy, like anybody could do it. Confused, he gazes at the woman. The boss. Her dark brows. Watching the inclination of eye as she does to him what he used to do to homeowners on their doorsteps. She's the sizzle countess. And the steak. But money here takes the marketplace to its kingdom come. And then Clive. Colette would trump him. Telesales was her idea. And already it drives 60% of bottom line at Holmes. Nothing escapes. Listening as she explains, Jimmy gets as much of Colette as can get seen.

"Hello! Jimmy, hello!" she whoops, hand waving at his face. She leans across the desk. Waving more. "Hello, anybody home? I know you're in there somewhere!"

"I was thinking about doorsteps. It's ugly out there. But I *was* listening to you."

"Still thinking about canvassing?"

"Well, yes. But I definitely want to move on."

"We're all tinkers in this life. One way or another. If it makes you feel better I did canvassing one year myself. It was *gross!*"

"Are you giving me a telesales job?"

"Let's take it from the top. I'll tell you rule number one. Hard-sell is out, finished! Those days are *so* yesterday. The next phase will be more, how can I put it, organic? We're not giving up on our homeowners. But we want the business sector. We used to have barrow-boys in telesales, but from now we'll only have graduates. History, or science, anything."

"Theology?"

"God sell home improvement? Come on!"

"Music?"

"Yes, yes. You did a music degree, didn't you? Yes, that's right. Well what we can do with that, what that means, music means you can hold a theme. You can listen. Listening is 90% of sales. Not patronizing you, am I? What d'you think? Any questions?"

"It's only about the money," he says. "The more, the better."

"Heard the one about musical cows?" Colette giggles. "You know, cows have their favourite tunes."

"They produce more milk listening to music?"

"Correct. So, play the music!"

"How's it work?"

"Do *not* come the prima donna with me! I'm trying to help you. I don't have to do this. Let's cut to the chase. You want money, you want a job that won't browbeat you, yes?"

"Honestly, I want it."

"Well, you've got it!"

"You mean it?"

"Listen and learn, Jimmy!"

"When do I start?"

"Tomorrow. We'll set some targets, but it's a numbers game."

"I know what that means. It's like going fishing."

Colette's eyes roll. Chatty earrings clatter her cheeks. "No, not fishing! Let me tell you, it's as tough as it gets. You must realize, for every two hundred phone calls you *might* get one tiny deal."

"That's a lot of calls!"

"Two hundred calls, a hundred and ninety-nine end in nothing. Oh, you could get lucky, sell some kit when you least expect it. A thousand calls can go by. Two weeks can come and go. Three weeks, and nothing!"

"That sounds bad."

"The big hitters have it in their guts. But they prepare, prepare, and pre-pare. Sounds familiar?"

"I think so."

"You *think* so?"

"No, I get it. I get it!"

"Good."

"Who'll I be talking to?"

"Players," she says, dryly.

"Yes. But who are they?"

"We talk to company directors. Sell to them. Regular guys. Far more chatty on the phone than face to face. Once you get past the secretary."

"For me, that'll be a breeze."

"Look, this is your bread and butter. You with me? It's a game. So think money, money, money! Got that? Beats doorsteps, yes?"

"Yes."

"Good!"

"Thanks. Thanks for the chance."

Something more than tobacco hangs the air. Another lung of smoke exhales as she leans back in the chair. "The *chances* I give you, Jimmy!"

"I won't mess up this time. Honest."

"One false move and you're out!"

"Sure."

"Now you can scoot off. Come back tomorrow."

"One last question."

"Make it quick!"

"How d' you sell furniture to the business sector?"

"I don't understand the question."

"Company directors don't live in the office."

"They don't? Let me tell you, those people don't s*tay* overnight in the office. But that's where they live, believe me. Live in the office, luv. Nine to five. They're all egotists, dogs by another name. They want a home from home. Bits and bobs, screens, discreet one-offs, wardrobes. We make and fit. Then there's the people who work from home. Even some very big hitters, finance execs, hotshots, lots work from home."

"I still don't get how my music helps. I mean, I can't just phone up some accountant and talk rhythm and counterpoint."

"No, no. Wouldn't get two seconds with that. No. You have a chat with the top man. Or woman. We give you a script, don't worry. We'll train you up. It'll take about a week. Once you get the feel of it you can go from there, you know, cut loose, improvise, do your thing. A music degree is fine."

"Politics grads?"

"What about them?"

"Are they the best at telesales?"

"*Politics*? We've had a couple of those here. Very revealing. It was all book. No flair. Hands always in their pockets. No, this job's about flair. If it's in there it'll come out, I promise. But we can't carry you. You have to *want* it. The bottom line is you deliver. You make money, we make money. Simple, or what?"

On the table, A4 magazines titled 'Homes, Homes & Homes'. Jimmy grabs a clutch. And quickly flips through March/April, the current one. Furniture. Wood-panels, desks, partitions, chairs. Anything wood can make. It surprises him what can get sold down the phone.

"What's the average cost of these things?"

Colette checks the time. "It doesn't work that way. With some bits, you're looking at a few quid. A reception suite could be a hundred grand. We did one suite for 380 thousand. Depends."

"There's probably bozos on the line as well as bright folk."

"Don't worry, we'll go into all that tomorrow. Any thoughts?"

He gazes at the Portrait Of A Girl print on the wall; a painting reminding

Colette of business goals. She nods.

"A definite grand a week is possible?" he says, lighting a smoke.

"Look, we've been through that. The deal gets better and better. As you go on, you get perks. *Oh*, the perks! How much you make is how much you want to make. Got it? If you want to win then you *do* win. But you have to want it. Want, is not even close."

"Who else sells this over the phone?"

"Oh, just a dozen other outfits. That bother you?"

"No."

"Why?"

"I rate myself."

"*That's* the spirit!"

Jimmy grins. "It's going to be great while it lasts."

"Ah!" Colette shrieks. "What did you say?"

"I said it's going to be great."

"You said 'great while it lasts' didn't you!"

"What's wrong with that?"

"Let me give you a little bit of advice," she says, frowning, "there'll be days when it gets tough. Tough as old nails. When that happens, and it happens to everyone, don't go talking of quitting. Not in the salesroom. And *never* in front of Clive. Remember that! Look, nobody gives a toss for the artist and his dream. Nobody understands vision here. Don't go on about your music, your vocation or what have you. You can't sit on some high horse, you know, like this was just slumming it. Don't say I didn't warn you!"

"Then what do they talk about in the salesroom?"

"Deals, deals, deals! Then more deals. Money, money, money. What's left, well that's your Michelin restaurants, travel. The usual suspects. That's how it's done. You make decent money, you spend it. And there's a right way to spend money, believe me!"

Instead of five minutes for the interview, Jimmy gets half an hour. Making him feel welcome. But wondering why.

# 59

Clean air. A quiet place, far from the tenement. After the interview, it's a walk in the park for Jimmy. And thinking about Agnes. The chats they used to have here.

He remembers how she walked; that rhythm-quibble as she walks. One day she was in high heels and he could hear shadows in the footfalls, making him wonder if anything was wrong with her heart, like maybe a bug in the chambers. Laughing, she said she could run down a gazelle. So they walked one more lap, took the old scenic route round the park. The glitch in that woman's walk stays with him now. Lonely this morning in the quiet. Remembering.

A one-armed painter at the pond's edge. For five minutes in the clamped air, gazing over the shoulder of the artist, Jimmy gets the blues. The painter stipples a paintbrush onto dun paper. His grass is grass. His trees, trees. Only the bird doesn't sing. And somehow the landscape splits away, splitting like tapers. He's preparing fault-lines of summer. But summer's more than a whole season from here. The artist turns. Says the birds they hear singing remind him of ambitions, the kind that finally realize in a domestic cage of finches. But the smallest birds can claim England with melody, Jimmy says; just like the birds singing from that small tree in the foreground. The whole thing stippled down on dun drawing paper by a one-armed man in a dank park.

Walking away from the artist, Jimmy wishes for wrapping paper. Weird, wishing for brown paper. Acres of it. Enough brown paper could wrap trees in the park, even wrap the roadway to the gate where fresh gravel joins loose sections of life like with sellotape. But he knows. This feeling is a bad mistake in a public place.

Leaving the park, mulling on the months canvassing, the mile after old tarmac mile, he's alone. But remembers good people out there. On some doorsteps ordered chats took place. Even talk of jazz, talk of how jazz was bugged by gibe.

One old lawyer said Jimmy was a born composer. And a woman that traveled most the world said Lullaby Of Birdland was composed by George Shearing, a blind Englishman. Then she said racial problems were bad now, but not bad as before. Eyes narrowed, she remembered segregation was so hardcore 50 years ago that they asked Charlie Parker to use the back door to get into Birdland, the nightclub named after him; yes, the same one in George Shearing's tune everyone knows.

# 60

Agnes has a blue sky laugh. Half the world in that woman's voice. The phone rings. Ringing, but zil. Nobody in that Cape Town house. Or nobody answering.

Alone in the flat with just the keyboard to kick, Jimmy gets a 10-paper spliff right. Tenement dogs will bark tonight. Sour dogs, barking the building down.

He wonders about Colette. Remembers the earrings earlier. Those things were loud as bells, tinkle to clatter, clitta-clatter, clitta-clatter. And earrings shouldn't do that. But the worst part is mute flesh, earrings that cascade mutely on flesh. One day she got to her car and as she looked up at the window saw him gazing.

Geraldine's so quick with words she makes Jimmy say more than should get said. She probes, and probes. All the time. Alarm bells ring. He wonders if she could be a sneak, like undercover for the media, or reporting back to Trading Standards. Naked hard-sell is big. And all the time civil liberties are getting left behind by sales the onslaught. The sales game does what it wants, calls it entrepreneurship and sips bubbly. Laughing the laugh, sales folk laugh the laugh and operate from the backseat of a car or a snatch & grab address in a business park. Or even from a perch in Canary Wharf; like urban eagles, on spiel. The mark-up at Homes is big. Clive goes to China every year, gets prefab at 5% the UK price. But customers complain all the time now: hinges fall off, panels warp, doors won't open. On bad days, 8 or 10 angry folk mill in the reception at Homes. But it's posing as customer-services managers, guys getting called killer-closers, the kind of guys that sit down in punters' living rooms and don't leave, never taking no for the answer. One k-c stayed 10 hours in a house, squatting the living room till they signed the deal just to get him out of there.

The spliff's alight. A damp swell on the wall. A new one. Geraldine. He wonders again if she's a snitch, a witch hover. Apart from chat about her marriage she never talks about herself. Yet she always wants to know more and more, about Jimmy, how Nathan earns a living, why Agnes went back to Cape Town instead of big London cash.

Nathan's hands have maybe three years. But he can build a ten-paper spliff. Perfect every time. That arthritis will get so he'll use a pipe and no spliff.

Hard for Jimmy to think. Geraldine was always up front on doorsteps, always gave it to the punter straight. Hard to think. He remembers their chats. Main thing, she wants to be with Brian so they can sit in front of open fires in a village pub and quaff ale. But now she's in limbo, at her mother's house, and later in the year their garden will glow with Hunza apricots. She knows the countryside. Not just names of birds.

Time to know. Time to find out who she is. But. Just as he's about to dial, he remembers. It's the clincher. No need to doubt this woman: some days she arrives for work with fresh flowers from her mother's greenhouse. The phone falls back on the cradle. Whisky pours. Looks like Geraldine is who she, he thinks.

Jimmy talks with two pals, ganja and alcohol. Only the ceiling to look at. And thinking of Agnes. Through the haze he can see her eyes. His eyes meet hers in a hemisphere of carousels.

# 61

"Glad you called," Geraldine says. "How did the interview go?"

Jimmy swaps a smoke with the handset. "Easier than I thought."

"Good."

"No more doorstep crap."

"Nervous?"

"Like stage jitters, but more."

"If you're *that* worried about it, maybe now's the time to walk away."

"Something addictive in the air. Got to check it out."

"Telesales, it can be like cocaine."

"I can be invisible. But I don't want to end by dry-retching for hours at a time on a floor somewhere, alone, you know, miles from music."

"De-dums!"

"You sound," Jimmy laughs, "like the ugly witch you are."

"Will you give it a go?"

"Definitely."

"Thought you would."

"Think I'll be any good?"

"Probably sell in your first week."

"How much are *you* making?"

"Oh, it's not too bad."

"Yeah, yeah. How much?"

"Not complaining. Best part of 600 quid a week, on average. I can live with that. Did I tell you there's a monster?"

"A what?"

"Somebody in the telesales office, a monster, earns three grand a week. That's *three grand* on average! And that's before his bonuses, trips to Hong Kong or whatever. Odd little guy, turns up in jeans and cowboy boots."

"I've heard about him."

"Colette mentioned him?"

"Yeah. It's true, then."

"True, blue."

"I can't believe it!"

"Yes, I know. The amazing thing is it happens in a jabbering little place. It's not even that. It's more a psychiatry workshop! One bloke deliberately turns up in shoes with holes in the bottom. I say a little prayer. Everyday, a prayer."

"The money-go-round."

"*Money?*" she gulps, voice echoing in the handset. "Not about money, my innocent. It's one-upmanship. That's what they're about. You know, some people have just *got* to win. It's the chase. The rush is what they live on.

Some stand on chairs when they sense the kill."

Jimmy laughs. "On the phone, standing on a chair in the office?"

"I can't explain it. The sales office, it's like being in a foreign country, where locals speak to phones all day and only ever speak to each other when gloating."

"You sound depressed," he says.

"Let's change the subject."

"Listen to my tapes this evening?"

"*What* an ego!"

"OK, OK. Did your sister deliver that vase yet?"

"Yes. She finished it just this evening. We'll get a shelf specially made for it. It's parked on the piano, for now. The aquamarine in this thing! It's got oblong petals, thin petal shapes. Wouldn't even call it a vase. She jokes about it. Says the reds are blood from thimbles of dwarves."

"What?"

"Come for a visit! Play the piano. We've got a concert grand."

"At Homes," Jimmy groans, "how many women in telesales?"

"Two, including me."

"Carmen, the other one?"

"Who?"

"The shy black woman."

"Oh, right."

"What's she up to?"

"Gosh, you are *so* out of the loop! Sacked. Colette got rid of her. Our dear little Colette is often a cheerless bitch. I was coming to that. Not sure you'd handle the ego stuff. Don't hit your sales target, and you're out on your ear. Colette slings you out."

# 62

"Boring!" Lorna yells.

"Well," Jimmy frowns, "if gravity was any less, even one little bit, planets would be helter-skelter round the sun."

"I don't care!"

"Why?"

"Enough to get on with in this life."

"Stars work behind the line of sight."

"Yes, Mr Spock. Of course."

Earlier this evening Jimmy was considering black holes. Transfixed, that not even light can escape their pull. Then Lorna phoned. She was too sad. Too thumped. She asked him to visit. Now he's here she wants to talk the whole world. But not gravity and stars. Not even about her brother. The hospital said Justin slipped a little.

"Planets really want to escape the sun."

"What do *you* want?" she says

"Me? I want to be going some place."

"As in, 'Where are we from, where are we going?' sort of thing?"

"Yeah."

"That's where faith comes in, isn't it?"

"So says religion."

"What do *you* say?"

"Five years ago one of my cousins came to England from Jamaica. That same week she got raped by a nightclub bouncer. Suicide."

"My God," she says, covering her eyes, "that's terrible!"

"A snake from nowhere."

She grabs the brandy bottle. But doesn't open it. Gets to the hi-fi and turns it off. "A feather," she breathes.

"*What?*"

"Every ton can fly, right? So feathers can try."

"I'll say it one more time, I do not believe in religion!"

"Because your cousin got raped?"

"No. Because there's no way to prove that stuff."

She turns away. "Mike Tyson was in Brixton."

"I know. Six, seven weeks ago."

"It was great."

"You went?"

"Fabulous! He unhinged the place."

"I watched it on TV."

"He was so happy. Teasing the girls, shadow boxing with kids. He's not as big as you'd think. See him on TV and it's always 'Get in my way and guess what happens next!' But he's really friendly, just a boy."

"They never wanted him to be just a guy."

"They still want a freak show," she says, brows furrowed.

"They want an animal."

"He had a great time in Brixton. So much in his eyes. *So* much. Wasn't what I expected."

"Hendrix had to burn his guitar. They wanted the freak, wouldn't make do with the genius. Ever seen the Isle of Wight gig? When his set is over he chucks the guitar to the ground. I mean, bangs it down! Then walks. Dead three weeks later."

"Tyson is like, he sets fire to his own heart."

"Those TV shots, that crowd swell in Brixton."

"He was 'Here's my body as I die.'"

"The way you talk it!"

"That's what I saw."

"This stuff never gets said. Maybe it's because you're a white man's daughter."

"That's how it is."

"What gets me is those black guys, the ones from sport, they can get a brand new Ferrari every month, fridge-loads of money, get onto chat shows, TV, but most of them only strut the bozo strut."

"And have the *nerve* to call themselves role models!"

"Compared to real talent those guys are only ninth rate. Tyson shuns their stench."

Lorna frowns. "I don't think Mike Tyson ever wanted to be a boxer. I looked at him and it was somebody plain. Like a farmer. A working man, somebody tending cattle or barley."

"Even a teddy-bear could fight him now," Jimmy says. "He was the last of a breed. But he can no longer fight. Doesn't *want* to fight. Not to crack open a man's head for money. Anybody can beat him now. But where were they when he was a lion?"

"Quaking."

"Yeah, from the safe side of the cage!"

"He's like somebody with no home now."

"That's seriously bad. A huge wrong."

"As a person of colour, there's too much missing."

"I know."

"What's wrong with the world?"

"There's nothing like a St Paul's Cathedral we designed."

"No black Shakespeare."

"Muhammad Ali and Mandela, they laid down good real-estate."

"You mean, people are proud of them."

"Yeah."

160

"Too few!"

"There's guys like Duke Ellington."

"Rosa Parks!"

"Yeah, and the rest."

"Mike Tyson's the big scapegoat."

"Talking about grace again?" Jimmy wonders.

"Why not? The ones that abuse Tyson, *they* have none. No grace!"

"This grace thing," he says, "there's too much sissy in it. Nobody, no man can use that stuff. You'd be walking round with grace in your trousers and etiquette polishing your shoes. How far down the road would you get with that? You'd catch your reflection in your polished shoes  and you yourself would laugh."

"Laugh if you want. I won't mind."

"Look, there's good stuff in the bible. Great stories. I don't deny that. But then you get to the part with a virgin giving birth, dead folk coming back to life."

"And?"

"That bible stuff, it grabs me less than stars. A lot less."

# 63

Lorna lays the plate with sausages. But no brandy tonight. Only coffee. She grins. "Brixton was the place."

"Emotions?"

"The day Tyson came to town," she says, "it was so unreal. The twenty-first day of the first month, new millennium."

Jimmy's fingers click. "Bop, bebop!"

"Snap, snap!"

"Wish it was that simple."

"Well, we've got to start somewhere."

"Those closet-racists played a neat hand with Mike Tyson."

"Didn't come here to see them, did he!"

"They didn't want him here, anyway."

"Where are they now? Back to being the little nobodies they are!"

"Sly bastards. The way they got their line ready, you know, getting on-side with somebody black. Somebody big-time. And only one name was big enough. Ali. Those woad-mongers cited Muhammad Ali, how he was welcome when in Brixton years back, how he's a model to us all. *To us all.* Next sentence, it's 'Tyson is a pariah, we must prevent him coming here.' Sly bastards!"

"They thought people in Brixton must be trusting fools."

"Even after '81, that riot."

"Tyson knew what they were up to. The crowd was near, people shouting 'We love you, bro! You pain is our pain.' Never seen anything like it!"

"The woad-mongers wanted a freak show."

"They couldn't really bar him, not if they wanted to save face."

"But they watched from a safe place, didn't they! Wanted him inside a cage, have dominion over him like an animal. Him to be obliging, him tethered to some uncle-tom cabin."

"I don't think it was *that* bad."

"No? Then how come they still talk crap? Calling him a rapist. Think they care about that Desiree?"

"What d'you mean?"

"If she was white, it would have been gloves-off time! Yeah, no civic gardenias to run to and tend."

Lorna's eyes glaze. She looks away, scans a distance. Remembering. It was a strange day, that Brixton afternoon Tyson arrived. Hearing that he was there she hurried from her desk. Twenty yards from the station, heart pounding, breath riding the bustle, pressed to a market stall and, for some-thing to do, grabbed some cane; nine yards of sugarcane from an old woman's stall. As she cut the cane into even lengths, the old woman smiled a wide Caribbean wide. Tyson was round the corner. The crowd yelling. A crowd crush. It could have run wild. But straightaway folk realized; they knew the woad-mongers wanted it that way, wanted a stampede, wanted to see the crowd turn like an animal. So it was discipline time. But the wait was hard. Tyson was just round the corner, moving it, getting close. The old sugarcane woman said Tyson would never have sweated slave sweat, cutting cane or picking cotton, getting whipped, wearing out day by day on a plantation. Lorna clutched the heavy carrier-bag of cane lengths, tempted, confused by sweetness, the end-game of tooth decay. Blood provoked to fire. Black folk ripped from their continent to slave sweetness in the field. 7 days a week. 14 hours per day. Man, woman, every child from 5 years old. She sighs.

A cup of coffee pours. But something bad. Not the blues. Not gospel. Nothing with a name. Not yet. Something sad.

"Hold it!" Jimmy says.

Handing him a blank sheet of paper, she nods, "For every ton of sugar a slave died."

"Sugar?"

"It comes from cane. First phase is molasses, gobby black stuff. Then the brown thing. Lots prefer white, most people, but white's the phase that killed the most slaves. You writing this down?"

Jimmy nods.

In Lorna's gaze, a lifetime. Her eyes know. "In the heart of Brixton," she says, " they've got a street named Atlantic Road. I was walking along it the day Tyson was in town, me and 27 cuts of cane. After he left Brixton, the crowd split up. Fives and sixes. Ones, twos."

"Did you get to talk to him?"

"No. I toured the area on foot, but refused a lift. Wouldn't get into some flash lime-green convertible in January."

"Pose wheels?"

"Yeah. Atlantic Road wasn't where to get a lift from a poser in a lime-green car. That road, peculiar name."

"It's in the shadow of ocean graves."

"Most people in Brixton know. They couldn't forget the millions who didn't survive the Atlantic. Not really."

# 64

"Hope your brother makes it," Jimmy says.

"Take a look at those," Lorna says, eyes fixed to snaps of skydivers on the wall. "He's in the mix."

"Who am I looking for?"

"The one with the cigar. On the right."

"Who is he?"

"That's him. Justin."

To Jimmy the face is like everybody in the snap. Looks white. Even to somebody used to the spread of black types, Justin looks white. In the photo, nothing like a white face turning from sunlight or tanned. No white face in shadow. Only Lorna's brother.

"He's got dreadlocks under that helmet," she says.

A screwdriver splayed Justin's lung. The worst of the gang fight. Been in a coma six months. A race fight. Black v white. Alley night. Jimmy can see how it could have happened.

"Doesn't look very black," he says, loping back to his bishop-chair.

"Names!" Lorna yells.

"What d'you mean?"

"Black, half-caste, mixed!"

"What's in a name?"

"Everything. Brixton's got more odd names than Atlantic Road. They've got streets named after the likes of Spenser and Shakespeare. Chaucer."

Jimmy frowns. "Chaucer Road?"

"Yeah."

"*That's* the ironic one."

"Why?"

"Chaucer was the guy that penned the Canterbury Tales, right?"

"So?"

"Archbishops of Canterbury had blood tales to tell their god."

"What?"

"Christian kingdom after kingdom!"

"What're you talking about?"

"Christian kingdoms poured blood in the ocean."

"*What*?"

"The Church of England used to have slave plantations."

"Don't be silly!"

"Who's being silly? Plantations."

"Where?"

"Barbados. During slavery, archbishops of Canterbury had a plantation there. Codrington. Stuff all about it on the net. Yeah, exactly the same

Barbados where your grandparents come from. Your black ones. And that Church of England, Jeez! Had billions in South African banks. During apartheid the church tucked away huge wedge."

"I don't think that can be true. I mean, are you sure?"

"Even today a priest lives in a mansion. Lambeth Palace."

"Look, is this going to be a sermon? A big Jimmy rant?"

"Archbishop of Canterbury, a priest, preacher, living in a palace."

"That's ridiculous."

"But true."

"Why would he live in a palace?"

"The church. Dead and buried, isn't it?"

Lorna's eyes bead. She can't answer. Over Jimmy's shoulder her eyes seek the bible on the bookshelf. She remembers being only yards from Tyson that Brixton day. Dazed, confused. Then saw his portrait on a market stall. Got it home. Got it up on the wall. It was late night. Then the idea of brandy with cane. No man in her life. She asked herself why she was alone. Alone with a brother in a coma, who now and then opens his eyes and says 'What, me?' The crowd was for Tyson. Group woe. That pain never getting talked. The answer wasn't on the internet.

She turns to Jimmy. "What're you thinking?"

"About a white dwarf."

"Stars, and stuff?"

"It's a star with gravity 350,000 times that on earth."

"I'm impressed."

"Hey, I'm just making small talk."

"Great, if you could find something else to talk about."

"What's up?" he asks, gently. "What is it?"

"Tyson. He was a bit like that knight of the Red Cross."

"Who?"

"Promise not to laugh."

"I won't laugh. *Knight?*"

"The one in the Faerie Queene."

"Jeez!"

"Don't laugh!"

"A fairytale?"

"Fiction, I know."

"Tired old fiction, from your A level days."

"The knight was grace."

"Not *that* again!"

"What's wrong with it?"

"Nothing, if it's a woman's name. Grace is a woman's name."

"The knight felled dragons."

Jimmy laughs. "Tyson, in the Faerie Queene?"

"You promised not to laugh!"

"Bullshit! Even *you* want to laugh!"

"I'll try anything."

Weary, he ups from the chair. Fed up. Looks around. Stretches a big cat's stretch. Ambles to the bookshelf. And out of pure sympathy, strokes the bronze cover of the bible. Then notices the grinning face of Lorna's brother in the skydiving snaps.

"No wonder you want a dose of fairytales," he says.

"And you're just too grand for that, eh!"

"Your knight, that's way off the scale."

"I know," she says, hoarsely.

"Look, Tyson was here to fight. That was the deal. A boxing contract. That's what brought him. The guy came to England to beat the crap out of a British black boxer. Money. Going to Brixton was from his heart, yeah, I believe that. But money was it. That's why he came."

Gazing at the bookshelf, Lorna says, "I've got nowhere to hide."

Trying for some soft thing to say, Jimmy asks if her parents ever visit the flat.

# 65

Bernice is Lorna's mother. A black woman born in England. At seven, she was supposed to go to Barbados. Go back home. That was the plan. But inch by inch, that plan got left behind.

Bernice was typical. Grown by stock Caribbean mother and father. A nurse and carpenter. They wanted strong education for their daughter. And she was dutiful. Books all day. But eventually, well, England switched with Barbados in their happiness. Then. One day in her teens she quaked. In front of the TV, shocked, afraid. Her mother and father quaking. Black and afraid in front of the TV, afraid to look. Afraid of the next word. Afraid of the last word. Enoch Powell. Powell was the TV item that evening, preaching his rivers-of-blood speech. That old evening, Enoch Powell talked numbers, five million black immigrants and their descendants will be all over England by the year 2000. The year Tyson was in Brixton. Enoch Powell was in full flow when the money in the slot-TV ran out. And by the time they got the right coins, he talked how white people have become strangers in their country, how England was a place where a white person can't go as far as the corner shop without being followed by grinning piccaninnies.

Jimmy lights a smoke. Lorna wipes her eyes. Voice breaking, she says her mother still knows that Powell speech by heart.

Brokenhearted, afraid to go outdoors, like even getting to work or school, the family wanted to get straight back to Barbados, to leave the mother-country lie, say goodbye. But something happened. A man called Benn was on TV, calling on England, 'Remember fair play.' So Lorna's grandparents turned up the volume. Tony Benn is a special white man, they said. So decided to give it a go, give England one more try. But only one year at a time. Bernice would get to Barbados one day. Marry and settle there. But even now, after all those years, she has never been. Not even for a holiday. After the rivers-of-blood speech she made a vow. Late that night she cried in the bath. Then drew blood. Took a safety pin and drew blood from her finger. And vowed. Sure, resolute in the night, she vowed. Then vowed again on the family bible. Two vows. Hand on the bible, she'd never settle in England. The next vow was never to get anywhere near a white boy. And that was how it was. Years later, when it was boyfriend time she had a go-getter guy, a guy born in Antigua who admired the black panthers and wanted to be one. But he was a business man more than militant. Buying and renting property. Everything was set. Bernice was going to leave her job, help out at the business. They wanted to retire by forty with a boat in warm Caribbean waters. But then. Square circle. Snow ablaze. No slavery. Something happened. One day, a Viking man loped into the dole office where Bernice worked. A tall, smiling man. Striding in motorbike gear. A man, not blank white. A tall white man with a trimmed brown beard. Not one of the oppressors. Alan Stanley was striding through town. Bernice married him.

Lorna turns to Jimmy. "I know what you're thinking."

"What am I thinking?"

"It's the bit about grinning piccaninnies, isn't it! You're thinking my mother and her half-piccaninnies, aren't you?"

"Is this going to be about grace?"

"No."

"There's one vow your mother made. The one about never having a white boyfriend. She should not have made it. Not on the bible. That's maybe the reason why her son's in a coma now."

"How d'you mean?"

"The bible? Jeez! That thing can get mystic. Like maybe it took her son away, you know, to pay that vow. Mystic business in the bible sometimes. Bronze or black."

"I thought you didn't believe."

"No, not the promises of religion."

"You don't rate faith. But it's really how much light you want. I mean, it's like 'Why bother with that baking sun when I have a little switch on the wall!' Is that you?"

"The bronze of your bible, it reminds me of blood."

"Stephen Lawrence," she sobs, "was a lot like my brother. I'm sad, sad. Only thing Brixton's got going for it is, it's no Eltham."

"What's Eltham?" Jimmy frowns.

"If he'd been in Brixton, not Eltham, Stephen wouldn't have stood out that night. Freaks never go to Brixton to find somebody black."

"Eltham is lily white?"

"Yes. But they're not all murderers. A white couple in Eltham, they tried to help. Tended to Stephen where he fell. Tried to keep him alive. The woman had his head in her arms, kneeling down beside him. The man tried. His shirt was drenched in blood. Stephen was slipping away. But they tried harder. Tried everything they knew. The next day was too difficult. He had the terrible burden of what had happened."

"And," Jimmy nods, "a blood-stained shirt."

"He'd washed Stephen's blood from the shirt. But didn't know what to do with the water, the blood-stained water from the wash. In the end, he took it into his garden. Poured it over a rosebush."

Numb. Bleary. Jimmy can't speak. He sinks to the floor. Stephen Lawrence would have been invisible in Brixton. But in Eltham that bad night he was in a skin overcoat.

"What that white man did! What he did with the blood-stained water.

That was huge. That shirt, it's a shroud."

"To be kept safe," Lorna says.

"Got to find a place for it. The memory of it."

"Where?"

"I don't know."

"Let's check the internet."

"Yeah, the chat-rooms."

"Oh, I know!" she says, eyes afire. "Let's do a poem."

Jimmy lights a smoke. Reaching the bookshelf, she pulls a volume by Omar Khayyam. Agitated, she flicks through it. Turning page after page, looking, saying 'Stephen, Stephen.' Then turns back to the start. One verse stands out. Quickly she amends a line from it, makeshift but calm: *And never blows the rose so red, as where some buried black boy bled.*

# 66

A sale. Halfway through the third week, a reception suite was sold to a college. Jimmy. Great sale for a novice. But till today it was bad news on the line; nobody buying from the novice phone.

The gambler was glad. And Geraldine. The gambler grabbed Jimmy by the elbow, said 'This is where the party starts!' But jealousy was huge. The salesroom blinked, squinted, gazed out the window, stared at the wall. Then clenched jaws. The commission is four grand. Serious for a first deal.

Two minutes after the sale's confirmed, Colette flits to the salesroom. Big champagne in happy arms, she beckons Jimmy. Skits to the window.

"If that's what you want," she says, nodding to the hardware in the parking lot, "then it's the pick of them. One word of advice: the road to cars like that is where you travel alone. Alone and light. No daydreams, got that?"

"No daydreams at the office."

"Want it," she says, voice hitting a sweet note, "with *all* you've got."

She turns to the room. Flicking from smiling to callous. Just like old snow. All the phones get downed. Except the gambler's. He's a solo here, beyond rules, the big earner with cowboy boots piling high on a desk. Chilled champagne pours. Jimmy's never seen this callous Colette before. It reminds him. He was watching the Thames from a warm apartment in Canary Wharf one evening and the water seemed to huff. A liquid cityscape, seeing it tart as darkness grabbed. The Thames was hopping one evening. It sapped. The onset of snow was so sudden. Snowflakes on the window pane. The woman was tired of her apartment. She shrugged, and said 'What a world'

Jimmy's deal is only a tool to Colette. She taunts the salesroom. Most only do mickey-mouse deals anyway and here's Jimmy, she says, one of the newest here and gets a deal with four grand commission already. There and then two get sacked, told to try a job on the checkout tills at Tesco.

Chilled champagne in hand, Jimmy nudges the window. Colette plays air guitar round him. And taunts the salesroom one more time as she goes through the door. The gambler laughs. Lighting a smoke, the high-roller says Colette's name should be on the bonus board. Geraldine asks why. Every week the top two in the salesroom get a bonus. Colette should be one prize next week, the gambler says. And it's Chardonnay, yeah, that's a dozen bottles for the winner. Colette's a good second prize, he says; laughing through tobacco the gambler says the runner-up should get a striptease or blow-job from the boss lady.

Geraldine shrugs. "These phones are only a prop."

"Well," Jimmy says, "one somebody here gets to be invisible. Nobody can tell a black guy's on the line."

"And you like that, don't you!"

"I get a kick out of it."

"Like any old horse trading," she says, "*anything* can be sold."

"Talking about me?"

"What makes you think that?"

"The way you said it."

"Guess what?" she says, wryly smiling. "Mars is up for sale."

"What?"

"Plots, overlooking what was the Mars ocean, they're being snapped up. Idiots in Texas, I think."

"Telesales doing the selling?"

"Yeah. Crazy, isn't it!"

"From some salesroom in London or New York, selling into stars."

"No problem selling furniture round England, then."

# 67

Glass three sides of the salesroom at Homes. Just like it was designed to jolt, get action from the sellers. Some days lightning threatens. Overcast skies.

Days pass when nobody in the room sells a thing; not even the gambler. That's when the bragging starts. Always somebody with a tale, a hot weekend some place, clubbing it in New York or Las Vegas, or a sloshed week in Zanzibar and old bazaars.

Then a sale. As sudden as lightning. By luck or design. And the lucky designer is mostly the gambler. The dash for cash. It starts all over. Cash, the cool, the drought-buster.

Some days the gambler ignores the phone. Listens to Chopin on his Walkman. Shuts off from sales noise to listen to the A Minor Waltz. To this gambler, this Chopin piece is wanting death to be alone in a winter field. In a field with fresh snow, dying can be good, he says; or watch a famous man die on the internet; a tyrant walks to a firing squad and folk get to see dying is no big deal.

From a telesales crew of thirty, four or five make money. But only one in the top-man seat. The rest come and go. Start getting to know somebody and next thing they've gone. The next cycle lasts maybe three months. The big one can take six months to pan out. And all the time, heavy footfalls on the way out.

"Summer's a whole season from here," Jimmy says.

Geraldine frowns. "And?"

"It's better with rain sometimes. No swelter. Better with wildness. Playing thunder, grab some lightning. But summer's still down the road from the sales room. Yeah, a season invisible from here."

"I thought maybe we'd gotten past the mystic phase," she says, wryly.

"That part of my body is not invisible."

"Colette is ruthless. Noticed? Her sales charts never lie. If your curve falls then you'd better explain yourself to the chart. You'd get more pity from those charts than that woman."

"Doesn't bother me," Jimmy says.

"That's because she's got a soft spot for you. She's normally business. Except for you. Funny, your middle-aged groupie is your boss!"

"Theatre's her thing. Music is incidental."

"You care?"

"No. Well, yeah. I tap into that soft spot."

"In your element, aren't you!"

"How d'you mean?"

"This phone malarkey."

"The invisible thing?"

"Yes. You talk to people on the phone who don't even consider the race of who's talking to them."

"Only because I don't have an ethnic lilt. I play in a word city. It's ace for me, colour-blind. Like a skateboard over graphite."

"Don't let it get to your head. Half an identity is *so* not you!"

"Nah! The phone is playtime. Sometimes a woman's there to play. And that's pure fun for guys. Especially if she's a slick, somebody wanting to excite, like go on a date, illicit and hot, or wants to meet for lunch. Nice to play lady execs down the line."

"Then you suggest she should buy a little something, like a boardroom suite?"

"I've heard *you* making eyes with guys on the phone."

"The odd flirt, yes. But never a chat up."

"Don't get prissy. That's how the game plays."

"Funny, what people can get away with on the phone!"

"Just think," Jimmy smiles, "white folk are invisible all the time."

# 68

Malt whisky pours. Two letters from Donna to Jimmy this week. Fuss diet, watching that body thing. But still cooking. His mother phones.

"Agnes should get a letter from you," she says. "You should go there. Go to South Africa. Get away from the rain."

"I've got the money. Enough."

"But?"

"Complicated. Somebody else. Confusing me."

"What's her name?"

"Donna. The one I told you about. The one I messed up."

"You said sorry?"

"Yes."

"Where is she?"

"In Jamaica right now. But I can't get her out my mind."

"What's the one thing you can't forget about Agnes?"

"Lots. This and that."

"Not, not this and that. Got to be *one* thing that makes her different."

"Well," Jimmy groans, "there's how she turned up out the blue one day. Arrived with curtain rods. And an Ornette Coleman LP. Hard to forget that, her fitting curtain rods at the window. I mean, high on a chair with 8 floors down to the street."

"That's a great sign!"

"Yeah?"

"Absolutely. So, what's the problem?"

"In her last letter a man drops by her father's house. A finance tyro. A guy with a voice like Paul Robeson, she said."

"She wants you to make your mind up."

"In one dream, I watched a lion looking out to sea. Later in the dream I was walking along a sea-front. It was edged by blue neon lions. A cold coast at dawn."

"Stop it!"

"I'm never going to grow up," Jimmy says, laughing loud.

"By the way, what happened to Arleene?"

"She got fed up. Couldn't take the on-off between me and her."

"Shame. Maybe you can write a song about it."

"Nah! I listen to Motown for that. Do it better than I could."

"Go for early Gladys Knight."

"Nathan handed down the whole Motown thing to me. Every cut from the 60's and 70's. I play Motown all the time. Ace. That music, it killed Jamaica how sweet it was. Marvin Gaye, Martha and the Vandellas, the Supremes,

"Holland, Dozier, Holland. You could learn from those guys."

"Amazing, I know. Don't know how they did it. Anything by them."

"Go visit!"

"Nathan said that. Pity, you and him."

"Worry about your own love life!"

"Hey, I love *all* the Motown females! Diana Ross. The nicest looking. Limber lady with a long gaze. Those videos. She was maybe only 19. Top Of The Pops. Her doing Baby Don't Leave Me, telling that story in her eyes."

"Maybe she's got a daughter you can meet."

"She's got two, three. Yeah, for somebody like me!"

"Get into your dreams, Jimmy. That's OK. But stay clear of lions."

# 69

"I know guys that can deal with it."

Lorna gulps. "Violence?"

"No problem," Jimmy says.

"No!"

"Lions don't roar at the sea."

*"What?"*

"Somebody must pay for Justin."

"The doctors said he dipped a little, that's all. Took a bad turn. Not looking good. That's hard to deal with. But an eye for an eye is not how this will end. My mother goes to a faith-healer."

"What about your dad?"

"He went out to the garden, took a sledgehammer and smashed the shed apart."

Jimmy's at Lorna's flat the second time this week. Hard to tell why she turns to him. She sounded bad on the phone tonight. And now only silence. Silent gazing at the bookshelf. She's ground down. Pain in her eyes. Expecting the phone to ring. Afraid. Restless in the room, pacing. Wanting somebody to hold. But Jimmy's not the man for that. Lorna wants a man, not a wounded music man. No fugitive from closeness. Apart from Agnes, women were only prey. Agnes was different.

"England is a white man's country," he says.

"England is England."

"Somebody asked me what handshakes mean."

"What?"

"If you get hit, then you counterpunch. Three times as hard!"

"There's no limit to violence," Lorna says.

"Your thing, it's a bronze bible. You don't see what must get done."

Upright in her bishop chair, she turns to him. "Violence is out!"

"Well, you could call revenge a form of violence."

"What would you call it?"

"Revenge is get-even-time."

"Vengeance is mine, said the Lord."

"That bible stuff! A guy walked on water. But one disciple walked beside him with a sword. What was Peter's sword for?"

"We want the law involved, OK? "

"What will that do?"

"Clear the air."

"What will it achieve, beyond a bunch of talk?"

"Bigots are bigots."

"What's your mother say?"

"It was difficult."

"What does she think?"

"They had a bust-up over it. Dad was 'I told him those dreadlocks would drag him down.' You never hear my mother swear, but she got into that and I was 'Go ahead, let it all out!' It went on and on. For days, really."

Wondering, Jimmy gazes at the skydivers on the wall. He knows that Lorna's no warrior woman. Not a woman beside a warrior in the race jungle. "Lady," he says, "you've got too much bible!"

"What have *you* got?"

"Thirteen."

"Thirteen, what?"

"Twelve tones and a keyboard."

"Thirteen," she says, frowning, "like at the Last Supper?"

Jimmy's eyebrows raise. "You know," he says, "you're the first person I know that gets that."

"It's rubbed off from you. Weird stuff going on in your head."

"Not as bad your head full of wishes!"

"Like what?"

"You're trying to dream your brother's coma away. But he can't dream. Coma's a strange place to dream. Then there's the part that maybe he got stabbed by one of his own posse, another black guy."

"I know. From deep down in the coma he said it again yesterday, said, 'What, me?' Hearing his voice, that's so painful."

"And the law will fix things, right?"

"Where else can we turn?"

"Going to the law is a big uncle tom's cabin!"

"What?"

"If it wasn't for colour you'd be English all day. I still can't believe Mike Tyson's in your dream."

"In my *what*?"

"Well, he's up on your wall."

"The picture in the hall? I switched a Guns & Roses one for it."

"There's spilt blood in your dreams."

The screensaver idles the room. The word *ricochet* annoying Jimmy. It shuffles the mute screen like a strangle cord, like somebody tossing rope from a nightmare.

"That screen is my friend," Lorna says.

"Why a word instead of a picture?"

"Because," she laughs, "*I* am all ricochet."

Coffee pours. He wonders if she'll catch her reflection in a coffee cup. No mixed-race waver in Lorna. Nothing like the girl he knew. He was 17, but now remembers a witch. The only good time was the day her syndicate clocked the lottery. She was hot that day. Beautiful with her own thrill. But the next day spoiled it. First thing was a safari suit. Her share was half a million and she was even going to get him a sports car. But getting a car from the likes of her would've been a bad move. Her witch-like would've cramped the car from going fast or far. She was 18, more a frisk than eyeful. Always telling what was obvious. 'Do you know it's Monday today?' But the bad part was the way she repeated how she's mixed-race; even reminding Jimmy, especially when in a crowd. The bigger the crowd the more the witch used to say, I'm mixed race. She was never black; *black* was for black people. And though her father was jet that didn't make her black; no matter what, she said. A girl with bats in her head. Maybe by now she's shaped up from the lopside, he thinks. She was in a Porsche Boxter the last time he saw her.

Lorna frowns. "What's wrong?"

"You're you. I'm glad for that."

"Is that a compliment?"

"Yeah."

"Thank you!"

"You're nothing like somebody I used to know."

"So?"

"So, nothing. There's no next move."

"Who was she?"

"A witch."

"What?"

"Probably lives in Epping Forest by now."

"A weirdo?"

"She never said black. It was always 'my father's people' and stuff."

"Jimmy, what's really the matter?"

"Funny old world."

"And?"

"Why are people different colours? Don't say look at flowers!"

"This is about my father. I can tell."

"To know, or not know."

"Honestly, there's nothing."

"Well. OK. Now you mention it, who is he?"

Upright in the bishop chair, she grins. "Well, he's a handsome man. Quiet. Pale brown eyes. Hard-working. Difficult with strangers. I mean, he won't let anyone get close. You'd get on like a house on fire."

"How come he does nothing about Justin?"

"Depends what you mean."

"Your dad should square things, that's what!"

"We don't know who did it."

"Think it's because he's scared?"

"*Scared?*"

178

"Yeah, scared he might find out something."

"Who?"

"Your father."

"What d'you mean?"

"Last week on the phone you said they'd had a big bust up."

"Who?"

"Your father and Justin."

"Christ! Did I tell you that?"

"How else would I know?"

"That was such a long time ago. Ages and ages."

"Maybe it's still there, floating around."

"There is *one* little thing," she says, voice lowered. "He couldn't take it when Justin came back with locks. Didn't speak to him for months because of it."

"Back from Barbados?"

"Justin was there nine months. Came back with dreadlocks and a broad Bajan accent. It was 'Look, this is the real me!' sort of thing. *So* cute!"

"What about your sister?"

"How d'you mean?"

"The black community. Her stance."

"Can't make my mind up. Haven't you got anybody?"

"Brothers and sisters?"

"Yeah."

"People round me all day?"

"Family!"

"Nah. I'm the only one. My mother didn't want any more. She'd wanted loads. But it didn't work out with my old man. Not sure what he was up to out there. With him, well, there could be twenty more like me. Never asked."

"Don't you feel anything? Get lonely?"

"Now and then. Would've been great if I had a brother. A sister."

"Roll a spliff if you want," Lorna says. "It's OK."

"What was Justin doing with a Bajan accent?"

"You'll have to ask him. He never really said."

"You sister ever been to Barbados?"

"No. In so many ways, it was a lot easier for her."

"The independent type?"

"Stop making those little-lost-boy eyes at me!"

Feeling clumsy, Jimmy turns to the bookshelf. He knows Lorna's watching all his moves. Talking of family in her apartment makes him feel alone.

"Want me to leave?"

"Sit yourself down!"

"Chat?"

"No more stars and holes!"

"Black holes," he laughs.

"My sister likes that stuff."

"Religious?"

"An atheist."

"Goes out with white guys?

"*What*?"

"You heard!"

"What's that got to do with you?"

"Getting touchy in your old age!"

"Her partner *is* white. Satisfied?"

"Bet your father jumps for joy at that."

"Not especially. It's not 'One blue-eyed boy for you.' No, not at all."

"That wasn't what I meant."

"I didn't think about colour till I was 16, 17. Then it was black guys I liked. More or less. Justin's the same. Always been black girls. It was easier for Elaine. Her own choices. Look, she's not trying to be white, if that's what you mean. She knows what's what."

Jimmy exhales a billow. "How come your father isn't with the rest of you in that picture?"

"The one next to Tyson's?"

"Yeah."

"I don't want to get into that."

"Sorry I asked!"

"No psychoanalysis, OK?"

"Me?"

"You sound like a therapist. It's 'Wait, there's shit to uncover here.' Well, you're dead wrong!"

"Just checking."

"We're a *close* family."

"I never had that," Jimmy groans. "It was only me. And my electric keyboard. Nine or ten keyboards down the years."

"Why the fuss about my dad?"

"Just a thought. Not trying to snoop. Don't get diced."

"You ask lethal questions."

He steps over to the skydivers' photos. One man's taller than the rest. Looks like an ex-boxer. Or military copper. Steel in his eyes. Lorna's father.

He turns to face her. "Your dad's sister, she still sings?"

"Not really. After the last tour she gave it a miss. But that was yonks ago. Fifteen years."

"She do any studio gigs?"

"Yeah. She was good. Even auditioned for a Jimmy Hendrix show. It was

60's soul music. Black music, basically."

"Otis Redding, Sam Cook. I love that stuff."

"Wilson Picket. Got any of his?"

"Yeah. And Sam & Dave. Irma Thomas. Solomon Burke."

"Christ! I thought you were jazz, jazz."

"My old man is *huge* on soul. Crucial. Did soul sessions. Backed soul acts for years. I have a load of soul. And all the Motown stuff he gave me."

"Stevie Wonder?"

"Yeah. The works. My old man knows Gladys Knight."

"Bet my auntie could give your dad a run for his money."

"Now," Jimmy laughs, "you're going *too* far."

"How d'you know?"

"I won't get racial about this."

"Only kidding. But she's up to speed. She made soul tapes. We play them at Justin's bedside. Funny how it turned out."

"Yeah, after the soul excursion your auntie put away her foolish things and went back to white."

Lorna's head shakes. "It was Newcastle, fool!"

"What're they like?"

"My dad's family?"

"Yeah."

"Geordies. Working class."

"How did soul music get that far north?"

"You've got to understand, black music took a hold. In the 60s everybody got caught up in it. "

"I thought they liked Elvis."

"Yeah. The big one was the Beatles."

"Great songs. Seriously good songs!"

"You listen to the Beatles?"

"Yeah, there's things I learn from them."

"Think those songs are going to last?"

"Lennon by himself, no. McCartney was the higher talent."

"Can't imagine you being a Beatles fan."

"I am. I can tell you obviously are. Got a favourite track?"

"Mull of Kintyre. What's yours?"

"Mull is pure McCartney. I think Yesterday is a serious work. By a mile. Beautiful harmonies in Yesterday."

"But not your favourite."

"I dunno. She Loves You, that's way up there."

"What, the energy?"

"The teeny lyric. Those old songs, they could have been Motown."

"Look," Lorna says, "my dad was a biker bloke. He didn't wake up one morning and think 'Oh, what a swank day, I'll just go to London,  become a fireman, and, oh, hang on a minute, I'll end up with a black wife and three kids.' There was no grand plan. It just turned out that way, OK?"

"Sounds special. From a nicer time."

"What d'you mean?"

"The way you describe it."

"Don't you believe me?"

"Your dad. Somebody could learn from him."

"Nice of you to say so!"

"I mean it."

"Mean what?"

"Chas Chandler was from up there, wasn't he?"

"From?"

"Newcastle."

"I think so."

"I bumped into this guy on the tube one day. It was Eric Burdon."

"Is that the House of the Rising Sun man?"

"Yeah."

"My dad sings it in the garden. All the time."

"Eric Burdon knows the blues. Had relatives in coal mines up north. Says they were the same as slaves."

"Wasn't much going on after the war."

Jimmy frowns. "Eric says it was either get into black music, or look for unexploded German bombs."

Lorna's eyes roll. "What's all this leading up to?"

"Chas Chandler was in The Animals. Him and Eric Burdon."

"So?"

"Hendrix wouldn't have come here if it wasn't for Chas Chandler."

"And?"

"Something's bugging you. It's obvious."

# 70

Geraldine sets cut flowers in the vase. Fiddles them round. And grins. One more time.

Colette nods. "From your garden?"

"My neighbour's."

"They're gorgeous!"

"Yes."

"Such reds!"

"Should lighten up the office a bit, shouldn't they!"

"Hope so. Been all doom and gloom this past week."

"It's the weather. Too mild. Punters need something to moan about."

"This time of year they're like cormorants."

"Cormorants?"

"Those birds scare the daylights out of fish. I mean, last summer I saw a cormorant swallow an eel and it was longer than you'd believe."

"I think," Geraldine says, "that's a long story."

"No, it's not!"

"I was being witty."

"Course you were."

"Any news of the bonus this week?"

"Ah!"

"Bet the gambler wins it, anyway."

"He's got the greatest need. Fancy a smoke before everybody else gets here?"

"Tempting. But no thanks."

"Will power, eh!"

"I'll probably start again. Yes, one day maybe."

"Bishops behind closed doors?"

"What?"

"A puff of white smoke at the Vatican, and a new pope!"

"You sound like a certain composer we know. *Exactly* like him."

"He's talented, you know. Love having him here."

"One day he'll just get up and leave. You know that, don't you."

"Yes. But there's something about him. Everybody can tell."

"He respects you."

"He does no such thing!"

"Well, he knows you understand him."

"He needs looking after."

# 71

"You *just* missed him," Lorna says. "Left about a minute ago."

Jimmy slopes in, closes the door. "Meet him next time."

Alan Stanley cooks Sunday dinner. Always. Seeing a recipe just once, Lorna's father remembers it years later. He can cook anything. English, West Indian, Yorkshire pudding, jerk pork, run-down, and some of the best ackee & saltfish on a plate anywhere. As a young guy Alan never imagined a black woman. The closest to that was a quick Vietnamese girl. She was from the local take-away. They used to meet in secret. But that didn't count. He was fifteen. And they never did the thing anyway. It tickles Lorna, her father having a thing for a girl from Vietnam. And all the time at home in the 50s and 60s, Alan's mother played folk tunes on the Hardanger fiddle. Lorna claims Viking blood. It's all over Northumberland, she says. She definitely remembers the first racial. In her early teens she tried telling Alan something Bernice just didn't want to hear. From maybe eight or nine, she'd started to notice. Seeing a black and white couple in the street always got the same reaction. They smiled. Because of her, they always smiled. Smiling towards her. Thinking it now, maybe it was just by seeing her that the black & white duo called up a blessing for their thing. But when Lorna told him, Alan only laughed. Every time he laughed, said her imagination was too far.

Her voice lowers. "Well," she says, "my dad's a kind man. Absolutely fair minded. Listens to both sides."

"Knights in white tunics."

"My father?"

"Yeah. You're proud of him."

"Obviously. Of course, he's got his hang-ups. We all have!"

"My old man sees red, white folk claiming they helped create jazz. Pisses him off. But that's not a hang-up. What's your old man's gripe?"

"Complicated. Even we don't go there. He'll be OK for months. I mean, ages. Then something happens. He snaps, goes on about asylum seekers."

Jimmy grabs a smoke. "What about the big one?"

"Black people?"

"Yes."

"Call me black, don't you?"

"Course!"

"There's some that wouldn't."

"Mixed race, it sounds clumsy."

"Awkward?"

"No music to it."

"My nan thinks mixed is a cut above black. Big deal!"

"Your white grandmother?"

"Well, yes."

"They all think that."

"They?"

"White folk."

"They don't *all* think that!"

Jimmy's fingers snap. "Lots of black people think it. Loads of guys prefer half-caste girls, think they're a cut above."

"I know that sort," she groans. "The blacker some guys are the more they lose their souls."

"During slavery, white indentured labour was in Jamaica."

"As well as slaves?"

"Yeah. The white indentured were only a tick over black slaves in the pecking order. But way above all indentured whites were the black freemen."

"So, you *do* read history books!"

"Not now. But I was into all that. And the bible, once upon a time. When I first went to Jamaica it was weird. You know, seeing white folk born and bred there. White Jamaicans moving to the same rhythm as black Jamaica. Laughing the same. Big surprise. One day a white guy used his huge teeth to rip the bark from sugarcane. *Way* past words. Even now. Know what I mean? Under the Jamaican sun the white Jamaican crunched that cane. Jamaican white guys, they mostly hook up with Jamaican black women."

"It's obviously the other way round here."

Jimmy frowns. "I've never met somebody like you before."

"Me?"

"Don't get prissy. You know what I mean. Your father's white. A white man. Looking at you, even saying *white man* makes me nervous. Makes me feel I must watch what I say."

Lorna's eyebrows could be hyphens. They split. Resolve over high cheekbones. "I understand," she says.

"Alan understand?"

"Yes."

"Sure?"

"It's not 'There's that Stanley bloke, the one with darkies in his house.' It isn't like that."

"Who said it was?"

"I know the facts, OK?"

"But you don't want me to talk about it."

"Look! Anybody brings crap to my dad, they do it behind his back or get their brains knocked out!"

# 72

Options at Lorna's flat. Jimmy's early. He thinks she's special tonight; her brother might die, but tonight she looks great.

"Never seen you in jeans before," he says, stepping inside.

"I hate them!"

"Then put on a dress."

"Let's not bother going anywhere."

"The night looks good for live music. Let's go."

"I feel like cooking. Could do with a good fry-up."

"Then," Jimmy laughs, "let's stay in, invite Norman Tebbit."

"Oh no! Not race again!"

"Only way you'll shut me up is ask me to leave. Or we go out."

"Thanks!"

"Stick your head in the sand if you want to."

"I'll do you a deal. We spend two minutes on your race thing, then we relax and have something to eat. Deal?"

"Can't resist the spell in your eyes."

"What music shall we play?"

"Coltrane."

"Coffee?"

"Got any of that cane-brandy thing?"

"It's all gone."

"I need a spliff."

"Most white people," Lorna says, head shaking, "don't care about race. Some get vexed by non-whites here. Some want blacks gone, still waiting on a new Enoch. Then there's those that want no more blacks in the country *but* they'll give the ones here a chance, you know, to earn their way."

"Then along comes Tebbit, right?"

"He was the lure."

"White folk, they all use some version of the Tebbit test. Only a few say it out loud."

"He was Margaret's genie. The sly one. A lot smarter than her. But he was bald. And bald heads don't cut it on TV. Bald heads, they're too close to the sense of dying. That skull was like a warning. Even his own side called him the Chingford skinhead."

"He's so heavy-duty English."

"Norman Tebbit was RAF, then civic. Top pilot. Flying at that level, well, that's probably when you get the worse flake-highs of all."

"Where'd you get this flake-highs stuff, anyway?"

"I work in human resources, don't forget. You guys get flake-highs. Talented white guys get it when passed over. Black guys get it all the time."

"Put on your red dress, baby!"

"What?"

"Not you. Well, sort of. It's a song my old man plays."

"That thing, the Tebbit test, it's facile."

"Always support England at cricket, right?"

"Cricket, football, whatever."

"If England's playing the West Indies at cricket, Tebbit wants black folk to root for the England cricket team."

"That's the nub of it, yeah."

"So if I want to be English I've got to support England at sport."

"For starters," Lorna laughs. "For starters."

"What happens when somebody black does a robbery?"

"I don't know what you mean."

"News on TV, the hold-up man's 'of West Indian appearance' or they say 'Afro-Caribbean appearance.' They might say black. No matter where the guy was born. But where's Norman when bullshit like that's on TV!"

"Paying the license fee?"

"Yeah. But he should be scraping loud crap from them Tebbit shoes."

"It's a bit more complex than that. A lot more!"

"Alan thinks that?"

"My dad?"

"Yeah, what's he think?"

"He's obviously not a racist."

"All kinds of ways to be racist."

"What're you getting at?"

"There's this BNP guy, got a thing for ethnic women."

"No way!"

"I'm serious."

Lorna frowns. "You're having me on!"

"It's dead true."

"That's sick!"

"Obviously."

"Got to be sick, hasn't he?"

"A psycho."

"A hypocrite!"

"Yeah."

"So what's the problem?"

"I can't see how a black woman can shack up with the BNP."

"She doesn't know."

"But suppose she does."

"She *can't* know!"

"Or she's got a split personality."

"*He's* the one with a problem."

"Look, the white man plays games."

"Not my dad!"

"Sure?"

"What d'you mean?"

"Explain to me how a racist white boy can lust after a black woman!"

"I think you're making this up."

"Somewhere on a nerd's computer there's pixels moving like waves."

"*What?*"

"Pixels, they move round as pairs of numbers. One number weds to another in pixel heaven. Even the ugliest shape is a maths matrix."

"I'm sure you know what you're talking about. I don't!"

"What about *ricochet*? It bounces on your screen like ants in a cave."

"Where," Lorna says through gritted teeth," did you hear about that BNP dog?"

"It was in the papers. He only went with ethnic women. Black, Indian. One Chinese. I kept the cutting."

"I want to see it."

"I'll get you a photocopy."

"Sure you're not making this up?"

"I'm not. They found a load of guns, knives in his flat. Pamphlets. Squad loads of manic stuff. Doesn't mean I'm accusing your father."

"Then why tell me?"

"Because the story only proves I must play safe with white."

"Well, you're *so* off the mark with my dad!"

"I play safe. I'm not accusing anyone. Not folk I don't know."

"He's got his moods. We all have. In our house we laugh it off. If cricket's on TV, Justin's like 'Come on West Indies!' Always been that way in our house."

Jimmy yawns. "Your brother might not make it. But who lives till a hundred, anyway."

"He's twenty two!"

"If a cat gets run over, a spinster sheds tears, bawls."

"*What?*"

"I don't know what life is."

"Look, the deal was we talk for two minutes. Then I do a meal."

"Know what? I'm not hungry."

"I'll make you a fisher of men, Jesus says."

"No after-life. Not for me."

"Then," Lorna sighs, "who's there to trust?"

"Mandela."

"They call this place England!"

"Then I'd give Ashdown the nod."

"Paddy Ashdown?"

"Yeah."

"Why?"

"Woad can be any place. Even somebody with brains."

"Yes, yes. But what's so special about him?"

"He was a guide. Seriously. It's got to be somebody that can talk life as well as death. Prime minister this, leader that, but if push turns to shove the leader must know more than talk."

"Why him?"

"Because he's a man of life and death, like a bullfighter, but way too smart to fight a hummingbird."

"What?"

"In England right now a herd of cattle moves, herded and content, trundling to a haystack saved from fire."

Lorna blinks. "I don't know what the hell you're talking about!"

"Ashdown," Jimmy says. "That guy knew danger and paperwork. Could break a man's neck with his bare hands."

"And?"

"Before politics, he was SAS. Could see stuff a mile off. Next to him, these politics folk only shit spiders on TV."

"One ready-made hero for sale!"

"Better him than Major, or Blair."

"John Major had two left feet," Lorna laughs.

"Major should have tried cricket. Not politics. Claims he was born in Brixton, but never had a thing to say about black folk."

"Blair's OK."

"*That* bible boy?"

"He's honest. I think."

"Gigging at the Dispatch Box?"

"It's only been two years. Two and a bit. Give him a chance!"

"Don't like the look of him. I hear he can fumble on guitar."

"Lots of guys can. Guitar, whatever."

"He shoves aside his law books then grabs a Buddy Holly song-sheet, strums that thing, Peggy Sue through and through."

"That's cruel, *terrible*!"

"Hey, let's forget Blair. When you see uncle Norman tell him something for me."

"*Uncle* Norman?"

"Tebbit. Tell him I'd maybe root for England one day. But only after it's OK to criticize the place."

Lorna grins. "What, you don't like everything in England?"

"Think it's funny? He'd have a heart attack if somebody black moved in next door."

"Wow!"

"This is life and death."

"Bow-wow!"

"Unless it's sport," Jimmy says, "they don't like you criticizing stuff. You open your mouth, zap! Unless it's sport or bling, there's always somebody to tell you to fuck off, dead pan, go back where you come from!"

Lorna gazes her feet. "My mother's got a remedy for that."

"Yeah. Act like a stooge, like that Oprah Winfrey."

"No, no! When they start, you blank them."

"They?"

"Bigots. They make their noise, she lets them get on with it."

"Puts sellotape on her mouth?"

"My parents get on!"

"Yeah, yeah. Never quarrel, right?"

"Everybody has flare-ups. It's not 'That's your side of the house, keep your thoughts to yourself!' It's a man and woman, twenty seven years together."

"I'd be worried, having a white girlfriend."

"*Why?*"

"It's obvious!"

"Like how?"

"No way I could tell her if I got called a black bastard."

"As long as *she* doesn't call you that."

"I couldn't get home and moan. Not to a white woman."

"If she loves you, then end of story."

"I still couldn't tell her. I'd feel weird."

"She wouldn't be guilty for somebody else."

"Suppose I was out with her and, well, racist crap comes over. What happens then? I'd have to be a serious thicko to live that way."

"Not my family!"

"Sure?"

"Never!"

"Congratulations."

"*What?*"

"You get to live a fairytale. Congrats, lady."

"What is this? I mean, it's like a vicious pack of witch-finders at the door. You're talking about my parents, understand? My mother, human beings, been together 27 years!"

"Astronomers take snaps of the cosmos. Folk have albums, family frolicking at the seaside. But big time physics looks for more than that. They hunt gravitons."

"What?"

"Heartbreak particles. Too small. They'd explain the universal sigh."

"That's it! Now I'm sure. You *are* from another planet!"

Weary, Jimmy lights a smoke. Then a nervous cough. Not a tobacco cough. The room's a pinch. The night a pinch. He turns to Lorna. "I wasn't getting at your parents."

"Then what's your problem?"

"It wasn't personal. It's how I talk."

"Talk? You obsess!"

"Look, I've met ace white girls. Up there for talent, looks. The whole package. But it's never come down to anything. There's no way I could be out some place with a white girl and somebody shouts a race name at me. I'd feel stupid."

Eyes glazed, Lorna turns away. Pulls on her hair. Thick, African hair. Vacantly, she twists her fingers in it. "It's different from the outside."

"I'd never take the chance. Never!"

"Not if you love someone?"

"Love?"

"People go round imagining. They make things up. All sorts."

"I get called a black bastard, so I'm making stuff up?"

"Things happen," she sighs. "Like you say. I know, believe me. But there's none of that between my parents."

A smoke ring glides towards the door. Jimmy aims a lazy punch through it. Then checks the time. "Time for the night," he says. "A good blues band at the Jazz Café tonight."

Lorna doesn't budge. She weighs the size of the sitting room. Checks the visitor, the bookshelves and walls. Jimmy checks the time again.

"Let's have something to eat," she says. "I've got lamb. We can have it with aubergines and honey."

"Not hungry."

"A few minutes in the microwave."

"I don't want anything. Got to get some live music tonight."

"Bigots are all the same."

"Yeah, yeah."

"There's traffic both ways. A two-way street."

"So you say."

"In the early days my mother and father used to go out together. A lot. Sometimes they'd run into guys that shouted names. Bad names. Out of pure spite. The day she knew she was pregnant with me they went to a West Indian restaurant to celebrate. A summer evening. So happy. But there were cruel words at the restaurant. A crowd of young black guys. Taunting, non stop. My father tried to ignore it. My mother pretended it wasn't there, staying quiet, but aching. The sheer spite. Jostling. To play safe, they left. But not before their mini-van got clobbered. Bricks and kicks rained down on that little van. The side caved in. They told us the whole thing. Every now and then we talk about it."

"That's your two-way street?"

"How many examples d'you want?"

"One car the other side of the road is *not* a gridlock."

"The guy I was with for four years," Lorna sighs, "he got wordy to my mother last year. A locks guy. Born in England. Talked Jamaican all day. Raw, like he was born there. *Big* racial hang-up. Unbelievable. Thing is, his parents. They're both mixed-blood Jamaicans. But he had a racial hang-up over my father. I was sure it would pass. But one day he went berserk. It was at my mother. A word storm. I mean, terrible. Used every Jamaican cuss-word under the sun. All at my mother."

"What was the problem?"

"He was rubbish. I thought 'Jesus, what a mistake this is!' And that was it, basically."

"Lots of black guys think like your boyfriend."

"*Ex*-boyfriend!"

"Your ex."

"Thank you."

"Guys feel protective about women of their race. It's natural."

"You?"

"It's what's out there. White guys, black guys. The bottom line."

"What're you getting at?"

"When I was door canvassing I met people with their guard down. Only a few, but nice people."

"White?"

"Serious white folk. No hypocrite crap. Funny enough, most of them were women. But if their blokes were ever in the house, having dinner, then watch out! When they realize their woman's on the doorstep with a black man, they drop the plate, run to the front door. World-class sprint. You'd have to see it. Guys with food slopping round their mouth. And all I'm doing is talking double-glazing!"

"So?"

"So that's what's out there."

"So?"

"So don't get upset if black guys feel the same way."

"Got it all worked out, haven't you!"

"Let's drop it."

"Why, afraid you might say something?"

"Lorna," Jimmy says, glaring at the time, "I'm going. It's late."

"Getting sensitive again?"

"Not sensitive. Disappointed."

"*Disappointed*?"

"Yeah! You think black guys shouldn't have their own balls."

"What?"

"Tebbit draws his line in the sand. But black guys can't like who they like, mustn't hate who they hate."

"My brother's in a coma because he's black!"

"Then what d'you want from me?"

Suddenly, like caught in headlights, she wonders. Gets herself from the look in his eyes. Then turns away. Slopes across the room. And holds the curtains like a friend. The thick drapes part. And she peers out into night. Jimmy checks the time.

"In one second," she says, "tears can well up in someone's eyes."

"In one second, the Hiroshima bomb killed a hundred thousand."

"If it had been London, there'd have been more junk. Lots more. But the same tears."

"Yeah."

"Nasty. The way things pan out. Some things."

"What're you looking for?"

"Don't know what I'd do if anything happened to Justin."

"With everything I have, I wish him back to your family."

"Can you stay ten minutes? Ten more minutes. Stay for five?"

Jimmy ambles over to the skydivers on the wall. Looks them up and down. Then moves to the hall. "Let's do that nightclub," he says. "Up for it?"

Lorna is first to the front door. Looking back, tugging her overcoat.

# 73

They were pleased in Germany. The music director sent an email, said thanks. Jimmy definitely got a better sense of the professional music scene there. His mother phones.

"How was it?"

"Great to get away. From telesales, the lot."

"Germany is a strange move."

"No it wasn't! It was the full deal. All day yesterday it was me leading a jazz band. Dusseldorf. Seriously talented. Most were via classical. The money wasn't bad, but the buzz was ace."

"Next thing you'll want to live there!"

"No! I'm not swapping black bastard for whatever it is in German."

"Where did you pluck Germany from, anyway?"

"Geraldine. A woman I work with."

"Anything between the two of you?"

"Nah! The gig happened because her mother's from Germany. It's a one-off place, Dusseldorf. Industrial looking, but calm. True what they say about Germans. The discipline, order. Bach couldn't have come from any place else."

"You went alone?"

"Yeah. I was going to invite Lorna but changed my mind."

"Lorna?"

"Somebody I get on with. We're circling round each other."

"Not another one!"

"I'm still looking."

"Like father, like son."

"I *will* settle down."

"Yeah, right. What else did you get up to?"

"The first thing was a boat. A rowboat. Breathe some air, not swabs. Then check sunset. Rowed up the Rhine. A great evening. I could've forgotten, you know, rowed off into the night. The boat-keep asked me 'Where from?' I said 'Jamaica, out of England.' He knew enough English to talk about the island, white Jamaicans of German extraction. Blue eyed Jamaicans with roots in Germany, he said. But it was the Rhine. Mystic. Water, but not water. No sense of old-time spirits there to greet. Absolutely no shades to force somebody below those dark waters to drown."

"You *are* the son I used to slap. But slow down, promise?"

# 74

Only standing-room in the pub. This Sunday afternoon the crush is bigger than usual. More than just one thing to celebrate.

Lorna waves her glass. "Happy birthday! Happy twenty-five!"

Jimmy's twenty-five today. Boozed. Bleary-eyed. Clinking glasses, malt whisky to brandy. "Twenty-five is scary."

"Twenty-five is great!"

"A year, and I'm way up the road all of a sudden."

"Compose anything to celebrate?"

"Nah. It would be too self-conscious."

"Painters paint themselves."

"Can't see why they bother. Hey, let's get another round."

"What've you got against painters?"

"Only the self-portrait ones! You should be looking far as possible. What's out there, it's too far to be looking at yourself all day."

Lorna grins. "What's it like to compose? What's it compare to?"

"How I do it?"

"Yeah."

"I can only talk for me."

"Talk to me!"

The barman plays part-time in a folk band. And all the time in the bar, sots round him. He wants to quit pulling pints. Wants to gig in the big time. And wouldn't mind tweaking Lorna.

Jimmy nods. "Well," he says, "let's see. Composing, right?"

"Yeah."

"How I do it?"

"Yes!"

"Hard to say. Don't know how it gets going. For me it starts with something nagging. Really bugging. It's kind of in your head, but not there. A bit like somebody passing in a car and they wave, but you don't get to see who and so you spend all day figuring it out. Then you get a phone call, and you're too embarrassed. Because you didn't think of them at all. Disappointed, even. Make sense?"

"Not sure."

"Brandy whispers in your eyes," Jimmy says.

"Tell me what's going on."

The barman gets it. Sees clues. That Lorna's a woman, not a sister worrying over a comatose brother. He sees a great looking woman. But Jimmy's still in soft-focus about her. Still finding talk where today talk should be the last thing to find.

"I'm a servant to music."

She laughs. "Don't know how somebody can even compose at all."

"Sometimes it comes out of nowhere."

"What about when it gets ropey?"

"Then, it's like a soloist grabbing a theme. Improvise. Gotta have a theme. Miles Davis, he's a good place to start. Musos got to the studio and every time Miles only handed out a theme. Theme on bits of paper, no bigger than a Rizla. Great players say that about him, the likes of Wayne Shorter, John McLaughlin."

"Miles Davis was 'Take this, now show me!' That it?"

"No! It was 'What can *we* do with this?' Huge difference!"

"Got it."

"Hey, this whisky's bland. How's the brandy?"

"I've had better."

"One more round?"

"Well, OK. Let's end on doubles."

Next to Lorna, a man and woman talk of Martian poetry. Laugh, mention Craig Raine. It was Craig who delivered, the woman says; the pages of a book fluttering as it falls looked like a bird swooping from Mars. The man plans to wrap an article on Martian poetry.

Jimmy turns to Lorna. "Stars only twinkle on earth. The atmosphere."

"What?"

"Astronauts get black sky. Stars don't twinkle up there."

"Yeah, yeah."

"Am I drunk?"

"Sober as beer!"

"Atmosphere on earth bugs your eyes. That's what twinkles are."

Head shaking, she tugs his sleeve. "Let's get away from here."

"Yeah."

"Hungry?"

"Eat a rhino."

"My place?"

# 75

Rain this morning. All morning. And pigeons fitful and grey. They coo from a window ledge

"Jimmy?" Geraldine pants. "Been trying to get you. Were you out, or just not answering the phone?"

"Right now, I wouldn't swap pigeon songs for a nightingale's."

"You're having me on!"

"No," he says, stepping reluctantly to the window from the cold flat; the gaze in the windowpane looks like it knows. "I'm serious. I was watching pigeons on my window ledge."

"What the fuck for?"

"Pigeons were on the sill. Two love birds. Didn't want to scare them off, so I couldn't move."

"You didn't answer the phone because you might upset *pigeons*?"

"They can navigate like a satellite."

"So what?"

"They don't have racial hang-ups."

"You OK?"

"Pigeons are seriously smart."

"Stop being daft!"

"Well, yeah. OK," he laughs. "How's tricks?"

"Me? I called to check on you, how the music's going. Feedback from Dusseldorf. You're some kind of new mind there."

"Seriously?"

"Yeah, they rate you. Can't wait to make you an offer. Don't say I told you, but there's talk of a permanent post."

"Teaching?"

"Teaching, arranging. Take your pick."

"Some of the most talented folk I've ever met. I mean, in my whole life. Quick off the mark. Could learn from them as much as them from me."

"But?"

"I can't commit. You know that. It'd be two, three years."

"Think about it!"

"Who knows where I'll be in two years. Might even be in South Africa."

"Agnes?"

"Could be."

# 76

All evening a child's smile on Lorna's face. Innocent. Jimmy listens as she talks. The way she talks of family. The Barbados part. And the white folk in Northumberland, the Stanley family on holidays. Every year they stay with the white grandparents, folk living in their own cottage that's over 400 hundred years old. Festivals on the 4th of July up there, bonfires on the green, dancing, bagpipes. And the potato & onion cakes their grandmother makes. Treks in the dales.

Nobody says boo to the Stanleys. Never a racial. Ever. Alan's sixteen stone and way over six foot, a fireman, ex-para, not the sort to play games, not if his family get messed with. Maybe things would be not so good if Alan was black and Bernice white; a white mother could live her life getting called the worst names in England.

The Stanley family was planning new photos at Hadrian's Wall. But not without Justin. No going north this summer.

Lorna rounds the coffee pot. "Black or white?"

Jimmy frowns. "Doesn't matter."

"Something on your mind?"

"Think I can't talk my mind?"

"Got something to say, say it!"

"I was going to ask a question."

"Want us to get married?" she laughs.

"How did all this happen?"

"What d'you mean?"

Jimmy tries again. "How did your parents meet?"

Lorna's eyes roll. "Well," she sighs, "are you ready for this?"

"Comfortable in my chair."

"Once upon a time there was a mummy bear, and a daddy bear, and, no, didn't I tell you this already?"

"Tell me again."

"One day, this big Geordie bloke swaggers in at the office where a young black woman works. A huge Viking. Motorbike gear. And, well, one year later I was born."

"One more thing. Remember that thunder at the zoo?"

"The day we met?"

"Yeah. That lightning, it was all sky. "

"Can't forget it."

"I spotted the blues in you. You move like a blues solo. The way you bounce. Yeah, it's like a flame."

"Are you proposing?"

"What did you get, going to Brixton?"

"That day Tyson was there?"

"Yeah. You grabbed sugarcane. Got near to Tyson. Then it started."

"What?"

"I think," he says, "you gaze into wishes. Get something called grace. Too much bible in your life."

"And you, what've you got?"

"There's serious stuff to deal with."

"Is this going to be about race? You *never* stop!"

"Let's talk about the weather then."

"Cyclones are cunning," she laughs.

"Are they?"

"I don't want to talk about race, OK?"

"Did you and your brother ever catch tadpoles?"

"What?"

"Race is out, so I thought of something more interesting."

"Thank you very much!"

"White folk define thanks."

"Oh, come on!"

"When did racism get solved?"

"You're being sensitive again."

"There's bozos out there," Jimmy says. "Idiots."

"I know."

"Some days you can't win the fight."

"*This* fight can be won. There's a new mood. Live and let live."

"I don't get that."

"Look again!"

"What about behind them the scenes?"

"Like who?"

"White folk, expecting us to be grateful for Wilberforce."

"Clarkson," she says. "It was Thomas Clarkson. Wilberforce was only the fag end."

"It could have been another fifty years, without him."

"He was a racist."

"*What*?"

"Wilberforce. He thought blacks could only be trained as servants."

"Where did you read that?"

"Check those," she says, nodding at the bookshelf.

"I hate history!"

"Clarkson. Granville Sharp. They were the real abolitionists."

"What about runaway slaves? They wiped out Napoleon's outfit in Haiti. And there's Maroons in Jamaica"

"Yes. But give Clarkson a chance."

"Those white boys, they were only off-loading guilt about Africa."

"Steady on!"

"Francis Drake was part of the charade."

"What?"

"Drake was a slave-trader. A slave merchant."

"You sure?"

"You didn't know?"

"Only stuff you learn at school. A *slaver*?"

"Butchered black slaves. Raped them. Stole their soul. Then gave England a piece of the blood pie."

"That was a long time ago, anyway. Not the England I know."

"You love this place."

"I do! I do! But not a blind love."

"I've just opened Mandela's book," Jimmy says, "at random. And look! He talks about being a slave in his own country, 'having no strength, no power, no control over our destiny in the land of our birth.' *That* was the 20th century."

"Trust you to find it!"

"When did you ever cut cane, pick cotton all day?"

"Try this book," she says. "It's by a freed slave, Olaudah Equiano. I think he gets past flag waving."

"Black people did *not* grab Africa with a flag."

"Slavery is over!"

"Folk still getting called wogs, coons, black bastards?"

"Bigots! It's all bigots."

"They snatched people into slavery, built estates from the profits, preached from the bible."

"Steady on!"

"They lied!"

"There were certainly a few who, you know, were evil."

"Lied! Lied, lied! Said it was some god told them to civilize Africa."

"You're going too far."

"Where's there to go?" Jimmy says.

"It's inside. The journey's inside us. All of us."

"Tonight, a moonbeam's on a baby in Africa. That child is right next to one crying from hunger. Their village will bake in morning sun. And their mother go to the river."

"Else when," Lorna whispers. "Live, and forgive."

Jimmy stands beside the skydiver pictures on the wall. Trying to keep calm. He blanks the room. Then stares at Justin. Wants air. But turns to Lorna. "I'm thinking of leaving."

"England?"

"Yeah."

"Leaving, as in *leaving*?"

200

"Yes. Give some place else a try."

"What's brought that on?"

"I've had enough. My old man thought by now it'd be better. Not great, but better. Time to move on."

"Where would you go?"

"Brazil."

"And do what?"

"Or Africa. No fuss."

"Africa?"

"Yes."

"Sell mobile phones?"

"I'd head for a village. Learn village music. Or the desert, learn about camels and donkeys, trade figs and dates."

"You'd be so out of your depth!"

"Don't know where my ancestors are from in Africa."

"Get a DNA test."

"Yeah. But I like the desert."

"You and your donkey in the Sahara?" Lorna laughs.

"The desert is spiritual. I was meant to be a nomad."

"Dream on!"

"There's Jamaica. America."

"No race problems in America?"

"Look, they only want uncle toms here. No disrespect to your old man, but it's people like him in the way."

"How does my father get into this?"

"I better borrow your sellotape, put some on my mouth."

"Keep my father out of it!"

"At night, the desert shrugs. That cold Sahara repairs arid air. The old camel routes turn modern road. But more than 7000 years back, rivers and cattle were there. Yeah, rivers where the Sahara is today."

"Tell you what," Lorna sighs, "it could be you, the lions and me leaving together."

"This is not some game."

"But you want me to approve."

"I don't care what you do!"

"Race relations *can* work."

"That's in the bible?"

"You can't just walk away!"

"Think I wouldn't understand if a lion speaks to me?"

"I'm not a mystic."

"But you read the bible."

"Look, what have you got against me? My faith isn't a lie."

"The bible talks about a merciful boss man."

"God?"

"Yeah. He wanted Abraham to prove his faith, so asked him to slay his son. That means he didn't know it all. Because he'd have known what Abraham would do. Or he was a theatre-director god, moving Abraham round like stage putty."

"Is this a Jimmy sermon?"

"Yeah."

"Can we do it some other time?"

"Get your diary!"

"By the way," she says, "you promised to tell where your name comes from. Jimmy-Lines, eh?"

"My name's my name."

"Tut, tut. Getting defensive again."

On the stereo, Coltrane cuts through smoky air. Lorna got the CD as a gift but she's into his music anyway.

"Stephen Hawking listens to John Coltrane," Jimmy says.

"Good for him!"

"He talks about this machine, a huge thing. It could speed particles to grand unification."

"Stop!"

"It was my grandmother."

"What?"

"My name, got it from my grandmother. A map fell out a dictionary. It was covered in lines. Neat lines my old man had drawn. My grandmother was over here visiting, and she said 'Nathan, you have to call this boy Lines.' So they called me that. For all of five minutes. But my mother said it should be Hendrix."

Lorna covers her mouth, and laughs. "Hendrix Dell?"

"Sort of."

"What's she like?"

"My mother's ace."

"What about your grandmother?"

"She had a big thing for Miles Davis. But the map was so mystic. My old man just let the whole thing ride."

"You get jazz from your grandmother?"

"More or less. My old man was a world class trumpet player. Still is. All he got was duff gigs. When I went to Jamaica my granny grabbed hold of me, looks me in the eye and comes out with 'Go with jazz, boy, and women will look for you.' Stunning!"

"She play?"

"She's dead. She used to whistle."

Lorna gets Jimmy now, watching him gaze to a longtime. "Are you Jimmy, or Jimmy-Lines?"

"They all call me Jimmy."

"Jimmy-Lines is definitely on your birth certificate?"

"Yeah. But it could have been Moses."

"Moses?"

"What a pig that would've been!"

Lorna wants to laugh. Giggling, she steps back. Giggling silly in her hands already. "Moses? They were going to call you *Moses?*"

Jimmy must lie. Tagging with that bible name could get too dizzy. "Moses, as in Ed Moses."

"Who?"

"You don't know who Ed Moses was?"

"Don't think so."

"Athlete. Gold medals every time."

"Oh, him!"

"You were thinking Moses of the bible?"

"The only one I know. Ten commandments, and all that."

"*My* name would have been down to Ed Moses."

"Got a ring to it, hasn't it? Moses of the Nile."

"One day I'll check that great river."

"Well, Moses," she laughs, "if you want to leave England, guess what? The English Channel isn't too far from here. Handy bit of water. You can let me watch. Let's see you wave your wand, you know, like you did at the Red Sea!"

## 77

Geraldine scowls. "Should be no such place as a salesroom!"

"It drives me mad," Jimmy says, "how artificial this is."

"Nothing in the world like it. Nothing!"

"Yeah. But this is where it happens."

"Some people shouldn't be here. No place to hide if not selling."

"Great weather in the top-man spot."

"That's why he's a gambler. The rest of us often get drought."

"The hard part is there's some place far from this where a whole tribe withers. Tropical folk, not pulling rain by crying."

"Gamblers rule the world."

"I could never bet it all. He's something else."

"Some days he forgets money. Listens to Chopin on his Walkman."

"At least he's got taste. Chopin, as far down the road as it gets."

"I'm sick of salesroom talk. Chit-chat, holiday spots or murky sex."

"Ever notice how when anybody gets back they always say England is beautiful?"

A big poster in the salesroom. A whole wall to itself. Everybody turns to it for relief. Even recruits; the minute they get here, new people go up to it. Everybody agrees: the picture's like something from a Beatles' song, like maybe from Norwegian Wood. Some days Colette hums that tune in the salesroom. She made the poster from a photo Geraldine brought one day. Trees stroll in it. On overcast days that poster is like floodlight shimmer, light dropping down to patrol shadows; tree drama with light wanting to out-fox shadows. And the whole scene from the bottom of Geraldine's garden.

On bad days, days when selling is just not happening, Jimmy switches off. Money down the phone but he can vision things in the poster: some days it's women, the type that walk the well-kept lawn beside the trees. Beautiful women. Beautiful, watching swans nudge the moon's shadow in the lake. Smart women. Talking of desire. Or talking of what could have lead anyone to suppose all swans white.

Some days music wells up. Notes, wanting to get united. Being alone at the keyboard would be the thing. But not to fool with white keys alone, like a lake strewn with white swans only. Some days are pure polychrome. But the salesroom. Never the place to count swans. Money the thing. And something else. Jimmy's hooked to the game. Hooked to play invisible on the phone. While there's money to be made that can buy a year to compose, it's the phone game for him. And by the time telesales gets camera-to-camera feed, he'll be a world away.

# 78

Accountant, engineer, lawyer, fund manager; all types to sell to. And all the time they're good as blind, never seeing Jimmy. Till one day.

Seven weeks into the stint at telesales, a weird day. Windows of the salesroom got cleaned this morning. Burnished bright. He was on the line to somebody in St Albans one whole hour today. Trying the extra mile for a sale. The man's son died in a car crash. And every time Jimmy got near to close the deal, the man mentioned his dead son. No matter what was said, the man talked grief down the line. He could use a new office suite, but talked grief. Thirty grand of furnishing he could buy, but the man wanted to talk of loss. And all the while the whine of a stacker-truck was going by. A stacker-truck whining down the line. Bad vibes in that St Albans voice; a non-believer, but he goes to church now. Jimmy tried to steer the call, to target the office-suite. This punter could spend a whole warehouse if somebody would listen.

The day the salesroom glass was burnished, the day of the call to the St Albans man, Jimmy got a brand new outlook. The man's son was driving back from London one night but swerved in the dark. He was trying to avoid somebody at the roadside but swerved straight to a ditch. Killed on the spot. Only dankest grief. Crying out loud. Even now, four years later, the St Albans man still gets the same nightmare. A recurring nightmare of moths. Colossal, fetid moths, settling round a pool of urine. Jimmy no longer wants the sale. The story's too weird, nether. Backing down, he wished the man well. Said goodbye. And was just about to put down the phone when up came a weird report. The man's son had swerved to a ditch and died because of only one thing. If it had been a white person at the roadside his son would have seen him in time, but impossible to see black people in the dark.

Half past three. End of the road. Jimmy can't go on. Not at Homes. Colette saw the whole thing. Quietly, he gets all his personal things from the desk. This the last time to play invisible. Hand to jaw, Colette's watching him. He remembers how one day she bent over so he could see her bosom bloom.

When she's in the salesroom, she sits behind a glass screen. From a master phone she can listen in to anyone. And she'd tuned in to Jimmy talking to the St Albans man. The man was thinking white. It would have been easy to put the record straight, but Jimmy said zil. Fact after fact cried out not to get denied. Jimmy said nothing. Was hiding in the invisible overcoat.

Now Colette's inside his private head. But not as a woman alone with a man. What happened with the St Albans phonecall means she knows. It bothers him. Troubles him that a white woman knows, got a key. From now she can get straight to somebody of colour only trying to get by. All because he liked playing invisible down a phone line.

He rings her extension. "Get your kicks, listening?"

"Not kicks!" she says.

He hangs up. Then moves to the poster on the wall. One last time. A last look at the wall poster, last look at mystic light playing beech on the wall. Waves goodbye in the salesroom. Nobody understands.

Colette is in the corridor. Waiting. "How I get my kicks," she says, "is *my* business. And it isn't with a telephone!"

"Then why listen?"

"What?"

"Why'd you listen to my phonecall?"

"I run this place! It's not a party here. I told you that. What to expect. It's not about being pals. It's money! You make money, we make it. That means I listen in to what goes on in there. If that's what it takes, then that's what it takes!"

"How does that square with being a voyeur?"

"Who the hell do you think you are?"

"You didn't have to listen to everything!"

"No? Then tell me who was acting the *wonderful* psychotherapist with that man. That poor, confused man. You knew there wasn't a deal, but you kept him going. That poor man!"

"I didn't want to hang up on the guy. That's why I let him go on. Wanted him to get it off his chest. But you! It's like you get energy from listening. I wouldn't want my money that way."

"You know," she says, head shaking, "you're a strange one. Never seen the likes of you. Nobody like you. You made seven grand in, what, six weeks? Now you want to kiss goodbye to fifty grand a year. Sixty grand."

Jimmy steps back. Wondering. Checking. Learning from Colette. Wanting to understand the salesroom boss, a millionaire white woman. Wondering why she explains herself to a young black guy in limbo. "Your earrings look like skateboards," he says. "Or like space anchors. Those hard bluish-white petals."

"What?"

"I'll get by."

"What will you do?"

"What did that St Albans guy hear?"

"How d'you mean?"

"Who did he think I was?"

"He heard a confident English voice. *Your* voice. Not colour."

"White is the default colour."

"England is multicoloured. Here and there. But most of us are white."

"That means it's not a black man's home."

206

"That doesn't follow."

"No?"

"No! You can't magic old attitudes away."

"Race isn't going any place. Not soon. It was in the salesroom all the time, but I blanked it."

"Salesroom talk? Braggers, spitting out their soothers!"

"It wasn't baby talk. Two guys in there always talked to exclude me. When talk turned to asylum seekers, or Britain with Europe, that was their big excuse, saying how Europe's the homeland of white people. Talking so I could hear."

"What sorts of things did they say?"

"One that got me the most was European."

"I don't understand."

"One guy said liberals who count blacks as European are the same nutters that look out their window and expect camels in the streets of London."

"*Who* said that rubbish?"

"I blanked them. But I won't grass them up."

Arms folded, looking him steady in the eyes, she says, "I'm trying to help you."

"I asked you to sort my life?"

"Weren't you supposed to give this a go? Your best shot? You need the money. I know you do. *You* know you do. Walk from this and you won't get it somewhere else. You'll do gigs, of course you will. But that'll be sweet goodbye to the music in your heart. Want that?"

Colette was always good to Jimmy. Times she went out of her way to help. She knows what it takes to be a music one. But that phonecall to St Albans, that's too much. One phonecall. His hand extends for goodbye.

"Appreciate it, what you've done for me."

"Funny way of showing it!"

"That money I made here," he says, "it'll take care of business."

"For a while."

"It was never going to be forever. The way I want it."

Now a new idea. Suddenly, a stark thought. He wonders what if it was not Colette. What if it had been the camel-fanciers that listened to the St Albans call. No going back to the salesroom, but it would be great to ask two guys there if they fancy camels by the street-load, or just one at a time. Jimmy will miss the salesroom. That poster on the wall, the mystic stretch of trees.

"All right," Colette says. "OK. I get it. I know where you're coming from. Want to be by yourself, your music. Ah! Wish my life was that cut and dry."

"You don't look too footloose."

She sighs, head shakes. "I'd better get back in there. Will you be at the theatre next month? Still got the ticket? The music is by a friend. I told him all about you. Come."

# 79

"Boy!" Lorna whoops down the line. "Listen to this!"

Jimmy grabs another malt swig. On the line, Bessie Smith crooning St Louis Blues. Bad regret. A woman alone, singing low, '*I hate to see, de evenin' sun go down. Hate to see, de evenin' sun go down..*'.

"Nice, isn't?" she says, switching the music off.

"I play it all the time. A great Handy tune. This version as good as any."

"What're you doing?"

"Why, you inviting me over?"

"Well, I could do with a blues concert tonight."

"Me and you playing it?"

"Concert for two, eh?"

"Yeah."

"What're you slurping? You drunk?"

Staggering to sit, Jimmy sings, "*Oh, how we danced on the night we were wed*, we *danced and we danced, though a word wasn't said.*"

"What's that?"

"Romanian folk song. Slapped around by Americans."

"You *are* drunk!"

"Bessie Smith was an old bruiser."

"What?"

"Sing for me," Jimmy mumbles.

"I can't sing."

"Then mime."

"Mime, on the phone? You're definitely boozed."

"Sing something."

Humming to St Louis Blues, Lorna hums low. And laughs. Humming the blues and laughing; a good sign, Jimmy thinks.

"Any news of Justin?" he says.

"Same as yesterday."

"What's the hospital up to?"

"They don't know."

"What's the faith healer say?"

"She's an idiot. Potions. God knows what! Lies."

"Want me to come round?"

"You're too drunk to drive. And I'd better stay by the phone."

"Yeah."

# 80

"An English bishop mocked two overseas bishops. It was on the radio this morning."

"Jimmy," his mother says, "you gave up religion, remember?"

"Say again? Your mobile's crackling."

"Why listen to religious fairytales?"

"Some of it was deep. Yeah. The guy doing the mocking was because the other bishops ordained priests by blowing breath on them. One guy laughed, said 'Lazarus gave you life!' Funny, eh!"

"Having second thoughts?"

"Religion? Nah! It's only noise in a cave."

"You OK for money?"

"For six months. A year."

"So, what's the problem?"

"Since I left Homes, I'm still up and down."

"What the hell got into you? That St Albans man should've been told: 'Listen, I'm black.'"

"It was a weird day. Weirdest phonecall."

"You stayed quiet because of the kick, didn't you! It was the kick. You got a kick out of passing for white on the phone."

"First time I've denied myself. I mean, deliberately."

"And the last!"

"A white face compared to a black face in headlights, like on a dark St Albans night near a ditch."

"Simple as that?"

"Yeah. But there's Colette. Why'd she listen so long?"

"Ask her."

"She used to look out for me."

"Look, you played invisible at Homes. But sick now for trying it!"

"It's like somebody getting a stroke, losing the use of my arm or leg. Or seeing right from wrong, but can't talk it. Like wanting to witness the door but only saying 'Close the window after you.' Weird feeling. Been with me days."

"Read your book, that one by the wheelchair man."

"Hawking. Yeah, I was checking it out when you rang. I can't get over how stars die. Why they die. But I'm no sucker for star dust."

"Good. So, let's hear you repeat after me: 'Listen, I'm black.'"

"Yes."

# 81

"I'm at Clapham Junction," Geraldine says. "Rain. It's *so* scatty here. Lots of people! Plastic raincoats. All colours. And big umbrellas. So many people, capering through wet junction roads."

Jimmy laughs. "Like wildebeest on the move?"

"Still thinking like a predator? Somebody should paint this."

"Lions can't paint."

"Funny, ha! ha!"

"Terrible, I know. Hey, how's tricks?"

"Great sale this morning. A reception suite."

"You're out shopping?"

"Why not!"

"Buy me anything?"

"You really *are* in a slick mood. Look, I must dash. Got to get home. Quite a hike. A taxi, jump on a train."

"Why the rush?"

"The theatre tonight, remember?"

"Ah! Colette's co-production thing. You going?"

"Of course. And you mister! No more doldrums for you today. Get yourself out of that flat. See you later at The Chair!"

Colette was always good to Jimmy. So seeing her again could do it. Say thanks, face to face. Or don't bother, but write a thank-you letter. But something strange. Not possible before the St Albans call. Turning from the rain he knows new risk. Not to do with other folk. But inside, knotted.

Being above race was kind of natural to Colette. The salesroom kills race-talk when she's around. But now she owns a key to private Jimmy. A key she can never give back. Nothing like a door key; not like changing the lock or get the key back before they copy it. Colette saw him concealed. Now she knows.

Seeing her again might answer it. He'll know from her eyes, know if the secret's safe. Or maybe she's already talked it, laughed about it over a lager somewhere. Maybe she's like the white couple that adopted a black child and one day went to the bathroom and the child was scrubbing and scrubbing itself with bleach. Jimmy must see this woman. Get the angle of slant. Those eyes will tell. The theatre ticket trips like a writ. He wonders. Driving rain starts. All over again.

# 82

Lavender. The new scent of it wafts through the foyer. A fresh trace, like a smile in the small chatty place. And women. Some wishing for candlelight. Some with no man beside them, looking like they're ready to play cards or get sneaked from a market.

"Jimmy!" Colette yelps. "So, you got here! You look fit. A bit hungry, perhaps. Yes. But let me stop. This is the guy I told you about. Kevin, meet Jimmy."

Geraldine doesn't know Kevin. Lavender's what she wears tonight. Lavender is Geraldine's bling. After a shower, lavender. Colette takes her arm and moves her away. And in one minute Jimmy knows this is the place to be. The foyer of The Chair is right-side emotion. Not a place to pretend. Kevin composed the music for the play and, as they talk, Jimmy sees the talent. Colette was right; this guy is one of the chosen. Big talent. Kevin hates the airwaves. Hates risk-free music that plays, flat-foot tunes, moron harmonies. He's forty three. Last year he made the shortlist for the British Composer Awards. But walked away, asked to be excluded from the chase.

This is a safe place. Nobody wears day-glo here. Respect in the air. Somebody says gypsies are it. And if it wasn't for the start of the show, two composers would talk and talk. They swap phone numbers, agree to get round a piano one day.

Snug between Colette and Geraldine, Jimmy checks out the play. And tries to blank lavender from one cozy near. But a secret. Something night-time. In the dimmed theatre light, a low laughing from Colette. Laughing low, thanking some secret thing. On stage a gypsy. A gypsy girl plays with light; an actress being a gypsy, playing with light, doing the gypsy. In the dimmed light she looks like Colette maybe used to look at nineteen. But the dance. It's the dance. The way the girl moves. Not a mere dance. More like floating over pagan lands. Colette wants to be the girl. Wants to be on stage. Her secret tonight. She'd understudy the gypsy, knowing the girl's part by heart, every gypsy move, miming to a polychrome gypsy line. The girl is a tart. And in Colette, something wants to be the gypsy girl tart.

As she quits the stage, Jimmy mimes, saying, 'Gypsy, do it tonight.' But he knows. This is a fairytale. Like a spiteful hand that beckons, this place is where applause can happen by a single hand only.

The stage is empty now. Only a sandscape there. Sand dimmed low. A place where weather gets punished by gypsy dance as violins play.

In the first act, Geraldine's arm was in Jimmy's. For a while her head sloped to his shoulder. Comforting, like a sister. He should've had a sister. Guys with sisters have better lives, they understand women better; or so his mother says. He was paying Geraldine no mind, but something close, tempting. Longing. He'd never thought of her that way. But the evening can't disguise one simple: he wonders what it would be like; not as pals for the evening, but for the night. The lights go down for the second act.

Geraldine's a married woman. But asunder from her man. Tonight she's spliced by lavender, fondling her wedding ring. Jimmy blinks. Confused by the woman's hand. It slides over the ring finger, back and to, again, again, deliberate, tight. Suddenly she tugs. Grabs him by the shoulder. Looks him in the eye. He knows. She can't forget the ring. Not even for a night. Must keep the faith. Even the ring remembers.

The theatre light drops a notch. The same enchantment, but a smaller place now. The gypsy girl is heartless. Her eyes take no prisoners. Eyes seeing the moon as simple. Sunflowers wouldn't bloom when she steps.

Colette, Jimmy, Geraldine. Not part of the cast here. But part of something. Awkward and quiet. Leaving their seat. Geraldine doesn't look at him. Not once. He avoids her eyes anyway. The foyer seems confining. Time to go. Or maybe get a quick drink then grab a cab.

"What a good idea!" Colette says. "Lets *all* go for a drink. There's a lovely little spot. Two minutes from here."

Not Geraldine. She must catch a train. With a strict goodnight, the lavender woman goes off alone into the night. Now, Jimmy's alone with Colette. In nervy night air, with a lavender trail disappearing, he's got nothing to say. So lights a smoke. Looks over what Colette wears, comparing the dress to suits she wears at the office. Her dark eyes won't go away. Her eyes compel like a gypsy gaze. He wonders how a woman way past 35 can understudy a girl 19.

"You're not really up for a drink, are you?" she says, sleepy-eyed.

"I don't usually drink on rainy days."

"What's the matter?"

He shrugs. Feels awkward. "Have you, er, got a clothesline in your back garden?"

Colette lights a smoke. Smiles. Nighttime swings in the folds of her dress. A cool aqua weave, the shimmy of the dress swerves like waves. Shimmying like a jazz score.

# 83

"That lobster's still alive!" he says.

Red wine served. The restaurant light is low. Just right, and close. Every table aware of how to keep chats private.

Colette laughs. "Jimmy, don't be silly."

"Then how come one leg move?"

"The lobster *is* dead. Lobster muscles remember, that's all."

"It longs for the sea. No way I can eat any!"

"Look" she says, "everything comes from the sea. Yes, at one time or another. And, you know, a lobster doesn't have a lot of brains to start with."

"No lobster for me."

She pours wine. But only half a glass at a time. "The lighting is so nice here. Mmm, nice and low. So restful."

"If it was any lower I wouldn't have seen this lobster twitch."

"You're *so* sensitive."

In the nighttime light, dimmed and calm, Jimmy could reach out and touch this woman; run a finger across her face. She's a woman, not the boss tonight. Thirteen years between them. A single mother, millionaire woman, a doer.

At the last half-glass each of this easy wine, she pours hers back in the bottle. Back to the glass. Then orders a new bottle from the waiter. Streetlights flicker. An hour goes by.

"I'm surprised," he says. "Can't get how easy it is, talking with you. We've even talked politics."

"But the best part is music. Love hearing you talk about Ellington."

"Folk should understand him. Ellington connects to them. And he played mean piano. Some days he could out-Monk even Monk. Yeah, and he scored natural feelings."

"I like it here," she says. "Mmm!"

Jimmy hums the melody to Mood Indigo. Her fingers tap. Then he segues to Sophisticated Lady.

"Yes!" she says.

"Want some more?"

"Yeah, more of the same."

"Well, this is Cotton Tail," he says. Hums, fingers clicking.

"Mmm, yes!"

"Great if I could hire a coach. Take the folk here through Brixton."

"*What*?"

"They'd get a better feel."

"For what?"

214

"I'm one black man that's never been to Brixton. Could be the likes of a Cotton Club there already. A young Ellington. Yeah, a place waiting to extend."

"I'm a blue woman tonight," Colette says, talking into the wine glass.

"Solomon was a king with a mile of women."

"So what?"

"Some guys have all the luck!"

"Think you could handle a house load of women?"

"I'd give it a try. Any time!"

"I wish," she says, "you were more my kind of age."

"The sun's got five billion more years to burn. Burn bright, then zap!"

"Is this your party trick?"

"How d'you mean?"

"I don't need stars, OK?"

Jimmy and Colette talk and talk. But never about the St Albans man. Maybe it's the lighting, discreet light, but chatty folk at other tables seem right. One couple mentions TV, they like the Antiques Roadshow, saying how unmissable it is, better than church on Sundays, yes, more spiritual, because some new adventure's always up the road, and that's only because the road winds and never ends. Colette thinks they're gormless.

The waiter is a part-timer here. By day, a postgrad. He's still hooked on Star Trek tapes. The first series. But he never wore the Captain Kirk suit handed down by his dad, and lost the ears for Spock. Star Trek made him choose physics. Wiping the water jug, he says there's more to water than smooth transparency. Water's quicker than even thoughts, he says. If you magnify it then you get a whole  new ballgame. Yeah, ballgame. Because what's way down the microscope are things like footballs. They're moving all the time. And that's not all. Because the whole show is made up of particles, tiny stuff, beautiful and small, attracting when close but repelling if pushed too close.

"You and that waiter, you're so alike," Colette murmurs.

"Your eyes are dark," Jimmy says.

"What?"

"I can't believe how dark your eyes are."

"You like my eyes?"

"Yeah. Darkest eyes in a white face. Except for gypsy white."

Eyes narrowed, she takes one last sip of water. "Now what?"

Squatting on double yellow lines, the Maserati is rose-red in night light. She hands him the keys. His first time ever in a Maserati, let alone getting to drive one. She curls in the passenger seat and, through every one of ten speakers, Roy Orbison laments on Blue Bayou. Her eyes close. Jimmy wonders what if the guys at the office could see her now; if the camel-fanciers could see Colette in the passenger seat of her own car with him at the wheel.

Criminal. The only word for the crazed horses in this engine, he thinks. But as it grabs road the Maserati's balance is sure, wild horses reined by a wild friend. The bouquet of a woman hints at part perfume, part sweat. Then the scent of new leather. She doesn't speak. Her eyes gaze past the hard-raked windscreen into frangible night. And maybe if she talks, even one word, then Jimmy would skew.

The taste of red wine lingers. And in the car nothing that can get said. Red car threading night. Horses trained to race hard. Colette's like more than one woman, he thinks. One woman's easy enough; tonight she's like a top-20 song, laying into senses. That woman will remember the St Albans man. But the second woman! She's alone, somewhere like in a cold attic room with skylight to unloved outdoors; that woman's too scared of the sky to hold the image of a man hiding in a phone. She doesn't wear big earrings tonight.

"Want to take her for a spin, really let her go?" she says, stroking the dark dashboard loom. "Let's go for it. Let's do the M25!"

The car pulls up at traffic lights. Jimmy gazes at the earrings, small, discreet, frail turquoise laced in silver. But the wine. Her eyes are clear but anxious.

"Traffic lights are like the giver of a do," she says.

"Lights, unpacking gifts of traffic?"

"Mmm, something like that. These are like party lights. Lovely."

"And me driving your car with nothing to say. Not with words."

With women, guys in Jimmy's family are the hunter ace. It's a family joke: Nathan and his brothers bring down some of the greatest prey. But for about a year Jimmy's been trying to walk from that. Maybe this is down to Agnes. Or Donna, the gap in her front teeth when she smiles.

Gypsy eyed, Colette says, "What gives?"

"I was thinking how, you know, neat this car shifts."

"But?"

"That wine at the restaurant."

"What's the problem?"

"We might get pulled over, breathalysed."

"Poor little policeman!"

He turns the music off. Time to think. Decide. Strange, but now he can see. It's stupid to bother with a woman unless she can see. Slowing the car, he remembers the first visit to Jamaica. He was fourteen. Most days under the Jamaica sun it was listening to Thelonius Monk, or learning from Bud Powell tracks. The sea was turquoise. But the big thing was folk having blood from all over. Full blood black, and full Chinese, full Indian, white. Then the mix. Folk mixed from every race. And white girls born in Jamaica mostly moved in that same wait-state as black girls. Making time in a stride. Now Jimmy wants jazz in a woman. Weird, but the only thing with a white woman was that Jamaican white girl. She'd never been to England. She was with him a whole week, chatting, circling, finding out. Jimmy, born in England with a snapped Scouse accent, and the girl born in Jamaica talking a Jamaican brogue. Then one noon towards the end of the visit they walked hand in hand along the beach. And stopped at a quiet place.

Colette removes the earrings. The scent of sandalwood somewhere. A low scent, like from the clasp of sprites. The earrings rest in the cushion of her lap. They glow a grant of silver. Like fireflies. Jimmy saw fireflies flashing on a verandah one warm Jamaica night. Earrings looking like magic sand in the woman's lap. Maybe the Jamaican white girl's been to England by now. Her letters stopped after a year. And by now she could already have the two children she wanted. Colette had planned four or five.

"Cat got your tongue?" she says.

The car slows. Dawdles. Stops. "Look," he says, "I don't want to go for a tear-up on the M25."

"No?"

"Don't need speed."

"Fancy a smoke?"

He looks at the woman as hard as she at him. "I'd like to get indoors."

"Tired, are you?" she smiles.

"No. Not tired."

"Drunk? Had too much to drink?"

"Not drunk."

"Then, what?"

"My flat is too untidy."

"And?"

"We should find a hotel. A quiet place."

# 84

"You're not yourself," Geraldine claims, fretting down the line.

"We, er, went for a drink," Jimmy says, more asleep than awake.

"Ended up in bed?"

"It's a blur."

"Hypocrite!"

"What?"

"You called her a cannibal, gorging on the unemployed. Forgotten?"

"No."

"What happened?"

"Last night?" he groans, reaching for a smoke.

"Yes."

"What a night! You're not going to believe this. Nobody would."

First thing last night, was getting to a hotel. Then make sure. Check again. Every pocket, one more time. But no condom. Not one rubber. Mentioning that was bad, but he said it; turned to Colette and said they'd better go get a packet. But she was aching for the ladies' room. Squeezing his hand, she said she'd better book them in. So he was back in the car. Back to the night. Alone on the road with a lusting Maserati. Motoring nice and easy, dicing. Then backing off to check the rearview. And then something weird. Mystic. Freedom was never like this. Maybe it was the car. Few people can afford Colette's car. After a minute the emotion was something else. It was like when a jazz band hits the groove; a new groove saying 'Play it!' The car willed him to try. And the streets ad-libbing through the steering wheel. Then the moon! It was low slung, nothing like a satellite. Streetlights heavy as paperweights. With all that, a moment to think. Thinking about actors on stage. And the street so silent, bruised by wandering, no applause from the tarmac keep. And he knew that somewhere far, wild flowers would be crackling like fire, somewhere where fever talks to flesh and cinch with stars. But he was in a zip car, thinking of the owner, how by now she was taking a shower at the hotel. Sure seconds. Gunning scarlet to the car. Bad down. Gunning. Wanting to get this thing on. Then a quiet quarter mile. Easing back, going through light traffic, breezing. Then moving it. The car was slicing land when the carphone rang. Colette. Sultry, her voice said 'Hi, luv!' She said Mr & Mrs Core have booked into room 15. *Who*? Mr and Mrs Core. The car diced to lights. Like a wish, it gave back a late-night chemist. Still open; like maybe waiting just for one somebody. Jimmy the one. In one minute he owned a new silk packet. Blue glaciers on the attendant's face didn't matter. He was back into night with a grin, breezing the car; whatever the attendant was thinking, he wasn't going back to the hotel to watch Colette hang washing on an arctic clothesline.

The air was clean air. Traffic scant. Traffic was like two ships in a hundred miles of ocean. Afloat, he knew Colette was looking at the world-sized moon from a hotel window. Bang! The zebra crossing. One inch from the bonnet! How'd the car stop? Old man on the crossing. Face of a confused old man. Beacons flickering, hi-tech orange in the night, flickering in the old man's eye. Shaking, Jimmy climbed from the car. Tried to keep steady. The old man only shrugged. The shrug implied that what had nearly happened was enough said. Then without checking the road he moved away. Eventually, faded round a turning. Nobody ever pushed pottery in a wheelbarrow the way that old man walked. Nobody else was even a mile away. Jimmy gazed at the car. Hazard lights blaring, driver's door agape, the Maserati was like a tart in a red bout of frenzy. Still shaking, he was on the move again. Slow, not sure, wanting to hang back. Then thinking the woman. Surging a while. Wondering if Colette's the kind of woman with eyes open when getting claimed. The night was a low blue, diminished. That near-miss at the zebra crossing. That was too close. But now it was hotel time. Motoring the Maserati. Going to get into one fastidious lady owner. Then panic! Cold sweat. Weird. A sense of grass with evening cargo; grass supplying lions with zebras getting blinded by stars. Stop the car! Before, the Maserati was a wild cat. But that red car changed on the crossing. It was like a lioness; a lioness crouching on a fresh kill of zebra. That was no zebra-crossing. The car was a lioness tearing zebra meat apart. Then a weird thought. If a real accident instead of a near-miss at the crossing, the old man could be dead. Then the police. Instead of a quick Mr Core hurrying to consummate Mrs Core, the night would be a plexus of low moon. Jimmy was no Mr Core, would have to give police the facts; how come he was driving it. Black guys get it. They know police can be police or psychos with blood for dice: they'd see a bullet car and somebody driving in a skin overcoat. But the old man's face, he knew Jimmy was no Brixtonite gazing the moon. Then again. The man from St Albans: the moon could have been any place else the night his son died. The car phone rang. Colette. Jimmy wanted to talk, but lied. Said the car was out of petrol. Then lied again, saying the next move was to get to a station, get a can, get to the car, then back to the petrol station, then the hotel; forty minutes, he said, lying to the handset. Lying to Colette wasn't good. But something was happening. The instant she asked where he was, if he was lost, that was it. *The* it. Going back to that the hotel was a no. Do what? That hotel room was not the place. It was a room reeking from folk making do down the years; like theatre seats, for drama or knots. He was lost. But not how Colette would know. Not lost that a map could cure. The engine hummed. The tank was quarter full. But what had to happen next would need a full tank. The way ahead was Liverpool. Get from London. Go north. Laze night at the Mersey, watch it ebb and flow. The Mersey on such a night would be fish frightened of fire, like a prostitute moaning for air in moonlit tide. Breezing the motorway, the car was heading north. Gazing at joy. That car was a red lady pounce. One hour up the motorway, he wondered about Colette. The way she poured wine. Her silver earrings sparkled in her lap. Her scent lingering in the car. One more hour passed. She didn't call. Maybe she'd guessed. Because of the St Albans phonecall, the lady got something from Jimmy nobody else ever managed. Nobody white. And nothing he could say or she could ever say could blank that. She owns a piece of his private thoughts. Like a piece of art. And no physicals ever could change that. Motoring on. But suddenly changing his mind. No longer Liverpool. Thinking of how somebody whispered to the Mersey. How the water was cross. The water listened to a whisper but didn't reply. Only spit. Liverpool was a slave port three hundred years. And in one fairytale, Poseidon vomits on a shore. Jimmy turned back last night. Headed back to London. But where to go? Brixton? Walk Brixton at dawn? Lions at London Zoo would be pacing. And all the time Colette in that hotel, showered, wondering. He got there half past five in the morning. Scribbled a note. Then slipped the car keys and note under the door of room 15. Walked away. Walking faster and faster. Then a door opened. In the corridor, Colette called a name. She called the name again. Jimmy stopped. The carpet was like Velcro. She called his name again. But he didn't turn round. Next thing, she's standing face to face, note in hand, wounds in her eyes. She asked him; the point of the note, she said. Wooden, he heard himself say 'Only a loner would understand it.' After a minute of bleary talk they left. Walking away in out-of-body mode, apart, in steep estrangement. Nothing was clear. Like somebody witnessing their own fate in the death room. He decided to take the bus home. In the early morning air, Colette faded down the hill. Both knew. They knew a man and woman looking but seeing only from mirror shards; seeing a woman out of sight and a man wringing his hands in a complex overcoat. He was at the bus stop alone. Birds singing in the churchyard. Some women on the bus looked Turkish, the rest African. At every stop, one or two more. Ten African women on the bus after a few minutes; Africa staring at vacant streets and huddling in their own arms, going to morning cleaning or getting back. Woman after woman. Detached but lovely, and out to wash London toilets to get by. Key in the door, the 8th floor flat was like a safe. Colette got to her house and kicked off her shoes then checked her daughter. Colette is not the kind to have Grieg on tap, not the A Minor Piano Concerto. Not the kind to close eyes and listen for woods and fields. And yet. She always hums Norwegian Wood; a neat tune, but only stubble next to Grieg. Jimmy wondered if she'd keep the note or only gaze at the mirror. No place to hide. Then Mozart. He played the A minor Sonata. Quieter than any time before. Then built a spliff. Then willed it alight. It was 8 o'clock. Time to think, watch sunlight take control. He was nudging sleep at 9 o'clock when Geraldine phoned. Her sister-like voice chirped the line. She knows about last night. Sort of.

"Sorry," she whispers. "Didn't mean to wake you. Sorry."

"It's OK," he says. "Nice to run last night past you. Weird, wasn't it?"

"Why didn't you just tell her?"

"Tell her what?"

"What was in the note."

"I didn't want awkward questions."

"Like?"

"Like if I had a problem with my manhood."

"Your *manhood*? Haven't heard that one before!"

"The state I was in, I couldn't face Colette," he says. But must lie. "Couldn't face feminist wisecracks. Not so early in the morning."

"You poor thing!"

"I don't need patronizing, OK?"

"Those women are still out there. But I don't think Colette is one."

"Which women d'you mean?"

"Your pin-up girls," she says, giggling.

"Who?"

"Your blithe feminists."

"*Who*?"

"Your feminist pals. There's still a good few out there. All kitted-up for parties. Pretty balloons, this way!"

"I'm not in the mood," Jimmy groans. "Got to get my head round what happened. The *last* thing I need is stupid parties, balloons."

"Then stay right where you are!" she laughs. "Wouldn't want you at one of those feminist gigs. Not really. I hear they blow their balloons up by farting into them, so keep away!"

# 85

Nathan laughs. "Yes, Hendrix was in a Burberry overcoat."

Lorna's eyes beam. "What was he like?"

"Shy. It was September '66. In a Soho club. Having a quiet drink. One day after touching down in England. I was here a year."

"Anything like the stage diviner?"

"No, no, no, no, no. Shy guy. Shy. Just a guy having a quiet drink. Talking with Mitch Mitchell. Mitch had a head full of soul music, into people like Curtis Mayfield. I was the only other black guy there. Kind of strange, but Hendrix had unusual eyes. Nobody in England ever seen anything like him before. Not that hair, the funk clothes. It was that bad guitar, the dread beauty. Alien, but, you know, straightaway it clicked. Human blues. But from some place else. Harrowing. That guy played beautiful guitar. Humble eyes. Folk didn't get it. Glitter, glitter. Not Hendrix."

"You mean, they didn't let him *really* play."

"Young lady, that guy would have played blues like it was never going to get played again! Folk listen to a blues like Red House, think that is it. But that was just the start. There's people that listen to him playing All Along The Watchtower, and the wise ones get a clue, a place no guitar from here ever went. Before, or since. Wings to the beautiful place, eternal home. The jawbones of a donkey got used on All Along The Watchtower. Two jawbones, acoustic guitars. Man, even Bob Dylan did not know what was caged in his own song. Hendrix set it free. That guy was right-handed. But played leftie guitar. Always. A shy guy. Shy about singing. Folk just do not realize how shy. I mean, All Along The Watchtower got taped where Hendrix was behind a screen. In the studio, behind a screen. Must not get stared at."

"A genie, not wanting to get watched singing from the lamp?"

"Yes, yes. And it happened to that tall bloke. Terry Waite."

"*Who*?"

"That envoy guy, global envoy to the Archbishop of Canterbury. Waite was a hostage in Beirut. Five years. Get back, had to eat alone. Huge guy, six foot eight, but shy for food after five forfeit years."

"So," Lorna says, hope in her eyes, "is this the time to try it?"

"Sing it right, and I start your music lessons."

*"There must be some kind of way out of here, said the joker to the thief."*

# 86

Geraldine guessed. Today she got to Jimmy's flat. Arrived out the blue. And brought a taxi-load of shopping. The first thing was to throw her coat. Then set the place in order, corner to corner. Then said it.

"Time you moved on!"

"Been thinking about lions. Wish I was a Masai."

Her eyes roll. "Yeah, yeah."

"Some dreams, lions nuzzle up to you."

"What?"

"Lions are friends. Good friends."

"Any women been here lately?"

"What's that got to do with anything?"

"Lions are mysterious. Fine. But staying indoors all day, I mean, even pussycats don't do that."

Jimmy laughs. She always makes him laugh. "We're like lifelong pals," he says. "Like I've known you all my life."

"*Our* life! You're not even a week older than me."

"You're the first woman here without, you know."

"Being involved?"

"Yeah. No involvement, right?"

"Why not come and visit? Come one weekend. Me and my mother. I told her about you. She plays your tapes."

Geraldine and Jimmy sit around. Talking and lounging. Play music. Plenty laughing and music. In the end, she can see why thinking of lions is not so weird; or so says, frowning, going through the door.

Alone again, he tries not to think of Colette. That night, the theatre. In the ivory foyer light, her dress licked the air. But watching the play was strange. Somehow she was the gypsy girl. And he wanted to go where the girl was going in a gypsy life. But she was only a stage part. Then the way Colette poured restaurant wine, dark eyes, pouring wine, looking elusive as it poured. But all the time it was the gypsy. A resolute girl, she was a no-mad on stage; gypsy owning no land. Then the motorway. That car ride, steering a red bullet through half England. Half looking for the gypsy life, wanting a woman nomad. Only a nomad would know. The way ahead was way more road than roadway. Only a gypsy gets the longing, the ache. Not knowing where to belong. Then being alone. Trying to figure it. Trying music. Listening to Brahms, and only Brahms, playing the Hungarian Dances half a day. Listening from the last dance to the first. Over and over. At last. Things made sense. The woman on the gypsy highway wasn't Agnes. Arleene came close. But she wants a man that loves her all day. Then Donna. A woman like Donna could dot it, but will domesticate somebody. Nathan rates Lorna; says she can't sing but there's good vibes in her soul. A gypsy woman can plant. Or she just moves on. Jimmy knew it: he'd been looking for a nomad. As the Hungarian Dances played, the gypsy girl was the first dance. The second dance was about an older gypsy female; one that starts fire at evening so she can undress in G minor, then carry water. Colette. She was always in the third dance. But she was not it. She was a signpost; a woman gazing at wine instead of ceiling tilt.

# 87

"I phoned, and phoned!" Lorna says.

Jimmy yawns. "Must have been asleep. Out like a light."

"I knew you'd be drunk."

"That bottle was taller than before."

"Whisky is taking you apart."

"The part we play, and all that."

"Look at the state of this place!"

"I'll straighten it up. Gimme a sec, a second."

"Did you understand what I said?"

"Yeah," he slurs, "your brother."

"Look, I've got to go."

"High ceilings."

"*What?*"

"Dead, you're buried. Then your ceiling is ground level. Folk upstairs in the life bungalow."

Dashing to the door, Lorna trips over cables on the floor. Suddenly the night's like a womb. She must reach her hand into it to deliver somebody to the world. But not quite. Wrong way round. The machine got switched off. Justin's dead.

"Pharaoh was the greed," Jimmy says. "Pharaoh wanted to check the god of Moses. Got the master-builder to figure a platform, you know, high enough to get up there, go and see."

"What're you talking about?"

"Pharaoh. That guy, *that* is what you call flake-highs."

"My brother is dead."

"Pharaoh's builder blanked the puzzle. Knew the god of Moses was too far. Too far to see. So he did a runner."

"You don't understand what's happened!"

"The river. Nile runs like forever. Till one day, dry. The place they call Sahara, Jeez! Green. It was green. Only seven thousand years back, that's when they changed it, I mean, it changed. Weather changed it."

"I'd better make you some coffee. Sober you up."

"African folk raised the Sphinx from stone, mummies two thousand years before Egypt was even born. But then it turned powder. The green land turned desert. Now your brother needs a tombstone."

"Look, I know you're only trying to help," Lorna sighs. "Try to sober up."

# 88

Bobby was glad. When Jimmy phoned New York, the bandleader said Minims is a goer. But tells it one more time: words about a blind lady must stay clear of bible talk; get it right by June, Bobby says, and it's a go!

Jimmy grabs A Brief History Of Time. Turns and turns the pages. Looking. Then slams it shut. No stars tonight. What's just happened to Justin hits home.

For a while Lorna's brother was coming along, doing well, looked like getting back. Today his mother was at the bedside with the faith healer. Doctors arrived with more doctors. But no use. He died. Lorna's brother is definitely dead.

Jimmy plays it low, playing Round Midnight non-stop. For four hours. Not a tune to derive in tenement Tottenham. A big-time football club is down the road from the flat. And nice women live in the area, step sweetly in the tricksy streets. But not a Sarah Vaughan. And definitely no Thelonious Monk whirling like a dervish.

"Round Midnight is like waterfalls," Jimmy says.

His mother sighs. "You *must* get away!"

"Waterfalls in a city. Cascade, cascade. Water from umbrellas or old yellow-cab windscreens."

"You don't have umbrellas in Tottenham?"

"Still think you're funny, don't you?"

"Come for a visit. I'm sick of this phone."

"Rain here. But not like downtown New York. Round Midnight, it's 1947 and the war's only 2 years over. Monk was the same age as that Faran on the cross. But this guy's ministry was to walk piano keys, talk with the sick, laugh with the lame. But not raise the dead."

"That's a bit morbid, isn't it?

"A grand piano should be here."

"A what?"

"Maybe a new idea could come along. 90 notes for Justin."

"Who's he?"

"Brother of a woman I know. Lorna, her brother."

"Well, you won't get a grand through that 8th floor tenement door."

"Assemble it. Piece by piece. If one was here instead of this keyboard, Lorna would've had no cables to trip over."

"You *are* in a bad way!"

"Weird, they switch off your machine. Some quick paperwork. You're dead."

"Bud Powell didn't need a concert grand."

"He was ruler of bebop piano. I'm not that good. Thing is, he was a bit like Justin. But he didn't die young. He was maybe only twenty but near death one night. New York police. Blow after blow. It was evil. Those truncheons. I mean, meaning to maim. Even kill. Those coppers coshed Bud because he was black. Left him in a gutter. Eleven weeks in hospital. Down the years his heart was breaking all the time. Remembering. In a way, he was a dead man that police night."

"But got back from the dead, didn't he!"

"Yeah, alive. Wobbling, but getting a life."

"Listen, I've got to go. Tell me the end part of what you're saying."

"Bud's Bubble is wince-time for me. Any piano player. Two years after that police attack, Bud laid that track down. It was '46, I think. Ever listen?"

"Of course! The bebop drum-breaks say 'Hey, put those truncheons away! Bop! Give drums a try, see what you could do. Bop! Don't mess law-and-order. Bebop!' That's the drums."

Jimmy laughs. "The piano's like drizzle. Bud's piano laughs, says, 'Wait, catch this, hitch these little raindrops high!' Ever notice?"

"Oh, yes. Yes I have."

"That's why I need a concert grand."

"Tools, tools, tools! Blame the tools."

"Guess what? I'm into modal again."

"Good. Still listen to Kind Of Blue?"

"I'll give it a spin tomorrow."

"Just get away. Tall skies, understand?"


Justin is dead. His girlfriend suckles a brand new baby he'll never see. Deep down in that coma, just before the machine got switched off, he opened his eyes one last time and said, 'What, me?'

Alone at the window, Jimmy's wondering. Kind Of Blue plays. Low on the hi-fi. Freddie Freeloader is the track that plays more than any. The only blues. He grabs a smoke. Wondering. This same Freddie track got inspired by a guy who supplied Miles. Freddie, the cocaine man that supplied Miles Davis. In '59, after the record got released, Freddie was tripping through New York, agile and proud, boasting. Telling everybody that the Freddie on the track refers to him. On every street corner he said, 'That's me, that's me!'

# 89

"Public meetings?" Geraldine says. "They tend to go on and on."

"That's what worries me. But I need to go to this one."

"Jimmy, your voice! Never heard you so serious."

"This guy was three years younger than me. Never met him, but I kind of knew him."

"Will there be a march? A public enquiry?"

"No march. Not for me. My old man tells me stuff they used to do in the 60s, 70s. It was marches, marches. People of colour and liberal whites, banners saying 'Freedom!'"

"Marching is silly."

"Yeah. It only marks time. Like religion. This religion or that. And the question where the marchers come from."

"The problem is where they think they're going."

"Yeah. Especially if the weather's bad. One day two summers back, I'd just got back from Brazil, and the woman in the paper-shop was beautiful, never complaining about the rain. 'What's it matter if your clothes get wet?' she said. Then cups of tea. Outdoors, the marchers' banners were raised high. High and multi-coloured. Hundreds, up high."

"Hunger for freedom," Geraldine murmurs.

"Yeah, that's it. But alongside the message was the cold eye, you know, eyes tough as flint. Waiting in the rain that day, folk jealous of tears."

"Try not to lose you temper."

"Before you phoned I took one more look at the leaflet. Lorna left a pile of them on the settee. Too hard to understand yesterday. She was a blur, tripping over to leave. Justin's machine got switched off. Now the leaflet's heavy as lead. That guy is dead."

"Does music help? Play, compose?"

"I was vacant. Stood at the keyboard. Hovered. The keys seemed weird. Those piano keys, looked like the damaged smile of a psycho. But somehow, diminished chords were in the room. Ghosts walked in, wanting the keyboard."

"Ghosts?"

"Yeah. Insistent stuff in your head. Ghosts hit the right notes. Every time. Get chords that say it. Say goodbye. It's OK, those chords said. It's OK. They said even suicide has another side, they know sometimes even waking is a chore. Wake up for what? Brush your teeth? For what? Get ready for the smile-game. I'll tell you, those ghosts want a lot more out of life than that!"

"What about life, the living?"

"I know. Can't duck that. Somewhere in my manuscript pile, there's one piece. You'll like it. It gets worked, more and more. It tries. I want to sync Bach's counterpoint to Coltrane's flow. The more I work it, the more fun it gets."

"More than ghosts can gag at?" Geraldine wonders.

"Hey, ghosts say life is only couture."

"*What*?"

"We all get to wear one. This mortal outfit or that. Indian, Chinese, black, white, mixed. Everybody in their skin overcoat."

"I'd better go. Mustn't keep you from your meeting."

"Ghosts do white keys. Pretend. Then try black keys."

"You're losing me again."

"No, I'm not! You know exactly what I'm saying."

"You *never* switch off. I can't bear it!"

"Then put yourself in my place."

"Sorry, I've got to go. Hope you finish your new piece."

"It's called Cobalt. A new Coltrane ghost and a Bach."

"Mind how you go," Geraldine says.

7 o'clock. Getting late for the meeting. Jimmy reads Lorna's leaflet one more time. Then says goodbye to ghosts. Folds the leaflet, tucks it in his overcoat.

## 90

"Call me BT," Trass grins, handing out business cards. "Feel free to call me BT."

Bosworth Churchill Trass. Regional director of race relations. Head race man. People in the community hall know about him. Some leave even before things start, but only because he's here. Somebody says Trass is a quacker, that his mouth moves like mud round a duck pond. The older folk try. They still allow. Trass is on TV from time to time, so they believe he talks for them.

Lorna is with her mother and sister at a table facing the meeting. Longing in the mother's eyes. The presence of a group of dreadlocked guys connects her to something; it could ease her worry. But agendas are already jockeying for prime time. Bosworth Trass is the high sly.

A neat black woman takes notes. Sitting next to Lorna and dressed in black, she jots and jots. And in the front row a girl with a buttercup face gets angry; Justin's girlfriend is a widow now. Nobody escapes her gaze. A week-old baby locks in her tight arms. Jimmy's phone rings.

His mother on the line. He steps outside. "The meeting hall hopes a messiah will happen," he says.

"Messiah?"

"Yeah. You know it is. It could be a word. The look in an eye. It's like a church, here. Religious ritual, them thinking a messiah will come. Give him time, give him time! They believe something will happen *this* time. Younger folk sit lower in their chairs."

"If it makes them feel better, what's the harm?"

"I'd better go back to it. Call you later."

An angry white woman stands. Says it louder this time, "Hunt them! Hunt them down! Use dogs. Like a fox at your chicken-coop!"

Two rows behind her, a chat about fox-hunting: that if it's ever on TV it's not the kill, it's the chase. Blood-red jackets buttoned tight and well. Horses chomping, running at hinterland. Prime land. Far from Brixton. Hunter horses have a sky-load of go, a woman says. It's great to see ruddy horsewomen pumping air, a man says.

"Dogs will find them!" the woman cries. "Use dogs to track down Justin's killers!"

Lorna gulps. Wanting air, but not air. From the look on her face she could be gulping painkillers. Tears in her eyes. But no memory. She checks the room, but not really seeing. Black folk of every age here. Every skin tone. Twenty or twenty-five white folk, mostly female. And a band of dreadlocked guys standing like a posse at the back of the hall.

The woman in black gets to her feet. "Good evening," she says. "My name is Marcia Hosannah. I'm from the Society of Black Lawyers. Not least, I'm a friend of the Stanley family."

From the front row, a white man bounds to the lawyer's microphone. Deftly, adjusts it for rake. The next move is neater. The man gets a white kerchief from his pocket and dabs Lorna's eyes. Gentle dabbing. Then runs the collar of her jacket in place. A soft squeeze of her cheek, nudge of chin. Alan Stanley. Father of the family. Alan gets back to his chair without a word to anyone.

Eyes fixed to the table, the lawyer sighs. "Thank you all for coming. I don't want to raise false hopes, so I'll come straight to the point. As you all know, there've been no arrests. So this community, *our* community, we must spell out our own terms of reference. I repeat, no arrests!"

Lorna's head shakes. "Let's get on with it," she moans, turning to the meeting. Then stands. "What's wrong with this community? We live here. It's where we live. But it's like we're in the dark, we're too scared to turn the lights on. What's Bosworth Trass got to say for himself?"

Trass gets up from a black swivel chair. "*I* will spell out what this is. Want to call it the terms of reference? That's fine with me. But first things first. There's no evidence attacks on black people. No evidence at all. Nothing that would stand up in the courts. And that's not an excuse, it's a fact!"

Lorna's eyes narrow. "Tell us what you call evidence."

Trass grins "Evidence is what you must have if the police are to act. You can't go to the courts with empty hands."

But he knows. Everybody can see. They know the old hypocrite arch. Only one swivel chair was in the hall and Bosworth Trass claimed it. The chair's like a pendulum in some old clock, somebody says; yes, a relic from an old colonial office. Chairs in the meeting-hall come from all over, but Bosworth had to go for the swivel. If it could talk, it probably would say *Evidence, spell it, police, spell, act, spell. Quite!* Trass will be a lord soon enough. Talk is, he'll be Lord Trass. And that's why he's here. To shore-up. To log woes the race industry can own. That's why he got the MBE last year, a woman claims.

"Can be only two hyenas in a pack," a dreadlocked man says. "Even thirty hyenas. When the pack done, no evidence. Hyena eat the hoof. Eat skin. And if horn on the prey, them eat the horn. And blood. Blood in the soil where the prey fall. Them wild dog, them eat the soil. That youth, Justin, him was in a dark alley. And even if what them say is true, that maybe it was one of him own posse by mistake, another black guy no less, then that is still the scavenger business. Justin maybe was passing for white by mistake. That alley light."

The meeting-hall is fetid. Folk gazing into who's who. They get to a community hall or church to wait for it to happen. But mostly nothing gets said that is not hyena talk.

Jimmy was late. He looks at Lorna now and then. But she looks away. So he switches off from the meeting, thinking of the keyboard. Eyes closed, he's like at the piano already, like up on the 8$^{th}$ floor at the flat. Quiet hands take it. Left hand at Bach's G Major from the Cello Suite. The right hand spans altered chords to Coltrane's Mr PC. Sweat pours.

Marcia is tall. Pained, but she's holding control. "Stephen Lawrence. Remember him, Mr Trass? Ever read the McPherson Report?"

"Evidence," Trass says, "is the start of everything. Where's the evidence for your race attack? Where's evidence for institutional racism?"

"*Evidence?*" Lorna shrieks, drilling every heart. "You go for a drink with the police, don't you Mr Trass. You take turns on the karaoke. That's what I call evidence!"

Jimmy can't escape. Not to music. Not from here. This lawyer, this Marcia Hosannah, a woman making guys disappointed in themselves. The meeting does not prevent her lips from lushing. But then. Lorna's in every heart. Tears well.

The community-hall is no home. But the April evening outdoors is just too nameless to leave now. And yet. Most here know what will happen next. They want Alan Stanley to talk, say something. Somebody should give Trass a pasting. Justin is only a stepping stone for Trass. Young and dead, Justin could get him to the Lords.

Lorna wipes her eyes. She grabs the mic. "Somebody, *please* say something. Even a whisper."

Jimmy's throat clears. "Where can black skin whisper? Enoch Powell got his numbers right. But a blind lady getting here tonight would have to choose. Take a white cane, step past dog mess on the pavement, or step inside this community hall and listen to bull."

"At the end of the day," Trass snorts, "it all comes down to what you can prove."

"Prove *what*?" Lorna shouts.

"If society is to work for us then we have to give the law something, do what the law understands. Can't run before you walk."

Marcia grabs the microphone. Her eyes curse Trass. "How many deaths will there have to be before we learn this walk of yours?"

A gaunt black man stands. Old, bolt. Kwame Urshell. Talk is, he was a panther back in the 60s. A black panther in England. To him, the race hypocrite is the problem these days. Each woman checks the business card she got from Bosworth Trass. All white women and the light skinned ones have two, three cards apiece. Some blacker women have none.

Hush. Slow quiet. Intense. A slow Mexican wave. Two by two, folk get it. They get how difficult it is to see any man in the race industry with a lady black as himself. Bosworth's got more reason than one to punch ethnic numbers. Nobody's ever see him with any woman that would be black in South Africa. A slim model from Lebanon goes the rounds with him now, but not here tonight.

Urshell adjusts the microphone. "Too much black folk stalk skin. De victim is sista dumb, brodda dumb. Dem no know seh dem a de victim. Dem no understan' de stalker man, de skin-tone man. Dis happen all de time. It happen in a de race industry. Man! Skin stalker a teach, skin stalker ina entertainment, sport. Hypocrite a talk multiracial dis and dat, but all dem do is chase light skin. Trass? Dis hypocrite a de top a de pile."

"Can't you talk straight English?" a white man says. "I get the drift of what you're saying, but I can't be sure."

"Standard English?" Urshell smiles. "Yes, of course. Well, we have a problem here tonight. A skin-stalker. Bosworth Trass. So it will not be possible to discuss the young man's death with Mr Trass. Don't get me wrong, this man is no fool. Not with a Cambridge MA. But come the time for honest talk, like tonight, then no chance! Mr Trass is gone! This man claims to be proud being black, but stray dogs grin from his mouth. And, you know, race officials talk folly, talk *inclusivity*. But, man! Most of them run from their own kind. Nobody knows for sure where Bosworth Trass is from. But a big queue of women get fooled by him. Woman after woman, light-skinned or white. We can *not* discuss honest things with this race hypocrite. Not here."

# 91

Headache from the fuss, Jimmy quits the meeting. Gets out to the night. But worried about Lorna. She's in there still. A grief woman.

At a zebra crossing, he's wary in a humid night. The evening is thick with folk heading up the road. Now and then a young blood laughs out loud, just like a Tyson or Janet Jackson.

"You were right," he says. "The meeting was only show. Theatre."

"But you had to go," Geraldine says.

"Yeah. But a race-industry man was there. Can you believe it, somebody called Bosworth Trass?"

"Nobody kicked him?"

"No. Black folk always know a Bosworth, a hypocrite over race like a mouse with cheese."

Geraldine's voice lowers. "Where are you?"

"In the car. Calling on my mobile."

"Then keep you eyes on the road. In more ways than one!"

"To think, all this started with a flag. Somebody waved a flag across the sea. That colonial cloth, it misled folk. 'Come to the motherland.' There were guys with Union Jacks outside the meeting hall. Laughing."

"It's who gets the last laugh, isn't it!"

"I dunno. Last week a BNP bloke got onto a town council, a place called Bromyard & Winslow. Because of how scat the law is, he didn't even have to get elected to claim the seat. Folk in community halls are still getting misled."

"What d'you think I can do?"

"*Exactly* what I wanted to ask you! White folk must do something."

"That's a hard one. Even you don't trust white people."

"I don't trust the historical white. But that's where you come in. You and people like you."

"How?"

"Admit what happened."

"Admit?"

"There's Holocaust denial. And there's white folk refusing to see what happened to the black man. The size of what happened. "

"That meeting must have been heartbreaking. You're *so* angry."

"I'm going back to the flat. Smoke ganja, do a bottle of whisky. Kick the walls."

"Better still, sleep with the sexiest woman you know."

"Not in the mood."

"Problems," she laughs, "with you manhood?"

"In a dreamless night somewhere, somebody walks in a narrow lane and gets moonlight reflecting in a puddle."

"Now, *that's* more like you! Go, my mystic, go!"

Weary on the road, Jimmy's gazing at folk passing by. Not wanting to get back to the 8th floor flat, a slab-hearted space. So the open road. Cold tarmac. Old graphite. And the petrol-gauge glowing the dark.

# 92

"Jimmy, it's me," Lorna says.

"Funeral tomorrow!"

"I don't want to go. Can't bear to think of what it means."

"Justin's life was a good moment. You can't see that right now, but his life will help clarify things."

"Are you seventy-five, or only twenty-five?"

"Honestly, you'd see it if you weren't so close."

"Go on, tell me about my brother, somebody you've never met!"

"He was no hypocrite. If the world wants to call somebody like him black then he was happy with it. Some that's dead grumpy, getting lumped with the black side."

"When does it end?"

"Don't know."

"You're not seventy-five, then!"

"I was six when the Brixton riots happened. A line in the sand. My old man was there, my mother kept all the cuttings. 10th April, 1981. Things boiled over. Weird, but that same day some strange things came together."

"Like what?"

"Bunny Wailer was doing his 34th birthday. A guy from the IRA was in jail but got elected as an MP. Somebody in a Brixton pool-hall got stabbed."

"Peculiar day!"

"Yeah. Bob Marley was getting ready to die. Reagan was shot two weeks before."

"What happened to the guy in the pool-hall?"

"He was black, obviously. Police rolled up. They didn't rush him to hospital, but stuck him in their vehicle and posed. You know, showing who's in control. Young black folk gathered round shouting 'Hospital, get him to a hospital!' But zil. The police just posed. Guy gushing blood and all they do is pose. So it was grab-the-brother-time. Grab him from the coppers. Dash him to hospital. That was the first day of the Brixton thing. The riot. Some call it 'The uprising'"

"Bricks rained down!"

"No, that was next day. Saturday. The police claimed a cabdriver in Brixton was carrying drugs. The cabbie was a black guy, family man, way away from drugs. Those coppers didn't learn from the first day. When young black folk folded round this time, well, things different. This time a line got drawn in the front line."

"From cuttings? You get all that stuff from cuttings?"

"That's why I'm a composer."

"What d'you do with it?"

"A new piece. It's called '11th April, 81.' Finished it last month."

"Jazz?"

"You decide. Want to hear the theme?"

"Shall I come round?"

"Too much on your plate. Funeral tomorrow."

"Not sure what you mean by theme."

"Ideas. But loose. Vocalists can play with it, move it around."

"Can you do it over the phone?"

"Yeah. '*Young and black, going your business. Redneck in uniform calling you thief, mugger, saying you deal drugs. Call you race names, names. Guffawing like from swamps, a swamp. Your shame, got cotton in your ears. Wear cotton for ears, ears. Bricks cruised Sat'day night. 11th April night in '81. Bricks, stones, fire. Concrete on fire in the night! That first petrol bomb, first one on the UK mainland that Brixton night. Burning, burned down the night! But. It was no April shower. No rain calmed things down, cooled the fire. Water-jets from a fire engine. That's what cooled it. Brixton, old tarmac after that water hose, hose. Old and cold. But no more shadow. Nobody hooking fingers round white cane. Nobody blind, blind. Black folk saying No way! No more groping in the street, not blind! Then somebody figured it, figured how Newton's apple falls from Eve's tree, tree; a pissed-off young, sick of Faran in paradise seeing fire, black pastors saying Praise the Lord! The Lord! Faran on the cross with a crown of thorns, thorns. Silent folk crucified in a Brixton overcoat, a skin coat. But between sunlight and shadow, light not tears. But nobody homing in from ethnic, ethnic.*'"

# 93

The morning sun is taller than high. Sunlight floating shade on every leaf. Up and down, calm dwellings define this road. Every house quiet and detached. Lawns tugging the sun like a child's kite.

Jimmy's glad for the green. The countryside wakes up round him as the car points through it. Till today he didn't know it, but St Albans is close to where Geraldine lives. The roads here are just like she said: 'You'll leave the turn-off, drive for a hundred yards and notice a bit of a smell, then go past rape blossoming in the fields.'

Two weeks since Justin got buried. Jimmy didn't go. And no wreaths from the flowers in any garden on Geraldine's road. The car stops. He lights a smoke. So, this is where she lives. This is what Geraldine does. This quiet road is way past. Every house safe, slow, taking time, watching early summer derive. Some way past the million.

The heavy door knocker drops. It clangs like thunder in the morning quiet. The noise is a mistake. Jimmy knocks again. Soft this time, like trying to atone. A dog barks. And the birds on this road singing up and down.

A woman smiles. "Come in, do come in!" she says, assessing. "So good to meet you!"

From how Geraldine talked of her mother, Jimmy expected an elfin, a woman way past 60. Instead, somebody of indistinct age at the door. She smiles again. And clowning in a green oilskin jacket, Geraldine grins in the hallway.

"So," the woman says, "you are Jimmy Dell. How are you?"

"Pleased to meet you."

"I just this minute got back," Geraldine pants. "Fresh bread, and a few things. You look tired."

"Was at Kevin's till late."

"Kevin? Who's that?"

"The guy Colette introduced at the theatre."

Hand to jaw, the old woman wonders. Quiet wondering. "We have blackcurrant bushes in the garden. Wonderful. Heavy with fruit in summer!"

Jimmy's never seen Geraldine this happy. This is maybe the first time in a long while she's snug in her own eyes.

She grins. "Find your way OK?"

"A doddle."

"Coffee? How about a nice mug of cocoa? I'm doing toast. Fancy a piece of toast? Half a loaf, if you want!"

Off the kitchen, a newish conservatory. Victorian. And a quiet garden relaxing through the glass. Geraldine walks the floor like girl mutiny.

"Mum's doing breakfast," she says. "Toast and cranberry. Nothing complicated. Oh, and a few eggs. Is that OK? Sit where you like."

"Did she already know the facts?" Jimmy says.

"What d'you mean?"

"How did you tell her a black man was coming to visit?"

Her blue eyes reach for the ceiling. Arms slumped. Shoulders poached. "Oh, come on! Are you going to be silly?"

"Well, I never know."

"Please don't spoil it."

Steam curls the mug of fresh-ground coffee. Geraldine's garden is a fairytale, Jimmy thinks. Gazing at the lush, he thinks the garden here is like music. A plate of toast on the table and her mother with a tray of cups, eggs and homemade jam. And white napkins, cutlery gleaming in sunlight.

"Thanks, Mrs Nash."

"Can't you call me Renate?" she says. "May I call you Jimmy? Yes, of course. So, call me Renate."

"Geraldine said you're big on pottery."

"Not pottery," she sighs. "That's Lydia, my other daughter. She's the one. But I was quite handy with sculpture. A bit more than just handy, perhaps. But now it's my eyesight and, well, why go into that?"

"See that thing in the garden?" Geraldine says, wanting to set the record straight. Her eyes indicate a zany blue sculpture. "That's what my mother can do. We call it Next Time. It won a prize when she was at art college. And winning prizes was a lot more difficult those days."

Renate smiles. "Ah, winning prizes!"

"Now it's just a free-for-all, isn't it mummy?"

"Like how?" Jimmy says.

"Nowadays," Geraldine shrugs, "you can chuck your guts up in a bucket and there's certain to be somebody out there awarding you a prize for it."

Renate laughs. "Jimmy, you *must* see the garden. We have some lovely wildlife. Visitors. Herons in the mornings, foxes now and then. Badgers and kestrels. All sorts. Absolutely fantastic. Something all year round. Some lovely instants at the far end of the garden. A real sense of wow!"

"I was thinking about working from home," Geraldine says. "Hate the traveling. I could sit in the conservatory, bring the phone out on a lead."

"Yes," Renate grins. "and be quite silly if you want."

"Stripped down to bra and knickers, making business calls."

Renate turns to Jimmy. "You went to the Royal College of Music, didn't you?"

"After my degree, yes."

"Bet they liked you there."

"A great year. Real music. Brilliant people. Hands on."

"Got to be pretty nifty to make it there!"

"Well, that's why you go."

"Why did you choose the piano? Or did it choose you? If I may say so, you look like, well, some other instrument."

"Sax?"

"Yes, I think that's what I'm getting at."

"I've heard that before."

"Oh dear, did I put my foot in it? Didn't mean to stereotype you."

"Renate, it was never the sax," Jimmy shrugs. "It was chords. Piano, because of chords. Piano makes you play big chords. Melody is great, but chord work is deeper."

"I always think of you with a little mandolin," Geraldine giggles.

"Any chance of a bit of music?" Renate says, curling a leg under a trim lady figure. "Can't wait to hear you play."

"Now?"

"No, no. Have your coffee, my dear. Bon appetit."

Sipping coffee, checking the mother and daughter team, Jimmy gets dazed with garden quiet. The lawn, a hushed green. And way down the vista, a half forest. Hunza apricot trees are out there. Geraldine talked about them all winter.

"Do you play much classical?" Renate asks.

"Yes. And romantic. But I'm with blues, atonal, jazz. Some days it's all one language, different accents."

Geraldine frowns. "What's the difference?"

"Between?"

"Classical and romantic."

Jimmy's eyes narrow. "Well," he says, "let's get to your piano. I'll do a demo."

"Can't you *say* what it is? I mean, in a word?"

"Classical and romantic?"

"Yes."

"Talking about the difference probably leads to bunkum. I hate that existence stuff. One day music will get so there's no ethnic slant. Purely abstract. Like maths. But looking backwards, classical is like standard Beethoven, Mozart. Highly structured. Romantic is like Schubert, or Chopin. Intuitive, freer. Something like that."

"But," Renate sulks, "there are so many, many exceptions! The Moonlight Sonata, for one. Beethoven's Moonlight is so profoundly non-classical."

"Romantic!" Geraldine says.

Renate nods. "*Any* of Beethoven's sonatas. Thirty two of them, I think. All deeply romantic."

Jimmy gulps a mouthful of coffee. "That only shows the bottom line, doesn't it! Music. Anyway, the Moonlight is a bad example. Listen while you watch the moon, hold that C-sharp minor, and the magic flits before your eyes. All that's there is the moon shining. I always imagine a bunch of reindeer. Ever see reindeer, them testing how safe ice is on a lake? They get more and more confident, then just run onto it. Maybe it's the key. Yeah. That C-sharp minor, it even grabs ice reindeer love."

"I must," Renate says, frowning, "try your reindeer image sometime. One moonlit night, naturally."

"Music is like clouds," Jimmy says.

"Why clouds?"

"Breeze going one way, you get nimbus. Another breeze gets you something else."

"That stuff," Geraldine says, "probably helps weather forecasters. But farmers know it in their guts."

Weary, Jimmy looks past the clear glass. Gazing out over the garden. Then turns to Renate. "Six months after the Brixton riots, Stephen Hawking was in Moscow. Went to talk quantum gravity. But they couldn't understand his wrecked voice, so somebody transposed his ideas."

"What on earth is that to do with music!"

"No instrument, no music."

Geraldine's eyes roll. Jimmy laughs. Then hums a bar of Minims. And laughs again. Hums more bars.

"To call your Minims tune folk music," Renate says, "is a mistake."

"Why?"

"Because, my dear, with folk music you just gather round. Something happens. Something heartwarming."

Geraldine agrees. "Folk music is like knowing a tree when you see one. Even if you haven't seen it before. Folk music is like that."

"I think the young man knows that," Renate reproves.

"He's a law unto himself," Geraldine says. "Or so he thinks."

"Is there one thing," Renate quickly cuts in, "just *one* thing about jazz why it differs from classical? I've so wanted to hear from the jazz side."

Jimmy takes a deep breath. "Where to start? No easy place. Jazz is like Picasso, abstract, minimalist, themes. Classical is photographs."

"And to somebody blind, how would you explain it?"

"If you want one word, jazz is Africa."

Renate frowns. "What about improvisation?"

"What's wrong with Africa? Too awkward?"

"This is going to be a sermon, mummy. It's how he is."

"Jazz," Jimmy says, "*means* improvising. Imagination. The next word is syncopation. Take rhythm from the universe, it goes up in smoke. As for the improvisation part, that's the purest music. Players know. We practice years, a lifetime. If you're good enough, the silent voice takes over, 'Speak for me, speak for me.' Hard to explain. An example might do it. Let's get to the piano. I hear you have a concert grand."

"Imagine I'm deaf," Geraldine says. " How would you tell me what you mean?"

"I'd tap rhythms on your forehead," he says, and laughs.

Renate sighs. "Beethoven was completely deaf at the end."

"Not trying to be funny," Jimmy says, "but when classical musicians improvise, a jazz muso says go back to doodle-school."

Renate isn't convinced. Jimmy's in a place having a concert grand, but all they want is talk. He turns to the garden. This could get difficult. It can't get done without showing. Renate's eyebrows raise.

Suddenly, a clue. "Bach!" he says. "Bach could've done this garden. So could Chopin. This garden's so complete. Nothing to add. But there's nothing here that Thelonious Monk would whirl at. In a word, it's your planted blooms. That's not jazz. No crunch. Nothing a Ferrari could park beside and not seem domineering."

Renate frowns. "Will you explain crunch?"

"I'll try. Matisse could have painted here, but nothing Picasso would have leaned on. These symmetries, they're too obviously 3-D. Nothing here on-hold in the sky. No spacesuits flapping in solar breeze. Does that make sense?"

"Clear as mud," Geraldine grins.

"Imagine water," he says, turning to the garden. "You get water doing its thing. A classical composer comes along, imitates it, gets the sounds, the sense. But there's still no idea what kind of water it is."

Renate's head shakes. "I don't follow, sorry!"

"Imagine a boat out on the water," he says. "Classical music, and that romantic thing, that music tells you there's a boat on the water. But if it's a speedboat, or yachts with multi-coloured spinnakers, then big trouble!"

"Nonsense!" she yells. "I mean, I don't agree."

Jimmy shrugs. "Don't apologize, Renate. Whatever you do, don't ask a composer. Not to tell the difference. But since you ask me, I always think of boats. There's the whole ocean to cut through. Lots of things can happen. Mostly you can't plan. You want to bring a melody home, get back, then you'd be looking at jazz."

"Then where," she wonders, "does Stravinsky fit? And, you know, Schoenberg."

"Those guys are roughly there. In the same ballpark as jazz. Well, not quite."

Geraldine pours more coffee. "Meaning what?"

"If you want an abstract theme," Jimmy says, turning to Renate, "then it's jazz. It's the most abstract form that holds melody. With classical, you always have shapes you can name."

242

"Young man, I don't get what you mean!"

"There's circles, squares, even a dodecahedron, but always shapes with a name. To me, that's the basis of classical. But with jazz! With that, you're looking at things with no name most times. Whole chunks of the ocean have no name."

The phone rings.

"Let it ring," Geraldine shrugs, tucking into toast.

Renate chugs from the chair. Must answer the phone. Jimmy grabs the jam jar. Jam so homemade, it could wink. Geraldine gazes at the garden as he ladles another spoonful.

Back in the conservatory again, Renate looks bleak. She puckers her eyes, gulps coffee. "Must go," she says. "Only a couple of hours, but I must go. Make yourself at home, Jimmy. I'll be back soon. Can't wait to hear you at the piano."

"You play?"

"Been trying for fifty years."

"Music," he says, "is a bit like religion. One set of prophets update an earlier set, then folk believe again. Over again."

"Herbert Von Karajan, he always drove the hottest Porsche money can buy."

Jimmy nods. "Heard about Nigel Kennedy? Recorded a homage to Hendrix."

The old woman's grey eyes blink. "Hendrix?"

"Yeah. Hendrix played jazz-type chords."

"Jazz?"

"Hey, there's more colours to jazz than a rainbow could weep at."

"Enough!" Renate laughs, hands thrown in the air.

# 94

The music on the radio stops. A chat in German starts.

"That radio only speaks German," Geraldine says. "I'll switch it off, if you like."

Jimmy checks the time. "No," he says. "Let it ride."

"Come to think of it, I can't remember that radio ever being tuned to anything else. My father didn't allow German in the house. Believe it? German in the kitchen, listening to that radio or talking to Renate."

Renate is sixty four. To Geraldine, her mother's a vibrant woman. Her father is sixty three; but looks younger, she says. Renate is a thinker. She was a fine-arts lecturer till last year. It was through her Jimmy got the Dusseldorf gig.

"You speak to your mother in German?"

"Yeah. Lots."

"Man!"

"Why the surprise?"

"If I wasn't here, you and your mum would be talking German?"

"The only English is when she might say 'You can say that again!' Or, 'What a load of rubbish!' Ditties, really."

"Your father's an army man."

"Definitely!"

"Wars and stuff."

"Retired now, of course. But still vigorous."

"They got divorced?"

"Separated. Bit of a bigamist when he moved in with the other one. Knew her before my mother got on the scene, then went back to her. Ten years ago. It all came to a head. Minor aristo, Lady Zip of Buttons. Are you interested in this?"

"All the way. Anything you tell me."

"An amazing man! Lots to the bloke, really."

"So what's the down side?"

"Like how?"

"He left you all."

"Leggy females!"

"Her nibs is a blonde?"

"Yes."

"Bitch toffs are always blonde."

"Yeah."

"Why's that?"

"Search me!"

"Still see him?"

"Yeah. 'The Colonel' when Renate mentions him. Pretty scary!"

# 95

One morning Jimmy phoned Agnes and somebody answered the phone but didn't speak English. Agnes speaks Afrikaans. And Zulu, Xhosa. Not to mention English. She can mimic Boers; gets the same noise of a pig plowing as when fat Boers talk, she says.

The radio breaks into German talk again. To Jimmy, something in the voice is strung like topiary.

He turns to Geraldine. "What're they saying?"

"The radio? Oh, not a lot. Just a bit of muttering. Resentment about the arts."

"If a bonsai tree could speak," he says, "it would talk German."

"What a *peculiar* thing to say?"

"Freed from a thousand year rage, a bonsai would talk German."

"Is that an insult?"

"Nah! Well, I didn't intend one."

"Don't you know any German at all?"

"Me?"

"Why would that be so strange?"

"For me, it would be weird."

"Who did the music degree, listens to Schubert?"

"OK, OK. I know a few words, the odd word or two. But speaking it, understanding stuff, that never really cropped up."

"Well, here's your chance!"

"Why?"

"For one thing, your contract in Dusseldorf."

"The folk I deal with there, they all speak English. In the orchestra, everybody, they know enough English. And it sort of leaves them with something, you know, me not talking German."

"Knowing the lingo could save your neck! Still a bit of simmering going on."

"Nazis?"

"Neo-nazis, the likes."

"Hey, they can keep what they have. Keep all the punk Wagner they have!"

"I've got cousins in Dusseldorf."

"Gardening shows on TV can cut tenement pain. Your garden is so else. Somebody could lay low here, a real home-from-home."

"Then, make yourself at home."

"If Steven Hawking's home is a wheelchair, where's the puppeteer?"

"What puppeteer?"

"The one that put a withered man in a wheelchair that can outsmart any puppeteer."

Geraldine's eyes roll. "Anyone for mysticism?"

"Today," Jimmy laughs, "is the first time I've noticed your details."

"My *details*?"

"Yeah. I can see the German side."

"Come off it! What's changed about me? You've had a coffee, noticed the radio's on."

"Don't know what it is. Could be your eyes. Your eyes never clicked before. The blue! How much blue. I thought your hair was blond."

"But it's really blond?"

"Yeah."

"Depends."

"On what?"

"Don't be cute! Depends on what I'm wearing, obviously. What else? What else d'you see?"

Looking across at Geraldine, Jimmy remembers that theatre night. And remembers Colette, a woman of olive skin. A little black mole's on Colette's cleavage. Somebody said olive-skinned white women have brown nipples. Geraldine's mischievous blue eyes gaze.

"Argh, Jim lad!" she laughs. "What do you see?"

"What should I see?"

"It's like you've never seen me before. So, what d'you see?"

"I see a surprise."

# 96

Half past ten. Beside the patio, two mimosas in full bloom. They look like gold puffballs over the green. A lush Hertfordshire garden.

"Mimosas are more at home in the south," Geraldine says. "In the sun. Somewhere hot. Portugal, Italy. But they get lizards. Couldn't stand the sight if a lizard poking out its tongue on a mimosa tree."

"Those people on your radio," Jimmy says, "they're like gyroscopes."

"Gyroscopes?"

"Flywheels. Spinning objects, holding in a stable plane no matter how their frames move."

Her eyes narrow. "*How* d'you know such things?"

Past the mimosas, the morning strides round in the garden. Ignoring the radio, Jimmy mulls; remembers last night. Being in the same space as Colette last night. The first time since that weird evening at the theatre. Last night was going great at Kevin's flat, getting chords to work in a new arrangement. Then she arrived. She and a teenaged girl. Her daughter. Never cropped up before, but Kevin was Colette's onetime. And even Kevin never mentioned it. But last night everything was clear. Colette and Kevin lived eight years together and have a daughter. But they've been apart five years. Seeing the full story, things suddenly made sense for Jimmy. He stood back from the piano, checking the way Kevin played with the girl. Colette chain-smoked at the far end of the studio. Their eyes met. A flicker. Something like regret. Quiet but quick. Something there, and always going to be. But Kevin's studio was family space last night and Jimmy didn't spite the innocent teenage girl. Colette's daughter. Kevin's daughter. The girl was like the Modigliani repro on her mother's office wall. It was time to go. Kevin got the vibes as Colette walked Jimmy to the car. Nothing was getting said, not till the engine fired. Then he asked if she kept his note. No, she said, puffed, puckering; then said he should check a psychiatrist. He asked if she wanted to know. Know what, she said. Well, that theatre night he was shoveling the Maserati for all it was worth and, even now, still wonders how it would have been instead of walking away. Waving him on, she said 'Doubt is good. Life's a bore without a bit of wild-card!' Jimmy said goodbye. Then went for a night of malt. Sober malt whisky. Last night was sleepless and definitely alone. By 3 in the morning the bottle was empty and the ganja clean out. But Cobalt was ready. It's been jigged and re-jigged and jigged so many times that now, well, no real reference in it to Bach or Coltrane.

Geraldine's off to Ireland tomorrow. So Jimmy's here three weeks earlier than planned. She could go for six weeks. Six months. So this is a chance for a tenement dweller to grab some quality time. Some quiet English garden time. She promised him a recovery day in her garden. And promised not to talk of Colette.

They sit on the patio. And a breeze wafts over a table with three chairs. Last week, Geraldine freshened them with ivory paint.

"Right!" she says. "Fancy a proper walk round, or sit and talk?"

"Your garden's a lot bigger than you said. Never seen anything like it. What's over there?"

"Oh, just half the world."

This garden and 5-bedroom house is where Renate lives by herself. The old lady must be glad, having her daughter back at home for a while, Jimmy thinks. He goes with Geraldine further from the house. Moving along, looking for more outdoors. A dog and two puppies arrive from where a wooden bench squats opposite a bird-box.

"The lawn here could do a football game," he says. "No, not football. Not here. Bowls. Something sedate."

"Let's sit here a minute," she says, checking the sky.

"Any chance of a UFO?"

"Today? Oh, we'll see what we can do."

"I believe that stuff."

"Aliens?"

"Why not! Something else *can* be out there."

At the far end of the garden, birds sing high in a plane tree. Jimmy's learning, listening to birds sing. A bird melody trips round a flat-5, low to the lawn, cascading, ignoring trees, then heads back to sunlight. And consecration. Then it starts again. Looks like Colette was right, he thinks; sometimes the only canvass is a wildcard. But this quiet place is nothing to Geraldine; not to somebody who's been in this place most her life and not noticing it now.

"I hate the thought of getting old."

Jimmy frowns. "Let's get back to the patio."

"What's the matter?"

"This is Zen."

"The quietness?"

"Yes."

"So natural?"

"Natural. That's the word for this!"

"Well, that's the point of having you here."

"I read somewhere that symmetry is huge in nature. Serious maths folk devised symmetry-breaking. Nature revealing patterns to the mind."

"Zen?"

"Yeah. And birds, they've been around so long."

"You're really quite reserved, aren't you!"

"Not as shy as birds," he laughs.

"There's one type in Borneo, mimics buzzsaws in a forest."

"A bird doing a buzzsaw?"

"Some imitate the noise of jets taking off."

"UFOs could be the next big thing for birds to mimic."

"But then, who'd know?"

"Cynical!"

Geraldine's outstretched arms indicate a clump of trees. "Recognize anything?"

"Don't ask me to name plants," Jimmy says. "Wouldn't have a clue."

"No, no. Look! Don't you recognize those trees?"

"What about them?"

"Look harder!"

"Tall. Green."

"Funny man!"

"Well," he says, "now you mention it. Yeah, something *is* familiar. That water and the trees. It's like some place I've seen. But where?"

"On a poster, maybe?"

"Hey, this is my first time in the countryside. This can get seen from a motorway. Or the train. But inside, it's a different thing. Birds singing, miles from a tenement."

"Cracked it yet?"

Suddenly, the puzzle snaps. The far end of Geraldine's garden is like the salesroom poster at Homes. But different lighting. She took a picture at dusk that Colette scanned into a computer and re-jigged to make it suggest a forest. But instead of a lake, like in the poster, only a pond here at the trees' edge. Light streams down through leaves, like from stained cathedral glass. After the phonecall to the St Albans man, Jimmy turned to that poster in the salesroom. But now, only gazing. Seeing real sunlight at play. The poster was a fake. No swans float on the pond. No swans here.

Silent, they go past flowers most people have never seen. Keeping quiet. Until she starts. Geraldine talks hard facts, the life causing them to meet. The past year's been too difficult, feeling a wipe-out, a failure, having to come back to her mother's house. But that was nothing. Not next to the hurt when her language agency failed. She gets broody, but maybe Brian's a blank. Tomorrow it's Ireland, check if anything's still there between them.

"I suppose the house makes you think we've got a few bob," she says. "Not true!"

"Could have fooled me."

"See that vegetable patch? It's definitely no hobby. I owe my mother her life savings. We chucked oodles of it at the business. Lost it all. I can't say how painful it was to come back, you know, get back here and twiddle my thumbs. When I turned up at Homes I'd have cleaned the toilets if that was all there was."

"Hey," Jimmy says, "when I first saw you it was class at first sight. Aloof, but classy. And kind."

"Aloof?"

"Yeah."

"Kind? You've never said that before."

"No need. You always knew where you were going."

"What about now?"

"Pure class."

"Are you pitching me? Trying on some spiel?"

"No, no. Class. That's got nothing to do with your plush house."

Getting misty-eyed, she turns away. "You know, I've never really thanked you. I count on our friendship. Lots. I admire what you have. Your inner strength."

"My inner strength?" Jimmy laughs. "What bit of my anatomy is that?"

"You're very chippy today!"

"Well, you asked for it. You *know* you're a class act."

"Enough about me," she says. "You now. How's it going?"

"You mean Colette, don't you?"

"Hmm."

"This is the part where you weren't going to mention her."

"I don't understand it, you and that woman."

# 97

"Petals," Jimmy says, "make great patterns. They fall from a flower, cruise your eyes."

Geraldine shrugs. "So what!"

"Slaves were sugar-dice. Or stuffed cotton in their ears."

"What?"

"Birds sing the blues. Some fly seriously high. A pilot was forty miles high one day and a flock of geese was up there."

"How high?"

"Forty miles. Some birds hop over farmers' fields. Then somebody comes along with a shotgun, sprays the sky with buckshot. That breaks their heart."

"What?"

"OK to smoke?" he says, yawning.

"Bit late to ask!"

"No, not tobacco. I need a spliff."

A letter from Agnes alongside the Rizla in his pocket; a six page letter and a photo from South Africa. So far, only the first paragraph got read: 'We went to the beach on Sunday. The women met for traditional songs. I'll send you a tape.' The letter arrived a week ago but Jimmy didn't read it. But thinking now of Agnes, of that woman wading in sea water. African woman waving from another continent. But the photo. Hard to understand the photograph with the letter.

"Still thinking about Colette?"

"Somebody on my mind," he says, "and it's definitely not Colette."

"Is it that South African woman?"

"Yep."

"How is she?"

"Me and her? No idea. Don't know how it'll pan out."

"Where does Colette come in?"

"Why mention her?"

"Because it's upsetting you."

"It's not Colette. Believe me!"

Geraldine grabs the spliff. This is the first time for a while. Now she's pulling on it, pulling and pulling. Blows bad smoke rings. Her smoke rings daze out to the trees.

"Know what I think?" she sighs. "I think you love your South African. Lost without her, but so wish you'd slept with Colette."

"Colette?"

"Yeah. You should have, you know. A bit of 'been there, done that.'"

Hard for Jimmy not to wonder. Time to time, wondering that weird

Colette night. That wildcard night. One thing was condoms; leaving the flat that night with none. Or the bed linen; if it had been clean that night. Or if no old man was at the zebra crossing, no old man nearly getting mowed down. None of that, and that woman would have lived her gypsy life. But then. The big question. The salesroom talk at Homes was that every now and then Colette singles out one guy to get close to. Jimmy was only the most recent one, they said; up-and-coming young black guy with new music, but only a trophy for the woman. And then. The big one. Hard to tell. Colette could've been doing a black-white fantasy that theatre night. Or maybe she was into Jimmy as a man.

"Your lawn is no wildcard," he says, turning to Geraldine. "Tapers of mown grass reach away, like to set alight the countryside."

"Pass the spliff!"

"Don't get greedy."

"Instead of Colette, what if it had been a black woman hearing you talk to that St Albans bloke?"

"A black woman?"

"Hmm."

"A militant black woman would suck her teeth. She'd turn away, say, 'What a big-time uncle tom!' Then again, they know. They understand. Most black women know how to try for a quiet life among white folk."

"Regret it?"

"What?"

"Not sleeping with Colette."

"No," Jimmy shrugs. "This poke, that."

"Yeah."

"Sometimes it's a bitch, anyway."

"I'll tell you how it is!" Geraldine groans, passing the spliff. Her eyes are distant, her voice dips. "Bad sex is like new clothes, the type you don't want but can't take back because you've lost the receipt."

"Yeah, I've been there."

"I almost started seeing someone. I was so missing Brian."

"Missing out?"

"Emotions, physical."

"I know the feeling."

"If I ever cheated on Brian, seeing someone, it would hurt."

"This going to be a confession?"

"Confession? So, you want one of those?"

"The dirtier the better!"

"Then hold on to your seat, mate."

"Hope this is going to be dirty. Filthy!"

"One day," she says, "it was just after Christmas and I went for a walk, getting away from myself, a bit of shopping, the usual. When I got to the checkout, I had a packet of condoms in my trolley. Search me, how they got there."

"Weird!"

"Think that's weird? You have *no* idea what's out there."

"People are weird, as weird can be."

"*So* lots of posturing."

"Why the condoms in your trolley?"

"How should I know? Find yourself alone and you don't want to, you know, you're not sure!"

"Why the condoms?"

"Plastic, plastic!" she says, flicking petals. "Seen the she-condom?"

"I heard about that thing. Wouldn't want to meet it."

"There's Fred and Gertrude, get it? Fred's sporting his new canary condom. Gertrude's chuffed to the nines with hers. What a scream! Oh, here they come. Mr and Mrs Flastic Puck! Anyone for ice-hockey?"

# 98

He wonders how this can be Agnes. Thinks the photo is somebody else. A sister maybe. Or a young aunt. But. The clincher: 'All my love, Agnes.' signed over it.

The sun wavers a stark sky. Rooks screeching high as Geraldine gets back from the house. Jimmy slips the photo in his pocket.

Setting the tray on the patio table, her eyes follow his, looking out at the distance. "You seem miles away."

"Weird, an hour ago it was birdsong out there. Beautiful. How did rooks get into this?"

"Oh, the noise! That's what's bothering you? There's a different choir on stage now."

"Sounds like one of those stupid teen bands!"

She grins. A mischievous girl's grin. "Fancy a riddle?"

"Riddle-me-dee, riddle-me-da?"

"Yeah, that's it."

"You like all that stuff, don't you? Riddles, puzzles, hidden stuff. Not so long ago they would've called you a witch."

"How can a forest pine for Hitler?"

"Trees?"

"Yes."

"Pine for Hitler?"

"That's the riddle!"

Hoping this is a joke, he checks her eyes. But nothing in blue. Not a blink. "It's one of those head jobs, isn't it?"

"That's not the answer!"

"Is it a tattoo Hitler had, a tattoo of pine trees?"

"No."

"Look, there's no way I'll get it. You'll have to tell me."

"It's about larch trees."

"What about them?"

Disappointed, she shrugs. "A forest can pine for Hitler when larch trees get planted in a pine forest!"

Jimmy toys with the marijuana sachet, but lights a cigarette. "I don't get it."

"This is the bad part," she says. "The strangest story of all time. Gothic. But true. Just outside Berlin, the old Nazis planted larch trees in a pine forest. Every autumn for the past 60 years the larch turned brown against the green pine. Larch, planted in the shape of a giant swastika that only ever gets seen from the sky. Like the Great Wall of China."

"That," Jimmy says, "sounds like something from Wagner."

"No, this is from now! Larch trees were used for centuries. Make great boats, apparently. But in that forest near Berlin they were a kind of lighthouse."

"Nazis looking for myths in autumn skies."

"I couldn't believe it!"

"Makes you think."

"Absolutely."

"The things you can do with trees!"

"Oh, they're gone," she says. "Chopped down. Gone now."

"How come it took so long?"

"Nobody knew. Honestly. Nobody sensible knew. We can surf the chatrooms, there's some really useful websites."

"Jessye Norman sings Wagner."

"Bet that raises a few eyebrows!"

"Colour-blind casting."

"Which opera was it?"

"Die Walkure. A black woman as Sieglinde to mate in the forest with blond brother Siegmund."

Geraldine grins. "Wagner, bet he's boiling in his grave at that!"

"He was the weaver of blue-eyed art. Arch weaver."

"Jessye Norman is amazing. Wonder how she dealt with it."

"I don't know why she bothered," Jimmy says. "Aryan fairytale. Sings her heart out then leaves the opera-house alone as black."

"What about Jessye the woman?"

"Bumped into her once. A large lady."

"Bet you fancied her, a younger version."

"Why not."

"Listen to lots of opera, classical opera?"

"Yeah. You?"

"Lots."

"You know Die Walkure?"

"The ring! The magic ring! Alberich the dwarf, maker of the ring, handing power to who can possess it."

"That ring," Jimmy says, "is a crippled fairytale."

"I can feel a sermon coming!"

"Or a rant, right?"

"And all because of a riddle about trees!"

"Wasn't really about trees, though, was it!"

"Without them, we're dust."

"Trees?"

"Don't take them for granted."

"As in, the trees in my 8$^{th}$ floor tenement flat?"

"Don't be hateful."

"You've seen where I live. How would I know about trees?"

"When will you get away from there?"

"When Mary J lets me."

"Who?"

"Mary J. Blige. Singer. Black wife."

"And?"

"She sings tenements. Sings them away. Singing to get green instead of concrete. About the same age as us, four years older."

"Let's swap," Geraldine says.

"Swap what?"

"Trees for music. Let's try it for a day."

"Leaves everywhere. So what?

"Where leaves go, they can take you with them."

Jimmy laughs. "Hey, trees. Spare a ride?"

"Spiteful!"

"Me and my tenement trees, right?"

"Got splinters in your eyes today, haven't you!"

"What?"

"Oh, forget it!"

"You started it!"

The dog and puppies investigate something lurching on the lawn. It's a frog. In one bound it gets yards away.

"So," Geraldine smiles, "you want to fight? I'm a judo black-belt. That lawn is a good place to show you."

"If I had a woman like you," Jimmy says, "I'd show you new moves."

"Watch it!"

"Brian doesn't know what he's missing."

She turns away. Scans to the countryside. Eyes searching. Thoughts beyond the lawn. "Can you always tell whether it's a man playing?"

"Music?"

"Yeah. The piano, anything."

"Depends."

"So, you *can't* tell!"

"What's this gender stuff?"

"You can't tell if it's a man or woman. Go on, admit it!"

"Well, no, not with classical. But with jazz, you're looking at a big difference. The boss players are guys."

"All of them?"

"Well, no. One or two women. Mary Lou Williams. Played serious jazz piano. Composed neat stuff."

"But?"

"It's guys. Same with blues."

"Isn't that because you already know who's playing? There aren't too many, who shall I say?"

"Oscar Peterson?"

"Right!"

"You know of him?"

"Renate's got a video. Him, playing with Andre Previn."

"Oscar is good."

"Not too many of him around, are there?"

"No. But he derives from Tatum anyway."

"Who?"

"Art Tatum? Blind guy from Harlem. "

"Black?"

"Yeah. Tatum was it. Ace, ace, ace, piano player of all time! Seeing him play, Rubinstein couldn't believe it. Rachmaninov. Rach couldn't believe his ears. Those guys freaked, knowing Tatum was in this world. And that Paderewski, one more classical ace that didn't believe it when Tatum played."

"Rubenstein, Rachmaninov, Paderewski. What a roll-call!"

"Happy philharmonics, guys!"

"What about Bill Evans?"

"What about him?"

"He was great. Great piano."

"We were talking clouds, now you bring it to tree-top level."

"*You* recommended him. He's on that record you lent me."

"Which one?"

"Kind of Blue."

"Listen," Jimmy says, "folk always praise Kind of Blue. It's the big scapegoat. Everybody, especially the ones that don't get it. Jazz comes from the blues."

"What're you saying?"

"People jabber. This and that. They even say Bill Evans got dropped for the Freddie track because there's no brains required for blues. They don't get it."

"Well, *I* don't get it!"

"Bill Evans could not *play* blues. And that Freddie Freeloader it's, man! Space-wide blues. Blues to spare. Other tracks, yes. Bill playing neat piano, but the deal is the 'kind of' in the title."

"I don't get it, sorry."

"Those guys on Kind of Blue, they did something big. Modal, deep. But it wasn't always jazz. That's what Miles meant by *kind of* blue."

Geraldine frowns. "It's always blokes, isn't it?"

"I'm not a gender maniac."

"Then," she says, "tell me about women in blues and jazz."

"Instrumentalists?"

"Yeah."

"I wouldn't say they're a genius. I mean, there's no Charlie Parker. No-body on guitar that's a female Hendrix."

"Why is that?"

"Dunno. But if you hear Sister Rosetta Tharpe, that woman played mean guitar! Funky playing."

"Black woman?"

"Yep."

"Proud of that, aren't you?"

"Proud?"

"Of your black musicians."

"You proud of the white ones?"

"What a daft question!"

"But only when I ask it, right?"

"You're being defensive again!"

"Chip on my shoulder?"

"In a way, yes. You love to strut. Strut black."

"And when I praise Bach or Mozart, what then?"

Eyes crinkled, Geraldine slopes in her chair. Her eyes gazing her feet. "Yeah. OK. I'd forgotten. Sorry."

Jimmy laughs. "Check out Libba Cotten. That woman was a serious player. Played till past ninety."

"Piano?"

"Guitar. She composed Freight Train. She wrote it young. Eleven, twelve. A lot of serious people say it's *the* theme of American folk."

Geraldine sighs. "Can you do me a theme? Not now. One day."

"I don't do love songs."

"That's OK. Any theme you like."

"Lions?"

"Why not? They were all over Britain before the ice age."

"I dreamt walking through a pride of them."

"A pride of lions?"

"Yeah."

"Sleeping lions."

# 99

Pacing, taking ground. Wondering. Thinking hard. Pacing the patio. Gazing at the lawn. Geraldine calculates. She could almost count every blade of grass on the lawn. "It's not the music," she says. "I think it's the title. They don't like Minims for Britain."

"When I first sent it off," Jimmy says, "that's what it was called. But I changed my mind. I faxed the change. And told them on the phone. That's why I rang. I said it's called Minims now."

"Minims, then! It still suggests immigrants."

"*What*?"

"Immigrants!"

"It's not about immigrants."

"Then why so defensive?"

"It's about people waking up, going for a better real."

"It's an odd title."

"Why?"

"Everybody thinks globally these days. Brits. Germans, the French."

"Hey, the French for minim is blanche."

"And?"

"If Minims was about immigrants I'd have called it something else, like Crotchets in Britain."

"Why?"

"I could've called it Crochets."

"What's crochets got to with immigrants?"

"You're the grand linguist, and you don't get it?"

"No."

"French for crochet is black. Well, noire. I could have said crochets."

"Well, mon frere, blanche means white!"

"Just proves it. Minims grabs that. And minim is a palindrome."

"Oh, stop the crap! Stop being such a clever-clogs, so superior."

Geraldine turns away. She turns to the lawn, like she was window shopping with a difficult someone; like maybe with a wayward nephew. A bill arrived last week from the hosts of her website. But the site won't get renewed.

"Ever had ackee and saltfish?" Jimmy says.

"Jamaican food?"

"Yeah, the absolute business!"

She tugs his sleeve. "Look," she says, "it's not how you explain your music. It's what they think it means."

"But who are they? They're just a bunch of bad mistakes."

"*They*, clever-clogs, are the gatekeepers!"

"Must be great living somewhere like this."

"Don't change the subject!"

"Stephen Hawking, he'd leave wheelchair-tracks on your lawn. I can see it now, him chasing his papers before the breeze."

"What?"

"Wheelchair, making tracks on your lawn."

"Stop the fog!"

"What's the matter?"

"Stop the reverie."

"But I must bow down to gate-keepers, right?"

"I'm going to speak my mind. Don't take it the wrong way." She turns to him. "Interested in what I have to say?"

"Just don't say there's a chip on my shoulder!"

"Really got your hackles up, haven't you! What's the matter?"

"Know what? The last thing I need is a pep talk. I could fill your house with all the 'Think positive, keep smiling' crap I've had!"

"Think negative then," she laughs.

"You should be so lucky!"

"Clive used to say 'My friends, no negatives please!' Remember that?"

"Shyster!"

"The cheek of the man! Him, his pathetic business motto."

"Hovering over the moon, all Neil Armstrong could think was girls in bikinis on a beach."

Geraldine's arms fling in air. "Here we go again! Planets, stars!"

"Who joins the dots?"

"Which dots?"

"Polka-dot bikinis. Why'd a swimsuit get named after where they tested the atom bomb?"

"Bikinis, on the moon?"

"Yeah. Neil Armstrong was thinking girls in bikinis."

"First *man* on the moon. Typical!"

"He was full of stars."

"He was an astronaut. You're not."

"Know why I do music?"

"It's so you, isn't it. Very, very good at it."

"Good was the easy part."

"Never look a gift horse in the mouth!"

"Music, because I had to get away from words. Live without talking."

"Don't be daft!"

"I mean it."

"What happens when the phone rings?"

"No words at all."

# 100

Geraldine yawns. Tired, she looks out at the lawn. Wipes her eyes. And yawns again. "I'm jealous of your music."

"I need a spliff," Jimmy says.

"Another one? The fourth one so far."

"So what!"

"No comment."

"That sounds like a put-down."

"Wish I could do a music degree."

"That's the easy part."

"How'd you manage it? Three years in two, that's *so* nerd!"

"That course was laced with politics. Not sure it was worth it."

"Plunks?

"What's plunks?"

"Round here," she says, "plunks is what we call politicians."

"I like that! Yeah, we had loads of those. Quacks playing mind games, claiming jazz wouldn't have made it without Stravinsky."

"Igor Stravinsky, jazz?"

"Yeah."

"Never really listened to his music."

"There's folk claiming he invented jazz! Check it out."

"Oh, let's not. Not today, please. It'll lead to talk of race."

"Read the story behind the Firebird," Jimmy says. "It's a big piece. Huge ambition. Even now. There's stuff going on when you listen to it. Ace. But no way he's a parent to jazz. He tried explaining himself when Firebird first came out, wrote a lecture called Poetics of Music."

"Any good?"

"Deep."

"Then your idiots should read it."

"Yeah."

"Cheer up! At least there weren't tone-deaf DJ's on the course."

"No? One day I had a punch. It was with a cretin. I boxed his ears. We were supposed to be talking facts, origins and stuff, but all he said was there'd be no Hendrix without Buddy Holly."

"Oh, my God!"

"Yeah, that bad."

"I see what you mean."

"Credit, where credit's due."

"Of course. Naturally. But then, aren't you just flag-waving? I mean, who cares who got there first? What's it matter?"

"Know who Charlie Parker was?" Jimmy says.

"You always talk of Charlie Parker. Always!"

"Ever see that film Clint Eastwood made about him?"

"Funny enough, we watched it one Christmas."

"And?"

"And he drank neat iodine."

"Yeah, that's him. The one they called Bird."

"I remember the plot."

"The plot's not the story. The film didn't quite get there, didn't get the depth of playing. You're looking at genius. The only word. Greatest improviser ever. Greatest."

"You're building up to something!"

"It's bull, claiming no Bird without Stravinsky's Firebird!"

"The film claimed that?"

"No."

"I think it got at the man, you know, the Parker back-story. You get the music any time."

Jimmy shrugs. "It's head-in-the-sand people, they're the ones!"

"Like, me?"

"When Bob Marley first came to England, BBC morons failed him at the audition."

"What!"

"Seriously. BBC plunks. They gave him the thumbs down."

"Bob Marley?"

"Yeah. They claimed he didn't know reggae."

"You're joking!"

"Bach used 16-note chords in Cantata No. 90."

"I know what you're getting at," Geraldine sighs.

"What am I getting at?"

"It's obvious."

"Dead right!"

"Then why split hairs? Isn't it the music that matters?"

"Yes."

"So who got there first doesn't matter."

"It's slander. It matters!"

Pretending not to get it, her eyebrows raise. "Slander?"

"Brixton!" Jimmy yells, pushing from the chair. Wanting to leave. Suddenly wanting to get away. Or scatter marijuana seeds on this garden; enough seeds to start a plantation.

"Slander?"

"If you're black and talented, good, then the gate-keepers might let you in. They might just bother. But only after they toss a coin."

"Can't you set that aside? For me? For one day?"

"Your garden, this quiet English space, not where a hurricane would happen."

"Enough mysticism!"

"Not a place from where to go barracuda fishing down the lane."

"*What?*"

"The green reserve here," Jimmy says, nodding at the garden, "no way a bird of greatness could escape. Not from somebody's ribcage, not even Stravinsky."

"Don't get mystical. Please!"

"What would Charlie Parker do here? A bird of greatness would never escape from here."

"Why?"

"Because this place is free. Free!"

"Then get a hold of some."

"They say I have a chip on my shoulder, an axe to grind."

"And *they* always know best, do they?"

"They make sure people like me know my place. So they come out with 'Just trying to help, don't take it the wrong way.' Any idea what I'm talking about?"

"No, Jimmy."

"I won't fill my head with stuff I can't own. How'd I own this house? Even if I clocked the lottery the folk next door would resent me. They'd move out."

"Talent! You own a talent. Special. Amazing, amazing!"

"I own is the chip on my shoulder."

Teeth gritted, Geraldine grates the coffeepot across the table. Head shaking, she pours a cup. Hesitant pouring. Then attacks. She spins the lukewarm liquid with a spoon, clink rhythm. Teaspoon on bone china. The cup wants to itself alight. For a full minute she says nothing. Cold emotion in a cup. Mud, not coffee. She stirs so fast that a wall starts in the cup, like a circus rider on a wall of death. The coffee rider can escape the cup. Or collapse, die.

She slings the spoon. "What was all that about!"

"What d'you mean?"

"I'm a grown woman. I think you want to trust me. What stops you?"

He turns to the greenery. Grabs a handful of space. "Any jasmine in this garden?"

"No!"

"Some people live for jazz."

"You don't say!"

"Some folk have never seen jasmine. Jelly Roll Morton. He worked piano, played in brothels. More than anybody, jazz is down to him. Jazz with jasmine. Jazz maybe gets its name from the flower. Jelly Roll was doing his thing, same time Stravinsky took a stint with Coco Chanel."

"Igor Stravinsky, and Coco Chanel?"

"He tapped Coco's bush. Way before she got perfume to market."

Geraldine laughs. "What's the point of the story?"

Jimmy remembers why he's here, why she invited him. 'What are you doing here?' her eyes say.

"I wasn't trying out my frustration. Not on you," he says. "You know how I get wound up. Stuff comes at me from all angles. If I think somebody's having a go at me, telling me I have a chip on my shoulder, then it boils over."

"If there *is* a chip on your shoulder I'll be the first to tell you, believe me!"

"I'm saying sorry, OK?"

"Doesn't matter now."

"Say what's on your mind!"

"I can never decide," she says, "whether you believe in  people, or in nothing."

"Is that all?"

"Isn't that enough?"

"I thought you had a lecture for me."

"What I was trying to say, what I *am* saying, no, it's no use, I can't."

"Bet it's something sloppy, like I should settle down and live."

"Yes. Get a grip!"

"I'm unhinged?"

"Stop feeling sorry for yourself!" she says.

The sun relaxes on the lawn. Quiet now, out and out. And Geraldine stacks cup in cup, clearing the table. Saucer in saucer. A soap-cloth's in her hand, drudging a table that was spick anyway. Wiping hard, like a blood stain there. No middle class brogue in a dish rag.

# 101

Two o'clock. The sun loiters. The photo of Agnes shucks in Jimmy's armpit. Gazing the lawn, he asks what would happen if a lion should suddenly appear. Geraldine's quick eyes cut in.

"Where would a lion come from?" she says.

"Black male, approximate age of seventy."

She doesn't understand. But wants to be baited. "Only seventy? Oh, right."

"Charlie Parker's postmortem report."

"What are you getting at?"

"Charlie was only thirty-four when he died."

"And?"

"Only a medically thick alien would think you're seventy when all you were doing was thirty-four. You can't look at a guy thirty-four, see some old man seventy. But that's what they did to Charlie Parker."

"Music lives on, attitudes fade."

"Stick that on a banner sometime."

"Love to! But what about a bit of consistency?"

"I talk gibberish, or is it mumbo-jumbo?"

"*Quick!*" Geraldine shrieks. "There's that lion!"

"What?"

"Quick, it's coming this way!"

Jimmy ups from the table. No lion can be there, but he reacts anyway.

"Slush for logic, mon frere!"

He laughs. "Yeah, you're the sister I never had. Sort of."

"Let's not get preachy. Not today."

"I like your mother. So motherly."

"Ever go to art galleries?"

"Yeah. But only when I want to lose a day."

"We went to the sneak preview at the Tate Modern. Me and Renate. Speechless. Art galleries are my mother's thing. This one's the biggest modern art space. Airy sections. Nice and quiet."

"Visual arts are a pain right now. You said so yourself."

"Did you vote for Ken?" she says, eyes sprinkling mischief.

"Ken, who?"

"Livingstone. You know, Mr Nose."

"What was the vote for?"

"Mayor of London. Where *have* you been!"

"Nowhere near a ballot box. That's for sure."

"London's got two mayors now."

"Who's the other one?"

"The lord mayor. But that's only ceremonial. Ken will run the city, like mayors in America."

"I wouldn't have voted. No way!"

"Such a fuss."

"Hey, look at those clouds! Rain clouds."

"That rain's been threatening all day."

"Right now somebody's dying of thirst somewhere."

"Yes. And wastrels blathering in a swimming pool."

"A lion laps water while zebras wait their turn."

"Fancy a drink? White wine."

"Only 90 seconds after the Big Bang," Jimmy says, "the temperature of the universe cooled to a billion degrees."

"Still preaching from that book?"

"Yeah. A Brief History Of Time. Kind of tedious, but a good deal."

"You and Brian would get on like a house on fire!"

"Loves Ireland, doesn't he?"

"Yes, but he's English. Born and bred in Burton Bradstock, lovely place in Dorset. Water meadows. They've got the River Bride flowing though hills to the sea. Thatched cottages. Everyone knows everyone. In spring, migrating birds shelter in the valley."

"Sounds like I'd like it there."

"Are you getting defensive?"

"In what way?"

"Tebbit. That thingy, the Tebbit test. Bothers you, doesn't it?"

"Obviously, I don't agree with it. But I see what he's getting at."

"I don't think he'd want your sympathy."

"Not sympathy. It's how cunning that stuff is."

"On second thoughts, can't we just enjoy the day?"

"You brought Tebbit into this. You started it!"

"And you want the last word."

"Sorry I brought my tenement head."

"Here we go again!"

"You've got your garden. Your neighbours have theirs."

"If you want a yardstick," Geraldine says, "then try Alan Turing. Know about him?"

"No."

"Computing."

"Ah, yes! You mentioned him before."

"Yes."

"He wasn't a lion tamer!"

"Our top man at Bletchley Park."

"Where?"

"The war. Code-breaking. Turing cracked the best German codes at

Bletchley Park."

"What's that got to do with me?"

"We'd all be speaking German."

"Bitte, bitte!"

"Kennst du das Land wo die Zitronen bluhn?"

"German?"

"Ja!"

"Hey," Jimmy laughs, "if I talked that arrogant bull I'd still be on the outside looking in."

"It's from a poem."

"What's it mean?"

"Roughly?"

"Anyway you want it."

"Well," she says, eyes tuned to the garden, "I'd go for 'Where's that country where lemons bloom?' Lush, isn't it?"

"Sounds like I should be grateful."

"For what?"

"Lemons."

"Lemons are *so* sunny."

"I don't feel grateful for the sun. No nostalgia for lemons."

"What's the matter now?"

"I was born in England."

"Then remember that!"

"So easy for everybody to forget."

"That's not fair!"

"Glad you see it that way. Lots don't."

"A few racist idiots."

"Way out in space," Jimmy says, "deep inside a spinning black hole, time-travel could happen."

"So sorry!"

"For what?"

"Us earthlings. Must be very boring for you down here."

"If a fat woman can see her toe then maybe we're all ready to go."

"Bullshit!"

"A genius called Kurt Godel. He was with Einstein at Princeton. Ace. *The* business. Those guys wondering what we can know in the universe. Godel. Huge brains. Showed all true statements can never be proved."

"Gobbledegook!"

"How many idiots are a few?" Jimmy says.

"Idiots?"

"Racists are a few idiots. That's what you said. How many's a few?"

"Quite the little accountant, aren't we?"

"How many?"

"How should I know!"

"Take a stab at it."

"What will that prove."

"It'll show you know what you're talking about."

"Three, four percent. OK, no more than ten. Ten percent."

"Then let's go for a walk. Me and you. Right now, down your road. See what your neighbours think."

# 102

Bales of clouds smudge the sky. From Geraldine's garden, a noise like somebody shouting for help. But it's only the peacock next door.

Her throat clears. "I once saw a little girl, tiny little thing, struggling down a country lane. I think it was in Mauritius. She was carrying a man-sized tray of mangoes on her head. She wanted to cry but her mother said she was her little peacock and peacocks don't cry."

Jimmy's eyes narrow. "Peacocks are weird, upsetting."

"I quite like them. Alan Turing was a bit of a peahen."

"I'd never keep animals. Ever."

"But you'd like a harem?"

"That's for me!"

"What would your girlfriend say, your South African?"

"This and that. Mostly."

"She'd run a mile from you!"

"Hey, got anything to drink?"

"Wine do?"

"What you got?"

"White."

"No whisky?"

"No."

"Then let's hit the trail. Ganja time!"

"Cherie's due any time now."

"Who?"

"Cherie Blair. Blair's wife."

"Coming here?"

"No, no. Their fourth child. It's due any time now."

"Didn't know she was banged up."

"So, what'll it be? Boy or girl?"

"Look," Jimmy yawns, "get to the point."

"The point is, you're scared of Norman Tebbit."

"Nah!"

"He's your bogeyman."

"Then whose fault's that?"

"Yours, if you let him get away with it."

"That's gibberish!"

"White-liberal gibberish?"

"Yeah, fancy talk. Language games."

"Then *do* something about it!"

"I'm not a politician. Not a plunk."

"You don't have to be. Turing did it, unmasked the language game."

"Turing sets me free?"

"Well, let's phone Brian. He's a wiz at this."

"Computers?"

"Language. Logic."

"I don't feel like talking."

"Let's give him a call."

"Don't wanna talk to the guy."

"He's very good."

"It'll lead to race. There's no way I'm going through *that* on the phone. Bet you know that Turing stuff anyway."

Geraldine's brows pucker, like a little girl found out. Her eyes say she wants only one excuse to flip. Phoning Brian, she'd say there's somebody visiting who can play piano.

She turns to Jimmy. "Suppose, just suppose you ask a computer and you can't tell."

"Tell?"

"Not sure I can do this. Alan Turing, difficult."

"Got stage fright?"

"Don't want to get it wrong."

"This was your big idea."

"In World War 2, Turing thought about German ciphers. How to crack them. It was maths. Heavy, heavy maths. And thermionic valves that today any pocket calculator would replace a roomful of."

"Bletchley Park, right?"

"That's where they cracked it"

"Then feasted on German corpses"

"That's war. But they played around. A lot. Had lots of laughs. Those codebreakers, frighteningly bright. Maths, ciphers. And they played word games with the Germans, silly stuff, like the difference in German between odd sentences."

"Like what?"

"Like the difference between 'toads squatting in autumn grass' and 'Scheherazade fretting in silk sheets.' Amazing!"

"Funny guys."

"It was 50-50. Half were women. Wish I was half that bright!"

"That Enigma machine, wasn't it?"

"Yeah."

"Where's Turing come in?"

She scuds from the chair. "OK, here goes! You ask two people the same question, what if you get the same answer?"

"Could be the right answer, couldn't it!"

"Suppose it's a computer and a person, and you can't tell the answers apart."

271

"Why would I ask a machine?"

"Something like the internet."

"Well, yeah. Search engines."

"The software knows."

"Yeah, but only like some kind of robot. A library assistant."

"The librarians *I* know are people!"

"And?"

"It means search engines are intelligent. Of sorts."

"Three cheers! Four cheers!"

"Don't be sarky, let me finish."

"What's this got to do with me?"

"I'd say quite a lot, really."

"The minute somebody like me gets close, think we've cracked it, that's when we get Anne Hathaway shoved in our face. Hathaway's daffodils, now some guy at Bletchley Park!"

"Haven't we done this anguish before? You never stop!"

"I visited Jamaica and they said 'English boy!' But they were only teasing. I was born in England but it's like I should get down on my knees here."

"Why?"

"I won't beg!"

"Calm down!"

"I can't live next door to Anne Hathaway."

"Who can?"

"Norman Tebbit."

"Look, that St Albans chap on the phone, he thought you were white. He couldn't tell. There's your proof!"

"Of what?"

"Tebbit's little bobbin won't work."

"How'd you arrive at that?"

"Racism is about what we see, hear."

"I don't need lectures in theoretical racism!"

"If colour doesn't figure on the phone then you're halfway there!"

"I should be content with halfway?"

"No. But it's a start, isn't it."

"What if it was a white Jamaican?"

"Sorry?"

"Suppose it was a white Jamaican that called the St Albans guy."

"Come off it! What's the chance of that?"

"If I knocked his door I'd just be a trespasser. That St Albans bloke. Him, and the likes. I knock their door and I'm not welcome."

"That is *so* defeatist!"

"A bunch of bishops learning to parachute, they end the same way as plunks polevaulting. Roman candles in the air, plunks on a pole."

"No white people you admire?"

"English?"

"Yes."

"Nigel Kennedy. Eric Clapton."

"Don't be daft!"

"Why?"

"Eric Clapton! He's only a rock guitarist."

"Blues. Listen him play the blues."

"He's a redneck, supported Enoch Powell."

"*What*?"

"Clapton said 'Keep Britain white!'"

"Where did you get that?"

"It happened on stage. In the 70s, I think."

"You sure?"

"It's all over the internet. That, and his other rants. Vile little man."

"Why didn't you tell me?"

"I thought you'd know."

"From now," Jimmy says, "he's definitely nowhere!"

"Mind how you choose your heroes."

"He was never a hero. I thought he was a good player, that's all."

"Admire people with more relevance."

"Turing?"

"Brains enough to keep Hitler from England."

"Then he paved the way for black folk coming here. Kind of."

"I suppose so, yes."

"Turing did a Newton. Black folk attracted here like gravity."

"And," she says, "just like Newton, Alan Turing had an affair with apples. One saw an apple fall, and wondered. The other guy laced his apple with cyanide and stopped wondering. Along came Steve Jobs and named Apple computers after Turing."

"That's relevance?"

"What would you call it?"

Jimmy grabs a smoke. "Relevance is a big word."

"Come on! You *must* know serious people."

"White?"

"White."

"I'd choose you. You're serious and white."

"Funny, ha!"

"Humphrey Lyttleton, then."

"Who's he?"

"Jazzman. Wrote a neat blues for Big Bill Broonzy."

"Try somebody we all know."

"Scarman. He was ace."

Bleary, Lorna rubs her eyes. Blinks an owl's blink. "Who?"

"Lord Scarman. Did the Brixton riots. Get a copy. Or Macpherson, his report on Stephen Lawrence. Serious white folk. But if it's *white* you want me to talk about, nobody anywhere greater than Bach."

# 103

Sunshine. The sun's brought butterflies out of hiding. From the quiet patio, relaxing in a calm green place, any tenement dweller could wish a life. Foxes and badgers, all the time; but now and then herons come and go from this semi rural place.

"We had Canada geese staying down there," Geraldine says. "They were at the water. Stayed three weeks. A month."

"Did you know," Jimmy says, "there's exactly the same number of Beethoven sonatas as glass capsules in the London Eye. He was way under 6 foot, but the London Eye's 450 feet tall."

"What's that to do with anything?"

"You wear high heels. Geese get high on clouds."

"*How* do you think of these things!"

"It was a big shock," he says, "hearing white Jamaicans talk."

"Oh, no! This is going to be a sermon."

"Hope not."

"Let's enjoy the day. No race, promise?"

"Must be great, living some place like this. Not getting overlooked."

"Sad, taking it for granted."

"I'd live on a private island. Get there by sea."

"Why private?"

"Some small place. You know, where maybe only a hundred folk live. No peeping tom with binoculars. No uncle tom with certificates in Latin."

"Quite a wish list!"

"I like the idea of geese chilling out here," Jimmy says.

"A fox grabbed one. I flew out of bed. Got there too late."

"You've got people with horses nearby. Jeez!"

"What's it like, I mean, white Jamaicans?"

"Thought you didn't want to talk race."

"No. Not the nasty stuff. What are white Jamaicans like?"

"If you look away when they talk, you wouldn't know."

"Are they properly integrated?"

"Yeah. Kingston's chocked with light-skinned folk. And quite a few whites. Whole enclaves of whites, some parts of the island."

"What's that like?"

"My first visit was a daze. The sun. Those smiles. How warm everybody was. You hear raw patois from Chinese, Indian, white. As well as black. Down-home patois from everybody."

"Can you speak it? That 'Yeh, man!' stuff?"

"Yeh, man!" Jimmy laughs. "Hey, why not visit?"

"Wouldn't I stick out?"

"Nah! Lots of white tourists."

"Love to meet a white Jamaican. Wonder what that's like!"

"One day there was this white Jamaican, he was trying to mimic my English accent. A black guy from England and a white Jamaican trying to imitate me. Funny."

Eyes suddenly overcast, Geraldine quits her seat. She ambles to the lawn. The two puppies play round her as Jimmy checks the green quiet, wondering about the question in her mother's eyes as she left earlier.

"These pups are disappearing one by one," she says, sighing. "One by one, get carted away in baskets. These are the last two. By this evening even they'll be gone. I tried not to name them. My sister's coming later to take one."

"Well," he says, "there's dogs, and there's life."

Jimmy's older than Geraldine. But only by a week. After twenty five years they met inside the tinsel world of a Clive Core, sales magician at Homes, Homes & Homes. But in late spring of 2000, they're alone. Each looking for more than dreams, less than a promise.

"Enough gloom for one day," she says. "Let's do charades."

"Nah, let's do another spliff."

"Oh come on, be a sport. Let's do a bit of Orwell."

"Who?"

"George Orwell."

"Let's get a spliff going."

"Big Brother's everywhere. Your mug's up on CCTV. In London, it's 300 times a day."

"You're joking!"

"300 times a day. Anyone for more cheese?"

"Fuck that!"

"In Germany there's a reality TV show called Big Brother. Corny, but it's coming to the UK. 50,000 idiots here applied. Thing is, only 12 slots available. They want to be on the first Big Brother show on British TV."

Jimmy gulps. "Cameras all over them?"

"A matchless view of their guts, 24/7."

"Zombies!"

"George Orwell, scene one, take one."

"That guy got 1984 wrong."

"So what? Anyway, it's not the date that matters."

"I need a spliff."

"At the third stroke, it will be 3:20 precisely, and time to sip your water! *Bleep, bleep, bleep.* At the third stroke, it will be 3:20 and 10 seconds, time to eat your greens."

"At the third stroke," Jimmy says, trying to mime Big Brother, "it will be 4 o'clock and definitely time to leave the table."

276

"Imagine," she laughs, "when it's 7:10 precisely and time to go to the loo, all six billion of us on the planet!"

# 104

Mid-afternoon. A skylark starts a song. Just as the peacock next door cries again. Two empty white wine bottles were left behind on the patio table. All this, and giggling in the kelly Hertfordshire landscape. Loud laughing in the garden.

"I had a dream," Jimmy says, "me, running away from lions."

"Better than hanging around!"

"They were coming towards me. This means something, but what?"

Geraldine laughs. "Didn't you ask them?"

"Next time. Yeah, next time."

"I used to come here when I was little," she says, guiding further in the garden. "I pretended not to hear when they called from the house."

"You lived your fairytale?"

"I got to be a princess. Daughter of the king of France and Germany. Courtiers all round. Dutiful people breathless everywhere. And over here, here is where they buried the king. Killed hunting wolves one day."

"Wolves, like in Little Red Riding Hood?"

"No. A proper princess."

"Why Germany and France? Why'd the king have to die?"

"Can't remember the bit about France. Might have read it somewhere. Anyway, my sister was doing German exams at school and every day I'd grab the dictionary, try to catch her out. Renate couldn't be bothered. Dad just said 'Bollocks!' That made me feel *so* in charge. She's only six years older than me, but to an eight-year-old she was quite something."

"Until I went to Dusseldorf," Jimmy says, "Germany was off the scale. I'd never wanted to go. Ever. But Dusseldorf, it's a tidy place. Kind of industrial, but beautiful for a factory city. Maybe it's the Rhine, legends of spies and things."

"I *love* it there. But let me finish my story. Where was I?"

"The king died."

"Yes, yes! As a princess, basically did what I liked. And that was so the thing!"

"Punishing the servants?"

"I was the king's daughter, after all!"

"Nasty little king's daughter."

"It's only a story. My little story."

"Sorry, I won't spoil it. Go for it."

"I, Princess Geraldine, had the best portraitist. A really young chap, always averted his eyes while trying to study my face. I was the king's cleverest child, so he changed the constitution so I'd rule."

"Then he dies before you grow up. Jeez!"

"Not quite. I still got to rule. But, well, the sad part."

"No fairytale ending?"

"It's my father. The other woman. He was away weeks at a time."

"Same thing happened to me. My mother asked my father to leave."

"Issues."

"Yeah."

"You hate being the only child, don't you."

"Let's get back," Jimmy says. "Another bottle of wine."

"Wine can wait. Let's listen to the garden."

"It's like Chopin here."

"Why?"

"Too many people hear rain, listening to Chopin."

"Noticed those clouds overhead?"

"Wish I could be that good. Chopin, nobody better."

"I read somewhere he was wracked by consumption."

"Yeah. He went to Majorca. Take sun. One quack looked at the stuff he coughed up, pronounced him dead. The second doctor said 'Frederic is dying.' But he still got the Preludes out of his system."

"You know them all, don't you?"

"Opus 28," Jimmy sighs. "Yeah, I play them all the time."

"Well, you'll find your own way. Soon. You're almost there."

"Die trying."

"Years ago," she smiles, wryly, "this garden was bigger."

"It's massive. Bigger than a football field!"

Two lime trees stand apart from the beech clump. The leaves of the lime opened last week. Geraldine was waiting for that. She gets to them now, choosing from the just fallen.

"We'll have these in the salad later," she says.

"Dirty old leaves from the ground?"

"Where d'you think potatoes come from!"

"Hey, I don't know want to get into food studies."

"Lime leaves make great garnish. Fresh lime leaves with potatoes, a bit of salmon."

"These leaves are the smoothest green I've ever seen."

"In a week they'll be hopeless. Tough as old iron by autumn."

"You could do a Delia Smith," Jimmy says.

"Where was I with my story?"

"The king died. You got to rule."

"Yes, I ruled with great sense."

"Kind taxes?"

"Of course! But then I blew it. Lost control to my suitor. I challenged him to a race one day. What was I doing in a ball-gown? Tripped over and lost. So then I was the odd one out. In the entire history of the kingdom, the only ruler ever to lose it."

For Jimmy, a strange day. Far from the tenement, a white woman in her garden gets back to dream her childhood. All inside secret England. Dreamy eyed, she almost owns the trees. But wants to play charades.

"Let's do odd-one-out," she says.

Jimmy looks up at the trees. Scans past them to the clouds. And checks himself in the context of a quiet green space. "If somebody else should arrive now," he says, "that person could be the odd one out."

"Why?"

"Because of getting here late."

"Try again."

"What if it's somebody white. I'd be the odd-job."

"Colour?"

"Yes. But if the third person's a white man, the man would be the odd one out."

Her eyes narrow. "Why?"

"Because a pair could be gender as well as colour must be opposed."

"That would be awful. Shocking, really. A race game."

"If female, say your mother, how would odd-one-out work?"

"What a day! Where did I get *you* from!"

"I need a leak," Jimmy says.

"Oh, just do it over there. I'll be the other side of the shed."

# 105

Far from Brixton, a peacock cries. Far from tenement fever, a sound like a huntsman's horn blares through the trees. Blares again. Not like Cootie Williams' trumpet in Ellington's band; no Mood Indigo in this countryside. Only a peacock crying.

Jimmy calls out. "You OK, back there?"

No answer. Rounding the shed, he calls again. But only trellis; a wiry trellis giving seclusion to the lawn. The lawn backs into blooms. Just like on a postcard. Flowers look so happy, like wanting to say hello. To Jimmy, the whole thing's like a TV gala with sound turned off.

"I just got stung by a bee," Geraldine moans.

Jimmy flops on a flower pot. It breaks. "This place could be Zen," he says. "The thing about gardeners and bees, well, that's like a spindle whirring. Whizzing in a godless universe."

"What?"

"Zen."

"Not that again!"

"If you want a sane world, talk to stars. Explain beauty."

"I don't know why I bother with you."

"Religion enjoys suffering. Then you get a garden called paradise when you die. No way flowers are the calling-cards of paradise."

"Enough gobbledegook for one day! Flowers are flowers."

"Flowers like these," he sighs, "that's enough after-life for me."

"You're *so* wounded."

"Blooms blowing in a breeze, or flowers in a paradise of wreaths? Simple choice from a tenement!"

Geraldine slaps soil from her hands. "Too often," she says, "bouquets get composed to tell lies."

"I had a row with a moron. It was about flowers, the ones that bloom between paving-stones. He said they can't be flowers. When I asked him why, he said whatever grows where you don't want it to must be weeds."

"Idiot!"

"Yeah."

"What happened next?"

"Shouldn't have said it, but I told him one hand can point outside the Milky Way, clap loud enough."

"Even hold and hug."

"Gardening's kind of spiritual."

"Hmmm."

"Better than religion."

"On second thoughts, maybe you'd better spell that out."

"Gardeners prepare for bees knowing that bees prepare for them."

"Well," she smiles, "just don't call me honey!"

"That's corny. So twee. I thought you hated schmaltz."

"Stop being so serious!"

"I like it, the way the garden and house gel."

"They focus well, don't they."

"This part is like a monastery."

"Renate's secret place."

A thread-fine drizzle. Flecks of rain attracting Geraldine's upturned face. Raindrops falling like faded notes on a score. Her arms make a circle enough to tame the sky.

"Who's afraid of the big bad countryside?"

Jimmy shrugs. "Not me, lady. Not me!"

"You know, I'm a tiny piece of this. No bees in my bonnet."

"Rain in a minute. We better head for the house."

"Oh, be a kid again!"

"What if I get wet?"

"You get wet! Come, let's show you the real birds and bees. Let's do the rest of the garden. Get rain any old time."

Hands signing and signing, Geraldine gives Jimmy a tour of garden plants. Little Dorrits and striped Pickwicks, over here. As they hurry towards the house she points to plants he's never seen before, names he's never heard of. Fritillary, dumb looking, heads bowing like in reverence. Tritonia. Wildflower. Dutch Hyacinths, frail, dabbing at knees, violets, dawn-tints and whites, wanting to step from the border, wanting to chat. But. Rain.

Jimmy tells Geraldine she could play jazz. She can look at irises and see baleful and pale, first-light, sham, incandescent, and more. Most folk catching the same irises see only white flowers.

"Red irises might be impossible to breed," she says. "But we'll keep trying. So far, the closest to red is the orange of the Fort Apache variety. Must keep trying."

"Even if it takes a hundred years?"

"Of course."

"What's this one?"

"Ah, this one! It's another iris."

"Iris?"

"Yes. Our little black beauty."

"What's it called?"

"Swazi Princess," she says, all smiles. "It's just for you."

# 106

4 o'clock. The rhythm of rain is like running antelopes. Vegetable soup steams on the table. Restless rain. Torrents stream over double-glazing. Rain, nothing like a fountain. The conservatory was added to the house in a fit of rage by the colonel. But to a tenement dweller, this quiet glass place is big as a house.

Jimmy says it again. "Geraldine, you could play jazz. Takes a few years to get the basics, but you'd be a natural improviser."

"I'd play romantic music."

"Jazz musicians have it," he says. "Nothing, no colour-tone is out of reach. Always know the chords to alter, arpeggio to cascade."

"I quite like Miles Davis."

"One of the best."

Giggling, she sets the hi-fi going. Vivaldi. Then pours wine. White wine. Unwraps the towel from her hair. "Drink up," she says.

Jimmy frowns. "I hear the music of failure."

"Vivaldi?"

"Yeah. He was wasted. 18th century, too early for him."

"Explain that. Oh, oh! On second thoughts, some other time."

Rain launders the conservatory. Geraldine's hair gets frizzed by a towel. A bottle of wine's on the floor between them. Their eyes turn to the downpour.

"What does rain owe land?"

"Owe?" she says. "Are you going to get mystic?"

"I think it owes respect."

"*What*?"

"There's stuff between land and water."

"We call it evaporation."

"No, not that. There's respect."

"Don't be daft!"

"You don't agree, then."

"With what? I mean, no wonder you didn't sleep with Colette!"

Downing more wine, he shrugs. "Maybe."

"Abstract tosh. Tormenting yourself. What if this, what if that!"

"At least, I didn't want to govern the Bank of England."

"Who'd want to?"

"Somewhere, right now, someone's picking lemons in the sun. It was one day in Liverpool, 25 years back, my father realized lemons are great for lemonade but shouldn't get squeezed to fake sunshine."

Geraldine eyes roll. "I hope you understand that stuff. I don't."

"In jazz, you show respect. The great ones give, get something more musical. Charlie Parker. Bud Powell."

"What about classical?"

"Vivaldi, from classical."

"*Vivaldi?*"

"Forget the time difference, and he'd walk into Benny Goodman's outfit."

"Renate adores Vivaldi. He's the theme to my family."

"He was way ahead. Ace at improvising."

"Do me some?"

"Improvising?"

"Yeah."

"Your piano?"

"Please!"

"Let's go."

"Show me!" she says, grabbing the wine bottle.

A Boesendorfer. Jimmy checks the loud pedal and, with big gestures, mimics a concert player. Tries some scales. But something else is wrong: Lydia's vase is on the piano; the pottery she claimed got it's hue from blood of dwarves. Geraldine's eyebrows raise.

"This thing needs tuning," Jimmy says. "Only a Tatum could play it."

"Can't you give it a go, anyway?"

"Beethoven got a new piano from London. 1818, I think. It was the explanation. They explained how a Broadwood piano was made. And that warmed him to it."

"What's that got to do with my piano?"

"Think of a blind lady, one with a white cane. She might remember white, but sighted folk get the white of the cane. That's the deal."

"*What?*"

"This piano's blind," he says. "I can't improvise it."

"Then let's smash its face in!"

"You're drunk."

"My libations are my affair."

"I can *not* play this blind thing. Let's get back to the conservatory."

"Boo-hoo. My piano defeated you. Heh, he-he-he-heh!"

# 107

Rain smirked the countryside. A wet Hertfordshire. And now the coy sun. Outdoors, a breeze hovers. Light and bright. Jimmy spots a camera in the conservatory.

"Any film in that thing?" he says.

"I think so."

"Fancy a snap?"

"Hmmm!"

"By the trees. Got to get proof of this."

"Proof?"

"Yeah, to show I was here."

"That's a bit ominous, isn't it! Not planning to come again?"

"Don't wind me up."

"You've gotta come again. A whole weekend next time."

"If you'll have me."

"Plenty of space. We can go for walks. Renate drool while you play."

"Get that piano tuned!"

"Even so, it needs a good seeing to. Somebody who really can."

"If you mend things with Brian you won't be back."

"If only!" she says, kicking off the flip-flops. Then wobbles outside to the sodden lawn.

Jimmy takes the first turn. As she trips to the lens, he can almost touch the smile. Set by clear air, her girly smile hurries from where it had forgotten itself; just like she's never left for the world outside.

"Two shots left," he says. "Want one against the house?"

"Got lots of those. Oh, I know! Let's do one together. Lydia's here in a minute. We can get her to press the button."

"No delay switch?"

"What? Yes, yes. There's a thingy. Not sure I can get it to work."

As she runs to the house, he plays with the dogs. Not what happens in the tenement, no tenement hounds here. And all the time in this lucky place, land sweetened by rain. Geraldine stumbles back from the house. Carries a bundle of newspapers to set the camera on. Different clothes now. She wears a blue sweater. And jeans. Just before the shutter clicks, they turn one on one. She says she's never been to the dentist since the age of twelve. He's never noticed before just how sad her eyes can be. The next snap, they link arms, wave at the camera. Then turn to the house. As if it could speak.

She remembers two skaters. Olympic skaters. All over again. Remembering them irritates her. In the memory, two swirling skaters leave a strange trail on ice. Their swerving is hard to forget. The woman's perfume was dashed on, nagging, seeping to the man's vaulting sweat. But it's their chitchats on ice; that's the problem. Their heads are sculptures on the sidelines. Heads are the only bad part, two wooden flaws over empty ice. And their bodies. Their sinews make great moves, redeeming their wooden heads. Their shadow on the ice is deciduous, thin, small, gliding down to the frozen wasteland in a stride. Dangerous parabolic glide; a great move! Two hyperbolas on the axis; great move, *great* move! Olympic skaters dancing and dancing, like water stencils maybe, crisscrossing cold competition light. Over here, this way, this way, try the ice over here! Yes, you can. You can do it! Then they slip. The man first. Then the woman, trying to steady him. Flushed, ground down, they collect one another in a wistful glance. In the memory they always zoom to the center of the rink, out and out. TV images of two Olympic skaters never quite going away for Geraldine, remembering them.

5 o'clock. Renate phones. She's half an hour away. At the far end of the lawn the puppies have something at bay.

Geraldine grabs Jimmy's arm. "Let's go see what's going on."

He imagines the old lady's eyes, cool and grey, flitting from her daughter to him. Then back to her Geraldine.

# 108

"What's white, got covered by yellow in the morning, then covered in blue by evening?"

Jimmy doesn't understand. It nags him. "Say again?"

"Something white," Geraldine laughs, "that was covered with yellow in the morning, then blue by evening."

"The weather?"

"No."

"A rainbow?"

"Not likely!"

"A magic carpet, unweaving after a magic ride."

"Not a magic carpet."

"I give up!" he says.

Woozy with wine, she's a mischief. Then, for a blink, points to her bosom under the blue jumper. "My dear friend," she says, "the answer to the riddle is my female items. This morning I wore a yellow jumper, now I cover my pale mammary glands in blue."

"Jeez!"

"Hmmm!"

"*Great* riddle."

"Thought you'd like it."

"I do, I do!"

"Don't count on a repeat. That was your lot!"

The London Eye was officially opened in March. Geraldine went. She had a rendezvous with Brian there. They talked and talked. And all the time the Eye was like a glass necklace on a giantess. Glistening.

"You've had too much wine."

"Think I'm drunk?"

"You're tipsy," he says. "You look sad. Sad tipsy."

"Think so?"

"Spell your name backwards."

"Where's that bottle?"

"Where it should be. Far from you as possible."

"Race you to the house!"

No time to think. Racing down the garden. Swerving, but racing. He starts to chase, but his mobile drops. Stopping, he remembers a story. They tell it in Jamaica. Happened in Port Royal a long time ago. A woman pirate plied the waves; a wayward lady, menacing, always dressed like a man. She was danger. Then one day she lost a sword fight on the quayside. But at death's door, just managed to rip the front from her shirt. The rip exposed the goods. Soft surprise. Her adversary blinked. Then goggle-eyed, paralyzed with surprise. Her sword flashed. Sliced the man clean through. The man didn't remember, he was gaping like a man at a woman. But in one flash his adversary changed. And his life.

After a bracing run, Jimmy slumps in the conservatory doorway. Gasping for breath. A potted-plant is in Geraldine's hands.

"Today was very nice," she says.

"Yeah. But somewhere, snowfall is a lot heavier than usual. And somewhere else rice gets gathered in scant fields."

"What's that mean?"

"A pebble can slow the ocean reaching the shore."

"Rubbish!"

"I had a great day here today."

"Good."

"It's back to the tenement, when I leave."

"Take this," she says, handing him the plant. "It will remind you. It's long-flowering. The petals will remind you. "

"Nobody ever gave me a plant before."

"Take care of it. Petals all year."

# 109

The plant in his hands makes Jimmy think of sad things. He remembers the letter from South Africa in his pocket.

"This is a photo of Agnes," he says.

"Oh!" Geraldine frowns. "She's not how I'd imagined."

"Like how?"

"Thought she'd be more, well, earthy."

"She's ace. A lot different to the picture."

"You know," she says, hand to jaw, "there's a lot of women coming to England from eastern Europe. More and more. Scientists, engineers. But now it's the hostess game for lots of them. Clubs. Strip clubs."

"And?"

"Just thinking."

The door-knocker slams. Straightaway, Jimmy's on edge. Must not seem at home. Must seem not calm. Moving by quiet instinct to the garden door, he sets the plant down. Grabs a cigarette. In the body of the house two women's voices exchange. Glad voices. They laugh exactly the same. And on the lawn, the labrador and her two puppies play.

Geraldine grins. "This is Lydia. My big sister."

"Your *only* sister," Lydia says. "So, this is the brilliant composer, the jazz man!"

Jimmy nods. "I try."

Lydia dislikes strangers. Or making eye contact. A lot taller than Geraldine. She's a bassoon player. Mozart is her special; earlier today she practiced the Bassoon Concerto. She'll take a coffee then collect her puppy. Jimmy mentions the vase, says the colour's unique but the shape is painful. Lydia wonders what a painful shape is. But a hi-rise dweller could tell it. She talks like a magpie, he thinks.

The wet garden spreads softly from the conservatory. And the sun. It's shining now like to blot rain it didn't prevent today.

Seeing the puppies on the lawn, Lydia shrieks. "Oh, look! There they are!"

"You'll need a towel," Geraldine says. "They're soaking wet."

"I can't see mine," Lydia moans. "Where's mine?"

"Mozart was five feet tall," Jimmy says. "Stephen Hawking's only the size of a wheelchair. But the London Eye, that's the highest lookout wheel anywhere. Sitting in capsules on the Eye, tears of laughing."

"Gerrie, I can't see my puppy!"

"Which one d'you mean?" Geraldine shouts from the kitchen. "There were only four. Those ones are the last two."

"Where's the one with the sad eyes?"

"The one with the blaze on his face?"

"No, no!" Lydia snaps. "The little nigger-brown one."

"Oh, that one!" Geraldine says, coming into the conservatory. "He was the first to go."

A slow arc in the glass. Jimmy smears an arc like an angel's wings. His eyes regret seeing the patio, seeing this place. His body regrets the story about swastikas in a German forest. Time is cut; a tempo chit.

Geraldine stands beside him. Wordless, her lips are chalk. Her whey face topped by illness-enlarged eyes. Head lopped. Nothing like this. Not anywhere. One word is ghoul. A mannequin ghoul hauls Geraldine to itself. She can't talk. Some cold thing. Here. Not anguish, not pain. But crowing. Cold, it crows between life and mortification.

# 110

Glasses frame Urshell's face. Gazing at the picture, the old man would rent it apart. "That woman is not for you!" he says.

Jimmy just gets to snatch it back. It was really Agnes. She's changed. Or maybe he didn't know her. It was hard, but he disconnected what was in the picture from how she was in London. The picture could almost be saying 'Go on, try me!' And that's not how Agnes ever was. Even with low light. He knows it now. The photo is cold change.

"Difficult situation," Urshell says.

Jimmy nods. "I know."

"Want things right?"

"Naturally!"

"Then do not move with a woman like that. In this life, you tell the truth. If you can. Spiritual thing. That woman is a lie."

"A *lie*?"

"A woman like that can get close. Only a fool lets that happen. She can use tears to fool somebody, but one day she betrays a man. A good man. Why let that be you?"

"She's the best woman I've ever had."

"Best?"

"Biggest brains. And the rest of it."

"Brains is not the end of anything."

"What's better than brains?"

"That woman is barely awake. But shouting at somebody. You?"

For two weeks Jimmy's been trying to visit the old black panther. Now, after only five minutes he knows the score. Only serious talk will follow. Plain talk. The problem with the photograph is huge. He knows that to put it back in his pocket will insult the old man. But leaving it on the coffee table, Urshell will destroy it.

"I hear you're a Maroon, Mr Urshell."

"In this life we get to a certain age. The lucky ones have the vision, light in the soul. Maroons did not get tamed by slavery. Not in Jamaica. The white man was compelled to concede."

"I hear Maroons were great fighters during slavery. Killed a lot of white people, slave owners."

"Not the white. It was the slavery. You have a right to kill anybody making you a slave. Maroons, never anti-white."

"But definitely for their own kind!"

"Yes. The endpoint of the black man's journey. But that is down the road. This one, this Maroon been in England 50 years."

Jimmy blinks. "Fifty years?"

"I can not believe it. Man! Folk look at Mrs Urshell, call her old."

"Age doesn't bother me."

"You know you old when a film on TV that you watched thirty, forty years back and the actors that used to be older than you now look young enough to be your son or daughter. That is something a young man would not understand."

"I'll get there!"

"Yes, son. Yes."

"*Fifty* years. That's why your accent's the way it is. Accents. You talk standard English, and full-on Jamaican patois. Now and then there's even a clipped south London."

"That photograph you have, the woman is a traitor."

Jimmy can't resolve Agnes. He read the whole letter, eventually. But that only confused things more. In the letter she wants to get deeper into traditional African culture. But the photograph is a different story.

"She used to braid her hair," he says. "That's how it was. All the time she was in London, it was braided."

"Now she at home in South Africa, her homeland, but the woman going to a place of torture."

"*Torture?*"

"Yes, going to some back street to torture that African woman hair. Chemicals. A hot iron."

"Why d'you they do that?"

"Red eye."

"What d'you mean?"

"Dat a how de lie start."

Jimmy frowns. And yet. Something was always asleep about Agnes. He turns to the old man. "What call it a lie?"

"This straightened hair in the picture is torture, ruined road. This thing is like somebody high up in a skyscraper, cry 'Fire, fire!' But all the time what must get put out is inside them head."

"Straightened hair is a fantasy?"

"No, not fantasy," the old man says. "Those women are afraid. Run from facts. No place to run, so them run to the sky."

"Ostrich, shoving its head in the sand?"

"No. Not a flightless bird."

"Like a pole-vaulter without a pole?"

"What those women do is sing the blues. Nobody ever see them without a smile. But, man! You want to bawl. Yes, you could bawl because of the hopelessness. Woman slaying Africa with hair."

"What?"

"She run to her fake sky fe cry 'Fire!' Yu get me?"

"Yeah, buttoning up in the skin overcoat."

"Smiling that sad smile."

"Yeah."

"Your woman, man! She not even smiling in the photograph. The lady doing something else."

"Breaks my heart!"

"Bad times, young man. Crucial."

"Yes. I know."

"Forty years back, black women straighten dem hair. Fifty, years. Those days just one show in town. Then the 60s."

"What happened?"

"Well, dat is what you can call difficult."

"There was that black-and-proud thing. I mean, it was all over the 60s. And the 70s. It's in James Brown tracks."

"Yes, before you came into this world."

"I was born in '75. But I listen to all that, and it clicks!"

Urshell's heavy head shakes. "Samson an' Delilah."

"I don't believe in the bible."

"Dem straighten black woman, dem murder Africa!"

"*Murder?*"

"Yes!"

"Then why didn't you do something? Your generation."

"Do what? Dem tell yu seh dem still black, in full control."

"You old black guys, you could have stopped it!"

"Son, dem woman want dem head fe look like bin liner, yu get me? Plastic bin liner. Plastic bag."

"What, the black bag in the dustbin?"

"Yes. Understand?"

Jimmy turns to the old man. "Yeah, you're talking waste."

"Another generation lost!"

"Man!"

"Delilah destroy Samson, but every time a black woman put a hot comb in her head, a black man turn into a mimic. Son, walk from dat!"

"You mean, go to Africa?"

"Africa is every place. Any place with black folk."

"It's in your head?"

Urshell takes a shot of rum. Clears his throat. "Every woman is a dream. Or nightmare. A black woman with laminated hair, or wear a white woman wig, that is nightmare time. Wake from that."

"I had a dream," Jimmy says, "not a Martin Luther King, but a weird one. Black women on a beach. A beach full of them. Me flying over in a copter. The weirdest thing was how they're all in that one place, on the beach together. I can see their eyes. Weariness. Lost longitude. They want to please, to oblige. But only have longitude for eyes. Then sly cheerleaders stepping up among them, twirling false hair."

The old man grabs at his heart. "That's a hell of a dream," he says.

"At absolute zero, substances contain no heat energy. It's only at a small range of temperatures that a fake can cause havoc."

"Wha' yu seh?"

"The dream," Jimmy laughs, "is a jazz-opera. I made it up."

"*Jazz*?"

"Yeah. Sometimes it's hard, dreams dice with vibes."

"Then it is not a dream."

"It was only vibes at twilight."

"That is jazz talk!"

"You don't listen to jazz?"

"Not much. I like the song people. Ella Fitzgerald. Nat Cole."

"Nat Cole plays mean jazz piano."

Difficult for Jimmy, facing up. Agnes is difficult. She should be the one making the way easier. He turns from the photograph. Mentions the other reason being here to see the old man.

For days, it was shrugging off what happened. That quiet glass room, Geraldine's conservatory. Some days were like being a stowaway in the 8$^{th}$ floor tenement or at immigration control. Geraldine was a friend. In a way, she was a fake friend.

Anxious for a smoke, Jimmy's fidgeting. The old man doesn't allow smoking. Drink a jug of rum, that's fine. Get grogged on malt whisky. But absolutely no smoking here.

"Tell me the full works," Urshell says.

An hour after leaving Geraldine's glass and green, Jimmy was back in town. Back to the inner-city. Feeling glad. Back to the old familiar. Said a quiet 'Thanks!' to the streets. Tottenham High Road was jammed. Saturday shoppers moving it along. Geraldine's image was hard-wired. It was the crowds. Gazing at the crowds, trying for that one hue in somebody's face, a colour saying nigger-brown. Every kind of face went by; every hue from jet-black to light tan. He looked at his own face in the rear-view mirror. The car stopped. And he waited. Watching for the one. Waiting for that one hue. People going by, coming, going, hurrying, taking it slow. Black people moving along, minding their business on Tottenham High Road on a Saturday evening. Eventually, it happened. The evening shut down. Crowds dwindled to nothing and shops closed. Later that night, was being alone. Alone, and doodling at the keyboard, whisky sloshed, ganja clouds in air. Then things got clear. The switch flicked: whatever nigger-brown was, only somebody white could pick it out. Messing about at the keyboard stopped. Nothing known to music was big enough. The view of night from the 8$^{th}$ floor window was fake stars; way below, jump-if-you-want lights. Headlights. Crazy lights. Where were those cars going? Somebody would know. But who? No answer from the keyboard. Deep into night the search went on, testing the keys. Minor chords, then diminished, then whole-tone runs, arpeggios, major, over and over, trying to get it. Trying to understand. One evening soon after they first met, Geraldine said she wasn't up to speed with race. Serious in eye, she said that that didn't mean racial barriers in her heart. But now Jimmy could see. When her sister said nigger, Geraldine was where she was at. She was the same place as her sister. It was 9 o'clock next morning when she phoned; on her way to Ireland, but wanting to square things. He listened to the white woman. She was speaking in a low tone, saying this, saying   that. More confusion after the call. But, weird, he remembered the good times. Remembering her kindness. This was the difficult part. And that's because it's hard to tell. He wondered if maybe a word can be more than a word: maybe a word can sneak up like a virus. But then it was words that cracked it: Nigger may never get used directly but it can be dormant in a language-mind. Field marshals and deaf philosophers would shake their logic-beribboned heads. But Jimmy built a spliff. Cold fire, half-consoling. He knew.

Urshell shoves aside the rum bottle. "Know what?"

"I realized even if Geraldine never said it, she used the old n-word.  She agreed it was a label."

"Somebody shouts 'Nigger!' and a street-load of people turn to look, which white person didn't see a nigger but only a black man?"

# 111

"*Good* news?" Jimmy says, disbelieving.

Urshell says it again. "Good news. Some bad, but mostly good."

"How good?"

"Lucky, lucky. The private part of the white woman got restless with her public life."

"I don't understand."

"Yu in a room wid no heat, de white woman put yu in touch wid de fire."

"What about Agnes?"

"That woman, well, she put you in touch with the sun. To learn things like that, that is special. And," he leans over, shaking hands with Jimmy, "to know something like that makes you a lucky man!"

Jimmy frowns.

Laughing, the old man begins to burnish the lens of his glasses. Heavy lenses. Old hands, smudging, burnishing. "Spread that luck around, son. Spread it round."

"Trying to work out what's lucky."

"Things was goin' on?"

That night of the theatre, after getting condoms at the late-night chemist, he was hurrying back to the hotel to get it on. That was going to be the simple part. But something else. Like maybe Colette was going to substitute for Geraldine. Maybe that's why he turned back for a second packet.

"Between me and the white woman? No. Nothing physical."

"Then wha' yu do? Play strawberry and cream?"

Jimmy doesn't answer. After the rain at Geraldine's house, it was while doing the photos that a twinge happened between them. A secret twinge on the wet lawn. For that moment, two seconds, no longer friends. Just man and woman. Keeping something unsaid. And nothing was said. Then white wine in the conservatory. And the really big thing was that glass room itself; the talk that must have taken place down the years there. That family looked out at the seasons and wondered, sipped tea, gin, chatted, facing the wordless countryside.

Urshell coughs. "Man, you turned into a white person to that young woman. The white girl. Your black balls got lost."

"Turned into white? *Me*?"

"Watch TV?"

"Sorry?"

"You ever watch TV?"

"Naturally."

"Then you have the answer."

"Mr Urshell, I need help. Tell me what you think."

296

"You and the white girl, the two of you, it was like watching TV. But a bad story."

"Fiction?"

"The woman was a story. You, a story. But the two of you did not consider the players. You and she, playing round one another."

"I told how it was, but you think something else happened!"

Urshell turns to the room, gazing at the picture above the mantlepiece. "With commercial TV, too much sell. Advertise dis, sell dat. Shit left, shit right. But you and the white woman, the two of you! It was like you fooling round in different parts of the city."

"How does nigger-brown come out of that?" Jimmy says, leaning from his chair.

"When your white friend said nigger-brown, that was it."

"It was her sister! It was the bitch who actually said it."

"When your friend agreed with nigger, that was always in the story. But you wanted something else to happen."

"Sorry, I don't see that."

"Man! How do I get you to understand?"

"If you think I'm stupid, I'm wasting your time."

"Son, when I get under pressure, *pressure*, then one bad Jamaican to the rest of the world. That is my private self. Understand? The white woman, her private self was restless with her public self. Simple as that."

"Me and her, we were only play-acting?"

"Playing, no."

"Look, I don't understand half of what you say."

"A man must not just watch. Learn that!"

"Geraldine accepted me as a man. Always. The story between us was always iffy, but we were friends. That n-word rejects me to the core."

"Yes."

"Hey, there was good news and bad news. What's the bad part?"

"Young man, you have what you can call a fantasy. Two."

"Two fantasies?"

"The first thing is Africa."

"I've never been to Africa."

"You believe you can get Africa by going with a woman from Africa. Well, no man can get to Africa because of a woman. Not a hundred. Where," the old man laughs, "would little you live with one hundred women?"

"What's the second fantasy?" Jimmy says, grim faced.

"That is the easy one. Guys like you believe you can stop racial strife by fancy talk with middle-class white folk."

"Not me!"

"The big story of the black man is not slavery, not *we shall overcome*.

The real story of the black man is the dream a person will have. When folk have the same dream, man!"

Above the mantlepiece, Mandela's portrait smiles in the room. Looming, but somehow not really present. A seer. Father, patriarch. A grandfather, friend.

"Sometimes, I dream lions. Lions, all round me."

Urshell's head shakes. "Your white friends know about that?"

Jimmy only half understands. The old man is difficult. Too much twine in his soul. Too much to unravel.

"Stephen Hawking's got a string in the Minotaur's den. Everybody's crying 'Stephen, show the way!' I like that."

"Keep your feet on the ground. Step light."

"Got any white friends, Mr Urshell?"

"What?"

"Why d'you stay in England?"

"England is a funny place."

"I couldn't be born somewhere else and get old here."

"Son, England will talk to you."

"Like when?"

"Make it happen!"

Urshell's hands clasp. Hands that remember pouring paraffin like wine, or striking matches in bed-sit rooms to dine. He was in England before Tony Blair was even born. Seasons coming and going. Round and round. Stock silent, Jimmy wonders if hands like the old Jamaican's could ever have cast seedlings into England's winter soil.

"One night," Urshell says, "three years back, some white fellows out front. Making a heap of noise. Evil noise. Six, seven of them. Anyway, I get outside to see what going on. And, man! They have pissed all over the fence. Drunk. I ask them to clean it up. One guy tell me seh dem can piss whe' dem like, because de country belong to dem. Me ask him if de fence belong to him. Him seh 'No.' So me seh, 'Who will clean the fence?' According to him I must clean it. Him seh I must do it because it is my fence."

"At your age? You fronted young guys, at age? No weapon?"

"Yes and no. I had the old poker up my coat sleeve."

"Yes!"

"My next-door neighbour is a white man. A ol' boy, like me, but when him hear de commotion him come out, him an' him cricket bat. And, brother! Dem tek one look, dem know seh him mean business. So dem back off. Dat a one of de most beautiful tings wha' happen. Anyway, I get back into the house and meditate on it."

"The fence thing?"

"Yes, the fence can be mine. But the country is their country."

"That is England?"

"Yes. The fence can be yours but the land might not belong to you."

"Then why d'you stay?"

"Why not?"

"Don't you think living here is a cage?" Jimmy says.

"Cage?"

"You're living in England, old man. A hold zone."

"Listen, I met my wife here. My daughters born here, four of them. The second girl, she 'ave her own likkle business. The next girl is a bank manager. The next one doing finance with the council, and the last girl is a TV journalist. England give dem dat opportunity."

"Big things are starting to happen in Jamaica."

"If I had stayed there, maybe it could have worked out. But not so well. No, not so well."

"Five daughters?"

"Yes."

"No sons?"

"None."

"What's happening with daughter number five?"

Old, Urshell ups from the chair. An old man remembering, getting to a hazed place. "Alberta," he says, "she was my first born. Jamaica. She came along before I left the island. My great-grandchildren come from her."

"Tell me about your friend," Jimmy says. "The white man next door."

The old man steps to the mantlepiece. "What is a friend?"

"How d'you mean?"

"Man, whe' yu come from! Yu don't know what is a fren?"

"It's a weird question."

"So wha' 'appen?"

"A friend is, you know, somebody you trust."

"How many people trust you?"

"A few."

"How many people you trust?"

Jimmy frowns. "One or two."

"If you mess up, your friends absolve you?"

"You mean, like forgive? Well, yeah."

"You, you forgive your friends?"

"Naturally."

"Then, young man, I have just one friend. My wife."

"What about out there?"

"That fence is my friend."

"The fence is your friend?"

"No fence, no friend."

"Jeez!"

"Simple as that!"

"Then," Jimmy says, "how come you stayed so long? Why'd you get old here? Why didn't you go back? Why not go back now? I do *not* understand."

Urshell looks past Jimmy. Way past. Years taxi-driving means he can tell. "Somebody in a hurry is somebody you can read."

"I'm no taxi passenger!"

Ambling to the door, he calls out. "Annette! Bring some tea. Tea please, Annette."

The old man's unblinking eyes haven't strayed from Jimmy's. Reading him like a street map. A spliff would help. Two black men talking of racism while waiting to sip tea in a front room in England. To make matters worse, a helicopter circles overhead; its propellers droning out lifelong noise. Then it scuds off into the night.

"That copter was like it wanted to land in your back garden, the way it hovered."

"A police helicopter," Urshell says. "A black police pilot."

A quiet woman is in the room. Stunning, to Jimmy. She smiles. Says a shy hello. Puts a tea-tray on the coffee table.

"This is my youngest one," Urshell says. "Last one to fly the nest. Two weeks from now an' you a married woman, eh Annette?"

Jimmy's eyes can't leave the woman. She's twenty two and, as she leaves the room, one whole day older.

She turns to Jimmy. "Absolutely!"

"Sorry?"

"The guy I'm getting married to *is* a lucky man. That's what you were thinking, wasn't it?"

# 112

It was a grey day in 1950 when Urshell got off the boat. The sea from Jamaica to England was old, getting colder, sentimental. He was twenty four.

In England he was supposed to take up the tailoring trade; maybe even build suits on Savile Row. But cloth was way down the scale. Too dull for the sunshine Jamaica boy. And anyway. Every place they took him for a simpleton; stuff he was great at they said he would still have to learn, but their way. So it was quit. And quit again. Moving round, job to job. Moving north, dawdling, checked the Midlands, checking north and south. Then one day.

The wanderer turned into a van driver. More wandering. But this time it was directed. That was how things got off the ground. High with miles. To start, it was local. Deliveries. This and that. Furniture, anything. Then the big one, the bright nighttime: a job with a Jamaican sound-system. Moving round the country. Nightclub after nightclub, house-party after party time.

Worry about the war years wrapped up the fifties and sixties. But a lady's voice. Vera Lynn. She was the mood, a lady doing ballads that moved healing along. So much heart was in the war-time ballads she used to sing. But.

England was tired. Time for something else. Some hot and dangerous thing. But not war. To start, it was guys calling theirs noise skiffle. Quick cabaret guys, like Lonnie Donnegan and Tommy Steel. Nobody could touch a black piano player called Hutch. Hutch diced jazz piano, played cabaret, doodled Mountbatten's wife. But jazz in England was only small-time. Glenn Miller was on radio. Duke Ellington from time to time. Then guys like Kenny Ball and Acker Bilk happened along. Bebop was way too tough for most Brit musos here.

Funny, but most Jamaicans didn't incline to jazz. Ernest Ranglin moved from the island, grabbed his guitar out of Jamaica and got to America to get jazz-legs. Same deal for Monty. Monty Alexander played jazz piano in America.

Independence in '62. Jamaica was independent. Black community after community in England. Jamaican music the glue, the buzz. Ska, blue-beat, the groove of rock-steady. Jamaica in London, Birmingham, Manchester, Bristol. Every big city. And the house-parties they used to have! The she-beens! With Jamaican music it was the first time England ever got music in one private house that folk could hear ten streets away. It was innercity nighttime. Years and years.

Then the sixties. Mid sixties. Young white guys made the difference, getting into Jamaican music; black music in general. White guys turning up at the black clubs, getting serious in Jamaican culture. Even now, UB40, white and black playing black music. But in the sixties it was mostly Clapton. Eric Clapton turned up at the Flamingo nightclub in London, played blues, learned Jamaican music from Rico Rodriguez. Clapton was the first white guitar player in England with a serious way of blues. Some folk calling him god. But only till Hendrix touched down in '66. Jackie Edwards was the mellow man, Jamaican crooner on the England subculture; in the 60s, Jackie penned two number ones for the Spencer Davis band. Nighttime was the Flamingo club. The place. Prostitutes, pimps, night folk coming from the night to cool down. And way before anybody was a hippy, Carnaby Street was the place for music in the night. Hot vision. The Roaring Twenties was a nightclub in Carnaby Street. Count Suckle, a Jamaican running the show, blues and jazz records there. And one night, in walks Georgie Fame. Georgie was a white guy that nobody checked white. He learned the latest tracks from Count Suckle. And other young white guys turning up, learning 10-rizla spliffs, dressed like Jamaican rude-boys.

Urshell remembers the white girls. At every Jamaican house party white girls came out of the night. One or two, to start. Then more and more, quick of eye, runaways needing a place to crash. Or brute force nymphomaniacs looking for big black whammy. Sad girls, pairing off with pine-head pimps.

In those early England years, Urshell was a Jamaican face-man. Good looks pulled him along. Place after place. Woman after woman. Some of the sweetest black females. Lonesome nurse girls. A slick face-man could pick off all the sly hairdresser types and office girls. Some nights Urshell went back to a nurses' home with one woman and find good booty, woman after woman alone. And him! One woman at a time, one wing of the nurses' home at a time. Months to get round the block. At one time he was even living in a nurses' home, sneaking in, out, shacked up full time with one nurse in her little room.

Jamaican music was bigger than white folk could believe. The dazzle, nighttime and dark. Pure ganja coming in off the boats. But it was never just peace and love. From time to time, ructions. Fights could be about anything. Jamaicans fighting in the night always end in blood. One man with a knife, another man a bottle. Somebody else walked with a razor. Urshell can't forget one red night. Two guys squaring up over a woman, and before the second guy could blink the first guy walked a knife across his eyes. On his knees, blood flowing from eyes and calling on Jesus Christ. In the night, Jesus Christ! Purple in the night. Losing sight, never going to see again. One night going wrong.

But nowadays. Guys don't bother with the knife too much. Psycho gets a gun. But only use the gun against another black man. Obliging ones go to church to sing, or grin on TV. It was a different game in the fifties. Even as late as the eighties, Jamaican music was deep down. From a true heart. And even if somebody got cut, mostly nobody died. Not the way of murder these days. Black murdering black.

The 60s and 70s, Jamaican music was magic bandage. Black folk coming from all over. Guys standing, meditating, alone or with spars. Ganja from JA. Man! Sharash was something the police didn't know back then; guys walking with a whole weight of sharash and the police searched them but never understanding it. But it was house-parties. And Barley wine, curry-goat. And black women. St Kitts, Trinidad, Antigua, Barbados, Jamaica, any place. The sweetest kind. Music playing. An' de woman dem in a dem nighttime dress. Nutt'n good like a woman wha' smile an' curl her body. Black woman serving honey at night. And if the woman right, you holdin' on to Jamaica all night! An' wid all dat, yu smoke an' smoke. Smoke herbs wid yu bredren. De bass-line a poun' de room, de whole house, de street outside, de nex' street. And the next. Bass line pounding your *whole* life. Jamaica bass-line was heartache in a life. Longing for JA. Bad longing. Man, this was no house-party. No shebeen. This was Jamdown. Friday, Saturday night. Monday could wait. Back to work. Regular work was maybe factory, or drive bus, or a white boy on a building site know your name but call you John, load that lorry. Some folk worked seven days a week, family back home, urgent money for shoes, medicine, pay rent. A man could be forty-five, having a mother and father back home and four kids to send money to. But while the music played and a sweet woman smiled her beauty in the room, that was what. That, and grounding with your brethren. To smoke, and smoke. Smoke herbs. Ganja wid yu bredren.

Years. Way into the 70s. 80s. Then things changed. Urshell himself was different, slowed down. Married. And knew. Remembered. He was a Maroon. Remembered the duty to live clean. After his third daughter was born, it was time to think. Time to accept he might never have a son. The impact of that retreated him from the street, the way of the street. Not knowing he was to have two more daughters. And no sons. In a way, he didn't quit the streets. Not all the way. He was a bus driver. Years and years. Then a London taxi. And nowadays, old and looking out the window, watching as old England goes by. Then one day to die here, never to see Jamaica from under Jamaica soil.

# 113

"How's tricks?" Jimmy says.

"*So!*" Donna snaps. "You think I'm worth a phonecall?"

"Been thinking about you. Good vibes."

"Somebody who can play all Chopin's etudes can try anything on the phone. Trying to play me? Well, no chance!"

"You've been on my mind."

"And?"

"Could do with some of your cooking."

"Wait there, I'll send some down the phone!"

"Hey, why the war? What have I done?"

"You want something, I can tell."

"Bobby Delaney invited me to tour."

"America?"

"Yeah. Ten cities. Then we record my jazz score."

"Minims?"

"Yeah. That, and a new piece I call Cobalt."

"Cobalt was your tribute to Coltrane and Bach, wasn't it?"

"That's the one."

"Mister, you're getting there!"

"In the right direction. Yeah, moving along."

"What happened to Germany?"

"Fell out with them. Well, with the folk who introduced me."

"Told you it wouldn't work, didn't I!"

"That's what you said, woman. More or less."

"Was it race?"

"Yeah. The folk here, not Germany."

"Well," Donna giggles, "here's my shoulder to lean on."

"How's the Jamaican sky?"

"In Portland it's big and blue today."

"How's the diet?"

"Tough going."

"And the chickens?"

"Got rid of them."

"Sentimental?"

"Too much hassle."

"Thought you like fried chicken."

"Mr Dell, I want a lot more than chickens. Any ideas?"

# 114

Urshell nods. "Come in, young man. Come in."

Rum on the coffee table. A new bottle. The brown face of Mandela smiles from the sitting-room wall.

Jimmy takes a seat. Then hands over the LP. "This is Lester Young, a serious record."

"Jazz?"

"Yeah, the Lester Young Trio. Him, Nat Cole and Buddy Rich."

"Nat King Cole?"

"Most people don't know Nat Cole was a piano player."

"Lester Young, is who?"

"Man! The least of it, he was the sax with Billie Holliday."

"I do not like that woman!"

"Well, it's Lester Young on this record. I was going to bring something by Charlie Parker, but this guy laid the groundwork."

"Rum?"

"Thanks. No chaser. Your daughter still getting married?"

"Day after tomorrow."

"Annette is a deep woman. I wish her well."

"Relax, son. Relax."

"I'm off to America. Touring, and stuff."

"When?"

"Three weeks. I could hitch a ride. A long ride."

"Live there?"

"Why not?"

Urshell is misty-eyed. His throat clears. "You dream of lions, yes?"

"All the time."

"Lucky!"

"Last time I was here, you talked that luck stuff. Beats me."

"A man like you can go any place."

"I don't even know which way's which."

"Go where a lion can respect you."

Jimmy nods at Mandela on the wall. "Like that guy?"

"That's the man. Just *one* glance, a man a lion can respect."

"Even in a city?"

"A man must be confident in himself. No circus lion. No funny blokes with earrings. No sun-donkey!"

"What's a sun-donkey?" Jimmy laughs, quickly thinking donkeys with straw hats & dark-glasses. "A donkey sipping Coca Cola under a hot sun?"

"Sun-donkey? That is a black man with blond dye. Funny hair-dye, red die, unnatural. Black man, black woman with that weird dye."

Learning a new talk, Jimmy grabs at the smokes in his pocket. But a strict no-smoke zone here; the old man's eyes say 'Take it or leave it!' Hard not to respect Urshell. And that's why only the right question will work. "Why didn't you go back to Jamaica?"

"You know Jamaica?"

"Never lived there, but I've visited."

"Let me tell you about JA. Every two years, myself and the family go out there. The plan was always to go back."

"Why not now?"

"Son, you move too fast."

"Is it that multiracial thing you like about London?"

"You moving too fast."

"Jamaica is *the* multiracial place. But you already know that. Better than me."

"Jamaica is a mix-up. Black. White. Chinese. Even a little Arawak."

"What's Arawak?"

"Arawak was original Jamaicans. Long before white and black."

"It was the mixed blood thing I noticed. It was everywhere."

"Many, many Jamaicans. Black mixed with white, or Indian, Chinese. All over the island, a big mix-up, brown people."

"They get on OK."

"More or less. But calling everybody black? Mistake! Brown people in Jamaica, what you can call a new folk. From Africa, yes, but not only Africa. And, you know, everybody aware of blood-line in Jamaica."

"If you went back, you'd have deeper thoughts. You're a Maroon! You should *be* in Jamaica, living with Maroons. Not get old here and getting called a black bastard."

"Jamaica?" Urshell says, weighing a tumbler in his hand. "That little island? The most beautiful place in the world!"

"Then go back!"

"Why?"

"Roots!"

"What is roots?"

Jimmy frowns. Instinctively, grabs at the smokes in his pocket. "That's a big question. Too big for me. But you, you could take the money you made here and live OK in Jamaica."

"Which money?"

"Your savings. Even your pension. Take that with you."

"Ever see a humming bird?"

"Lots."

"Where," Urshell smiles, "is the home of a humming bird?"

Jimmy fumbles the cigarette packet. Slowly, hand to hand. Toying with the thought of tobacco, gazes up at Mandela. Then turns to the old Jamaican. Laughs. "I know what you mean," he says, nodding.

"Next time yu go JA, check Blue Mountain."

"Yeah. And those women, they're it!"

"Yes, yes."

"Don't you miss that?"

Urshell turns to the door. Jaws clenched. He turns back to Jimmy. "Every day. Even after fifty years."

"That's old-man's nostalgia."

"Jamaica?"

"Yeah. What's the big thing there for you?"

"If yu go country, a woman cook her food outside. Sweet! Mek you cry. Simple things, son. Simple."

"Then why d'you stay here?"

"Why I stay?"

"Too difficult? Is it too difficult to talk about?"

"How?"

"Too hard to find the words?"

"Well, four of my daughters born here. And I have my grandchildren. Kids born here. You get to like a place. You like a place that you live there so long. I would miss springtime here. The leaves. Son, never take those leaves for granted. Some days, no place better than England."

Jimmy laughs. "You're joking, right?"

"When I first came, it was what you can call different. Yes. We could not believe how everything was grey. The sky. Every house. Even the birds! I used to beg my father, please send me back to Jamaica. And the weather. *Cold?* Live in one room. Those days, man! No central heating. Paraffin heater all day. Everything, grey."

"When you retired, why didn't you go? You could have gone back, set up your own thing. Why didn't you dust the grey, go back?"

"Well, after a while you realize. For a period of time you just did not notice a white person could smile. Not smile true. Everybody was in a hurry. *Morning! All right? Oh, Good! Nice to see you. Bye-ee!* Man!"

"Yeah, the old smile game!"

"But you get used to them, get the true smile."

"What about Jamaica?"

"JA? I ask myself that question every time I go home."

"See, you said it!"

"What?"

"You said *home*. I knew it!"

Urshell smiles. "Jamaica is home."

"Then go home, old man!"

"England is home."

"Go back to roots, Mr Urshell."

"In Jamaica, people call me a foreigner. Even my own family. You get what you can call suspicion. No, more a kind of tension. Jamaica people believe because you live in England you have money."

"Even your relatives?"

"Man, me 'ave dis cousin, him do me a ting las' time me out deh. Me an' de wife a get ready fe de airport, an' dis guy a look pa' me shoes, him wan' me fe tek off me shoes an' gi' dem to him!"

"Did you?"

"Another thing, in Jamaica they expect a man my age to go to church. But the noise! I could not stand the noise. Too much hand-clapping. Wha' massa God mus think!"

"Your daughters got a good education here."

"Yes. One son-in-law is a science lecturer. Education, son."

"Education is *not* why black people stay."

"Yu, why yu stay?"

On his feet, Jimmy grabs at the smokes in his pocket. But remembers. He gazes again at Mandela's picture on the wall. Then slopes back to the chair. "Weird, but I feel connected in England."

"Because?"

"There's things I must do. Anyway, I was born here. Even my mother, she was born here and they don't even know where her birth parents came from."

"Mek a tell yu someting. Funny business goin' on."

"That's why I've come to see you. You have the answer."

"Me? *I* do not know the answer, son. God will know the answer. You don't believe in God?"

"No."

"A young man, so sure. God too big for any man. Young or old."

"Where was this god thing when black folk got scooped into slave ships?"

"I cannot answer that."

"At one gas-chamber, a chief rabbi invited his god to show divine power, intervene, put things right, chastise the Nazis, teach the world."

"Well, my young friend, it was not God that was not there. It was the devil that was."

"I've heard that whitewash before!"

"Slavery was the easy part. The start of the black man's story. The hard part, that is up ahead."

"How'd work that one out?"

"A dog can shed blood. But a liar can not repair history. Learn that!"

"*What?*"

"No liar can fix history."

"And this god business is, what, the fixer?"

"You want my opinion, you have it."

"God doesn't do it for me!" Jimmy huffs. "All that praying, that dumb groping round, blind, asking favours from something that never answers back."

"Man, you have lost your way!"

"The New Testament says 'Wherever two or three are gathered in my name, there will I be.' Know that?"

"I know it."

"Then how d'you explain kids getting raped by priests?"

"Too sad for words."

"Raped!"

"Yes."

"Inside the church building!"

"Yes."

"Or a black congregation get bombed in America."

"No, I can not explain that."

"Mr Urshell, there's better ways than religion."

"Nelson Rolihlahla Mandela. In the autobiography, Mandela talks it out loud: 'I can not pinpoint when I became politicized, when I knew I would spend my life in the liberation struggle.' Son, that is religion."

"You read the whole book?"

"Five times."

"What's it say about my generation making it?"

"Well, you have making it. Then you have *making* it."

"Where's the part where they don't say nigger any more?"

"That chapter is for you, your generation to write."

"In a multi-millionaire house tonight, Margaret Thatcher's probably revising her memoir. Or watching TV, toying with Vermouth and scrambled eggs. Her eyes probably dart from the picture of her son to Tony Blair on Newsnight."

Wry, Urshell smiles. "Sir, you are what I call a tricky customer. A tricky, tricky customer!"

"Because I don't believe in religion?"

"You believe in your future?"

"My future disconnects from getting called nigger."

"For a smart person, you too sure of yourself."

"When it comes to my future, you're dead right I'm sure!"

"Then, I can not help you."

"Want me to go?"

"One evening," Urshell says, head shaking, "a white fellow asked me if black people have ten times as much boy babies as girls."

"Why?"

"The bloke wanted to understand something. I want to understand that same thing. Maybe you can tell me why so many black boys with white girls."

"What d'you mean?"

"That jamboree, that business every year for celebrity black folk. I was in big trouble. I could not explain it to the white chap. Every black guy arrived with a white girl. Black and white minstrel show."

"*Minstrel?*"

"Celebrity black guys, every one of them was with a white girl."

"That gives minstrels?"

"Yes. The Black & White Minstrels. It was a show on TV in the 60s. A showbiz situation, white folk using black boot polish to pretend."

"Blacked up their faces?"

"Yes."

"*Why?*"

"Well, that is what I mean by making it."

"How? How?"

"Dat black-up business, it start wid a white bloke. Al Jolson. Black up him face, sing Mammy! on stage."

"But," Jimmy says, "some black guys baked their hair. I've seen those old films. Nat Cole. Ellington. Black guys with hair gel, grinning their heads off!"

"That stuff was on TV all the time. Yes, son. The minstrel show was every weekend. We used to sit and observe. But after a period of time some of the black folk born here said it was liberties, the black-up was taking liberties. Dem get de show tek off de air. '78."

"That's where nigger comes in? I don't get it."

"For an educated fellow, you take long."

"White people with boot polish on their face, that gives nigger?"

"Not by itself."

"What's the answer?"

"Your generation must cure the fetish. Banish minstrel fetish. Not one black guy was with a black girl."

"Maybe," Jimmy says, rustling for a smoke, "it was a coincidence."

"Coincidence? Son, nine or ten would be coincidence. Three or four, natural. But it was every single one of them."

"All of them?"

"All! Old and young. Every one of them. Tuxedo, white female."

"Maybe it's because more white girls than black ones in England."

"More black girls in South Africa than white girls. But celebrity white boys there, they do *not* have black girlfriends. Not one!"

Jimmy's eyes narrow. He remembers something Agnes said. When she talked of mixed-raced in South Africa, some are happy being called black, but most feel closer to the white side.

310

"Celebrity black guys in England," Urshell says, "in a bad situation in this life. Mus' get a white gal. Dem get nightmare 'bout Africa."

# 115

"No dreams of lions," Jimmy says. "Only pantomimes."

Urshell nods. "Right now in Israel, folk resent the Falasha. Resent being the same Jew as black folk from Ethiopia."

"Jews from Ethiopia?"

"White Jew, why not black Jew?"

"I didn't know there's black Jews."

"Israel opened every door to folk from Russia. Tens of thousands, even when half those people can not be Jewish."

"But white, yes?"

"White."

"Hey, let's talk black."

"Moses married a woman from Ethiopia."

"Really?"

"Numbers 12, Verse 1."

"I don't count bible stuff. Money you can't spend."

"You don't care?"

"If I was a Falasha, I wouldn't leave Africa. Believe me!"

"Son, now you dressing a wound that will not heal."

"I'm trying to understand."

"All people come from Africa. Even whitest white."

"That big migration stuff? A long, *long* time ago! Before the ice age."

"This thing is simple."

"Too complicated for me."

"Then, let's do it the hard way. Name me a celebrity black guy in England having a black lady."

Jimmy frowns. "There's lots, I mean, there must be loads."

"Give me a name. One name!"

"I can't think."

"You have any sisters?"

"No."

"Those black boys want nothing to do with black girls."

"Right now in Zanzibar," Jimmy says, "even in some UK spots, there's women wearing the veil. Originally it was to protect them from desert climes, but some inner-city women say the veil is their religion."

"Talk, but talk sense. Drop this veil business."

"A man gives a woman a rose, doesn't have to see her mouth smile."

Urshell slaps his knees. Laughs. "You? A *tricky* customer!"

"Galaxies wear veils. Till a telescope comes along."

"You talk like a man."

"I'm twenty five!"

Grabbing his glasses, the old man sighs. Then pans to Mandela on the wall. "Guys copy Bob Marley. Dem believe seh Bob talkin' to dem. Young guys. Bob never talk dat white faada business, but it bug him. Good people know. Everybody in Trench Town was a blacker skin tone. It used to bug Bob."

"My father says it's the mimics' fault."

"Wha' yu faada do?"

"Music. Ace trumpet, when his hands work."

"Him know Jamaica."

"More than you! He knows about the false-heads."

"Dat false-head business? *Dat*?"

"Yeah, I know. Six months ago I got rid of my dreads."

"Wha' yu know 'bout Rasta?"

"It's more than dreadlocks."

"A lot more! Bob Marley, that business start with a record deal. Man used to walk the same street as Bob. Serious man. Man like Bunny Wailer. But a white guy name Chris Blackwell happened along. Bob light skin."

"Chris is a white Jamaican, isn't he? Just like Bob's father."

"Chris Blackwell born in London."

"Whatever. But no way Bob didn't get the score!"

"Well, every man fe talk wid him faada. Dat natural. Bob talk when him sing. Rasta know dat, an' it nuh stop Rasta."

"How do they tolerate the mimicry?"

"Listen, every hypocrite mus' face up. Time fe man up! Face the truth. Mimic fe look in a dem own face, check if dem faada look like Bob faada, even like Bob."

"Man!"

"Son, when you only have girl children you have just one safe place in this life. Only one direction you can travel. One day you get old. You know what is out there. You try to keep your daughters from certain guys. My daughters are black women, son. Would not be good enough for the tuxedo black boys. To guys like them, black women not delicate enough."

"They're a load of bull!"

"Yes."

"*Way* out of order!"

"Most of them your age. You never notice?"

"Well, it's not something I bother with. Got my life."

"What?"

"I never check the street. Doesn't interest me."

"Son, that is what I mean."

"Sorry?"

"Making it, or *making* it."

Jimmy remembers the Jamaican white girl. Even her parents were born in Jamaica. Even her grandparents. One day she'll visit England. Her flaxen hair was blowing in the breeze, her skin was white and tanned. It surprised him. The sun hovered that afternoon as she showed a shy way up the beach.

"In Jamaica, it's the other way round. If it's black-white, it's usually white guys with black women."

Urshell nods. "That is Jamaica. But below the surface, oh boy! Jamaican people have some of the *biggest* hang-ups over race. Complexion. Even now, light skin better than black. Things like that."

"What about England?"

Urshell turns to Mandela's picture. "Wicked business going on. This race business, it bad. Some black girls never go with a black guy. Not so much as look at one."

"England?"

"All the time. Mostly, the darker skin women. Some of them never look at a black man."

"What're they up to?"

"How yu mean?"

"They're in denial?"

"Dem woman deh? Dem tell demself seh dem a mek it."

"Well, they can stay the fuck away from me! Sorry, I didn't mean to swear. Not in your house. Don't mean to disrespect you."

Weary, old, Urshell hauls his frame from the armchair. "With some black women, black men are never good enough. Some black girls, to them black men mean trouble. Their situation, man."

"Their situation makes me sick!"

"Many black folk hate black."

"*Why*? Tired of the downside, maybe. But not hate being black."

"Black folk, young men and women, get a mission. Live clean, live honest. No fetish."

"I'll drink to that!"

"Some black females run from black skin. Any white bloke will do."

"Death, by fantasy."

"That girl," Urshell grunts, "the one from South Africa. Let her go. Forget the woman. Thirty five million blacks to four million whites there and, man, you should run the country in your image. To deny the natural African hair means you do not understand."

"I know," Jimmy sighs. "Cuts me up inside, her fantasy in the sun."

"Who can spell fantasy?"

Turning from the old man, he shrugs the question. Suddenly, remembers the tropical plant in Lorna's front room. A tease. A botanic fantasy. From a distance the plant was like wafer glass. A solo flower flecked it like blood.

She brought it back from Barbados. Waters it and cries.

"Fantasies are hard to nail."

"Skin is not fantasy," Urshell says.

"I'm not begging England. Not chasing tuxedos, white girls."

"Every man will have a fantasy one day."

"Maybe."

"Your fantasy?"

"I don't have one."

"The South African girl?"

"I think about her. I don't *fantasize*."

"Because the woman is black does not mean she is not fantasy. You love the idea of a woman from Africa. Some black guys have the white fantasy. You, the fantasy for Africa."

"Listen, I'm black!"

"You know Africa?"

"Never been anywhere near."

"No?"

"I mean, I dream of it. But I've never been."

"No man can love a continent. Who," Urshell laughs, "can chase a continent round the bedroom?"

This is getting to Jimmy. Fun, now and then. But bleak all the same. And maybe it's true. Agnes herself accused him. She said he was only checking her out because she's from Africa, not for who she. Said all he was looking for was a way to square things; getting compensation, being with a woman from Africa. He didn't understand. This heated talk was in a music shop one day and, for a while, dazed browsers got slack-jawed because of a hot-tongued woman getting angry.

"Mr Urshell, why'd you ask if I dream lions?"

"That dream, only a lucky man will have."

"How come?"

"Somebody dreaming of Africa will have a lion to walk with."

"Think black folk care about Africa?"

Urshell used to smoke. At one time, 40 a day. This is where he'd reach for a cigarette. Instead, studies his guest. Over and over.

"Yes and no."

Jimmy frowns. "What about English folk."

"White people?"

"Think they understand lions?"

"Lions see human. Not colour."

"Meaning?"

The old man wavers from his chair. Begins to pace. Short, deliberate steps. Slow pacing. Quartering and quartering the room. Studying Jimmy. Like maybe he's a whole new kind of map, or from some place with no map.

"White folk," he says, "most white people will not think of a lion."

"They shoot lions! Put them in zoos!"

"Then it is not the lion. The gun is the thing. Or the cage."

"Old man, that's too much like religion."

"Well, you know, things never black and white. Many white folk are better than racial. I know English people that look at life the right way."

# 116

Sprinkling rum on the carpet, right hand on heart, the old man says, "Lions never see nigger. Never!"

"Hope not!" Jimmy laughs.

"Understand a lion, the slave business can not get to you."

"That's way too biblical."

"If you understand the lion you can not fear a circus."

"Racism is not a circus?"

"A fool can perform."

"You never smiled the smile?"

"Yes."

"You jumped to the ringmaster's whip, like everybody else!"

"But no nightmares about Africa."

"Nightmares. What's the point?"

"Those people are all over the place. Ask them."

"Sun-donkeys?

"Yes. Start with them."

Urshell can never forget one nightmare. In one African war zone, children talked how easy it is to kill. Or chop off limbs. Kids as young as nine, ten, getting the bone thrill. Human bones don't refuse a machete; that's why they're bones! Those kids played the saddest game, bet which severed limbs jump round on the ground longest. Which legs. Which arm. No need for childish toys in child-crazed war spots.

Mandela's eyes seem to narrow from his portrait on the wall. The face is alert, wry. But something distant in the eye. Mandela seeing far.

"His face seems oriental," Jimmy says. "A smiling face, but mostly his eyes are a long distance away. Africa, orient and far."

"All types of African."

"No way Mandela would stay here!"

"Why I stay in England? Well, we hang around because we are what you can call lost."

"Like nomads?"

"Nomad?"

"I *like* that word!" Jimmy says. "Nomad is me."

"That slave business, black folk, we must look beyond it."

"Too much denial. Most people in denial."

"How?"

"Living in the same England that made slavery happen."

"This place, that place."

"White people don't want to know. White liberals, here and there. But most don't want to know. It's always 'That was so long ago.'"

317

"Coming here from the West Indies was tough enough."

"American blacks don't have that problem."

"West Indies people, we in a situation. Go back to the sun or, well, time to move on."

"Black folk can't be nomads. Not in Britain."

"Son, you can put down roots. Move in city life."

"Like where?"

"Start a business."

"Anybody can do that! Intelligent blacks want something more than a business."

"As we go along, yes, we can get big-time."

"Merchant banking?"

"Stuff like that."

"Top lawyers."

"*Lawyer*?" Urshell scoffs. "Man, lawyers are some of the weirdest folk on this earth. Selfish people. And, you know, ninety percent are not honest. Even intelligent."

"Hey, blacks need lawyers. Good black lawyers."

"Why?"

"How you gonna guarantee getting serious in court?"

"Lawyers talk. But most of them can not do simple science."

"We want justice. That's got nothing to do with science."

"No?"

"You don't need a physics degree. Not to put things right. What about Margaret Thatcher? She did chemistry at Oxford, but look how she witched down. Hexed her own white folk, the working class."

Urshell smiles. "The smartest person I ever saw was a man from Ghana. Economist. And, brother! To him, the useful thing is science. Agriculture. Engineering. Medicine."

"But he still mouths off from his little economics hill."

"No! That honest man walked from that. Back to university. Biology. Yes, science is the place."

"Well, they can call you nigger any time. It's in their toolkit. Never matters to them how educated you are."

"Then who needs the education, you or them?"

Jimmy yawns. "Folk switching to science, it'll take a hundred years."

"When white folk stopped using nigger, it was coloured people. Thirty, forty years."

"Now we're just black. But they still hit you with nigger."

"Now and then. That is true."

"It was blacks in America. They made it OK to say black."

"That was the start."

"Old man, that was *it*!"

"Then why keep up the folly."

"What d'you mean?"

"Stuff you guys do."

"Music?"

"Entertainment is only relaxation, son. Smart persons should be in a lab. Cure the sick. Fuel. Irrigation. Things."

Jimmy's eyes lower to the ground. "I dropped science at A level. We can't all be scientists."

"Music is for spare time."

"I think that about politics."

"Politics is folly. Global warming going on. Bad, bad business. Politics is a backseat driver talkin' piss-pot!"

"Come on, Urshell! I mean, Mr Urshell. They've got to be literate."

"You ever look in the eye of a dentist?"

"I don't think so."

"Politicians sit in a dentist's chair, talk the dentist's two ears off!"

Jimmy laughs. Driving a black cab in London so many years, Urshell picked up half a world. Heard science talk in the cab. And politicians talking pap.

"I agree. Nobody would rate Stephen Hawking if it was literature or politics."

"Even music," Urshell says, smiling.

"Hey, great music is up there. Right up there with science!"

"Great music is luxury. Bad music is want."

"Replace politicians with scientists?"

"Respect."

"Pride?"

"Some good people came along in the 60s. Black folk with pride. The Afro thing, it was part of pride. But look what happened next!"

# 117

"What was it like, being a black panther?"

Urshell's eyes squint, like hit by sun. His gaze is a haze. An old man, remembering. He turns to old Mandela on the wall. Gazing, but can not decide. His heavy glasses lumber down, eyes wondering if Jimmy's one of the black recruits sent by government undercover.

"The folk at MI5 know all about me," he says. "So what the hell!"

Jimmy grabs a cigarette. But can't light it. He tries again. "Panthers were here in England?"

"Yes."

"How did it work?"

"Like what?"

"How did the hush happen."

"Hush?"

"Yeah. Black panthers in England are still a hush. Black folk here don't know. When blacks first arrived, they were like fresh gravel at a winter park gate. Makes me think of water-birds coming in from scree, you know, blue with arctic to break the ice. The first immigrants that wintered here were just too cold. Except to start a song sometimes. England was vivid white. Especially the countryside in winter. Even now, hedgerows look pinned back from surgery. Ice-cold secateurs. Those cuts. Exact cuts in the firm. To the early immigrants the sight of grass must have been a summer of swabs. Or maybe it was never only grass. Colours on the grass were maybe flocks of parakeets that died, too thirsty at the grey edge of the pond."

"You talk wise talk, son."

"Panthers," Jimmy says, "wanted to change all that. They wanted to send shivers down that winter spine."

"Panther?"

"Yeah, that's the one. Black panther!"

The old man frowns. "One day in '69, 1969, Bobby Seale was talking with his mother, deep talk, how American black folk will never go back to Africa. Reagan was governor of California. Eldridge Cleaver called him out, a duel, called him a sissy, a coward, Reagan must accept the challenge or call him Uncle Eldridge. Man, we laughed!"

Jimmy tries not laugh. "The good old days?"

"60s. Late 60s."

"And it got, where?"

"Everywhere. And no place."

"Jamaicans started the panthers here?"

"Jamaica, Trinidad. This place, that."

"I heard it was Jamaicans."

"Jamaican folk used to feel, well, sort of more ahead. But we put aside the squabbling."

"So, what was what?"

"How yu mean?"

"Who was who? The levels."

"Only one level."

"Some panthers were educated, weren't they?"

"Yes."

"I heard those were the biggest fakes on the planet."

"Well, you know, some did not understand the white man. Black power was their way to sleep with white. Live next door to white."

"Yeah. I heard that crap."

"Not much dazzle for white in Jamaica. We had Maroons."

"How'd you get to be a panther?"

"Powell! Enoch Powell. Mr Powell was the devil himself."

"And him having a name like that!"

"Name?"

"Enoch was father of Methuselah."

"One more Enoch was the son of Cain."

"Man!"

"England was a tough place because of Powell."

"So it was panthers' time!"

"Well, every black person could see how that man was wicked. A very evil man."

"Who was head panther?"

"Everybody."

"How come?"

"Everybody in the movement was Ivan X."

"*Ivan*?"

"Yes."

"Like the Jimmy Cliff part in, what's that film called?"

"The Harder They Fall."

"My father's favourite film."

"That was '72. The panther movement was starting to stumble by then. Ivan was the first vanguard. Everybody, Ivan X. You get arrested, the only thing you said was 'Ivan X!' Even the women."

Jimmy grins. "Women calling themselves Ivan X, that's ace!"

"Bobby Seale's mom would have been a Black Panther. She told Bobby she was just too old. But young women all the time. Plenty young black women. Militant black women in America, side by side with guys."

"The women were as fully armed?"

"Yes, yes."

"Did you meet them?"

"Who?"

"Bobby Seale, Huey Newton. Eldridge Cleaver."

"No."

"What guns did you have?"

"Gun?"

"Guns, like in the photos of those dread guys."

"Who?"

"American panthers. Serious artillery!"

"Son, black power was not guns. It was rebirth. That is stainless. Nothing more beautiful. For a period of time, the black man was a lion. Mandela was a fighting man in Africa. No need for guns here."

"That's not what I heard."

"Wha' yu hear?"

"I heard there was a place called the Black House."

Suddenly wary, cold beads in Urshell's eyes. "Well," he says, "maybe. Yes, maybe there was one guy. Half white. Michael X. Michael used to deal from the Black House."

"Walked with a gun!"

"Yes."

"Only him?"

"Maybe."

"Panthers, but no claws and teeth! What did you do?"

"Guns is not everything, son. The main thing was education, learn about the slave business. Things run clear once you learn that. Colonial this and that. Dat stuff still out deh. England was never America."

"But they say nigger here. Not just America."

"Dat worry yu?"

"Not only me!"

"Check out Black Skins White Masks."

"Books? What about the action, the real thing?"

"Action, and *action*."

"No disrespect, but you're getting away from the point."

"The point is?"

"Calling yourselves Ivan X. What did you do to live up to that?"

"We put things right in the community."

"Like what? What did you really do?"

"Organize. Legal defence. Projects. Buy bulk, cut the middleman. The aim was to get self-employed. Things."

"What about the real action?"

"Action?"

"Why were you afraid, Mr Urshell?"

"Like how?"

322

"Afraid of guns, man. What's so terrible about a gun?"

"Yu no si wha' happen wid de young boy dem! Dem tek gun an' a kill dem oneanadda."

"Not *that* type of gun."

"Which type?"

"The type where you refuse to get brutalized."

"Wha'?"

"Race mongers. Police. They still gang up on black guys."

"That will never change. Not soon. More time, a cop is somebody with a fly in the ointment."

"What?"

"Young, fit guy like you? Look in the eye of a rogue copper and only a puppy gaze back."

"They gang up on black guys."

"That was the 60s."

"It still happens!"

"Yes, but less and less. Look, I am not against police. Not all police. My neighbour was a cop. 40 years."

"The one with the cricket bat?"

"We go back thirty, thirty-five years."

"England has tamed you, old man. Sold you a bogus dream."

"You ever read Seize The Time?"

"No."

"I remember one part, Bobby Seale first setting eyes on Huey."

"Huey was the one with the shotgun, wasn't he?"

"Yes."

"That's the action I mean!"

Head shaking, Urshell ambles to Mandela's photo on the wall. In one move, his hands swivel the frame round. Another photo on the reverse. Two black guys. Militant, dread. A defining moment. Not just being on a victory rostrum, each guy with a gloved fist in the air.

"This," he says, "is the greatest picture in the world."

"Those black power guys at the Olympics!"

"The '68 Olympics. 200 meters ceremony. This is Tommy Smith. And this man is John Carlos."

"What a scene!"

"Start of rebirth."

"*That's* what I call panthers!"

"Those two boys were not panthers. Tommy Smith was not. Yes, the black-power salute. But that was greater than panthers!"

"When the picture was taken those guys were about the same age I am now. Their dread stance. Anthem to the black man."

"Yes."

"It was a one-off," Jimmy says.

"Tell me what you see in the picture."

"Two black guys, one white guy."

"Gold for the winner. Silver for regret, only a step away. But bronze! Bronze is for blood spilled just getting to the rostrum at all."

"Why hide it behind Mandela's picture?"

"December '56, Mandela got arrested. In front of his children. Early one morning. Accused of treason."

"In his own land!"

"The name of the arresting policeman was Rousseau."

"Big deal."

"A policeman with the same name as the French philosopher, the one that said 'Man is born free but everywhere in chains.' Learn that!"

Jimmy turns to the picture. "Two guys, like they're lighting a torch in the sky."

"That is the meaning of the gloves."

"I get the clenched fists, but how come they bow their heads?"

Urshell's own head bows. To his chest. His hands clasp. "John and Tommy? Those boys praying. They had to go back to America and the Ku Klux Klan was watching. Lynch mobs still going on. Uncle Sam glad for the medals, but happy to turn a blind eye if they got lynched. Bad situation. Bad! Martin Luther King assassinated that same year."

"Jeez!"

"Tommy Smith, that boy's grandfather had been a slave. Tommy was the one to turn the victory rostrum into a witness. But John Carlos, man! John was the real deal. The one with vision. The American team was full of uncle-toms."

Jimmy's eyes glaze. "What's going to happen?"

"A slave can win a medal, but only freedom can own the shine."

324

# 118

"Urshell bamboozlin' yu?" the old woman says.

Jimmy laughs. "Miss Marva, your husband is a serious man."

"England," she says, "too much confusion. Black sportsmen, brother! Them can't wait to drape in the Union Jack and flutter round."

Urshell nods. "Fool, after fool. Proud of the flag, even when redneck in the crowd hissing like serpent."

Marva frowns. "It's one thing to run fast, kick football, box great. But if that's all you do, if you don't have principles, then you better just bank your million. And shut your hypocrite mouth. Tommy Smith's teammates claimed the power salute cost them millions, you know, sponsorship. But beyond a medal, even a world record, those same black teammates did nothing. Tommy and John changed things."

"What did the panthers in London do?" Jimmy wonders.

Urshell turns the picture round, showing again Mandela's photo. "Son, that is a long story. Marva, you tell him."

"You better at this sort of thing. You tell him."

Jimmy turns to Urshell. "You weren't real panthers. That must have hurt!"

"No guns. But we used to drive parasites from the community."

"Like who?"

"Low-life black guys."

"Pimps?"

"Yes. And toms."

"We used to leaflet the toms," Marva says. 'Dear Sir Lord Tom, straighten up and fly right.' Beautiful times!"

"Then," Urshell says, remembering, "then the dilution."

Jimmy's head shakes. "You started a fire, but had no fuel."

"Mandela said Rousseau did not handcuff him that morning in '56. He was well capable of beating Rousseau to death, or just give him a beating, but allowed himself to get taken to the station."

"What're you saying?" Jimmy wonders.

"Well, one thing with the panther movement here was money. Money is basics. We had to have things."

"But not guns!"

"Equipment. This was the 60s. Some smart white folk following Marx. Early 70s. That flower-power. White girls burning brassieres in the street."

"But you had Marsha Hunt. Fantastic looking woman! American, wasn't she? I've seen posters. She was something else!"

"Yes."

"She was in Hair," Marva says.

Urshell nods. "Hair was a hit show. She used to dazzle white boys."

"She had the biggest Afro in England!" Jimmy says.

Marva shrugs. "But no respect for black men. She was the sign of what was coming. But some folk, we were aware of serious black guys. Ali, Mandela."

Jimmy grins. "Hendrix."

"Great guys," Urshell says. "Because of them the panther movement was like a magnet to English folk, famous white."

"Anybody big?"

"Oh yes. Musicians, actors."

"You needed their help, that's life, but what did *they* want?"

"Who?"

"White people."

"Well, some of them curious. Or rebellious, had to be different. The militant black people here, we gave them a buzz! Some of the brothers were educated guys. So it was easy to talk, black with white."

Jimmy laughs. "Sounds like white people wanted to join up. Join the panthers. But seriously, how did they know where to find you?"

"You know," Urshell says, "it was never underground. Everything was up front. English folk would help out. Good people."

"White people?"

"Yes. Dem bring equipment, money. Tings like dat."

"What they did want?"

"How yu mean?"

"They gave you money, but what did they want in return?"

"Well, when you look back tings not soh clear."

Marva laughs. "White guys wanted to sit, smoke ganja with black folk. Serious discussion. Good talk. Good people. English. Brilliant guys. And the white girls! Those girls could talk. A lot of them were very bright, more serious than the blokes. Some of those girls couldn't wait to get to know the brothers. Dazzle for black guys."

"Because of Hendrix and Ali?" Jimmy wonders.

"Yes," Urshell says. "Dazzle. Middle class white girls did not care if a brother looked like a jackass, had to get near that black man dazzle."

"*That* was the panthers here?"

"I know. It looks bad."

"You allowed dazzle to trump?"

"Allow?"

"Razzle-dazzle, bling-bling!"

"Young man, how old are you?"

"Diz! Dazzle, bling!"

"What?"

"Hypocrites!"

"Who?"

"The so-called panthers! Every one of you, every Ivan bling X!"

Marva sighs. "Jimmy, too many people calling themselves Ivan X were on a trip. Happy to drink beer, sleep late, read Karl Marx. Exactly the time members of the Black Panther Party were getting murdered in America. Government assassins, gunning panthers down. Dozens and dozens, murdered by rednecks or uncle-toms in America."

Urshell scowls. "It was only a few of the brothers here."

Jimmy turns to the old man. "I heard the educated guys were the biggest hypocrites!"

"The movement could not hold together without educated people. But, yes, a lot of hypocrites."

"One guy," Marva says, head shaking, "tall, good-looking, really neat, he resented the white girls, you know, mashing down the movement, but he was with a white-looking Asian woman."

Disappointed, Jimmy turns to Mandela on the wall. "Hard to believe how it works. It was  hypocrite bling time."

"Human nature," Urshell says.

"That's why you didn't walk from the crap?"

"Me, personally?"

"Yes!"

Urshell tries a smile. But knows. He must deliver. For a while, Jimmy's the son he never had. His throat clears. "Who could walk away?"

"Honest people could."

"Son, nobody could walk away. Everybody was up in the sphere. The greatest times. And some white folk, people you could respect."

"Like who?"

"John Lennon was a good guy. George Best. The boys out there that play football now, man, nobody in England good as Best."

"How come Hendrix was never big with blacks here?"

"Jamaican music. A few Jamaicans used to play jazz records, but black in general did not know blues music. Jazz."

Jimmy scowls. "Hendrix was a blues man. Miracle blues. But white folk baited him with cheap thrills."

"We had James Brown," Marva says. "Aretha Franklin. We loved that music. The best record ever was Solid Gold Soul."

"My old man's got it. But the rest of that era was a fake."

"Fake?" Urshell says.

"Yeah, your stint with the panthers was a fake."

"Jimmy, that is disrespectful," Marva says. "It was not a show."

"What was it?"

# 119

"On a wicked bookshelf," Marva says, "some bad place, a book how blacks got too close to a Bunsen burner in the Garden of Eden."

Jimmy jumps from the chair. "Burn the shelf!"

"The day in '42 when Mandela got his BA, he was very proud. But somebody wise told him the score. Education necessary for freedom, but not sufficient."

As Marva leaves the room, Jimmy could do with a smoke. Nervy, he turns to the old man. "I don't mean to disrespect you."

"Talk what you must talk."

"You sat around, pretending being panthers."

"Everything, things happened so fast. The movement was like a party. And with every party, folk that can not hold liquor."

"Black women getting insulted. Was that the party?"

"No."

"What kind of fun was it?"

"Well, you learn as you go along."

"Who was the sun-donkey? The minstrel?"

"You have a fire, Jimmy. But get it right, son."

"That's why we're still getting called niggers. That's why!"

Old, wracked, Urshell steps from his chair. "That is only one side of the story. Most of the brothers had their black woman."

"We're going round in circles!"

"How?"

"Why didn't you deal with the hypocrites, break their skulls?"

"You know, this is not a simple business. Those guys used to attract rich English folk. Educated people."

"You were supposed to be panthers!"

"Yes."

"Black *panthers*!"

"Yes, son."

"*Black* panthers!"

Urshell wipes his brow. "I am old enough to be your grandfather."

"Guys like you get old. I need information. All you do is remember."

Jimmy's mother's foster-sister left Liverpool in 1970. She wanted to get away. Joined the panthers. And straightaway it was life & death. Plans, the struggle, education on economics and slavery. Some classes were by serious folk from LSE. The panther movement was motoring, going the right place. Then one day. She realized. The money donated from showbiz white folk linked the movement. Too many guys getting called black panthers but all the time ogling white; just didn't get the difference. So she went back to Liverpool. Got back into jeans and plain T-shirts. And honest work in a car wash.

"I remember one particular brother."

"There you go again!"

"Son, let me finish. I remember a bad thing, a stupid guy."

"A tom?"

"Yes. A graduate guy, going with a brainy white girl."

"And calling himself a black panther!"

"For one year, she suck de brodda wood. Him black wood. One day she call him a wog. A bloody wog."

"What, with the same mouth?"

"The precipice."

"What did he do? She was talking to all of you."

"I know."

"She was talking to panthers!"

"Son, calm down. That girl was talking to your generation. Twenty, thirty years before her time."

"Sucks my cock, calls me a wog? I'd have shoved it under a bus!"

"You have a fire, Jimmy. A fire."

"You treated Marx like he was a god, smoked ganja with dropout white guys, and had the nerve to call yourselves black panthers!"

"A situation where some of the brothers were confused."

"Scared of guns!"

"Guns, that was never for in England. Not thirty, forty years back."

"No, just white pussy. TV chat shows. That's exactly why types like Bosworth Trass are out there."

"Then learn!"

"The big lesson in town is hypocrites multiplying."

"Black folk, people of colour, we will never have a community. Not in England. Only folk with skin."

"The white man does *not* see it that way!"

"You talk for white?"

"No. But the white view is at the hub of the problem."

"Some of the brothers could see what was coming."

"Guys like Mandela, man, they put their lives on the line!"

"Yes. Big part of the journey."

"Panthers here didn't reach for the stars."

"No, son."

"There's still maypole dancing on English village greens. You too?"

"Watch your mouth!"

Jimmy can see worry on the old man. Old, with no place to go in his own home. "Sorry. I didn't mean to talk out of turn."

"Chairman Mao."

"Who?"

"China. Socialism. Communism. The panthers learned."

"How?"

"1930, Mao's wife got beheaded by a warlord."

"That was his allure to panthers?"

"Mao was still a young fellow in '30. China in big trouble. Years after all that, the Chairman helped folk in Africa."

"What did panthers see in China?"

"The black struggle."

"*Black* panthers?"

"Every time the Chairman talked peasant, we talked slave."

"Or uncle tom."

"Jimmy, act your age!"

"Toms are everywhere."

"Yes. That uncle tom business, out of control!"

"How d'you deal with that?"

"Too hard. Your generation can do better."

"You saw things going backwards, didn't you?"

"We wanted to hold it together. But, woosh! Honest folk got talked down by one educated jackass after another. America, folk wanted the middle ground, live between Martin Luther King and the panthers."

"Rosa Parks," Jimmy says, "was way more than King and his bible."

"No cotton growing in the fields of England."

"Where does nigger-brown come from?"

"Ask the white man."

"Are all those dog panthers still around? I'd like to kick one."

"Son, those guys were island boys. From small spots in the Caribbean, glad to walk round here, shop the big stores. In Jamaica we call that gladdy-gladdy. Those guys, what you can call a gladdy-gladdy. Maybe me along with them."

"Not panthers."

"A panther will go where a panther must go, day or night."

"Too right!"

"Go to South Africa. Check out Robben Island. Mandela said it was a place with no black warder and no white prisoner. All prisoners forced to wear short trousers. Grown men, even Mandela."

"Robben Island is only a metaphor," Jimmy says.

The old man pours a tumbler of water. Sits bolt upright in the old chair. Heavy glasses slope from his eyes. His throat clears. "Nobody could explain how the movement slipped. Panthers in America got into big trouble. Traitors. Police informers."

"*Informers*?"

"Any black thing, always somebody that will run to the white man and tell. Remember that!"

"Can't you tell who's who?"

"How?"

"Isn't there some kind of test, weed out the informers?"

"No."

"Why not?"

"Somewhere down the line you trust somebody."

"That's all there is?"

"Some panthers had to leave America, lay low. Algeria, Cuba. The police was starting to gun them down. Big shock. Man, everybody was in a daze. Could not explain that. Everybody in a different direction. Meet somebody in the street, more time you going separate ways."

"What a let down! Panthers here, a bunch of mickey-mouse."

"England is not America, son. Never any real need for panthers here. England was always different. English folk different. After a period of time you realize that. You meet the English with a higher vision."

"Old man, you're losing me again. I don't understand."

"Reagan becoming the president. That definitely got a big something to do with Michael Jackson."

"How?"

"Roll the dice, one illusion."

"Up face, or the down?"

"A stupid B-movie clown becoming president of the US of A. Yes. And watch this! Roll the same dice, and a weird thing, a black boy by name of one Michael Jackson. Black boy wanting to turn into a white man. A weird person. Yes, that little guy is nimble on the feet. But who can call that a black man?"

# 120

"Murder!" the old man yells. "Million upon million witnessed that man get killed, that young black man. The murderer walking free."

Jimmy frowns. "Michael Jackson?"

"A white man calling himself Michael Jackson. That man committed a public slaying, killed black Michael, put on dancing shoes, went out on stage to celebrate."

"You're not joking, are you?"

"Never more serious! Michael was brown-black. Now a lie-white, a computer Michelle more than a Michael. Inside the junk, that individual bawling."

"He's old enough to be my father. More or less"

"Somebody could be African, or mixed, British black, all that stuff. Black as night or fair like light, everybody was black. Simple as that. For a period of time we looked at things that way. Not now."

"Black is cool," Jimmy shrugs. "I'm OK with it, well pleased! No way I want to get called something else."

"Want my opinion?"

"That's why I'm here."

"Calling everybody black is, what? Not liberation. With that boy, that Michael Jackson, the whole thing gone up in smoke."

"Michael is ill, Mr Urshell. A disease. It sapped the natural colour from him."

"Disease?"

"Vitiligo, or something."

"Disease with a nightmare about Africa!"

"Not his fault. He couldn't help it."

"Even now that little man calling himself black. Even now!"

"In America, they say African-American."

"All black people are not African."

"Then what are we?" Jimmy laughs.

"Africa is not a stain."

"How does stain come into this?"

"Nowadays, all kinds of folk. Irish-American, Italian-American or Pol-ish-American. Dis an'dat. But dem never seh European-American. So who the hell is this thing, this African-American?"

"It's because they don't know. They don't know where in Africa the slaves came from, which slaves from where exactly."

The sitting room is all of a sudden too strict, too bare-knuckle. Time for a smoke. Apologizing, Jimmy heads to the door. Must get outside. Fresh air. Flex. Think. Sip nicotine. Upstairs, Urshell's daughter sings along, just in tune, with Aretha Franklin.

# 121

An amber light shines from the front room of Urshell's neighbour. House of the old English man with the cricket bat one drunken night. Amber shining through the curtain. The road stone quiet.

Jimmy pulls back from an urge to knock the door, wondering if the man knows Urshell was once a panther. Black panther, sort of.

Nice laughing from the house. The man is the outdoor type. Years as a copper on the beat. And a mooring in the Lake District. One summer he took Urshell on a slow car trip up there, touring from Kendal to Windermere. The smell of juniper drifted in and out. Marva gathered mosses for the rockery in her garden. But she was wary; old black lady thinking the ground would swallow her up as puzzled English folk watched and watched. But mostly that day was smiles. And buzzards on high, soaring, toying with the landscape, getting high, then grabbing rabbits to gorge on them. The man said that to buzzards rabbit blood is maybe just like gin.

Somebody gazes out at the night from the his first-floor window. Then draws the curtains. Tight. In a minute, the laughing starts again. But stops as the amber light switches off.

Jimmy takes a long drag. Fills his ungenerous lungs with tobacco. And almost spiting himself, wondering. Jealous of the man Urshell's daughter will marry day after tomorrow. Thinking. Mulling. Then dials his mother.

"I was wondering about tarmac and boot-black," he says.

"What d'you mean?"

"I don't know why star-filled nights tar lungs searing for release."

"I love Cobalt," she says. "The best thing you've done."

"I feel a bit of a fraud."

"Why?"

"It started with me doodling to Bach."

"Well, there's no trace of that. And nothing of Coltrane."

"Rather be dead than a plagiarist."

"Come and visit before you go."

"America scares me. It's where I have to be. But big nerves."

"Don't leave any unfinished business behind. No broken hearts."

# 122

Urshell pours two shots of rum. "Watch the Cup Final last week?"

Jimmy nods. "A good match."

"It was close."

"Nah! Chelsea outplayed Aston Villa."

"Name of the guy that scored?"

"Di Matteo. Roberto Di Matteo. That match was the last one under the old Twin Towers. They'll tear down the place, build a seater for 90,000."

"Ever play at a stadium?"

"Not yet."

"My daughter saw you at a jazz thing. Last year. You can play."

"I'm no Bud Powell."

"Lester Young, you rate him?"

"With no Lester Young," Jimmy says, "no Charlie Parker. Lester switched from drums to sax and in no time nobody could believe it. The control, the scope. Billie Holliday said his playing was the closest thing to singing, ever."

"Jazz was never my music. Not too big on it."

"Start with Lester Young, this record I brought you. Catch the timing, the space. Just listen. You won't believe it."

"Lester Young was a kind of genius?"

"Well, that's a step too far. Half a step. He was great. *The* great sax player before Charlie Parker. On the ethnic side, there's all kinds of ways to look at him. A black man, but green eyes from his mother."

"*Green* eyes?"

"And light skin."

"But they called him nigger still."

"Yeah, they want to be the ones to tell you who you are."

"Tar brush, big in America. Somebody passing for white? Not near a redneck! Even now, even the bluest eyes, blondest hair, if that tar brush there somewhere, then rednecks will get what they call your true colour, call you 'Nigger!' Learn that!"

"Lester's wife was a white woman. First wife. They had a daughter that Lester never told anybody about. Her mother's all-white blood combined with his part-white blood that, man! No trace of black. No black showed. Ten years ago me and my father were in America and somebody pointed her our. She absolutely passed for white. Went her own way, lived as a white woman till she passed away."

"She run from something. But what she getting at?"

"You tell me!"

"No, son. Your turn. *You* tell this old black man the score."

"The start was black America."

"Which start?"

"With no African-Americans, you know, folk like Lester Young doing something big, then the struggle is mickey-mouse."

"What is this African-American business?"

"What d'you mean?"

"Lester Young. Pale-skin gent with green eyes. How you get African-American out of that?"

"That's what they call themselves. *They* say African-Americans."

"Yes. But a jacket is not a suit."

"Then," Jimmy says, gazing at Mandela's photo, "name some suits."

"Sydney Poitier. Louis Armstrong. Oprah Winfrey."

"Martin Luther King?"

"Oh, yes. Alice Walker. Eddie Murphy."

"Colin Powell?"

"No."

"You're only going for the blacker ones."

"Powell is not African."

"He's black!"

"Yes, and no. As much Europe in that man as Africa. Maybe more."

Upstairs, a record of Martha Reeve singing with Marvin Gaye. A love song. Simple and soft, two people no longer lonely. Urshell's daughter is preparing to fly the nest. But tonight, swooning with Motown.

Jimmy smiles. "Berry Gordy, is he an African?"

"That is plain. A canny African. The Supremes, Marvin Gaye, Smoky, Martha & The Vandellas. That was all Berry Gordy. Then you get The Jackson Five. Michael Jackson. That boy was great, a black man as late as Thriller."

"You hate Michael!"

"The talent, no."

"You hate the man."

"Man?"

"Who're you to judge?"

"Somebody set fire to a house, the next one could be your house."

"I know," Jimmy sighs.

"The whole Jackson family, so damn good looking!"

"Yeah. Janet is beautiful."

"Aretha Franklin is beautiful. Something inside."

"Hey, it must have been great living through that Motown thing."

"As you can hear from upstairs, my daughter is a Motown sweetheart. She nicked all my old records."

# 123

"There's a mixed race woman I like," Jimmy says.

Urshell frowns. "Choose one woman. One woman at a time. One."

"Is mixed race a problem? I mean, for the way ahead."

"Some of the baddest militants were mixed-race."

"Then how come so many blacker people envy light skin?"

"That one is old as time."

"Did you see lots of mixed in Africa?"

"No."

"I get the sense you don't like mixed-race."

"The word, not the people. It does not mean connection with Africa."

"I still don't get who's who."

"All Africans are black. Some black people are not Africans."

"What?"

"Millions of black people are not Africans."

"How d'you get that?"

"Face to face with a lion, a white man never says nigger."

"So what!"

"If yu look African, then yu African!"

"You're saying there's Africans and blacks. Then folk in between, like Colin Powell, with no exact name."

"White folk call some people *black African*. But not white African. White South African, yes, that is cool. White folk from Zimbabwe. But not white African. Africa is homeland of the black man."

"Of course."

"So *black* African is a tautology."

"A what?"

"In Jamaica patois," Urshell smiles, "something like a tautology is a bang-a-rang."

"Old man, you draw big lines in the sand."

"Black folk from England, black from France, Belgium, black people from Holland, and where not. Nobody is a black European. Nobody is a white African."

"Wish you could look into the cradle?"

"At my age?"

"Because of your age!"

"Then tell me the *one* name a black man can not call another."

"Black guys say 'What's up nigger?' Happens in the States."

"Thirty races of mankind get called black these days."

"*How* many?"

"Thirty."

"Like pieces of bible silver?"

Urshell says it again. "Want to pretend?"

"Confused," Jimmy admits. "I mean, you want to divide people."

"You can not divide what was not united."

"I don't see that. What's the point?"

"Point?"

"Mandela, he's still in the struggle."

"How far from eye to eye?"

"Hey?"

"Shortest route from a picture to person?"

"*What*?"

"Collect different type of black folk and, man! You need a big room. A dance-hall."

Weary, Jimmy ups from the chair. Fed up. Wanting to leave. Wanting music, get back to the flat, eke light from piano keys. And yet. This old man talks what never gets talked.

Marva brings coffee. And a plate of hot fritters. She definitely is the reason why Urshell never left, Jimmy thinks. With a wife like that, old or not old, a man could be any place and not notice. Small room, big room. Africa, England, Jamaica. Any place.

Jimmy grabs a fork. "Mr Urshell, you're talking Noah's Ark."

"All black people are not the same race! *That* is the problem. Only a microscope can tell some have anything to do with Africa. Black is a short-cut word."

"Hey, blacks call themselves black."

"Black is a stain?"

"No way!"

"What is black?"

"It means you derive from Africa. Visibly. Whole, or bits."

"Good!"

"So what's the problem?"

"Lester Young, that man's daughter is not African-American. Not black. Not even mixed-race. She's white. Only a scientist can get the tar brush."

Jimmy laughs. "You sound like a preacher. You talk like Solomon."

"That fellow had a black mother."

"Yeah. Called himself black. His father was Semitic."

"In the bible Solomon was wise."

"He was ace!"

"I must be a fool."

"Hey, I don't want to talk bible. Solomon, because what you said about black and African is like that cleave-the-baby-in-two."

"Solomon tell Jerusalem woman 'bout himself."

"With women," Jimmy grins, "he was it!"

The old man's eyes lower. "Solomon was afraid."

"*Afraid?*"

"Nervous."

"The guy had 300 wives!"

"Him tell Jerusalem woman seh him black but comely. Black *but* comely!"

"I'd take those wives. Tonight!"

"Those women, every one of them had to be true to Solomon."

"Jerusalem was ladies, frankincense and spice!"

"Solomon dip dat tar-brush. Deep."

"Bring it on!"

"Be honest with who you are. Whole African, or part. Every part worth the same."

"That's not what's out there."

"Every part worth the same. Every part!"

Jimmy sets aside the plate. "How much is a part?"

"How yu mean?"

"Suppose there's some other blood."

"If yu look African, then yu African!"

"Even if born some place else?"

"Even Jamaica."

"London?"

Urshell sucks his teeth. Turns away. "If yu African, yu African!"

"Tiger Woods," Jimmy says, "calls himself a Cablinasian."

"Who?"

"Woods, the golfer. He was fed up getting called African-American."

"Why?"

"He's more from Asia than Africa. His mother's Thai. His father is a black man with bits of white and red-Indian in the mix."

"Every part worth the same."

"No tigers in Africa."

"Africa in Tiger Woods."

"Too much pretence is out there."

"Man, that is the worst nightmare about Africa!"

Jimmy nods. "Posers, sky high."

"Hypocrites have the loudest mouth, want that Woods boy to call himself African-American, deny his mother, talk false."

Urshell's daughter's been in the room for a whole minute already. But saying nothing. Only wondering. She collects the cups and plate. But can't decide. Not quite. Looking long at her father.

"Wish you a happy wedding," Jimmy says.

Frowning, Annette turns to him. "It's hard to get what's going on. With some guys it's 'Your life is worth nothing.' I hate that."

"Why blame guys? Takes both sides."

"Yes. Some of us women are crying out, but only inside. From the soul. Crushed petals. Ever seen crushed petals? I've never seen them bloom, not where grass exhausts a jeopardy with blood."

Jimmy blinks. "Wicked!"

"Think it's a fable?"

"No, no! It's the way you talk. Like poetry. But real."

"If black women wears a white woman's wig into hospital to give birth, what's real?"

# 124

"It's territory, " Jimmy says

Urshell's head shakes. "What is territory?"

"It's where you do your thing."

"Mandela at Robben Island was like in another country. Qualified lawyer, his own land, but forced to wear short pants like a boy. Next place was Pollsmoor. Meat was there. Vegetables every day."

"Pollsmoor," Marva sighs, "was a bad concrete place. Stark and grey. I remember a line from the book: he was missing the natural splendour of Robben Island. July '90, he was getting used to being out of jail. But the rate from black-on-black violence was fifteen hundred dead. In that one year! Mandela was old, weeping like a child."

"Territory is a dirty word!" Jimmy says

The old man nods. "You young guys, you do a thing that is not life."

"Me?"

"Too much black guy have red eye!"

"Blood red," Marva says. "Coffee, Jimmy?"

"No thanks."

Urshell stands. Tall as the door. "If yu eye full wid blood, blood is yu territory."

Marva bites her lip. "Young black guys fence down the community with knife. Even gun. Us older people point a finger, or go to church. But young guys feel the only thing to point with is knife or a gun. Them point at somebody that look like them. Last week one guy killed a younger black guy and his mother cry out, 'Dem kill him because him wear de same darkglasses.' Bad times!"

"Even if you own the fence," Urshell says, "you do not own the country here. If you own shares in the country, then you take care. Your life. But guys with the red eye arrive. The way of red-eye is bad, content with second best. The business in a red eye is kill."

Jimmy slaps his forehead. "The one thing I can't stand, is black folk strutting a skin overcoat."

Marva agrees. "Red-eye guys murder them own. Night. Morning. Day or night."

"And all the time," Jimmy says, "the woad-man's laughing. Rap doesn't help."

"Rap?" Marva shrieks, heading for the door. "*That* larceny? Oh, man! Somebody wanting to talk like a machine gun, call it music? That is the hell. Red-eye protect red-eye from sunlight. Somebody with a name that is not even a name."

Jimmy turns to Urshell. "Why did you take an African name?"

The old man wipes his brow. A tired wipe. He gets the glasses from their case. Pondering hands begin to polish them. Awkward. Troubled. Thinking. Mulling a name. "You know," he says, "American black folk have names for white. Here, blacks only have *white man*. When I was your age I used to call myself African."

"Afro-Caribbean?"

"African."

"A back-to-your-roots feeling."

"Yes."

"First thing was to change your name?"

"Of course."

"What was it before? Hope you don't mind me asking."

"Errol. Errol Fitzroy Urshell became Kwame Urshell."

"What'd your folks say, your mother and father?"

"My poor mother cried. My father was still alive so I had to hold on to Urshell."

"Then it was Africa, getting there?"

"Yes."

"Whereabouts?"

"West. Myself and two brethren."

"Roots?"

"All the way!"

"What was it like? How long did you stay?"

"Two years. Man, that place beautiful!"

"The land, the women?"

"Son, you would not believe it. The natural African woman!"

"Hey, I have a thing for African women. Love them."

"Woman wid dem big backside."

Jimmy grins. "That killer body. Those smiling eyes."

"Then why you don't go?"

"I want to."

"Motherland!"

"Those women didn't anchor you. You left."

"Yes and no."

"You left!"

"Yes."

"*Why?*"

"Well, it was things. Lots of things, son."

Jimmy sees the old man get queasy and old. Then again, he knows a man's age is not enough. Not if that age is only to hide from something. "Mr Urshell, what was the reason you quit, left Africa to come back here?"

"Well, it was the vibes. Superstition. Somebody with a bible in one hand, witchcraft in the other hand. Every ten miles a man calling himself a chief, or a general. Things like that. Tough. I could look at my roots, yes, all the while. Man, looking in the face of folk that look like me. I belong to those people. Belong to them! But I just did not know what to talk. Made my heart swell. Those people could not talk to me, not proper talk. Everybody expecting me to praise England. Wanting to come here."

"The ones *you* met. The town people, maybe."

"Ask dem why dem come 'ere!"

"Who?"

"African people."

"You call yourself African. Why did you come?"

"I come from Jamaica! African, yes. But from Jamaica."

"Lots of places in Africa you could have disappeared in!"

"Travel, yes. But stay wid yu roots!"

"Where in England are your roots?"

"The branch is important as the root."

"Studies."

"Wha'?"

"Africans I met at college were the most serious folk on the planet!"

"Dem go back to Africa?"

"The ones I know, everybody went back."

"Africa is dem homeland."

"It's that colonial thing. It's the same for them."

"Yu tek me fe a fool?"

"I wouldn't be sitting here if I did."

"African from Africa, dem 'ave some place dem belong. But dem come ya. Fe wha'? Cry? Dem have dem language, dem culture, dem family, but dem come a England fe shovel shit."

In the street, two teen voices go by. Jimmy turns to Mandela's portrait on the wall. "Nelson Rolihlahla Mandela."

"A serious name."

"Weird, him named after Horatio Nelson. Nelson was a slave-owner. A sly. Mandela, yes. But *Nelson*?"

Urshell turns to the portrait. Quiet, he adjusts the glasses on his old face. Almost doesn't recognize his mentor on the wall. His eyes narrow. Old hands remove the glasses, fold them away. Throat clears. "History will always come and go."

"A man is not his name?"

"Yes, and no."

"What's the no part?"

"Son, it was Greek folk. Africa is a Greek word."

"Where did you get that?"

"Before the white man, Africa was Alkebulaan."

"You should have gone to the villages. I heard village folk in Africa are it."

"That is true."

"Stephen Hawking describes supergravity, a theory."

"What?"

"Particles having different spins are different aspects of the same super-particle."

"Son, you moving too fast!"

"What's village life like in Africa ? If I went, it'd be villages. Or the desert."

"A young man can always have a fantasy."

"I'd go to Mali, check out Ali Farka Toure, learn from him."

Urshell smiles. "Marry him daughter?"

Jimmy laughs. "What's it like, waking up in an African house?"

"Africa is a big place. Continent. City, town, village."

"What's village life like?"

"A dirt-poor family, one goat, kill the goat so you can eat."

"Hospitality. That's not enough."

"Yes and no."

"How does no get into this?"

"Hospitality was open door for the European. The nightmare."

"You went to lands of your ancestors, enjoyed the scene, hospitality, but you left. Will you die here?"

"I traced my roots. One part of my roots. The part in Jamaica. It was somebody in 1760. A man that used to round up wild horses. Sell them. Funny thing, he was called Driver. Cudjoe Driver. Somewhere in the spirit world, Driver smiled at me driving black cabs in London."

"I hear Maroons believe in a spirit world they can talk with."

"Yes."

"Africans took that to Jamaica with them?"

"Yes."

"Africa, in Jamaica."

"Yes. Because of the slave business, one day I realized. I am from Africa. That is plain. But I am a Jamaican. I belong more to JA."

"What are you now?" Jimmy laughs. "Jamaican British?"

"What?"

"British Jamaican?"

"African-Jamaican. Alive in England. Yes, 50 years here."

"Old man, you'll stay!"

"Well, you know, you stand your ground. If all you know is talk then you run when you must fight. Fight when you must move on. Things like that."

"Like Mandela?"

Urshell nods at the portrait. "I hear what yu sayin'."

"I worry about the big identity thing. English born."

"You want to be English?"

"I dunno."

"That could get bad. Bad."

"It should be simple."

"Son, black English is a *long* way down the road. Your grandson, grand-daughter."

# 125

A car-horn blares in the night. In the street a woman says hello and, for half a beat, her voice could mourn. But she's going to throw the night away. Somebody will hear her whisper tonight. Jimmy wonders.

He tells Urshell about a lion dream. Two lions. They move at evening by the Thames, one each side of the breezing river. In hushed twilight the male lion's at the water's edge, mane high on the riverbank, claiming the cool river. The lioness swims across to him. And then. The best part. Two lions walking the river, beside it, lion with lioness, the same side of the river, moving along.

Wry, the old man smiles. "This is a simple dream. This is you with Agnes in mind."

"Your name should Joseph," Jimmy says. "Like the dream-sayer in the bible."

"Joseph is a big story. Too hard to carry. Tea, son? Rum?"

"Rum sounds great. But I'd best keep my head clear."

"Try the tea."

"No thanks."

"Shot of water. Iced-water?"

"What happened after Africa?"

"Roots?"

"What else!"

"Well, it was time to observe."

"Observe *what*?"

"I was back to England. Regular driving work. Bus work. Then the taxi business. Years. Jamaica was too hard to go back to. Going back was defeat. Then one day the whole business was plain. That lady was on the scene."

"Maggie?"

"Mrs Thatcher."

"*Mrs* Thatcher?"

"The same."

Jimmy squints. "You respected her?"

"That individual was a good woman. You know, the early days."

"Sounds like you wanted to dance with the witch."

"Watching the woman was because, well, all my children are female. When a woman hits the top you stand back, observe. She was what you can call a woman."

"She *hated* black people."

"Hate is a strong word. Bad word."

"What would you call it?"

"The blokes in the government, man! Some could not dance with a woman. Blokes taking shelter in the office."

"That's what made her get so high?"

"One year at Number 10, she was a pretend duchess."

"Mouthing off about Brixton, Handsworth, the rest."

"Yes. She badmouthed black people. 'We will not be swamped by immigrants!'"

"How'd they rein her in?"

"Rein?"

"I heard she was mellow towards blacks at the end. Less callous."

"Carnival. Notting Hill carnival."

"No way! There's no way that woman got influenced by that."

"Why?"

"Carnival is *huge* on black."

"You ever check carnival?"

"That tropical itch? Nah!"

"It was the white people. Carnival got bigger every year. Nobody could see how far you would go. It was white folk, them saying 'We want the carnival.' Man, that was making you think new."

"Like you could be OK in England? Black and OK?"

"Yes."

"One weekend every year, a phony weekend!"

Urshell's eyes close. His arms take the arms of the chair. "Yes, son. I know."

"When carnival started here, the physics community thought protons and neutrons were the bottom line. They never bothered with a dead German called Leibniz. Now they know. Quarks are it."

Urshell frowns. "Study, Jimmy. Study physics this time."

"I'm a composer. That's enough on my plate. I'd like to do half what Duke Ellington did."

"You talk plenty about this Ellington."

"Yeah, the music. But he was big on race. Seriously into race. In 1943, Carnegie Hall listened to his Black, Brown & Beige suite. Wasn't just skin-tone. Life. Mahalia Jackson sang it: *Black for labour, brown for black soldiers in the army, beige for American black music*. He even adapted Caribbean lilts for parts of it."

"Cuba is a boss music scene. The whole Caribbean."

"I think carnivals started there."

"Carnival means meat."

"You ever go?"

"Not me! Something wrong when a sweet woman can wear bird feathers, prance down the road with a whistle in her mouth."

Jimmy laughs. "Maggie, dressed in bird feathers?"

# 126

"What about Tebbit?"

Urshell frowns. "Who?"

"Lord Tebbit," Jimmy says. "He must have freaked at carnival!"

"Who is to know?"

"You had activists in your day, but nobody now. It's like blacks can't wait to get patted on the head, like if enough know about the Tebbit test there'd be queues to pass the good-little-black-boy test."

"I support West Indies for cricket. New Zealand for rugby. England is nice for some things. If you want a chance, England is a good place. But I am a Jamaican for Jamaica sun, Jamaican for Jamaica woman. I am a big Jamaican for Jamaica!"

"Did he ever use your cab?"

"No. But I met the man one day, what you can call a polite fellow."

"Can't imagine you and him rapping."

"Norman Tebbit is a very clever man."

"I didn't say he wasn't. I'm saying he's a big-mouth!"

"That man does no less, and no more, than anyone proud of their country."

"I understand that. But he's no friend of black people."

"Look, nowadays you can get a black-cab any colour."

"What's that go to do with it?"

"Lord Tebbit can ride in a red black-cab, a green, or a blue. Not to mention a black black-cab."

"Yeah," Jimmy laughs. "What about a white black-cab?"

"That too."

"A white black-cab with a black cabby, get what I mean? It's the part where some snob's on a pavement, flags down a white black-cab, then gets something to talk about later, like 'I flagged a black-cab, a white one actually, and the colour was a bit off-putting but I didn't mind, had to get off my feet, then as I got to it there was this *huge* black man at the wheel.'"

Urshell slaps his knees. Mulling, remembering. Then a slow laugh. An old man laughing to himself. Disbelieving. Laughing louder now. Way out loud. One old Jamaican folding down in a bad laugh. Jimmy's glad. The two of them chopped down by laughing. Bad laughing. This is like panto time. A black cabby, driving a white black-cab in London.

Marva bolts to the room. Annette close behind. A young madman, laughing. An old man, laughing. Urshell wants to explain, wants to stop, tries to stop. But can't. Nothing can halt the belly laugh. Laughing through pain now. Laughing getting close to clinic zone. Jimmy laughs through tears, grabbing at air. But. Seeing how worried the women are, Urshell gets to stop. Tries to tell it. But not for long. The women start.

"The *huge black man at the wheel*," Marva says, "that's the killer!"

As soon as one bout of laughing winds down, somebody says something, anything, and new laughing starts. Over again. Nobody should laugh to death. Laughing this way, somebody might die. They all know. Somebody definitely could die here.

Annette says it again. "White black-cab, with a black cabby."

Laughing splits the sides of four black folk in a London front room. Late. Way past midnight. In the end, the clock stops it.

Tears of laughing in his eyes, Jimmy checks the time. "Outside in the night," he says, "taxi drivers are hustling for fares right now."

"And a rainbow arcs over the Rift Valley," Annette says.

Marva's eyes clear. "One nightmare of Africa was Miriam, sister of Moses. The bitch was upset because of the Ethiopian woman Moses married. Miriam got chastised, got a bad skin disease because of that nightmare about Africa."

"Jimmy," Urshell says, "now, that dilution thing."

"You mean, how the panthers fell apart?"

"Yes. Foolishness, calling yourself a black activist these days. Too much conceit."

"Deceit?"

"Deceit, conceit. Anyway, a short while before I quit work I used to have this regular punter, a young black fellow. Born here. Thirty, thirty-two. Mother and father from the West Indies. The first few times in the cab he was too uptight to talk to me. But after a period of time, man! You could not stop him talking. Book talk. Zeitgeist this, zeitgeist that. The plum in that boy's mouth! Talk about his white great-grandfather. All the time. But when you looked at that boy, he was black as me. He bought a little place in France, starting to run between London and Paris, but man! A bigger uncle-tom I have *never* seen!"

"When yu get somebody dat young," Marva says, "you know big trouble up ahead. Big trouble!"

"Heartbreaking," Annette says, wincing.

Jimmy nods. "I feel sorry for the sucker."

"Son, let me put it this way. I used to have a big-shot punter, a white fellow, a city gent. Never used to talk. Quiet, doing the cube. Remember the cube? After five, six minutes I used to drop him at the office and that cube was solved. The right fare was always ready. The exact amount, always in the same hand as the cube. But, brother! That gent made sure the white side of the cube was facing me. *Every* time. That bloke was telling me something, but man!"

Wry, Marva shakes hands with Jimmy. "Nobody," she says, "can put race back together like a Rubik's cube!"

## 127

Lorna reads the list. Again. "Tony Benn, Bob Geldof, Paul McCartney, Jools Holland, Ray Mears, Elvis Costello, J. Paxman."

Jimmy's eyebrows raise. "You sure?"

"Yep. That's your lot."

"Women should get listed by a woman. Even one woman."

"Let's go!" she says, grabbing the car door.

"Hang on."

"What's the matter now!"

"There's one too many. You've got seven."

"Really?"

"Yeah. Got to be six."

"Come on! If it works for six, even better for seven."

"The rules say six."

"Stuff the rules!"

"Why bother playing?"

"It was your idea."

"Anyway, you were five seconds over. Strike the last one off."

"What?"

"Paxman. He's the last."

"No, not him!"

"You get conned too easily. Only one of these would be on my list."

"Crossing one off, that'd be like letting somebody down."

"They're not here in the car, are they? Can't hear what we're saying. Come on, cross somebody off."

"No."

Fresh morning air rolls in from the slowed sea. Jimmy lights a smoke. Sulking, Lorna takes the list. Gazing at the sea, she begins to fold it. Then folds it again. And again. As the folds get too tight to fold more, it unfolds. Lazy folds. The list opens and closes like a concertina.

"Tell you what," she says, "*you* cross one off. It's your game!"

"You wanted to play."

"Look, we should be getting some of that beach. You know, before the crowds get here."

"Just close your eyes, stick your finger down. Random elimination."

"You sit here if you want to. I'm going for a walk."

Remembering the serious point of the game, Jimmy grabs Lorna's arm. "Cross off the one you're not sure about. Got to be one like that."

"I'll do you a deal. Let's walk the beach before it gets packed out."

"What's the deal?" he says, stubbing the smoke.

"We go for that walk. I mean *now*. Then I lose one name when we get back. How's that?"

Before today, Jimmy and Lorna haven't met since the funeral. Time after time he picked up the phone. Words failed, every time. He sent a card of condolence. But more than anything, didn't want to crowd her private space. Six o'clock this morning she phoned. Steeled up, he was expecting Geraldine's voice; but it was Lorna. Suddenly it was the whole world, hearing that woman, her noonday voice. She wanted to talk. Talk anything, everything. Maybe go for a walk somewhere. Then she said sorry about the time; early, but not obscene because the sun was already smirking. Jimmy suggested the seaside, especially with no crowds there. The state he was in, the sight of water would be a treat. The model-boat in the flat reminded him; a model yacht with mainsail and jib getting tired on the window sill. She asked if he's still driving that old car. Better go in her car; better safe than sorry, she said. It was just after 7.30 when they got to Eastbourne. Lorna wanted a quick visit to Beachy Head. Jimmy said all they do there is suicide; folk swap stars in their eye to leap for mud; the cliffs at Beachy get more leaping than salmon leaping, more folk leap there than any place else in England, he said. Lorna rubbed her eyes. Stopped the car. Then turned back, headed down the sea-front, alive in sea air, past the string of hotels. The car dawdled past the pier and bandstand and, eventually, nudged in a neat spot. The morning sea. Strong coffee was in the flask. And then quiet. No talking. Watching boats at anchor. All sizes, easy on the swell, all nodding feints to the wind. Just the sound of the sea was the thing.

"You love the sea, don't you!"

"Wish I was at my keyboard," he says. "A new song in my head."

"Really?"

"Yeah. It needs setting down."

"What's it about?"

"A woman by the sea."

"Sing it. Please sing it!"

"Hate singing."

"Then whisper it."

"Nah! I'd feel silly."

"I *always* knew you were a shy little boy."

"Can't sing. Terrible voice."

"Then speak it. I'll get the music from how you say it."

Eyes on the ocean, Jimmy shrugs. "*Somewhere, a solo woman. Solo woman by the sea, alone, lonely, dreaming the same somebody today, today. Raindrops on external worship, longtime togetherness, longtime. Jade bottle on a table, pale flowers in it. Pitter, patter, rain falls. Rain falling, saying 'Listen, hear the water tiptoe. Oh, anyone can hear. Close your eyes, put your water-slippers on. Your slippers on.'*"

"That it?"

"For now. Can't wait to get to my keyboard."

Lorna laughs. "Water-slippers?"

"What d'you expect from a lady by the sea?"

"Your piano is really you, isn't."

"Yeah. I like most instruments. Guitar. Wes Montgomery. That guy played octaves that you wouldn't believe, block chords, lightning ace. The invention. And there's Tal Farlow, saying it with notes, zipping."

"Where's that come from?"

"My song?"

"Yeah. What gave you the idea?"

"Boats, they're a lot like music."

"How?" she says, getting her feet wet.

"Boats can best waves. Same for music."

# 128

Lorna, Jimmy. The ocean. Side by side. Nothing to say. As the sun gets higher, something opens inside her. A small flower opens in her heart. Now it's clear: she can never leave England.

"Just think," she smiles, "you get in your car and in an hour you're sitting in sand, looking at boats on the water. Beautiful. Too nice to leave, eh!"

Jimmy slaps his forehead. He remembers something Urshell said. "The old man reckons on four more generations."

"For what?"

"England to be stable enough. Colour could be easy by then. No talky whites on TV to chat immigrants anymore. No blacks talking diversity while ducking under fakery, no blond wig on their ebony."

"*Who* is this Urshell?"

"Not a prophet. But he sees things."

"Nostradamus?"

"Don't get cute! That old man is for real."

"Take me to meet him."

"He was at that meeting for your brother."

"The tall old guy talking about skin stalkers?"

"Yeah. He talks stuff. You know, like how one day a black person can arrive in a certain kind of car. A brand new Jag. Make sure you don't arrive in a Jag at a village pub these days. You'd cause hushed talk. Somebody black driving a Jag through green England would be chase time. So if you go, go in a mini. Or in Porsches, Ferraris."

Lorna frowns. "Why not a Jag?"

"Because a Jag is what the English gent drives in his English country-side."

"Don't be silly! I mean, your Urshell."

"He's got a point."

"As soon as I can afford it, I want a Jag!"

"That's up to you."

"Bit of a pessimist, isn't he!"

"Toss a coin. You decide."

"When does the gloom end, according to him?"

"When a black man or woman in a yacht turns up, somebody with the skill to solo the ocean. All five oceans. Or win gold in Olympic sailing. When that happens, racials will be fewer. Yeah, few and far between."

"Dream on!"

"Well," Jimmy says, pointing to the ocean, "Africa's over there. But blacks are everywhere. A big African diaspora."

"And?"

"Me and you, bits of Africa on this shore."

"Not that stuff again!" Lorna says, stomping sand.

"What's the matter?"

"I am *not* an African! Can't dump the white half, chuck it in the sea."

"Hey, who asked you to?"

"Black half swims to Africa, white half stays on the shore?"

Jimmy laughs. "Fussy mixed race woman!"

"I don't feel *mixed* anything."

"Your mother's from Africa."

"Barbados!"

"Born in England, out of Barbados, but African all the way."

"What?"

"You heard."

"Well, yeah. OK. African."

"That's where my soul is. Love to settle there."

"I'm not getting picky, but Africa is so different."

"Then," Jimmy says, "better hold on to black. Hold tight!"

"Fine with me. So many colours. A million greens. Billions. Blues, reds."

"Plenty of huffing over black."

"Where does it end?"

Jimmy grabs a handful of sand. Squats, gazing at the ebb and flow. Wondering. Mulling. Bit by bit, seeing things clearer and clearer. "You agree with Tiger Woods?"

"How d'you mean?"

"Calls himself a Cablinasian."

"What," Lorna blinks, "the hell is *that*?"

"His ethnic bits. Caucasian, black, Indian, Asian."

"Jesus!"

"His old man's black, bits of Caucasian and red-Indian."

"His mother's Thai, isn't she?"

"Yeah. In America, orientals get called Asians."

"I have a friend, half black, half Jewish. Calls herself blewish."

"Big change from nigger."

"That word!" Lorna says. "It sends shivers down my spine!"

"Know who the Falashas are?"

"Never heard of them."

"They're black Jews."

"So?"

"Your blewish friend got it wrong."

"Oh, stop slitting hairs!"

"Know what? You'd better call yourself a blite."

"*Who*?"

"A blite," he says. "Or a whack."

354

Suddenly, Lorna's eyes pop. "Wait, wait! Rican, that could do it."

"A what?"

"Rican. That would do, wouldn't it?"

"What's a Rican?"

"Part-African. Why not? So cool. Rican, Rican!"

"Hey, mind you start something."

"Honour your mothers and fathers, right?"

"There's enough of you to make Rican stick, make sense."

"And there's a good few Icans out there. And Cans."

"The ocean's getting older, but no nearer to any place."

"Oh, don't get mystical. Not now. Let's be quiet a minute."

"Quiet?" he smiles. "Stay quiet about what?"

"OK. OK!" she says. Her eyes roll. "Let's do the big mystic."

"Let's listen to the sea."

"Running away again? What a surprise!"

"I hate false quiet. Wouldn't know where to start."

"Then let's do the list. Explain it."

"The list is a race-gauge."

"How, for Christ's sake?"

"You name six white folk that never say nigger in anger. Celebrity whites."

"I get that bit, obviously. But what's the point?"

"Time. The trick's the amount of time it takes. Closer to 20 seconds, better the state of play."

"What if it takes a minute?"

"Not good."

"Suppose it's more than a minute?"

"They only produce toilet paper."

"Then what?"

"You decide."

# 129

Squinting from sunlight, Lorna turns to Jimmy. "What's going on?"

"My life?" he says. "Wish I knew."

Agnes on his mind. Again. That woman's so scared of flying she put up with seasickness for two weeks on a ship. Talked it to him by mobile as the ship sailed away. Today, he remembers her voice: a nervy voice, saying she couldn't see him at the quayside so could he try waving both arms this time. He wondered if he'd ever see her again. Hurt was in her voice as she talked of water, the ship was slipping and sliding. Menacing water, she said; water rolling like mules on a slush hill. The ship turned blue to grey, getting small, smaller and smaller, so small, and, eventually, too much wisp. Grey fog snatched it away.

But today, he's walking a beach in England with Lorna. A light breeze whirls across the sea as gulls package idling air. Sails furled and stowed, boats in water cradles. Lorna frowns. But keeps her thoughts.

Jimmy mulls on that first visit to Urshell; remembering Marva, the old man's kind-hearted wife. As he was about to leave, she slipped the photo of Agnes into his pocket, knowing how it fazed him. Back at the flat, the picture was of an alien woman now. Destroying it was too hard. Impossible. Sending it back seemed the best thing. But that would have been spite, like some rotten fruit a hand picks in the dark. And then. A new idea: run the picture through a computer, swap that straightened hair for natural. At the photo shop, the technician tried hard. Trying out natural hairstyles on the photo. In one style, Agnes had braids. Beautiful again. Then more styles. And ten more. But the one with the Afro was the one. Afro was the best style of all. And that's when he could see. Yes, something was wrong; something out of kilter, too wrong. No matter what hairstyle the technician tried, all that happened was Agnes' fantasy for straight hair was getting swapped with his fantasy of how she could be. How she was in London. That was too hard for words: swap false with natural, and still get a fantasy. He took the photo, said sorry. Then it was clear. Seeing what was wrong was easy. Urshell wasn't wrong. But that old man wasn't right. Not quite. Fantasy was not the word. It was affirmation. Not fantasy; all the time Jimmy was longing for affirmation.

Lorna's footsteps in sync with Jimmy's as she walks beside him on the beach. "Affirm, what?"

"What d'you mean?"

"You were mumbling away."

"Must have been sleepwalking."

"You can't take your eyes off the sea."

"It's not about mermaids, OK?"

She laughs. "Am I a mermaid?"

"Are you?"

"Can barely swim."

"Hey, let's get to what's what. Let's talk."

"Yes."

"That's what today is about, isn't it."

"I want you to help me talk though it."

"It's been bad?"

"I don't want to cry. Let's get back to the car."

"Tears in sand, better than dashboard blues."

"That's *so* glib!"

"Take yourself too seriously, and you won't make it."

"Where shall I start."

"What happened after the funeral?"

"It was hard. Kept to myself the whole time. Took a month off work."

"Couldn't face the world?"

"No. Locked myself in the flat. Most days probably didn't even draw the curtains. It was 'What's the point!' Couldn't get my head round it."

"Then you phoned?"

"Yes."

"Why me?"

"Tons to get straight. Didn't realize just how much there was. Funny thing, I couldn't face my mother. After the funeral we were all together at the house. Spent the night talking. Coffee. That was the worst part. Nobody could accept it, Justin never coming back through the front door. We broke down, everybody, crying."

"I don't need to know. Don't want to intrude."

"Intrude? Some people get counseling, learn to hang it all out. With me, I talk to you and it's 'Yes, now I understand!' Know what I mean?   I can't really explain it."

"Why couldn't you face your mother?"

"Too difficult."

"Time like that? Jeez! I'd need my mother."

"I know. I thought about it and, Christ! It was like cold fish. I was never able to just throw my arms round anyone. Even her."

"How'd you cope?"

"Couldn't think. The only thing was Mull. I played it non-stop."

"Mull of Kintyre?"

"Yeah. Non-stop. But the more I played it, it was 'You've got to do this one more time.' So I played it, yeah, over and over."

"Why?"

"Because, because!"

"The lyrics, the tune?"

"How should I know?"

"For me, it's the bagpipes. Bleak pentatonic."

*"Oh mist rolling in from the sea, my desire is always to be here, oh_"*

"Yeah!"

"Can't explain it," Lorna sighs. "I mean, there was only pain. You yourself, you want affirmation, don't you? Mull of Kintyre. Lock your door, phone off the hook, Mull will sort it."

"I like the song," Jimmy says, "but a bunch of bagpipes wouldn't keep me from *my* mother. She needed you."

"I know, I know! It's doing my head in. I stayed away. Had to. I didn't know what was going on. Thought I was losing it. Then I thought of Beachy Head. I listened to the shipping forecast. Every, every day. Get a coffee, tune in to Radio 4. Listen to 'Viking, 40's, southerly 3 or 4, but occasionally 5, becoming cyclonic later.' Every day, something like that."

"Slow down. I can't see where this is going."

"Occasional rain, then thundery showers, moderate with fog patches."

Lorna is at a place Jimmy doesn't know. He wants to go, get back to London. The sea's like it's getting breached by emotions, even with no one else but the two of them on the beach.

"Ever seen a boat that was on the seabed a long time?"

Lorna frowns. "What?"

"Barnacles, stuff clinging."

"Hope *you* know what you're on about. I don't!"

"Your mother needed you."

"I couldn't face that," she says, sand trickling from her grasp like an hourglass.

Jimmy lights a smoke. "What spooked you?"

"Family."

"Pain, now Justin's not there?"

"Things, there's things that never get said in families. And my dad, well, not the talky-talky kind."

"Finally accepted it?"

"What?"

"Accepted his son was black?"

"What d'you mean?"

"Don't act like you don't know!"

"No, I *don't* know."

"With a helmet on, Justin looked white. You know that!"

"No!"

"Looked white."

"What're you getting at?"

"The facts."

"Witch-hunting again!"

"Me, the magic man?"

Out to sea, a speedboat rears its bow above the waves. And shoots a tower of spray at the shore.

Lorna turns away. "Yes, you're right."

"Pain?"

"You know," she sighs, "my brother's dreadlocks, that was the start of something. His mates were black guys. Right up till the funeral I don't think my father really ever wanted him to be black."

"White?"

"Don't put words in my mouth!"

"Whitish?"

"I'm serious."

"If you're going to talk, talk!"

Lips pursed, she reaches down. Grabs a fist of sand. Lets it play through her fingers. Tries it with both hands. Then flings at the sea.

"Sometimes," she says, "he'd mention how Justin looked like him. Tall. The same pointy-nose. On and on! Like if it wasn't for his frizzy hair, Justin was white. On, and on!"

"What did he think?"

"My brother?"

"Yes."

"Thought it was a joke."

"That stuff," Jimmy says, flitting the cigarette at the sea, "it's half a world from me."

"There's more. Promise I can tell you."

"What is it?"

"Don't know who to talk to. Can I tell you?"

"Depends."

"If I tell you, then it stays put. I need to know."

"I'm not the one. Hate secrets."

"Promise!"

"Who would I tell?"

"You won't mention it? Even to me. Promise!"

He turns to face her. "I swear."

"Summer before last, they took snaps together. My father and brother. Just the two of them. All smiles. A hot day."

"*No!*"

"You know?"

"I think so."

"What was it?"

"In the photos they had crash helmets on?"

"Yes," she says, eyes welled with tears.

"So Justin would look white."

"Yes! What else was there?"

"Why didn't you do something?"

"We never really saw it, what was going on."

"When did you find out?"

"After the funeral I was going through albums. Old family albums. Checking it all out. Coming to terms. There's me looking at old snaps, the family, and every picture my little brother's grinning his face off. I couldn't stop crying. Then the helmet ones. I'd seen them before, but something just clicked. Suddenly I knew what they meant. So I pulled them out. Wanted to get rid of them, bury them somewhere. But then my dad comes into the room. I tell him I know what he's done, what the pictures mean. Doesn't say boo, does he! He's like 'You think you know it all' and I'm like 'No, but I wouldn't deny my own son!' And he gets so sad, old. He takes them off me, stares at them a minute. Then just sort of wilts, really. He looks so old and everything. Not himself at all. I was crying again. He asks me what I want to do with them, and I knew that was it."

"What'd you say?"

"There's no way they're going back in that album, I said."

"Then?"

"He gets out his lighter. Puts them on a plate. Sets fire to them. We just sort of went numb together. Me and him, watching them burn."

"I knew it! You shouldn't have told me."

"Why not?"

"Nobody outside your family needed to know."

"Jimmy," she says, "*never* mention it. Not even back to me!"

"Never."

"But?"

"I'm just a foot-loose."

"You promised!"

"Why me? I mean, things like that you keep in the family. I don't know your father. Never even set eyes on your brother. Not alive. So I should never know this private thing. Too private."

"You can handle it," she says, and wipes her eyes.

"I'd tell the sea something big as that."

"What?"

"Why not?"

"Oh, grow up!"

"The sea's got a bigger heart than me."

"Pickled, spiteful water."

"What about your mother? She must have known that helmet thing."

"She knew. I didn't know she knew. I looked at her and it was 'Yes, I've known this all along.' Christ! All those years and my dad's suddenly admitting Justin's mixed-race. Black, or whatever."

"Black?"

"Yeah."

"How'd it turn round?"

"What d'you mean?"

"Your dad, the facts."

"Oh, he said let it go. My uncle had come down from Newcastle, brought a gun, huge shotgun."

"Now you're talking!" Jimmy says, pumping a fist. "I thought the guys in your family were passives."

"*My* dad? You're joking! Ice cold. When Justin was little he wouldn't tell if there was a problem. Black, white, my dad sorted them!"

Jimmy lights a fresh smoke. And turns away. Wishing. Watching the ocean. Listening it call, respond. Water in convention with the shore. Music in waves, sad solo from a sound-box sea. And then, Agnes. Wondering what she's doing, what her photograph means.

"Way across the sea," he says, "blue whales are chatting. But the sea is no hearing-aid, not for pangs of somebody longing."

"No mystic talk. Please, not now."

"What happened with the gun?"

"Oh," she says, eyes glazed, "they sat around, you know, glowering. Staring at it. For days, a week. My dad talked my uncle out of it. It was 'Time to put our own house in order.' And that was that. They didn't know who to go for. There was that nagging feeling it was a mistake. One of Justin's own mates admitted using a screwdriver in the fight."

# 130

A good-looking day. The beach is warm. The place to be. No city. Not for Jimmy. Not for Lorna. They gaze at yachts capering on waves.

"Fancy a swim?"he says.

"Swim?"

"Yeah. Swim in our underwear."

"Remember the opening scene from Jaws?"

"Sharks? Nah!"

"Good day for a territorial great white."

Jimmy remembers Lorna's quip about Moses, mystic of the Red Sea. As he turns to face her, he knows she remembers what she said. Shrugging, he turns away.

"Sorry," she says. "Can we forget that Moses thing?"

"Yeah. I'm no Moses."

"You love the sea, don't you?"

"Home from home. If my music takes off, I get a boat. Sail far."

"When! *When* your music gets there. When!"

"Yeah. Could be just round the corner."

"Look," she says, "I must know. Are you free?"

"As in?"

"Not involved with anyone else. The woman from South Africa, is she still a factor?"

Jimmy must think. He steps away. Slow steps. Must be alone. Agnes. She took a set of his keys to South Africa. When he asked 'What if you don't come back?" she said 'Then you needn't change the lock.' He remembers her at the flat that first time, shy but smiling. But the phonecall last week was hard. Yes, she'd straightened her hair; but only as a joke, she said. She realized if a man loved her then what her hair was like wouldn't matter to him because she wasn't the same as her hair. Women play their hair, she said; even white women straighten it, hurry to the hairdresser to rinse and straighten. But straight is natural to white, Jimmy said; then asked, 'You're in the heart of Africa, why wear a skin overcoat?'

Walking the beach, he must be sure. It looks like things are all over with Agnes. And maybe she's already got something going with the guy that talks like Paul Robeson. Then Donna. Next week it's New York; flying to the States to tour, get Minims on CD. Jamaica is one step from New York. Donna will fly out and meet up in Manhattan. She said she's got a surprise. And Lorna; she's wired in his head. But Donna's deep in the soul. Maybe because of what happened, the hurricane that first time, the soft peal the last time, but only today on a quiet beach in England that things look clear.

# 131

Down the beach, Lorna sits alone in empty sand. She turns to watch as Jimmy gets nearer.

"I've got a lyric in my head," he says. "Maybe it's only crowd fodder, like for a football terrace, but I might use in a song one day."

"You're not going to sing it, I can tell."

"I'll give it a go," he says, fingers clicking. "Ray Davies might have thought of it. I'll borrow the melody from Waterloo Sunset. Ready?"

"Go for it!"

*"The blacks of Brixton, met the brix of Blackston, halfway to Leicester Square."*

"Rubbish! Off with his head!"

Jimmy laughs. "I know. Even I want to cringe."

"At least you admit it."

"I'll be myself when I get to New York."

"Don't get starry-eyed. Not about America. It's got sundown towns."

"Sundown?"

"Yes. It's 'Nigger, don't let the sun go down on you here!'"

"*What?*"

"Surprised?"

"America?"

"Yep."

"These days?"

"Here and now!"

"Like where?"

"Towns," Lorna says, "like Anna. That one's in Illinois."

"Anna was a witch?"

"Anna stands for 'Ain't no niggers allowed.' Hard to believe?"

"And here," Jimmy says, "Britannia wears a stone corset."

"America's a two-way. Brilliant blacks in Wall Street, the military. But sundown towns."

"They get away with it?"

"I read about an albatross," she sighs. "A yellow-nosed maverick. It was in America last month, visiting Martha's Vineyard. So far north. I mean, way beyond its home in the southern hemisphere."

"So what?"

"It was alone. I think it was trying to find a mate. Great sea-bird, this myth, trying to pal with gulls in Martha's Vineyard."

"A mistake."

"*Bad* mistake!"

"Powell's parents flipped a coin," Jimmy says.

"Hey?"

"Colin Powell. He was born in America. Jamaican parents. If they'd come here instead of America, he'd have ended up as a sergeant in the British army. That's what he said. Big 4-star American general."

"Christ!"

Jimmy knows for sure now. Lorna's joined to England. Loves it. Even though her brother's in the ground here. But she's definitely not the type that will come along again and again. She wakes some spiritual thing in him. A quiet hold. But Donna. She's deep, deep. To Jimmy, Donna's the same beautiful as fresh black olives. That heavy woman will get on a plane from Kingston to New York. But. That's next week. Lorna's here, today, now, this side of the ocean.

"Remember that day at the zoo," he says, "the day we first met?"

"I'll never forget it."

"What d'you think happened to the lions?"

"I'd like to go back one day. Go back to find out. We can go together sometime."

"I was thinking the same."

"Today? Look, I'd love to see them. I dreamt them one night and they were like 'When will you come again?' Funny, eh?"

Leaving the sea, side by side, Jimmy and Lorna will go on a journey. Getting back to London, they'll take the old road through Brixton. Then while some time in the market before crossing the Thames.

Half a day's getting left behind here. Like baggage. In one way this is maybe how it was meant. Not stay with the beach to loll, make small talk, watch folk arrive with downcast eyes, not get melancholy being a part of a sunny English day, laughing, toying in sand, not even build a neat sandcastle from a ton of it. After all, every ton can fly.